KT-549-816

Joss Wood loves books and travelling—especially to the wild places of southern Africa and, well, anywhere. She's a wife, a mum to two teenagers and a slave to two cats. After a career in local economic development, she now writes full-time. Joss is a member of Romance Writers of America and Romance Writers of South Africa. Visit her Author Profile page at Harlequin.com, or josswoodbooks.com, for more titles. You can also find Joss Wood on Facebook, along with other Mills & Boon Desire authors, at Facebook.com/harlequindesireauthors!

A former Hollywood studio executive who gladly traded in her high heels and corner office for yoga pants and the local coffee shop, **Susannah Erwin** loves writing about ambitious, strong-willed people who can't help falling in love—whether they want to or not. Her first novel won the Golden Heart® Award from Romance Writers of America, and she is hard at work in her Northern California home on her next. She would be over the moon if you signed up for her newsletter via susannaherwin.com. Visit her Author Profile page at Harlequin.com, or susannaherwin.com, for more titles. You can also find Susannah Erwin on Facebook, along with other Mills & Boon Desire authors, at Facebook.com/harlequindesireauthors!

Discover more at millsandboon.co.uk

HOMECOMING
HEARTBREAKER

JOSS WOOD

WHO'S THE BOSS
NOW?

SUSANNAH ERWIN

MILLS & BOON

First Published in Great Britain 2021
by Mills & Boon, an imprint of HarperCollins*Publishers* Ltd
1 London Bridge Street, London, SE1 9GF

www.harpercollins.co.uk

HarperCollins*Publishers*
1st Floor, Watermarque Building,
Ringsend Road, Dublin 4, Ireland

Homecoming Heartbreaker © 2021 Joss Wood
Who's the Boss Now? © 2021 Susannah Erwin

ISBN: 978-0-263-28298-6

0721

MIX
Paper from
responsible sources
FSC™ C007454

This book is produced from independently certified FSC™
paper to ensure responsible forest management.

For more information visit: www.harpercollins.co.uk/green

Printed and bound in Spain
by CPI, Barcelona

HOMECOMING
HEARTBREAKER

JOSS WOOD

Dedicated to Karen Booth and Reese Ryan,
my smart, talented, funny friends.
Working with you guys is always a blast.

One

Well, he was back.

Mack Holloway raked his hand through his black hair and rubbed his stubbled jaw, steering his Benz into the turn-off to the old logging road, a mile or so from the stone gates of Moonlight Ridge, the exclusive inn and resort owned by his adopted father, Jameson Holloway. This time he wasn't home for a one-night stay or a flying visit on his way to another city; he was here for a couple of months. And yeah, the thought made him grind his teeth and his throat tighten.

Mack cut the engine and pushed open his door, exiting his low-slung, stupidly expensive sports car. Slapping the door closed, he forced himself to look over the roof of the Benz to the thick forest of yellow pines. He swallowed, panic crawling up his throat. He didn't want to make the short walk up the road, to look at the place where his life had changed. He'd lost so much that night, his family, stability, *Molly*...everything that mattered.

Jamming his hands into the pockets of his pants, he forced his feet to move, feeling the cold fingers of a light mist touching his face. He didn't want to look at the scene of the accident but if he was going to be living here for the foreseeable future, then confront it he must.

Mack walked on and the mild spring wind lifted his hair and plastered his shirt against his chest and stomach. After a few minutes he stopped and looked around, realizing he was standing at the exact spot where the truck had left the road, and he swallowed, trying to ease his suddenly tight throat.

But instead of reliving that night from start to finish, as he expected to, he only recalled the screams, heard the high whine of the engine as the truck rolled.

He'd lost control of the truck and his temper. He'd failed to look after his brothers, Grey and Travis. He was the oldest and they had been his responsibility.

It was one night, fifteen years ago, but it had had enormous ramifications. He'd thought himself invincible, they all had, but that night taught him that actions sometimes had massive consequences. As a result, he was rarely spontaneous and never made quick decisions. And keeping calm, rational and controlled was vitally important to Mack. It was his guiding principle, his compass point.

He couldn't change the past and the stupid decisions he made but he could control the present and plan for the future. To do that he needed to push the past aside and focus on the here and now…

On what he could control…

He was back in Asheville, temporarily returning to Moonlight Ridge because Jameson—the man who'd rescued him from the system shortly before his eighth birthday—recently spent a week in the critical care unit in Asheville's premier hospital after experiencing a brain episode.

They'd operated, Jameson was home, but the next few months would be critical to his long-term health. His adopted father's recovery was contingent on keeping his stress levels at a manageable level.

And Moonlight Ridge was the source of most of his stress...

On his way back to where he'd parked his car, Mack glanced to his right, knowing the boundary to Jameson's super luxurious resort, a smaller and more exclusive version of their neighbor, the famous Biltmore, was just a few miles to the north. Both properties were institutions in Asheville, North Carolina, and over the past seventy-five years Moonlight Ridge had been the retreat of kings and politicians, ultra-reclusive Hollywood celebrities and international billionaires.

And Jameson, as the owner and operator of the stunning stone-and-wood inn, had been the face of Moonlight Ridge for decades. He lived to work, and the luxurious resort where he'd raised them was his world. People energized him and he knew every guest by name.

But Jameson's individual attention to their guests was going to be, for the next six months at least, impossible.

After many tense and terse arguments with his brothers, and with Jameson himself, they'd finally come to a compromise: each of Jameson's sons would temporarily relocate to Moonlight Ridge. Mack, because he was the oldest—and despite knowing how hard it would be face Molly again—volunteered to take the first shift. It was the least he could do to try to atone for the devastation he'd caused...

Mack knew that complete atonement was impossible, but he had to make the effort.

But God, how he wished Molly wasn't still working as Moonlight Ridge's manager and living on site.

Mack placed his butt against the side panel of his car

and stretched out his long legs, rolling his head to relieve the knots in his neck.

He met Molly even before he met Grey and Travis, his adopted brothers. He'd been eight and she, the daughter of Jameson's accountant, seven. He'd been entranced by her corkscrew blond curls, olive complexion and her fascinating light green-blue eyes.

Molly's complete lack of fear of Jameson, a big, burly, dark-skinned man—so different from his slightly built, mean-as-hell Korean biological father—helped him become accustomed to his new dad and his many rules and regs. With Molly's help, he soon realized that Jameson was all bark and no bite. Over the next few months, he started to relax and then to thrive.

He had Jameson, he had Molly and he felt, *finally*, loved and secure.

Six months later Grey joined their little family and two months after him, Travis. They might not look the same, Jameson told them—Jameson and Travis were African American, Grey was white and Mack's father was of South Korean descent—but taking his name made them his, they were Holloways and they were a family. Diversity was strength, Jameson had told them; differences were to be celebrated and skin color was irrelevant.

Jameson, as he'd found out later, always wanted kids but never found the right woman to give him any. On hearing how difficult it was for older kids to find a forever home, Jameson scooped up Mack, a kid who lost his mother at childbirth and was abandoned by his dad when he was seven.

Mack knew how lucky he was. And, he figured, he couldn't have been that bad because Jameson went on to adopt two more boys close to his age.

That first year, with all three boys trying to find their

feet and their place in their new family, was unbelievably tough. They all had trust issues, a fear of being disappointed, preferring to keep themselves to themselves. But Jameson kept a firm hand on the wheel and steered them through the storm, frequently reminding them that they were a family, and they'd better get used to the idea.

They listened and, despite not sharing a drop of blood nor a strand of DNA, became brothers in every sense of the word. For almost a decade he had a father and two brothers who, he believed, would go to war for him.

And he had Molly, his north star.

He supposed it was inevitable, given how close they were, that his and Molly's relationship would turn romantic, and those last four months they'd spent together had been the best of his life. They'd laughed, loved and explored their sexuality, convinced that they'd spend the rest of their lives together.

Then the accident ripped apart his family and lost him his oldest friend and his new lover…

After the accident, believing that he wasn't deserving of his family, of any type of love—Molly's included—he'd left Asheville and everything he adored behind, cutting all ties with surgical precision. It was his way to punish himself and he'd been stunningly successful in doing just that.

For years he'd been a walking, talking emotional bruise.

Mack scrubbed his face with his hands, reluctantly admitting that, sometime after college, he could've approached her, made some effort to be, at the very least, polite. But no, because he was stubborn and stupid and, yeah, scared, he let the years fly by without contact and now he felt as alienated from her as he was from his brothers. If he'd reached out sooner, made the effort to connect earlier, their upcoming meeting would not be a fraction as awkward as it was bound to be.

Moonlight Ridge was Molly's home, probably more than it was ever his. She'd lived on the property as a child, worked for Jameson in her teens and was his father's favorite-ever girl, the daughter he'd never had.

And she was now the manager of Moonlight Ridge and, because he was going to assume Jameson's duties at the resort, he would be working closely with his ex-friend and ex-lover. The woman he'd thought he'd make his wife, the mother of the children he'd once wanted.

Completely fabulous.

Mack slid into his car, punched the start button on his dashboard, but instead of pulling away, he stared at the emblem on the end of his hood, feeling edgy, tense and very unlike the supercool, controlled businessman he normally was. All he wanted to do was to return to Nashville.

Asheville, Moonlight Ridge, Jameson and Molly were all agents of change and he didn't want variations; he'd designed his life and liked it exactly as it was.

But he owed Jameson. He'd do anything for the man who gave him stability and love, security and a family, when he needed them the most.

But his past and present were about to collide…

More than ever, Mack needed to stay in control.

Molly Haskell stood at the window of her third-floor office, her eyes on the long driveway. She'd had a brief message from Mack, telling her he'd arrive this morning, and she cursed her elevated heart rate and dry mouth.

He'd left fifteen years ago; surely, she should be over him by now. Molly, frowning at the thought, gave herself a mental head slap. She was over him; *of course* she was. She refused to be anything *but* over him.

But Mack's return to Moonlight Ridge as Jameson's stand-in was going to complicate her business life—she refused to let him affect her or her emotions!—and put a hitch in her plans to revitalize the resort.

Just before he fell ill, Jameson promised to listen to her proposals to make the resort the premier destination in the South, but before they could meet, he collapsed and was rushed to the hospital, unconscious. His brain episode—another word for his narrowly avoiding an aneurysm—scared her senseless and all she'd been able to focus on was whether he'd recover or not. Now that he was out of danger, she could give her attention to Jameson's beloved business.

He was her mentor, her second father, the man she adored, loved and trusted and there was nothing she wouldn't do for him, including reviving his resort.

But as Moonlight Ridge's manager, she'd didn't have the authority, financial or otherwise, to make dramatic and sweeping changes. She'd now have to—*ugh*—get permission to implement her plans from, according to Forbes, one of the country's most brilliant young businessmen, Jameson's oldest son, Mack Holloway.

And Mack, because he was a leader not a follower, a visionary who liked to forge his own path, was bound to poke many holes in her plans.

Molly released a low growl, then a hard sigh. She was already annoyed with him and he hadn't yet arrived.

No, that wasn't true; being annoyed with Mack was her default setting. She was simply more annoyed with him than usual.

"I will not let him stand in my way."

"Talking to yourself again, Mol?"

Molly turned to see her best friend stepping into her small office. They'd met when they were ten or eleven, when Autumn's wealthy family vacationed at the resort two years in a row. When she didn't return for the third year, they exchanged postcards until their friendship faded in their early teens. Two years ago, a scandal involving Autumn's father—a famous Hollywood producer—chased her out of LA and she landed at Moonlight Ridge as their independent wedding planner.

Their friendship sparked again and these days Autumn ran all their weddings and events on a shared profit basis, and also arranged functions throughout Asheville as an independent contractor.

Autumn pushed her black glasses up her nose and joined Molly at the window, placing a hand between her shoulders. "Are you okay?" she quietly asked.

Of course she was. Maybe.

Molly stared at the Degas print on the opposite wall. The ballerina wore a frothy tutu, was on pointe and tilting down. In her teens Molly had been a talented dancer, one with a lot of promise, but she'd lost her beloved ballet that long-ago summer, along with so much else.

"Not really," she quietly admitted. Turning, she placed her bottom on the wooden windowsill and shrugged. "I'm hurt that, despite having worked here my entire life except for college, Jameson feels the need to bring in his sons to oversee operations."

"Maybe Mack will be too busy with his own work to get involved," Autumn suggested.

Hope flared in her chest. "Maybe. Maybe the brothers just told Jameson they'd stick around to get him to take it easy. You know how implacable he can be."

Molly tipped her head up to stare at the decorative ceiling in her office, trying to make sense of her mixed emotions. She was worried about Jameson, feeling nervous to be meeting Mack again after a fifteen-year absence, irritated that she wouldn't have free rein to manage Moonlight Ridge her way and terrified that Jameson's long-absent son would come in and tip over her carefully arranged apple cart.

"Am I allowed to still be angry that Mack dumped me?" Molly asked Autumn because, yeah, she was.

Autumn frowned. "Molly, it's been a long time. You were kids. Ninety percent of teenage relationships end."

Sure, but Mack had been so much more than a teenage fling. Before he'd become her boyfriend and her first lover, he'd been her best friend. Her refuge, the *one* person, besides Jameson, who had her back.

His leaving, without a word or explanation, eviscerated her. The months following his departure had been the loneliest of her life and contributed to her making the worst decision of her seventeen or so years, a mistake that still haunted her today.

"Talk to me, Mol," Autumn said.

What could she say? Autumn knew that Molly's father was Jameson's treacherous CFO. She knew Molly's history with Mack. How Molly and her family were forced to leave Moonlight Ridge when she was thirteen but how this place held everything and everyone she cared about.

But Autumn did not know about her *crime*.

"Mack and I working together is going to be awkward, uncomfortable. Mack has been home to visit Jameson before but, despite me living and working on the property, he's never sought me out to apologize for dropping out of my life, for not replying to the million text and email messages I sent him, the frantic voice mails I left on his phone."

Molly would never forgive him for treating her like she was disposable, like she was an object that he'd used and no longer valued.

She had her family for that.

There was something to be said for growing up. These days she was confident, assured, assertive and ambitious. She straightened her shoulders. "But I can handle Mack Holloway."

"Good. How?" Autumn asked.

He'd be expecting an attitude, Molly realized. He'd be prepared for a tirade. As a child and teenager, she'd expressed every thought, wore her heart on her sleeve, and Mack would expect her be as she was before.

Molly refused to be predictable. "I'm going to treat him as if he were any other employee, any other boss," Molly told her friend. "I'm going to be polite, friendly but distant and, above all, professional."

Autumn's arched eyebrows lifted. "And you think you can do that?" she asked, sounding doubtful.

Sure she could. She hoped. Trying to look, and sound, confident, Molly nodded. "It'll be a piece of cake."

Autumn patted her shoulder. "Well, you're about to find out, sweetie, because there's a car coming down the driveway."

Go time.

Molly returned Autumn's hug, sucked in a deep breath, left her office and headed for the tight, small and prosaic servants' staircase. The old, sprawling mansion—with two large wings added to house many guests—sported a massive, imposing staircase, but the staff needed to be discreet and that meant flying up and down the narrow staircase at the back of the house.

Molly used one of the many secret passageways—in the 1930s the original owners ran a speakeasy for their wealthy friends and used the secret tunnels to stash their illicit booze—and slipped into the imposing hallway/lobby via a discreet door. Waving to Harry, who manned the front desk, she walked through the hall dominated by the magnificent staircase and stopped to shove a tulip back into a bountiful arrangement of fresh flowers.

Moonlight Ridge was Jameson's, but, emotionally, it was hers, too. She came back to work for Jameson after college because she'd felt so damn guilty—she still did—but these days there was no place she'd rather be than within the walls of this thick building, with its antiques and silver, art and antiquities. She loved the luxurious rooms, the ivy covering parts of the building, the extensive, lush grounds and the gorgeous lake that was a centerpiece on the property.

Molly stepped outside and watched as the matte-black, low-slung sports car made its way up the long, tree-lined driveway. Molly scowled at the wide-shouldered shadow behind the wheel.

Mack was back...

She gulped.

She'd moved on; she *had*. She hadn't spent the past fifteen years pining, for God's sake! There had been other men, not many, but she'd dated. But no one managed to capture her heart. To be fair, she hadn't allowed her heart to be captured. She was perfectly content to be single.

Besides, she'd rather avoid the drama men brought to her life, thank you very much.

Mack pulled to a stop and cut the growly engine to his car. Molly sucked in a deep breath and put her hands behind her back, her fingers tightly interlocked. She hoped she was portraying her polite, friendly "Welcome to Moonlight Ridge" face but she couldn't be sure.

This was, after all, the man she still wanted to run through with a rusty pitchfork.

Chill, Molly. It all happened so very long ago.

Mack stepped out of his car and Molly slammed her teeth together to keep her tongue from falling to the floor. At eighteen, Mack had been gangly, all long limbs and unruly hair, a little awkward and uncoordinated. That wasn't something Mack needed to worry about now.

Molly tipped her head to the side and considered the man who'd been the center of her world so long ago. The boy she knew was gone and he was now a man, in every way that counted. His once shaggy hair was now expertly cut and styled, as black as a night in the Carolina woods. He'd inherited his Korean father's looks, his eyes—a deep, dark black-brown—and the shape of his face hadn't changed, but the light, sexy stubble on his jaw and chin was new.

But it was his body that had undergone the biggest change. He'd hit six foot two in his early teens but he'd always been skinny. He'd bulked up, his shoulders were broader, his thighs bigger, his chest wider. His shirt hinted at huge biceps and the wind slapped his white shirt against a stomach that was flat, hard and, she was convinced, ridged with muscle.

Mack, it was obvious, worked out. Hard and often.

Yum.

Molly felt the heat between her legs, the tingles in her nipples, and swallowed, looking for moisture in her mouth. *Yum? Really, Haskell?* He was a great-looking guy and, *rats*, she was still as attracted to Mack today as she'd been when she was a teenager. But unlike that naive, trusting girl she'd been, she now knew that there was a chasm between sex and love, that the two didn't normally have to walk hand in hand. She could appreciate a good-looking man; it was just conditioning and biology. Molly knew that she, and every other woman in the world, was hardwired to look for the strongest, best-looking mate, the one with excellent genes to give to her children.

She'd grown up, thank God, and it took more than a hot bod and gorgeous face to impress her these days.

Mack took his time acknowledging her and when he finally turned to look at her, his face was as imperturbable as she hoped hers was. "Hello, Molly."

God, even his voice was deeper, sexier, like well-aged red wine.

Molly inclined her head and didn't move from her position, annoyed to realize that her knees were now, and suddenly, the consistency of Jell-O. "Mack."

Mack placed his hands in the pockets of his pants—black, designer—and walked around the hood of his car to stand at the bottom of the steps. He looked up at her, his eyes shuttered. "I'm on my way to see Jameson…anything I should know before I head over there?"

Molly understood his asking; he knew she and Jameson were tight. Molly lifted one shoulder. "He's irascible and demanding. He fired another nurse this morning."

Frustration flickered across Mack's face. "That's how many now?"

"Nurses? One this week. Two last week."

Mack pushed a broad hand through his slightly wavy hair. "He needs a nurse, Molly. He can't be on his own."

Molly heard the accusation in his voice and bristled. "Hey, I'm trying to run the resort as well as keep an eye on him. There's only so much I can do but I did persuade his current nurse to stick around until you arrived today. He needs to accept help or, better yet, you find someone to nurse him who won't buckle when he yells."

"He doesn't mean it. He's just frustrated."

Molly scowled at him, annoyed that he was lecturing her about the man whom she'd known and adored all her life and worked with since she left college. The man she'd, sadly, betrayed a few months after Mack left Moonlight Ridge and Asheville.

Don't think about that now, Molly.

Irritated that she'd let him get to her, she forced herself to smile. "Did you have a good trip?" she asked, her tone completely, to her ears at least, false.

"Do you really care?"

Not a whit, she thought, keeping her smile in place. His

eyes narrowed as he tipped his head back to look up, taking in the three-story stone building, covered in thick ropes of ivy. Like her, he'd grown up in shadow of this stone-and-wood building. He in Jameson's house a short distance away, she, until she was thirteen, in the manager's house situated beyond the orchard at the back of the property.

A picture of a young Mack, maybe eight or nine, looking up at the mansion in the same way—bemused and impressed, as if he was wondering what he was doing here—flashed on her brain's big screen. She'd often seen it on his face over the years, as if he still couldn't believe he got to call Moonlight Ridge home.

"Are you moving into Jameson's house?" she asked Mack.

Mack looked like he swallowed a sour lemon. "Since he doesn't have a nurse, I suppose I, temporarily, have to."

Molly narrowed her eyes at him. When they were kids, Mack had hung on Jameson's every word, and Jameson hadn't been shy to tell, and show, them how much he loved his sons. He'd been tough but fair. As one of Jameson's longest employees—she'd worked for him temporarily since she was fourteen years old and permanently since she was twenty-two—she'd seen how the feud among the brothers impacted her boss. Jameson managed to still be the consummate host, the charming innkeeper, but Molly saw him in his unguarded moments, and his sadness had been tangible.

And, okay, she was being a bit fanciful here, but Molly was convinced that Jameson's moods affected the inn. When Jameson felt upbeat and buoyant the mansion seemed to glow, its windows, always clean, sparkled and the ivy danced. It seemed to shimmer, radiating his vivacity. When Jameson felt despondent or angry, the inn seemed to shrink in on itself, the stones seemed colder and the wooden frames, and doors, appeared dull.

To Molly, the inn was another character, the mad, rich, *adored* geriatric aunt everyone ran circles around. Well, she and Jameson did; the three Holloway boys left them behind a long time ago. Like Jameson, she didn't want to live anywhere else but here. One day, when Jameson heard what she'd done, she would have to leave, but today wasn't that day.

"A nurse I am not," Mack said, yanking Molly back to their conversation, "but spending some time together will give us a chance to catch up."

Molly gestured to the ornate doors behind her. "I need to get back to work and I'm sure you want to see Jameson. I'd appreciate it if you could take over the search for another nurse for him. Maybe you'll find someone who'll stick around."

Because he, sure as hell, wouldn't.

Two

In her messy office, Molly heard a rap on her partly open door and wearily lifted her head. Perfect. Just one more person she didn't want to see…

With her tiny build, waist-long blond hair and bright blue eyes, Beth looked like an angel, but Molly knew her brother's girlfriend was manipulative, demanding and self-absorbed. She fit into the Haskell clan really, really well.

"What do you want?" Molly asked her, her voice flat. Six months ago Grant demanded she find Beth a job at the resort and she'd handed her CV to Jameson, hoping and praying nothing came of it. Beth's résumé wasn't overly impressive but she had, apparently, bookkeeping experience, and Jameson hired her.

The books had been a mess before and Molly knew that Beth had made a bad situation considerably worse.

Before Jameson's collapse, Molly had expressed her concerns to him and he'd promised to look into the situation. If Molly had her way, she'd fire Beth but the hiring and firing of senior staff started and stopped with Jameson, and she didn't have the authority.

Great news for Beth; bad news for her.

"I heard that Mack Holloway has arrived."

Molly just stared at her, hoping to keep her expression bland. "If you've stepped in here to make asinine observations, you can just leave."

"I know that you and Mack had a thing way back when but if you are thinking of confiding in him, I would caution against it."

Molly rubbed her temples with the tips of her fingers, conscious of the headache building behind her eyes. A month or so back, tired of hauling around guilt and remorse—and after discovering her brothers took the money she'd recently given her mother to pay the gas and water bill and lost it playing blackjack—she'd, once again, told her family she was done and that they were on their own.

On hearing that she'd no longer fund their irresponsible lifestyle, her mom cried and told her she was unkind and a bad daughter. Vincent informed her that she could spare the cash; she was single, was being paid a mint and she owed them. Grant put his hand through the wall of the living room.

And when they calmed down, they did what they always did; they resorted to blackmail. If she didn't do as they asked, they'd tell Jameson she stole two thousand dollars from him when she was a teenager. They'd also imply that she hadn't stopped stealing from him, that she was more like their father than he ever imagined.

Jameson fired her accountant father for embezzling more than a hundred thousand dollars from him to fund his blackjack habit and charged him with theft. With her dad out on bail, Jameson gave them two weeks to vacate their house and the day the movers arrived, her dad dropped to the floor. Her last memory of her father was watching him leave Moonlight Ridge in an ambulance.

After his death, and despite the scandal, Jameson allowed the Haskell family to remain in their house on the grounds. It had been a wonderfully kind, magnanimous gesture but her mother and siblings never saw it that way. After her dad's death, Molly vividly recalled many conversations between Jameson and Vivi: him asking for her to exert some control over her rebellious older brothers, her blaming Jameson for her husband's death on the stress of being fired and facing prison.

After a series of incidents involving her brothers— skinny-dipping in the lake, playing their music far too loud, their harassing some VIP guests—Jameson insisted they leave the property. Despite being thirteen, Molly fully understood why Jameson didn't want any of the Haskells around. She couldn't blame him; she never wanted to be around her family, either.

Weeks ago, knowing that there was only one way to end this cycle of blackmail—and tired of living with her family's threats, with her burning secret, with the heavy guilt— Molly resolved to find the courage to tell finally Jameson the truth. She had the money to pay Jameson back, with interest, and if he fired her, well, she'd reluctantly accept his decision.

Being canned and being cut out of his life was no less than she deserved.

But Jameson collapsed before she could confess.

Now, because Jameson had to avoid stress at all costs, her confession would have to wait. She'd also considered moving Beth to another position within the resort but that meant hiring another bookkeeper and she didn't have the authority to do that.

No, the best course of action was to let Beth continue in

her role, keeping her on a short leash and scrutinizing her work. And she'd keep funding her family until Jameson was stronger and could handle stress better.

Molly stared at Beth, not bothering to conceal her loathing. "You do realize that this is blackmail, right?"

Beth shrugged. "You shouldn't have threatened to stop helping your family."

Molly slapped her hand on her desk, her temper bubbling. "My brothers are older than me and haven't held down a job, ever. My mother has never held down a job for more than three months. Why should I help them?"

"Because Jameson pays you a ridiculously inflated salary and you can afford it," Beth replied, looking nonchalant.

"Jameson pays you a good salary, too!" Molly pointed out.

"They are your family and my money is mine."

Molly felt the old, oh-so-familiar wave of frustration. "When Jameson is better, I will tell him what I did. He'll probably fire me and I'll be out of a job. And the free ride will come to an end for all of you."

Beth had the audacity to smile. "You don't have the guts to cut them off, Molly. If you did, you would've divorced yourself from your family years ago. No, you still think they are going to snap out of this slump and you are all going to be a family and sing 'Kumbaya' around the fire."

Molly dropped her eyes, knowing that Beth had nailed her biggest wish, her secret desire for a loving and supportive family. Her mom had never been there for her—she didn't think Vivi even liked her much—and her brothers were consistently unreliable. She didn't need a psychologist to tell her that part of the reason she attached herself to Jameson, and his family, was her need to be part of a unit that loved and valued her. In Jameson she had a father figure and a mentor, Travis and Grey were her brothers, and

Mack? Well, she'd thought she'd have her own family, the family she'd always wanted, with the oldest Holloway son.

Dead wrong there, Haskell.

Molly looked up and met Beth's icy eyes.

"The ball is yours to play, Molly. Don't confide in your old boyfriend, keep paying the family's bills and none of us will tell Jameson. He might or might not believe us but either way, it will upset him and we don't want that, do we?"

No, they definitely didn't.

Beth sent her another mocking smile and Molly considered throwing a stapler at her head. But before she could finish the thought, Beth stepped back into the hall and glided away.

Holy crap, could this day get any worse?

An hour later Mack stood outside Molly's office door and instead of knocking and entering, he took a moment to look at his onetime best friend, his first love. She was still as slim as she'd been at seventeen, with impossibly long legs, rounded hips and breasts that once fitted his hands perfectly.

Move your eyes up, Holloway.

Molly's body was world-class but her face still had the power to stop him in his tracks. Her grandfather was from Cuba, her mother's family had Scandinavian roots and she was a mixture of ethnicities. Her hair was still a riotous mop of blond, tight curls and he loved her sun-kissed, clear, gorgeous skin. Her nose was long and straight, her mouth wide, with a full sexy bottom lip he'd loved to nip.

But it was her eyes that always had the ability to drop him to his knees. They were a curious color, sometimes an aqua-blue, sometimes a light, direct green, sometimes a combination of both and touched with silver. The ring holding in all that color was a deep, dark blue, close to black, and her lashes were dark, long and thick. Her eyebrows, shaped and dark, were perfectly arched.

He'd loved her once, intensely, crazily. Fifteen years ago she'd been the reason why the sun rose and set, why birds flew and waves crashed. She'd been all that mattered.

That all changed the night of the accident and, last night, he'd spent many hours last night recalling every detail of that night from hell.

And, as always, he couldn't forget that it was his biological dad's voice he heard as the wheels of his truck left the road. *You killed your mom and now your brothers might be dead, too. Leaving you was the best decision I ever made!*

The memories hadn't faded, not even a fraction. The storm had been wild and wicked, both inside the truck and out. Grey sat next to him on the bench seat of his F-150; Travis had been next to the door. The wind rocked the vehicle and his wipers battled to keep up with the pounding rain, and his headlights barely cut through the darkness. Travis was pissed that he and Grey hauled him away from his then girlfriend and hadn't stopped bitchin' since they left the restaurant's parking lot. He'd told Travis to shut the hell up, that he was trying to concentrate on the road but, instead of silence descending, Grey, normally the peacemaker, added gas to the bonfire when he ripped into Travis.

The combination of low visibility, speed and temper caused him to miss the curve of the road. Someone had been yelling as the truck became airborne and the right-hand side of the vehicle slammed into the side of the ravine.

And it was all because he'd lost control; he'd acted without thinking. He'd almost killed his brothers and while he and Grey escaped with minor injuries, Travis shattered his leg, lost his football scholarship to a prestigious college and had to rethink his life and make new plans.

When he lost control, bad things happened. And the person most able to make him lose control was Molly. And that was why he walked away from her, without a word or explanation.

To Mack, love meant losing control, and he was damned if he'd ever let that happen again.

Mack rubbed his chest above his heart and hauled in some air, remembering that a few years after he'd made peace with Jameson, he'd come home to visit his dad and, feeling cocky, decided to end the years of silence between him and Molly.

They weren't, he reasoned, kids anymore and they could put the past behind them. Shortly after arriving home on a fantastically hot Saturday in July, he'd gone in search of her and eventually tracked her down to the pond on the far northwest boundary of the property.

They used to make the walk often, crossing the steel-covered bridge and taking an overgrown path through a small copse of trees to the little lake. The guests never made it to the pond; the trail wasn't well marked and he, Molly and his brothers considered the pond to be their private swimming hole. It was where they built their treehouse, where they'd camped out under the stars.

He recalled approaching the pond from the trees and she'd been standing on the bank, dressed in a small bikini, poised to dive into the water. He instantly swelled in his shorts, desperate to reach her and haul her into his arms, thinking they could make love on her towel, in the sunshine. The need to have her, taste her, to make her his again had been overwhelming.

Memories collided with lust and he recalled the plans they'd made, the house they were going to build, the kids and dogs they were going to adopt, the life they were going to lead. The longing that swept through him at lost dreams and unfulfilled wishes caused his knees to liquefy, and he placed his hand on the nearest tree trunk to keep his balance.

Molly made him lose control and because control was *all* that was important, he turned around and walked away, determined to embrace his life of surface-based relationships and being responsible for only himself.

Subsequently, he'd only come back to Moonlight Ridge for flying, in-and-out visits. But now he was stuck in Asheville, overseeing the resort for two months or so. When his time was up, he'd hand over the responsibility to Grey. Or to Travis.

But in the coming weeks, he needed to talk to and interact with the manager of the hotel.

And that person was Molly.

Crap.

Mack rubbed his hand over his face and told himself to get a grip. He was here to do a job and nothing would be accomplished by his standing in the hallway outside her office.

Time to stop thinking about the past and get to work, Mack told himself and rapped on her door. Her head shot up and those sexy eyebrows lifted in surprise. Then her eyes widened and she stood up abruptly, pushing her chair back so hard that it slammed into the credenza behind her desk. "Is it Jameson? Is he okay?"

"Why wouldn't he be?" Mack asked as he stepped into her chaotic office.

"You have a weird expression on your face."

He'd thought he'd perfected his implacable expression but obviously not. Damn. "Jameson is fine, Molly. I checked in on him and he's asleep. I thought sleep was more important than letting him know I was here, so I didn't wake him up."

Molly closed her eyes, her expression one of pure relief. When she opened them again, she looked puzzled. "Okay, good. Then what can I do for you?"

"As you know, the only way we could get Jameson to take time away from the business was if one of his sons came home to oversee the resort while he is recuperating."

Molly's curls bounced as she nodded. "But I'm here so you don't need to bother," she said. "I'm perfectly capable of running this place on my own. You can concentrate on your own businesses."

Mack steeled himself to burst her bubble. "Jameson was adamant that there's too much for you to do and manage on your own."

Mack saw dismay and hurt flicker in her eyes before they iced over. "He doesn't trust me."

Now that was just stupid. Jameson trusted Molly almost as much as he trusted them. "Stop feeling sorry for yourself," he snapped, "and think."

He ignored her sharp, annoyed intake of breath. "This place is enormous and Jameson has always had a pack of managers. Now it's only you. Why is that?" Mack demanded.

He saw her hesitate and watched as she looked for a reason that would placate him. Mack hoped she wouldn't lie.

Molly held his eyes for a minute but then all that stunning blue slid away. She dropped into her chair and pushed her curls off her forehead and out of her eyes. "I'm not sure what you mean, Mack."

"If you don't then you shouldn't be the manager of this hotel," Mack stated, keeping his voice cool.

Molly muttered a curse too low for him to hear. Gesturing to the chair, she ordered him to take a seat. "Okay, do you want the truth?"

"I always want the truth, Molly."

She didn't even bother to hide her skepticism at that statement. "Sure you do." Before he could ask her what she meant by that low, bitter statement, she told him about rising costs and falling income. The resort was unfashionable, needed updating, it was cash strapped and the guest occupancy was too low to sustain the business. She also informed him that the room decor was outdated and the food served by the kitchen was good, but not great.

Well, at least she wasn't looking at Moonlight Ridge through rose-colored glasses.

"Also, I think there's a perception out there that this place is for people of a certain age, so younger people with money don't come here," Molly added.

"And have you any ideas on how to turn that around?" Mack asked. Talking business with her was a lot easier than delving back into the past but he wasn't a fool; at some point they'd discuss why he left without saying goodbye.

But since she was treating him like he was just another business consultant or colleague, maybe he'd dodged that bullet. He hoped. And prayed.

Molly bent sideways, yanked open a drawer and pulled out a file, which she slid across the desk to him. "Actually, I do. I've spent an enormous amount of time working on a proposal to revitalize the resort. Jameson and I were going to dissect our business model, reconsider our marketing strategy and look at ways to cut costs. But then he got sick."

Mack tapped his finger on the glossy cover of Molly's file. "I'll read it as soon as I can and we can have that discussion you were going to have with Jameson."

Molly sent him a scathing look. "I'll believe that when it happens."

Yeah, there was no ignoring her sarcastic tone. "I don't lie, Molly. If I say I'm going to do something, I do it."

Molly shoved her chair, stood up and walked over to the

window, folding her arms across her chest. "Forgive me if I don't trust anything you say, Holloway."

Mack gripped the bridge of his nose. So they were going to go there here and now. Oh, joy.

He'd apologize and then they could put this behind them and, hopefully, move the hell on.

He mentally tested a few sentences and when none of them felt right, he settled for simple. "I'm sorry I left you without saying goodbye, Molly."

She didn't respond for a long time and when she finally looked at him, he saw one raised eyebrow, a sure sign of her displeasure.

"That's it? One measly sorry?"

Mack lifted his hands, knowing he was on unstable ground. He recognized the temper in Molly's eyes; it burned as brightly as it did the day her brothers put a frog down the back of her dress.

"So no apology for not contacting me to let me know that you were okay? No sorry for not giving me an explanation, for dropping me from your life, for treating me like I was disposable? We were friends first, Mack! You don't treat people like you did but you especially don't treat your oldest friend like that!"

A wave of shame, hot and acidic, broke over him, and Mack closed his eyes, wishing he were anywhere but here. He wanted to be back in Nashville, in his office, or at one of his many breweries, talking about dry hopping and fermentation, yeasts and yields. He didn't want to be here, doing this.

Mostly because she was right. He'd treated her badly and his only excuse, if there was one to be had, was that he felt that he didn't deserve her; he didn't deserve anything good in his life. Giving her up had been one more way to punish himself.

It had also been a way to take back control. Love, in all its forms, was uncontrollable.

"I'm sorry I hurt you." What else could he say?

Molly turned slowly and her direct gaze pinned him to the chair. "But you're not apologizing for leaving me alone, for running, for not having the decency to say goodbye face-to-face."

He couldn't tell her that if he'd done that then he wouldn't have left. If she'd asked him to stay, he would've because he'd loved her so damn much.

He'd failed his brothers and father. He didn't deserve her love, to have a family. It was far, far easier to be alone.

That was a truth he freely admitted, but only to himself.

Molly slid her hands into the pockets of her black pants, her expression remote. She nodded to the door. "I'm sure you want to unpack, get settled. While you do that, I'll get a housekeeper to dust and air Jameson's office, which, as you know, is right next door. It hasn't been used for a few weeks."

Subject closed, Mack thought. Thank God.

Mack nodded. "Thanks, M."

Mack winced at her old nickname. Jameson used to call them M&M when they were very young and the name stuck. But they weren't eight and seven anymore, and if he was going to work with Molly, he needed to keep things professional.

Before she could lambaste him for being overfamiliar, Mack changed the subject. "When Jameson wakes up, I will talk to him about him firing his nurses."

Molly looked skeptical. "And you think that will help?"

His dad was as hardheaded as a concrete block so...no. Not really. "I can only try. Maybe he has an idea of whom he wants to nurse him."

"Yeah, right." Molly's expression suggested he was grasping at straws.

"I'll make a plan." He was very, very good at getting what he wanted. When he had a goal in mind, it took a nuclear missile strike to knock him off course. It was how he built up a chain of indie breweries and gastropubs, becoming a millionaire by the time he was thirty.

He was single-minded and ruthless and had tunnel vision. Very little was of importance to him outside his work.

Molly had once been everything he ever wanted, desired or craved. And a part of him was terrified that if he allowed his guard to fall, even a little, she would become important to him again.

Not happening, not ever again. Control. He needed to find it. And hold on to it.

"Once you find him full-time help you could move into one of the lakeside cottages if you want to."

Mack stared at her, noticing the blue stripes beneath her lovely eyes. She was tired and more than a little stressed. He knew she loved Jameson and was worried about him, but he was on the mend. The hotel might be teetering but it wasn't about to go under. And even if it was, Molly had to know that, between them, he and his brothers would, and could, inject a healthy amount of cash to keep it going.

So what was really worrying her?

And why did he care?

Mack rubbed the back of his head and considered her question. The cottages were pretty, had awesome views but weren't private. "No, I don't want to bump into any of the guests. Any other options?"

"My old house—the manager's house—is vacant at the moment."

He heard, from Jameson, that the three-bedroomed staff house had been converted into a self-catering villa years ago. Mack suspected that it hadn't, like so many other of the resort's rooms and free-standing cottages on the edge of the lake, seen many guests lately.

"Why don't you live in that house, like the hotel managers usually do?"

"It's far too big for me," Molly replied. "I asked Jameson if I could convert the rooms above the stables into an apartment and he agreed. I live there."

The stables were a stone's throw from her old house, the only two buildings on the west side of the property. The enormous parking area and a large swath of woods separated the two buildings from the other staff cottages.

The house, he recalled from visiting on those early playdates with Molly, had a wide veranda and great views of the Blue Ridge Mountains. Yeah, he'd be comfortable there.

"Your old house will work for me. I'll get the key from the front desk."

"Don't bother." Molly walked back over to her desk, her stride long and sexy, and bent over slightly to open another desk drawer. She pulled out a key and tossed it at his head. Mack, knowing she couldn't hit a barn door from two feet with a BB gun, lifted his left hand and snatched the key out of the air. He had excellent reflexes, but Molly's throws had never been much of a challenge.

That, at least, hadn't changed.

Molly rubbed her forehead with her fingertips. "If there's nothing else, will you excuse me? I'm hours behind and it's not even ten yet."

Mack nodded and slowly stood up. Unable to help himself, he walked over to where Molly stood and gently, so very gently, pushed a crazy curl behind one ear. His fingertip brushed her cheek and her skin was still baby soft but her scent was sexy, a little wicked.

"It *is* good to see you, Mol."

Molly, because she was Molly, slapped his hand away and stood back. "Too little, too late, Mack. Now go. I have work to do."

Mack lifted his hands and backed away, resisting the urge to haul her into his arms and kiss her until her knees buckled and sexy little groans emerged from deep in her throat. He still, dammit to hell and back, wanted her.

Not going to happen, Holloway, so get that thought out of your stubborn brain.

Focus on what you can control. And that was work. Talking of…

"Please schedule a meeting with senior management at two this afternoon. I want a SWOT analysis—strengths, weaknesses, opportunities and threats—"

"I have a post-grad degree in business, Holloway. I know what a SWOT analysis is, for goodness' sake!" Molly told him, looking offended.

Right. He remembered hearing she'd gotten her master's in business administration sometime back. If he didn't think she'd bite his head off, he'd congratulate her on that achievement.

"I want them to do one for their department, one for the organization as a whole, then you and I will take those, see what we're missing and work out a plan of action," Mack told her.

Molly nodded at the file on her desk. "I have already done all that."

"Bring copies of your documentation to the meeting, but I want their perspective, too," Mack stated.

Molly stared at him like he was losing his mind. "They can't get that done in—" she checked her watch, a cheap knockoff of a well-known brand "—five hours."

"I'm not looking for a perfectly printed glossy brochure,

Molly," he replied, looking down at her bright and detailed folder. "I just need a list, a starting point."

"Still…"

"Two o'clock, in the conference room. I presume it's unoccupied."

"You presume right," Molly said, her tone sarcastic once again. "We haven't had a conference here for quite a while."

Why not? It didn't make any sense.

Mack placed his hand on the door and pulled it open. Looking over his shoulder, he frowned at her. "I hope you aren't going to let the past color our working relationship, Molly."

He saw the anger flash in those extraordinary eyes, the flush that tinged her cheeks pink. Man, she was beautiful…

And off-limits.

She pointed to the door and her voice, when she spoke, was shaky. "Get the hell out of my office."

Mack, recognizing the signs of her temper, thought it prudent to step into the hallway. Pulling the door shut behind him, he rested his forehead on her door and gently banged it against the thick panel. *Right, excellent attempt at making amends, friends and influencing people, Holloway.*

Not.

Three

A week later, as was her habit, Molly left her office, walked toward the rose garden and veered right onto a path designed to meander through the wild garden. Mack still hadn't found a nurse for Jameson and, instead of overseeing the resort, he was filling in as his father's nurse, with the once-fired Rylee stopping by twice a day to check vitals and dispense meds, and to be on call for emergencies. Judging by the constant barrage of text messages she'd received from Jameson, it wasn't going well and Jameson had fired his son on three occasions. Mack, as he'd told her when she stopped in to check on them yesterday, told her to keep bail money ready because blood was about to be spilled. He didn't specify whose.

Molly slipped through the gate that allowed her access onto Jameson's private property. After greeting Jameson's golden retrievers, Trouble and Nonsense, she stepped into his huge open-plan kitchen and dining room, the double-volume space dominated by exposed wooden roof beams. A few years back Jameson converted the barn with an eye to the future, creating large bedrooms with en suite bathrooms on the second floor and installing a massive dining table to accommodate his sons, daughters-in-law and all their children.

So far not one of his sons was falling in line with his plans.

Families—they were such weird entities, Molly mused. Jameson once had the perfect family, but it was ripped apart by the hand of fate. She had two brothers and a mother but she had no illusions of her importance in their lives; they neither loved nor liked her. She was, simply, their personal cash machine, a means to an end. But she still had trouble emotionally, physically and financially divorcing herself from them.

She'd never had much of a family, but she was stronger now than when she was a child and she could, and would, tackle the world on her own. And she might have to, if Jameson banished her from Moonlight Ridge after she confessed her sins.

Molly felt her stomach knot at the thought. She'd lose her home, a job she adored, the respect of the man who'd guided, advised and loved her all of her life. Was her self-respect, being able to move forward with a clear conscience, worth the price she'd have to pay?

Molly shoved her hands into her hair and tugged, feeling herself whirling away on a tornado of self-doubt. Was losing Jameson too high a price to pay? *Yes.*

If she remained silent, could she live with herself? *No.*

She was stuck between the devil and the deep blue sea. And she was drowning.

But this wasn't the right time to confess as his neurosurgeon warned them that Jameson couldn't be subjected to any stress, that he had to be, for a few months at least, shielded from any anxiety-causing issues. The knowledge that she'd stolen from him would send his blood pressure skyrocketing, risking an actual brain aneurysm this time.

Molly placed her hands on the cool wood of the dining table and stared at the golden surface. She couldn't confess and she couldn't talk to anyone about her it-keeps-me-awake-at-night worries about the resort.

So what could she do?

Molly straightened her shoulders. She could do her job and manage the resort to the best of her ability. So far working with Mack had been tolerable, mostly because she could, mostly, pretend he wasn't there. He was spending all his time with Jameson and, she presumed, keeping tabs on his own business empire. He'd call every morning at nine o'clock sharp and ask if there were any problems.

The only problem was his deep, sexy voice, the one that fueled her X-rated dreams. Mack, naked, his expression intense, saying her name as he—

"Molly?"

Molly stood up so fast her head swam and she grabbed the back of the nearest chair to keep her balance. Within seconds Mack's strong hands were holding her biceps, steadying her. Then she made the mistake of breathing deeply and she inhaled his scent, immediately transported back to summer nights, hot and muggy, skinny-dipping in the pond before climbing up into the treehouse to lie on the rickety deck beneath the stars to intimately explore, with inexperienced hands, the wonder of each other's bodies.

Molly lifted her eyes to his and his fingertips dug into her bare skin as he pulled her closer. She wanted to step back, thought she should, but her feet wouldn't obey her brain's suggestion. Mack's hands slid down her arms to link his fingers in his and she watched, fascinated, as his mouth dropped to hers. He took his time to reach her mouth and, impatient, Molly couldn't wait so she stood on her tiptoes to taste him. Her eyes closed as his lips met hers and she sighed, ignoring the thought that this felt right, that she was finally home.

Mack placed a hand on her lower back to pull her closer to him, close enough for her to feel the hard, very hard, ridge of his erection pushing into her stomach, close enough to feel the shudder that ran through him.

They shouldn't be doing this, but his mouth on hers was the sweetest honey, the tartest spice. Sexy and demanding and amazing.

Entranced, Molly wound her arms around Mack's neck, her fingers pushing into his silky hair. Holding her palm against his head, she kept his mouth on hers, needing him to take the kiss deeper, harder. Mack heard her silent plea and slid his tongue into her mouth, finding hers and leading it into a hot, desperate dance. Time and memories faded and she was seventeen again, lost in his touch, happy to follow where he led.

Teeth scraped, tongues dueled and hands raced as they fell into the moment, the deliciousness of the forbidden. Mack rediscovered the shape of her butt and she realized that his chest was broad, muscular, and his shoulders wide. Mack pushed his thigh between her legs and Molly just managed to resist rubbing herself against him. But she couldn't resist pulling his shirt from his cargo shorts, discovering the smooth skin of his back, feeling the hard muscles of his ladderlike stomach.

They had to stop this before they couldn't...

But not yet, not just yet. She wanted more, his fingers— or his mouth—on her nipples, between her legs...

Molly ran her hand over his fly, heard his groan as he

pushed his erection into her palm, his mouth on her neck. She moved her thumb to rub his tip but encountered…

Nothing. Fresh air.

Molly blinked, shook her head and realized that Mack had stepped away from her, hurriedly yanking his blue button-down shirt over his shorts. Not knowing where she was or, frankly, *who* she was, Molly hauled in some air and tried to get her brain to fire up. As her eyes started to focus, she raised her eyebrows at Mack, who nodded to the kitchen door.

"Company," he mouthed.

Blushing, then grimacing, Molly turned to look at the half-open stable door. Molly instantly recognized that dark head and the tiny frame. Giada worked for Jameson as a housekeeper at Moonlight Ridge years ago, and Molly hadn't seen the tiny lady for far too long.

Her embarrassment forgotten, Molly hurried across the kitchen and opened the bottom half of the stable door and pulled Giada into a hug. After they separated, Molly kept hold of her hands. "Oh, it's so, so good to see you."

Giada raised her hand to hold Molly's face. "*Cara mia*, you are so beautiful. And all grown up!"

"When did you get back to town?" Molly demanded, pulling her into the kitchen. "Are you still living with your sister in Florida?"

Grief skittered through Giada's eyes. "She died a few months ago."

"I'm so sorry," Molly murmured. Hoping that her face was no longer bloodred, she gestured to Mack. "Obviously, you remember Mack?"

Mack bent down, and down, to kiss both of Giada's cheeks. "It's so good to see you, Giada."

"Mack." Giada ran her hands up and down his well-muscled arms. "My, my, you have grown into a beautiful man."

Mack's smile was wide and genuine and Molly's traitorous heart flipped over. And over again. "Not as beautiful as you, gorgeous. As Molly said, it's wonderful to see you."

Giada's eyes, filled with amusement, darted from his face to hers and back again. "You are being too kind. From what I saw, you two are probably cursing me to hell and back for interrupting."

Molly winced. Giada never did beat around the bush when she could plow through it.

Mack slid his hands into his pockets. "I presume you are here to see Jameson?"

Right, judging by his inscrutable expression, no one would suspect that he'd just had his hand up and under her shirt. She had no doubt that someone half-blind could see that she'd been thoroughly kissed. Though *kissed* was too tame a word for what they'd done...

Inhaled each other might be a better description.

"I am. Is he up to visitors?" Giada asked.

Mack nodded. "He's in his sitting room, down the hallway and on your left. I'm sure he'd be very glad to see you," Mack stated. "We'll join you in a few minutes."

They both watched her walk away and when Molly was sure she was out of earshot, she forced herself to look at Mack. Feeling a little shaky, she pulled out a chair from the dining table and sank down onto its seat, dropping her head.

Holy, holy crap.

Molly heard Mack moving toward her and watched as he rested his hip against the table, not far from her head. He was too close and it gave her ideas...

Bad ideas...like reaching for his fly and picking up where they'd left off.

God.

Help.

Her.

"That shouldn't have happened."

Molly lifted her head to look up, stopping at his impassive expression. His eyes were shuttered and he looked like he was about to launch into a discussion about cash flows and profit margins. "Thank you, Captain Obvious," Molly muttered.

"In case you are wondering whether we are going to pick up where we left off, that's not going to happen," Mack said, his voice cool but sharp. "I'm only here for a short time and I'm not looking for a relationship. I don't do relationships. Hell, I barely do flings."

Her mouth fell open, not quite able to believe the words he was spouting, that he could be so damn arrogant to assume that, just because he was here again, she wanted to dive back into his arms and bed.

She'd just kissed him, not proposed marriage or offered to have his babies…

The *moron*.

Molly pushed her chair back and stood, all traces of her embarrassment gone and replaced by cold anger. She met his eyes and when his widened, she knew that he'd clocked her temper. "Are you freaking kidding me? Why would you assume that?"

"Uh—"

Molly slapped her hand on his hard pec and pushed him, annoyed that she couldn't budge him. "How incredibly arrogant of you to think that, just because you are back in my life, I'd welcome you back into my bed. I may have missed you, but you left me without a word. I haven't had a proper conversation with you in years and I'm solidly, completely, massively pissed at you! You acted like a jerk and I'd rather sleep with a snake!"

"Then why did you kiss me like I was your last hit of oxygen?" Mack demanded.

Calm down, Molly, and do not let him see how rattled you truly are.

"C'mon, Mack, we've been combustible since the first time we made out. We may have changed but that hasn't," Molly said, trying to lighten her tone. "It was just a kiss, no big deal."

"It feels like it's a big deal," Mack countered.

Arrgh, why was he pushing this? "I'll admit you broke my teenage heart but I'm very over you, Holloway."

Mack scrubbed his hands over his face and when he dropped them, Molly saw remorse within those dark depths. Too little, too late.

Knowing he was about to apologize and not wanting to hear it, she lifted her hand to speak. "Let me just say this, Mack, and then, hopefully, we can move on. I missed my boyfriend, but God, I *mourned* my best friend. And you will never, ever get the chance to hurt me like that again."

Squaring her shoulders, she pushed away the tang of acidic emotions and stepped into the hallway. She'd visit with Jameson and Giada and then she'd head back to her office. It was getting late but she had work to do, reports to read, staff schedules to post, requisitions to authorize…

A business to save.

Mack watched Molly's lovely figure walk away and pushed a frustrated hand through his hair. He was all about control, it was his guiding principle, a core tenet of his life. As an adult, and intellectually, he knew his mom's death was not his fault—how could it be?—but that hadn't stopped his biological dad from blaming him and taking his anger out on his young son.

His dad's uncontrollable temper scared him and he loved

Jameson's steadiness and lack of volatility and tried to emulate his nonblood father. The one time he lost complete control had disastrous consequences, so these days he always thought twice—thrice—and acted once. He never ever allowed emotion to guide him and what he wanted was always tempered with thoughts about what he needed and whether he could live with all the possible consequences of his actions.

Since leaving Asheville he'd been careful, thoughtful, conservative...

But Molly Haskell could blow him out of the water. She still smelled the same, looked, in many ways, the same, but there was a strength to her now that intrigued him, a confidence that hadn't been there fifteen years ago. And that, he supposed, made sense. She'd grown up.

And, Mack thought, remembering her perfect breast under his hand, the curve of her stupendous butt, she'd grown up damn fine.

Stop it, Holloway, for crap's sake. She's just another gorgeous woman. He'd met, and bedded, quite a few since he was eighteen. But none of his past lovers had Molly's ability to crawl under his skin, upend his life and muddle his brain.

Molly, damn her, wasn't someone he could easily dismiss.

So far life in Asheville was anything but boring. In between trying not to throttle his irascible and demanding father, Mack kept tabs on what was happening with his chain of breweries and gastropubs and, when he had a spare moment, tried to get a handle on what was happening with the resort. But uncharacteristically, he was often distracted by the memories of how Molly loved him so long ago. His lips on hers, her hand on his shaft...

The memory of her pain and disappointment slapped at him, hard and fast. If they were going to work together,

Mack reluctantly conceded, they were going to have to address the past. Properly. Their brief conversation last week had barely scratched the surface.

And…

He'd rather have a hot ember rammed into his eye.

But he'd hurt her and he regretted that. Mack wondered what she would say if he told her that he spent many nights thinking of her, missing her with every atom of his being. Would she be surprised to hear that, in the weeks and months after leaving, he'd often woken with a wet-from-tears pillowcase, feeling like a bowling ball was residing in his stomach? That he, on a hundred occasions, maybe more, picked up his phone to call her, just to hear her voice?

He was pretty sure that she had no idea that when he'd left, he cut out his own heart, too.

But he hadn't been able to stay. The guilt had been intense, his relationships with his brothers were annihilated and Mack couldn't fathom how Jameson could love him after what he did. In losing control, he'd failed his father and his brothers.

After he left Asheville, school slid into work and he immersed himself in his business, establishing brewery after brewery, adding gastropubs to the mix. He had a fancy loft apartment, a cabin in Whistler, cars and toys and a crap-load of cash in the bank, numerous women he could call on if he needed company…

He worked. Played a little. Worked out. Worked and worked out some more.

Existed.

But kissing Molly was the most alive he'd felt in years. When she stepped into his arms and her mouth touched his, she became the watering can and he the starved-for-nutrients plant. Excitement and need coursed through him and if Giada hadn't banged on the door, he knew their kiss would've moved from hot to nuclear.

Mack held his palm parallel to the ground and shook his head when he saw the slight tremor in his fingers. She made him feel like this: shaky, weird, out of control.

That wasn't acceptable.

Right, he needed to nip this in the bud. He'd have a decent discussion with her, apologize for leaving her and ask whether they could put the past behind them. Once she accepted his apology—Molly had never been one to hold grudges—they could move on. He'd keep his interactions with her as brief and as professional as possible.

It would be fine. It *had* to be fine. He would not let Molly—and his being back home—make him lose sight of what was important.

And that was keeping control. Keeping it together. He was determined to leave here with his heart intact, his world unchanged.

Sorted, Mack thought as he walked down the hallway to join Giada and Molly in Jameson's downstairs sitting room.

It annoyed Jameson that he couldn't leap to his feet when Giada walked into his small sitting room off his large, ground-floor master suite. He was an old-fashioned Southern man and it galled him that he neither had the energy nor the strength to leap to his feet like he always did.

Energy was something still in short supply and he was sick of feeling like crap. Jameson ran his hand over his stubbled jaw and, briefly, wished he'd shaved. But he wouldn't let Mack help him and he still tired easily. But if he was better at accepting assistance and if he had a little more patience, he'd look a lot better than he currently did.

That wasn't a problem his ex-housekeeper had.

She barely looked any older than she did when she

worked for him twenty years ago. Her hair was still thick and wavy and he liked the threads of gray breaking up all that rich brown. Her blue eyes were as direct as ever and Jameson shifted in his chair, thinking that she could look right into his soul. Her body was, maybe, a little curvier, and there were fine lines at the corners of her take-no-bull eyes. For a woman in her late fifties, she was damn sexy.

He felt like day-old roadkill.

Jameson inhaled her perfume as she bent down to kiss his cheek, surprised at the hint of action in his pants. Okay, so his attraction to Giada hadn't changed. He'd been into her a long time ago but circumstances—her working for him and the fact that he had his hands full running Moonlight Ridge and raising three boys—conspired against his making a move.

"Jameson—" Giada kept her hands on his shoulders and shook her head "—you look like hell."

Great. Exactly what he needed to hear. "Giada. You're the very last person I expected today."

Giada sat down in the chair opposite him and lifted her shoulders in a languid, oh-so-Italian shrug. "I came back to Asheville, heard that you have been ill and thought I'd check up on you." Her eyes moved to the ashtray sitting on the side table next to his easy chair, and a deep frown pulled her dark, thin eyebrows together. The smoke from his cigar drifted toward the roof.

"Mannaggia a te!" Giada muttered. He didn't speak Italian but he recognized curse words when they were directed at him.

Before he could respond, she surged to her feet, picked up the cigar and crushed its tip, mangling it into a mess.

"Hey, those are expensive!"

"You've had brain surgery! Surely, your doctor told you to stop smoking?" Giada demanded, her hands on those luscious hips. She was short, the top of her head barely hit his shoulder, but she was feisty. And fierce.

He was saved from having to find an excuse, not that he had or needed one—if he wanted to smoke he damn well could!—by Molly stepping into the room. Jameson accepted her kiss and when she stepped back, noticed she was looking tired. And stressed.

He had no doubt that she and Mack had exchanged words.

M&M, he used to call them, his two peas in a pod. His oldest son and the daughter of his heart. Watching her heart break after Mack left had been pure torture, but apart from putting her to work to keep her busy and her mind off Mack, he hadn't interfered.

Raising three boys had never been a walk in the park but those few months directly after the accident had been a shit show. In hindsight, he knew that most of his energies had been directed toward Travis, spending hours and hours with him at the hospital. He'd been there for his injured son, but he'd failed to realize his two other sons were as psychologically damaged as Travis was physically hurt.

Grey retreated mentally and emotionally and Mack had dealt with his guilt and pain by running. There were still walls between him and his boys—lower than they'd been before—but still there. Jameson wanted them gone. And he wanted his sons to be brothers again, as tight as they were when they were kids. And if it took a freaking brain aneurysm to get his boys back and talking to each other, then so be it.

Failing that, he'd just bash their heads together…

Molly rubbed her thumb over his frown lines. "You're not supposed to be worrying, Jameson."

Jameson captured her hand and pressed a kiss onto her fingers. "Don't fuss, Mol."

"It's what I do best," Molly told him, sitting down next to him on the sofa.

"Did you see Mack?" Jameson asked her.

Jameson heard a snort of laughter from Giada and lifted his eyebrows, silently asking what she found amusing. Giada just grinned and shrugged.

"Yep." He frowned at her terse answer since Molly was normally a talker. Hopefully, while they worked together, something would spark between them again. *Two birds, one stone*, Jameson thought.

M&M were destined to be together and when they pulled their heads out of their butts, they'd catch that clue.

Jameson, conscious that he hadn't paid his guest any attention—and he wanted to—turned to Giada. "I heard from someone that you went to nursing school and that you graduated." He'd once offered to pay for her education but Giada, like Molly—God save him from stubborn women!—refused his offer. They'd both worked part-time jobs to put themselves through school and he admired their effort but it had been so damn unnecessary.

Really, life would be so much easier for all involved if people just did as he commanded!

Giada nodded. "I moved to Florida to attend school and to be closer to my sister. After I graduated, I worked in the ER for more than ten years. A year ago I took a sabbatical to nurse my sister through terminal cancer. I'm not sure what's next or where I want to be."

Jameson offered his condolences before asking his next question. "Are you thinking about moving back to Asheville, finding work here?" He really hoped so; he would like to see her again. When he was well, and back to full strength, he might even ask her out to dinner, to the theater. And then into his bed…

He really, *really* wanted her in his bed.

Giada's eyes twinkled, as if she knew where his thoughts had veered to. She'd always had the ability to do that, to look below the surface and see what he was thinking. He wasn't sure if he liked it.

Giada crossed her legs, tanned and smooth. She wore wedge sandals and her toes were painted bright orange. He had a thing for pretty feet, lovely legs and gorgeous Italian women…

"My sister left me quite a lot of money," Giada replied, "but I'm easily bored so I might look for some work soon. But not in the trauma ward. That's a little too intense for me. I need to find something to do. I get into trouble when I'm not busy."

That, he could believe. Luckily, there was lots to do in Asheville, he wanted to tell her. She'd just walked back into his life; he didn't want her walking out again so soon.

"What about a job looking after a cranky, stubborn, annoying survivor of a brain episode?"

Jameson whipped his head toward the door to where Mack stood, his legs and arms crossed, leaning into the door frame. Jameson lifted his hand to make a slashing movement against his throat, scowling madly.

He did not want, or need, the lovely Giada nursing him, fussing over him. No, thank you; a man had his pride. And he had more than most.

"That's a really good idea," Molly said, her eyes brightening.

No, it wasn't. It really damn wasn't!

"She's qualified, she's tough and, best of all, you don't scare her." Molly looked at Giada, who was looking as shocked as he felt. "What do you think, Giada? Jameson is spectacularly grouchy and none of his nurses stick."

"You are exaggerating and I can manage just fine on my own," Jameson muttered, sending Giada a pleading look. *Please say no; please don't consider this idea.* He couldn't bear it.

But he also didn't want her to leave the area. God knew when he'd see her again.

"You need a nurse," Mack told him, his voice brooking no argument. Jameson heard the authority in his voice and realized that his son was a man. And a man who took no crap.

Well, he was a man, too, and he'd never taken any crap. He started to stand up, realized that he couldn't and silently, but violently, repeated a long, vulgar string of curses.

He was weak, dammit. And maybe he could do with a little help.

Mack stepped into the room, his eyes on Giada. "We really do need someone to help him, Giada. We're driving each other insane. The salary is generous and, because we know how annoying he can be—" Mack's lips quirking took the sting out of that comment "—we'll make sure you have plenty of free time."

Giada looked like she was seriously considering Mack's offer. Oh, God, help him.

But God wasn't on his side because Giada tipped her head to the side and pursed her lips. "Would I stay here?"

Mack nodded. "Pops converted our bedrooms into three guest suites, one with an en suite bathroom, and the other two bedrooms share a bathroom. The biggest guest suite has a sitting area and a small desk and is ready for immediate occupation. Jameson's study is right next door and he has a huge collection of books if you are a reader. The resort's kitchen will provide you food. Housekeeping takes care of the house. You just have to deal with Mr. Grumpy."

Funny. *Not.*

Jameson held his breath, not wanting her to agree, but because he really wanted to see her again, hoped she would.

"He won't be allowed to smoke," Giana warned them.

"Fine with me." Mack swiftly replied.

"And me," Molly chirped.

Traitors. "Not fine with me," he growled.

"I want to talk to his doctors and get proper instructions on his care," Giada insisted, her pretty lips pursed.

"I'll make that happen," Mack told her.

"I am sitting right here," Jameson told them, raising his voice. "Do I not get a say in all of this?"

Three sets of inquiring eyes rested on his face. Mack lifted his hands. "Sure, go ahead, Pops."

"I'm not comfortable with this. I'd prefer to have a stranger nursing me."

"Then you shouldn't have fired the past three intensely professional nurses the agency sent you," Mack told him.

"And Giada doesn't take any crap," Molly said. She darted a look at Mack. "Do you remember her losing her temper when she found us in her linen cupboard?"

"That was because you ate chocolate in that cupboard and put your sticky fingers on my fresh white towels," Giada shot back.

Molly grimaced. "I forgot that part."

Giada's grin was a little smug. "I didn't." Her eyes slammed into Jameson's and within them, he saw the silent challenge...

Can you handle me, Holloway?

At full strength, with one hand behind his back. And any way she wanted him to. Right now? He wasn't so sure...

If she came to work for him, they'd fight but at least he wouldn't be bored. The nurses he'd banished had either been too insipid or too bossy but Giada, at least, was interesting. She wouldn't take his crap.

And he wouldn't take hers.

Yeah, he wouldn't be bored.

"Is that a yes?" Giada asked, her voice soft.

"Suppose so," Jameson replied, less than graciously. He looked down at his mangled cigar and grimaced. "Just don't mess with my cigars."

Giada sent him an evil smile. "I won't need to because, from this moment on, you are not going to be smoking anymore."

Right, gloves on. She would need to learn that she couldn't push him around. "Not happening."

Giada stood up, placed her hands on her hips and glared at him. "Want to bet?"

"You wouldn't dare!"

"Watch me!"

As they squared off, neither of them noticed Molly and Mack tiptoeing out of the room.

Four

"How long do you think it'll take for blood to spill?" Mack asked her, his voice low as his broad hand on her back guided her through the wrought iron gate and onto the path that would take them, if they went south, to the main lodge, and north, to their respective houses.

Annoyed that his light touch could send tingles along her skin, Molly stepped away from him and pushed her hand into her hair, holding a bunch of curls off her face. "An hour, two if we are lucky."

"Well, my money is on Giada. That lady is tough."

Molly nodded, feeling awkward. What did one say to a man whom she'd once loved but who was now little more than a stranger? Someone she'd barely spoken to for the past week, despite kissing him like he was her last hit of oxygen? Someone she was still attracted to, a man who still managed to light a fire in her belly, who made her tingle down…well, everywhere. Her body had front-row seats to her heartbreak; how could it betray her like this?

But maybe she was also overreacting. It had been a tough few weeks, she was overwhelmed by work and terrified that Moonlight Ridge would fall apart under her watch. She'd been desperately worried about Jameson, and her family was bugging her for cash again.

Kissing Mack was a way to step out, to avoid reality. And to remind her that she was a normal woman with normal needs. Needs she'd been neglecting for a long, long time. Man, this was all so complicated, and she didn't have time or the energy for complicated.

Molly sighed, wishing he'd just go and send one of his brothers to deal with Moonlight Ridge. Travis and Grey she could handle. Mack? Not so much.

Or at all.

Molly gestured to the path. "It's been a long day. I'm going to go."

Mack placed his hands into the back pockets of his cargo shorts, causing his blue button-down shirt to pull across his broad chest and to bunch around his impressive biceps. Molly resisted the urge to fan her face. "I'll walk with you for a while and stretch my legs. Then I'll go back and finalize the arrangements with Giada. Hopefully, she'll be able to start immediately because I'm a shocking nurse."

"And Jameson is a shocking patient," Molly murmured before shaking her head. "You don't need to walk with me, Mack."

Mack scrubbed the back of his neck. "It'll give us a chance to clear the air, Molly, and I think that's what we need to do, especially since we are going to be working closely together for the next few weeks. We should've done this days ago, but taking care of my dad was more time-consuming than I'd thought."

Molly wrinkled her nose. She was hot, tired and out of sorts and she wasn't up for a discussion about the past. And

Mack, she was sure, was only broaching this subject because it was expedient for him to do so. To oversee Moonlight Ridge, he needed her cooperation. Mack had always been single-minded and stubborn and Molly had no doubt he was ruthless, as well—few men achieved his level of success without that trait—and he'd do what was necessary to get the result he wanted. And if that included smoothing the ruffled feathers of his irritable ex-girlfriend, that was what he'd do.

She had no intention of making life easy for him.

Stepping away from him, Molly crossed her arms and tapped her foot. "A hot kiss and a quick chat after fifteen years won't change the past, Mack. Are you really that arrogant to think that I would be so grateful that you are back, so happy to be in your arms again, that I would fall into line like a good little soldier?"

She saw surprise flash in his eyes and knew he had been thinking just that. *Arrogant much, Holloway?*

"We were kids, Molly. It was a long time ago," Mack said, his tone reflecting a hint of annoyance. "We can move on, surely?"

He wanted her to, that much was obvious. And under that inscrutable face, she caught hints of his frustration. It was in the tiny tick in the muscle running down his jaw, in the tightening of the fine lines next to his eyes. In the flattening of his lips. Oh, most people wouldn't pick up the subtle changes in his expression but she could look beneath the surface better than most. After all, his had always been her favorite face.

"As I said, I'm not mad because you broke up with me, Mack," Molly told him, keeping her voice level. Losing her temper would only make her look childish.

"We would be having a completely different conversation if you actually *told* me you were leaving, if you only left after an explanation and a goodbye. But you didn't call and when you came back here, you avoided me. Every single time. Not once in fifteen years did you try to talk to me, to check up on me, or attempt to reboot our friendship.

"You've been back many times and on any one of those occasions you could've tracked me down, had a conversation, made a goddamn effort! Not because we once loved each other but because we were best *friends*, Mack. Friends don't treat each other like that," Molly added.

Mack dropped his head to stare at the stone path, his mouth pulled into grim lines. "For what it's worth, I am sorry, Curls. I never meant to hurt you and I hope you can forgive me."

Her heart did a triple beat of his old nickname for her, but one she hadn't heard for a decade and a half. But she couldn't let that distract her...

She finally had the proper apology she'd been waiting for. She'd been waiting for this moment for fifteen years but now that it was here, she didn't know what to do with it, how to handle him, what to say, what to do next. All she knew was that she was exhausted and that she didn't want to argue anymore.

"Thank you and your apology is accepted." Molly managed a small smile. Ha, look at her, adulting here!

"I'm going to go," Molly added when he failed to break the uncomfortable silence between them.

"Maybe we should talk about what happened in Jameson's kitchen," Mack stated, jamming his hands into the pockets of his shorts.

Oh, God, she didn't want to talk about the past but neither did she want to discuss her insane reaction to his mouth and hands and his strong, sexy body. "It was a *kiss*, Holloway. Don't get excited." Molly smiled to take the sting out of her words. "You're a good-looking guy and I got caught up in the moment. It won't happen again."

The tiniest hint of a smile turned his stern face a degree warmer. "Oh, I think it will."

"You should talk to someone about your delusions, Holloway." Molly forced herself to hold his intense gaze, to keep smiling. She would rather be pulled through a field covered in barbed wire than give Mack an inch. "It was momentary madness. Don't read more into it than that."

"The chemistry between us is still running hot."

Thanks for pointing that out, Einstein. "We kissed. It was a *mistake*. Let's forget about it and move on."

"Easy to say, less easy to do."

"Well, we can damn well try," Molly said, cursing the agitation in her voice. "Mack, I'm exhausted. It's been a long, long day and all I want is a huge glass of wine. As for us working together, I will be professional but that's it. There will be no personal conversations and no physical contact. Are we clear?"

Mack opened his mouth to argue—she recognized his need to always have the last word—but instead of speaking, he shook his head.

Thirty seconds passed before he spoke again. "We can try. I'm not sure how successful we'll be."

He thought she was just going to fall back into his arms, oh so grateful to be with him again. Was he completely nuts? Okay, their kiss had caught her off guard, but it was a mistake, and she couldn't allow herself to repeat past missteps. Mack hurt her; she'd never allow him to do that again. As for their attraction, well, he was a good-looking guy and it had been a long time since she'd had any bedroom-based fun.

And if she was overdue for some naked fun, she could

head into town, find a bar and pick someone up. She'd never had a one-night stand but how hard could it be?

What she wouldn't do was let Mack Holloway upend her world. Once bitten, twice shy, blah, blah...

Molly looked up into Mack's face and sighed. If only he wasn't so damn sexy. High cheekbones, that square-ish jaw and pointed chin, his straight nose. That hot, sexy mouth and the rough stubble on his cheeks. He was such a *man*...

But he wasn't the man for her.

"Have a good evening, Mack. I'll see you in the morning," Molly told him, pushing past him to walk up the path toward her apartment above the stable. A part of her was done, ready to collapse into a heap; another part of her wanted to grab her leotard and tights and head into Asheville to work out her frustration in a hip-hop class. It wasn't ballet but it was still moving her body in time to the music. It counted.

She might dance first, collapse later.

All she knew for sure was that she had to put some distance, physical and emotional, between her and Holloway.

The next day Mack, on his way to Jameson's office on the third floor of the inn, caught movement out of the corner of his eye as he passed Molly's office. Stopping, he looked through the half-open office door and frowned when he saw a woman looming over Molly's desk, her index finger under Molly's nose.

Beth, Moonlight Ridge's bookkeeper. He'd met her at last week's senior management meeting. And he hadn't been impressed.

Mack cleared his throat and two heads whipped around to look at him. Frustration and annoyance skittered across Beth's face while Molly just looked relieved...

What the hell was going on here?

Mack leaned his shoulder into the door frame, crossed his foot over his ankle and lifted his eyebrows. "Am I interrupting something?"

Judging by their expressions, he very obviously was. Molly was frowning and her lovely eyes—light green today—reflected her anxiety. And her annoyance.

And the fact that this woman—tall, slim, generically beautiful—could make her feel like that annoyed *him*.

"Is there a problem here?" Mack demanded, keeping his voice even but making sure Beth heard the authority in it.

He'd be a fool not to see the warning glance Beth threw Molly's way. Oh yeah, she was stirring a bubbling pot with a long-handled spoon.

Beth flashed him a smile that was meant to impress, or distract, him. It did neither. "Good morning, Mack. Molly and I were just chatting about the family."

"And what family would that be?" Mack asked.

Beth fiddled with a button on her too-tight shirt, a movement that was supposed to draw his eye to her impressive cleavage. Not wanting to play her game, he kept his eyes on her face and noticed her tiny pout.

"Why, the Haskells of course," Beth replied, her too-high voice still cheerful but her eyes flat and wary.

"Beth and Grant have been together for the past six months, Mack," Molly reluctantly explained.

Ah.

Beth touched the messy bun on the back of her head, the movement lifting her chest, and breasts, up. Mack did an internal eye roll. *Okay, I get it, you've got great tits.*

Strike one.

As Mack walked into the room, his eyes moved on to Molly and he spent a minute taking her in. She wore a white sleeveless top that showed off her toned arms, and through the silky material, he could see the outline of a lacy bra. A pendant, a purple stone tipped with silver on a long chain, was wound twice around her neck, and her crazy curls were pulled back from her face by a multicolored scarf. Her makeup, unlike Beth's, was light and fresh and he could see the freckles under a light layer of foundation. Her eyelashes were long and coated with black mascara, making her eyes seems lighter and brighter.

God, she was gorgeous. And, despite the way they left things last night, he still wanted her.

Mack pulled his attention back to what had initially caught his attention—Beth leaning over Molly's desk, her finger in his ex's face. Nobody treated Molly like that and he was surprised she put up with it. Molly was, after all, Beth's boss.

"You weren't having a friendly, let's-catch-up chat," Mack stated. He locked eyes with Beth and studied her, keeping his expression flat and cold.

She brazenly held his eyes for ten seconds, then twenty. At twenty-five, she started to waver and by thirty her eyes had dropped to look at the floor.

"You were looming over her desk and your finger was in Molly's face—"

"We were discussing a family matter—" Beth interrupted him. As a child, before he came to live with Jameson, he could never ever finish a sentence without his biological father overriding or deriding him. As a result, he loathed being interrupted.

Strike two.

"Mack, just leave it alone," Molly jumped in and he heard the I-can-deal-with-this in her voice.

He ignored her and kept his eyes on Beth. "Molly is your boss. Personal discussions can take place outside of work.

And if I ever see you looming over her and jamming your finger in her face again, you will be dismissed, instantly."

Beth's expression turned ugly. "You can't do that."

"Mack!"

Mack ignored Molly and sent Beth a cold, hard smile. "Do you want to test me on that?"

Beth opened her mouth to blast him, thought better of it—clever girl—and sent Molly a vicious, I'll-see-you-in-hell look. Picking up a folder from her desk, she slapped it against her thigh, released a frustrated huff and barreled toward the door. Mack just managed to move out of the way; if he hadn't, her shoulder would've bumped his arm as she passed by.

Good thing she didn't or else her ass would be toast.

Mack turned to watch her storm down the hallway, a little uneasy. Yeah, he instinctively didn't like her. He was quite sure the feeling was mutual and didn't give a damn.

Turning his attention back to Molly, he looked across the room to find her glaring at him. He lifted his hands in a what-did-I-do gesture. "What?"

Molly put her hands on her desk, shoved her chair back and shot to her feet. "That was a private conversation and you had no right to interfere!"

Mack jammed his hands into the pockets of his chino pants. "That wasn't a conversation. She was threatening you."

"She was not threatening me!" Molly retorted, so quickly that he knew she was lying. "And, even if she was, I'm a big girl. I can fight my own battles. I don't need you to defend me anymore, Mack."

He'd been her protector as a kid, standing between her and her bigger, older, meaner brothers. She'd been an easy target for those two bullies until he, and his brothers, made it clear Molly was off-limits.

Back then the three Holloway brothers had been a force to be reckoned with.

The day they heard Grant and Vincent would be leaving the resort, they cheered loudly, happy to be rid of them. Then they realized that Molly would be leaving, too. Mack begged Jameson to allow Molly to move in with them; they needed a sister, he'd pleaded.

He hadn't spoken to Jameson for two days when he told them that Molly had to leave with her family.

Mack looked into her flashing eyes and felt the stirring in his pants. Yeah, it had been a long, long time since he thought of Molly Haskell in a sisterly way.

Mack dropped into the chair on the other side of her desk and placed his elbows on the arms and made a triangle with his index fingers and thumbs. Something was going on with her and Beth and he wanted to know the source of their quarrel. Why? He had no damn idea.

"What did she say to you?" Mack asked.

"None of your damn business," Molly said, sinking down into her chair again and pushing her fingers into her curls, dislodging her scarf. She cursed, pulled it off her head and tossed it onto the desk and her beautiful corkscrew curls fell over her face. He remembered her curls brushing his chest as her mouth trailed across his skin, brushing his stomach…

He hardened instantly and Mack silently cursed. *Display a little control, Holloway, for the love of God!*

Molly lifted her head, straightened her keyboard and mouse pad before turning to look at him again, her eyes shuttered and her expression blank. "Was there something you wanted from me or did you just step into my office to annoy me?"

Mack sighed and dropped his hands. She had that "go away" look on her face that he remembered so well. He knew that if he pushed her now, she'd close down and clam up and she'd never trust him with the truth.

Molly had her own fair share of stubborn.

Mack pulled his brain back to business, to the reason he was on the property where he grew up.

"In between looking after my dad, I spent time going through paperwork in his home office. He keeps a lot of the accounting records there," Mack told her, still trying to pinpoint the source of his unease. Something was off with what he'd seen and he couldn't put his finger on why he felt uncomfortable.

Molly reached for the phone and paused, her hand on the receiver. "I need coffee. Do you want some?"

Mack nodded. "Sure. Thanks."

Molly placed the order with the kitchen and sat back in her chair, looking professional and polite. He doubted either would last; there was too much passion between them.

But they could try because finding themselves tangled up in each other again would be a complication neither of them needed. He certainly didn't. When he left again, he wanted no regrets.

"I have a few questions for you…"

"Okay, I'll answer what I can."

Mack thought about the disorganized and inefficient mound of papers he'd recently plowed through. "Why the hell aren't the books on a computer-based system?"

Molly threw up her hands, obviously frustrated. "Because they aren't."

That wasn't any type of answer. "Molly…" he warned and noticed her squirming in her seat. Ah, he thought he knew what this was about.

"M, I know how much you love my dad, how much you love Moonlight Ridge. You always have. But you *can* criticize my dad and the business decisions he's made. In fact, I'm asking you to because if you're not totally truthful with me, I won't get an accurate picture of what's happening."

Her shoulders slumped and relief flashed in her eyes. "I've been trying to get Jameson to switch over to a computer-based accounting system for years but he insists on doing things old school. I did manage to persuade him to allow us to create a web-based booking system but that's as far as he would go. We've had quite a few arguments on this subject."

He could imagine: Jameson hated change.

"Even with the department reports and your proposal, I still don't have a clear idea what's happening, financially, with the resort, but something's not right."

Molly stiffened and looked away and Mack's senses immediately went on red alert. "What aren't you telling me, Molly?"

Molly rested her forearms on the desk and picked up a pen and tapped it against the surface of a blank notepad, leaving tiny black dots over the white paper. Her eyes, when they met his, reflected her anxiety. "As I told you earlier, in my opinion, the resort is on the edge of a tipping point, Mack. My gut instinct tells me we have six months, maybe a year, before the company runs into trouble, serious trouble."

Mack's eyes widened. Damn. He'd hoped it hadn't been that bad.

"Twenty, thirty years ago, this was the ultimate hideaway for the very rich, looking for a home away from home, a place that guaranteed privacy. The guests would bring their children for six weeks, two months at a time, and this place pumped. In fact, the way Jameson tells it, it was a little like the resort in the movie *Dirty Dancing*."

Mack grimaced. "The one you made me watch a hundred times when we were kids?"

Molly wrinkled her nose. "Twice, maybe three times. Anyway, back then the resort was crazy busy. But these days there's so much competition and we're just another luxurious resort in a market with lots of options. Costs are up, sales are down and staff is expensive."

Employing thousands himself, he knew exactly how costly staff could be. And, like Jameson, he'd believed in paying his staff well, provided they performed. But to Mack, it looked like there were too many staff members at Moonlight Ridge; the staff-to-guest ratio was insane.

"Who does the hiring and firing?"

Molly considered his question. "The individual managers put in a requisition for a staff member and once it's approved, they hire whoever they want to. Jameson believes in allowing his staff to run their department their way. Jameson handles all firing, but it's rare."

Mack gripped the bridge of his nose. He loved his dad, he did, but Jameson's strengths were in guest relations—he was a bon vivant and a genial host, a magnetic personality—but the nitty-gritty of business bored him.

A ruthless businessman he was not. In today's cutthroat business environment, you had to keep an eye on every aspect of your company and make crucial decisions—staff hires, expense approvals and asset purchases yourself—or the business could run away with you.

Molly, he believed, was the glue holding this place together.

"Tell me what you think of the senior staff," Mack commanded.

Molly grimaced, obviously not wanting to dish dirt. When he didn't back down, she sighed her displeasure.

"Well, you met them all last week. Beth runs the accounts department—"

"She's done a piss-poor job of it," Mack muttered.

Molly nodded her agreement. "The catering and events manager, Ross Barnes, is amazing. He's been here for about five years, has a lot of experience and he's very good at his job. He works closely with Autumn Kincaid. She's our independent wedding planner.

"Milo Horton, our maintenance manager and groundskeeper, is a hard worker. Fern Matlock, our executive chef, is competent. She used to be Henri's sous-chef—"

He remembered Henri, the resort's expat chef and Travis's mentor, with fondness.

"Harry Levin runs the front desk and guest relations. Other than Jameson, there's no one better with guests than Harry." Molly continued, "And I try to keep all of them from killing each other."

"I skimmed over their ideas born out of our SWOT analysis meeting," Mack said, resting his linked fingers on his stomach. "Some were interesting, some were pie in the sky."

A knock pulled her attention off Mack. A young waiter opened the door and strode in, holding a tray laden with an expensive coffee jug and china cups and saucers. The tray he carried was silver and was part of the silver collection—along with the art and antiques collection—Jameson inherited from the previous owner, Tip O'Sullivan. Jameson had been his manager at the time and Tip, who'd never married and was childless, thought the world of Jameson.

The waiter placed the tray on Molly's desk. "Thanks, Larry."

Mack took the cup Molly handed him and rested his ankle on his opposite knee. "As I expected, yours was the most intricate, detailed and sensible plan."

"It's the proposal I'd already compiled, in preparation for my meeting with Jameson," Molly told him, wrapping her hands around her china cup.

She was good at business and he felt a spurt of pride at her prowess. "If I gave you carte blanche to do three things, what would they be?" Mack asked.

Molly didn't hesitate. "Update and renovate the rooms. Update the menu. Instigate a massive marketing drive to look for segments of the market we might've missed. We need younger, richer people to visit Moonlight Ridge, Mack. We can't rely on our old guests to keep this place running."

He agreed.

"But I'd also like to add that we need to attract upmarket weddings and conferences. Those are our best moneymakers," Molly continued, passion in her eyes. He wished she was looking at him with the same passion, but her focus was solely on Moonlight Ridge and how to restore it to its former glory.

And if there was anyone who could do it, Molly could. She was knowledgeable and dedicated, committed and smart, and Jameson was damn lucky to have kept her for this long.

"As you saw in my proposal, I have detailed budgets for each suggestion. I have ten more ideas and ten more budgets," Molly said, sounding deadly serious.

Of course she did. "Would you like to come work for me?" Mack asked, only half joking.

"We'd spend all our time arguing or—" Molly snapped her teeth together and blushed. Mack grinned, knowing what she was about to say.

"We'd either argue or get naked," Mack told her. He smiled before speaking again. "I have little appetite for the first and a great deal for the second."

He'd always told her the truth and had no intention of changing that now. "Full disclosure, M, I want to sleep with you again."

Molly's eyes, when they met his, were cool and her expression distant. "Not going to happen, Holloway."

Mack sipped his coffee and eyed her over the rim. They'd just see about that. He had a feeling that the desire they felt for each other, the need to see each other naked, was too big, too intense, for either of them to resist.

Five

Full disclosure, M, I want to sleep with you again.

Disconcerted by Mack's statement, Molly stomped through the back corridors and used the old servants' staircase to step into the sunlight through a door adjacent to the bright and lush conservatory. She knew the mansion like the back of her hand, knew where to find her favorite paintings, when the silver needing cleaning, how to access the secret passageways and the cellars, what was stored in the attic. She loved running her hands over the walls that had sheltered so many people at different times over the past century.

Right now she wasn't thinking about the history of the hotel. She was too busy trying to get some sense of her tumultuous feelings. Her dominant emotion was anger...

She was furious with Mack...

Or was she? *Really?* Maybe she was angry at herself for still wanting him so damn much, for allowing herself to feel anything other than cool disdain.

She was definitely angry with Beth. She was always mad at her family.

And she was a little upset with Jameson for being ill.

Oh, and she was also pissed that Jared, Autumn's fiancé, dumped her a couple of days before their long-planned wedding a few weekends ago. Autumn was acting like it was no big deal but Molly knew she was hurting. She had to be.

That's an awful lot of mad, Haskell.

Slumping against the back wall of the property, she pulled her phone out of the back pocket of her pants and punched in Autumn's number. She tried to check in on her best friend a couple of times a day, just to take her emotional temperature. Autumn had yet to break down, to cry, and Molly worried about her.

Autumn answered her phone and Molly asked where she was.

"Actually, I'm hiding out in the bar, trying to catch up on paperwork," Autumn told her.

Perfect. "I'll see you there soon."

The bar was a small stone building detached from the main resort, situated between the art studio and Moonlight Ridge's heated swimming pool. Modeled after an English pub, the small space was dominated by a handcrafted wooden bar, behind which sat a world-class collection of whiskeys. At ten in the morning, the place was empty of guests and staff and Molly took two bottles of water from an under-counter fridge and walked over to where her friend sat, the table in front of her piled high with paper.

Molly sat down and inspected Autumn. Her honey-colored hair was bundled up onto the top of her head and secured with a clip and her black-rimmed glasses dominated her face. She looked a little harried and a tad frustrated but nothing like an almost-jilted bride. She'd barely been able to breathe when Mack left but Autumn was acting upbeat, like her nonwedding was a brief blip on her radar.

"How are you doing, sweetie?" Molly asked her, handing her a bottle of water.

Autumn shrugged. "Fine." She gestured to the chaotic table. "I'm just trying to undo the mess not getting married created."

"Have you spoken to Jared?" Molly gently asked her.

Autumn pretended to inspect her laptop screen. "Nope. It's over. There's nothing to say."

Molly bit her lip, wondering whether to push her to open up. Autumn needed to rant and bitch, to scream and sob. Keeping all this emotion bottled up wasn't helpful or healthy. But she was also an adult and entitled to deal with her emotions any way she thought fit. "If you want to TP his house or key his car or slash his tires, I'll be there, okay?"

Autumn smiled. "Thanks, Mol. Now, what sent you running from your office? Beth or Mack?"

It was scary how well Autumn knew her. "Both," she reluctantly admitted.

Autumn rested her forearms on the table, her attention on Molly. "What happened?"

"Grant wants money to invest in some business his friend is establishing," Molly admitted. "Beth was passing along the message."

Autumn looked skeptical on hearing her brother's latest scheme. "What business?"

"Ah, that's where she got a bit vague. She knew exactly how much he needed—ten thousand—but the details around the business itself were a bit sketchy."

Autumn did a massive eye roll.

"She got a bit intense in her demands and Mack caught her looming over my desk," Molly continued. "He called her out for threatening me."

"Good for him," Autumn stated.

Molly rested her water bottle on her forehead. "My family is so messed up, Autumn, and they are damn embarrassing. Mack never liked my brothers, none of the Holloway boys did, and honestly, I can't blame them for that."

"They are toxic, Mol. They aren't good for you. And if you tell me that you are responsible for your family, then I'm going to tell you, yet again, that you're talking rubbish."

Molly looked at her friend, grateful for her fierce attitude and insane loyalty.

"They are adults, Molly. They can support themselves. It's not your job to pay their rent, or to give them money for gas or to pay off a credit card. You've got to stop enabling them, babe." Autumn took Molly's hands and squeezed. "Mol, you have to cut ties with them."

Autumn would always, no matter what, be there for her. She knew this like she knew her own signature. Just being with Autumn helped her remember that she would be okay, that she had a great track record of recovering after things went south.

"You need to get Beth out of your face and out of this organization, Molly. She's bad news."

Molly considered her suggestion and immediately dismissed it. Beth wasn't great at her job but Jameson's lack of systems didn't help the situation. Beth hadn't made any huge mistakes, and her intense dislike of the bookkeeper wasn't enough to have her canned.

She didn't have the authority—dammit!—to fire a senior staff member so she'd have to take her request to Mack. It was obvious that he didn't like Beth, but before firing her, he'd dig deeper, scratch under the surface to understand her motivations for wanting Beth gone, and that would lead him to discover Molly's secret. Jameson might, one day, forgive her for stealing. But Mack? Not a chance.

Even as a kid Mack had a code of honor, a steel rod in his backbone, lines that couldn't be crossed. Because his dad had been so unreliable and immoral, he valued truth, taking responsibility for one's choices and integrity above all else. He had incredibly high standards and, on hearing about her teenage crime, she'd fall short in his eyes.

She still couldn't bear to disappoint him, dammit.

Besides, Mack had always fought her battles as a kid, but she was an adult, and she didn't need him to do that anymore. No, Beth was her problem, her mess, and it was her job to clean it up.

"Moving on from the never delightful Beth, how is it going with Mack?" Autumn asked, curiosity on her face. "Are you still attracted to him?"

Attraction was such a tame word for her yearning and burning emotions. But basically, yes.

Hell yes.

She wanted to know what making love with him, as a grown-up, felt like. She wanted to explore that incredible body with her hands and mouth, taking time to discover all the ways he'd changed. And all the ways he'd not.

It might take some time, but Molly was very okay with that…

Lord, she was in a world of trouble.

"You are, aren't you?" Autumn crowed. Then her eyes narrowed. "Something happened," she stated.

A lot of somethings had happened… "I love you dearly, Autumn, but I don't want to discuss Mack…or not just yet," Molly said, resting her bottle of water against her forehead.

Autumn pouted, disappointment in her eyes. But because she was a lovely friend, she nodded. "Okay."

Autumn looked at her watch and sighed. "I need to head into town for a meeting with a newly engaged couple."

"Try and persuade them to have their wedding here,"

Molly said, standing up. Weddings brought in a lot of money and they didn't have enough booked for summer.

"I always do," Autumn said on a small shrug. "Unfortunately, the mothers of the brides love Moonlight Ridge but the brides want less country house and more cool."

It was a criticism she'd heard before and something she wanted to change. Molly walked around the table to drop a kiss on her friend's head. "Thanks for the chat."

"Anytime," Autumn replied. "Trust Mack, Mol. I really think you can."

Molly disagreed. She didn't trust anyone, except Jameson. Everyone else had, in some way or the other and to different degrees, let her down. And sometime in the future, she'd do the same to Jameson.

The thought made her want to throw up.

At around eight that night, Molly shut down her computer, finally done with the day. Not wanting to go back to an empty apartment, Molly considered visiting Jameson. But it was getting late, he would be watching TV, possibly dozing, and she didn't want to disturb him.

She stood up and walked to the window of her office, staring into the shadows down below and rested her throbbing head on the cool window. She was mentally drained and physically exhausted and the thought of dragging herself across the grounds to her apartment above the stable block was, right now, too much to contemplate.

She glanced back to look at her laptop screen and grimaced. Having spent most of the day doing calculations and projections, she came to the unwelcome conclusion that the resort was in more trouble than even she suspected. Oh, she'd had her suspicions for a while but it was worse than she'd thought.

The reality was that they were facing the quietest summer season on record; the bookings they had wouldn't cover costs. She needed to do something to pull people in, something to bolster the cash flow. If she could get authorization to implement her ideas, she'd have a chance at saving the resort.

She couldn't let this fabulous place slide away or shut its doors. Without people, Moonlight Ridge would lose its magic.

Dammit, if only she and Jameson had discussed her plans for the resort before he got sick; that way she could instigate her strategy to revitalize Moonlight Ridge and he could concentrate on getting well.

She wanted to succeed because she loved the resort and could see its immense potential. And also because Jameson had been so good to her and she couldn't tolerate the idea of letting him down. He'd offered her a job at fourteen, paying her half her wages in cash and putting the rest into a bank account she hid from her family. In her senior year, shortly after she stole the money from him, he offered to pay for her college degree. Molly, consumed with guilt, proud and already in his debt, refused, insisting she'd apply for a dance scholarship. When she damaged her knee, she knew she'd have to find another way to fund her dream of a decent education.

The next few years had been tough but she managed, eventually returning to Asheville and sliding into a management position with Jameson.

Moonlight Ridge was still the only place she wanted to be. And if she didn't do something quickly, it would fade into obscurity. She refused to let that happen; there *had* to be something she could do.

She could ask Mack, Grey and Travis to throw some money at the problem; they were all self-made millionaires, a fact Jameson was exceptionally proud of. But even if Jameson agreed to that, and he never would, their infusion of cash would be like placing a Band-Aid on an open wound. It wasn't a long-term solution.

Molly heard the knock on her door. Sighing, she turned and watched as Mack stepped into her office. It was brutally unfair that, at the end of a long day, he still looked as good as he did this morning. His white cotton shirt wasn't wrinkled, and his pants looked like he'd pulled them on ten minutes before. The only hint that it was the end of the day was the dark shadow of stubble on his jaw and his less-than-perfect hair.

"It's late, Molly. Time to pack it up," Mack told her, stepping into her office.

Irritation bubbled; she wasn't a child who needed to have her hours regulated. "I'm very capable of deciding when my workday should end, Holloway."

Mack sent her a sour look and dragged his hand through his thick hair. "Dammit, Mol, do you have to fight me on everything?" Mack muttered. "You have dark stripes under your eyes, you look pale and any fool can see that you are shattered. You need a good meal and a solid night's sleep. That's all I meant, for God's sake."

Molly grimaced and dropped down to sit on the edge of her two-seater couch. Resting her elbows on her knees, she sent Mack an apologetic look. "Sorry."

Mack sat down in the wingback chair opposite her. He leaned forward and placed his big hands on her knees, and Molly felt lust and need and want flow through her body, instantly reviving her. How did he do that? And why was he the only one who could?

"Molly, look at me."

Molly lifted her eyes to connect with his, the deepest, darkest black, mysterious and rather wonderful. Mack squeezed her knees, his fingertips digging into her skin under the skirt of her figure-hugging dress. "In case nobody has said this to you lately, and I doubt they have, thank you for all your hard work and your dedication to this place. I have no doubt that Moonlight Ridge would be in a more precarious position if you weren't here, Curls."

Until Mack said the words, Molly hadn't realized how much she needed to hear them. Telling herself not to let him see how deeply his words affected her, she looked away.

There had been a lot of talk when Jameson installed her as his second in charge, Molly told him. "A lot of people thought the apple wouldn't fall far from the tree," she added.

"Jameson raised us to take responsibility for our individual choices. Your dad's choices were his own."

As were hers.

"Besides, you're an orange, not an apple. Or, judging by your prickly attitude, a cactus," Mack commented. The flash of humor in his eyes, and the way his mouth lifted up at the corners, told her he was teasing and she remembered that, back when he was young and fun, Mack used to mess with her.

When they were much older, he took his teasing to their lovemaking, and, despite how young she'd been, it had always been a fun and loving experience.

Strange that Mack at eighteen was still the best lover she'd ever had. At thirty-three and having had some time to hone those skills, he'd be, she had no doubt, freaking amazing.

Her panties felt warm and a little damp and her nipples pushed against the lace barrier of her bra. Yep, he still could set her blood on fire.

"What were you thinking about just now?" Mack asked, lifting his hands off her knees and leaning back in his chair. He rested his hands against his flat stomach, curiosity on his face.

Molly rewound and remembered her concerns about Moonlight Ridge. She could discuss her plans for the resort with Mack; it was a subject they had in common. And it would help her to ignore her insane sexual attraction to this infuriatingly sexy man.

"I was thinking about what we could do to improve the place."

"That's why I stopped by. I've been thinking about your top ideas and the easiest one to begin with is updating the rooms. We can get started immediately by repainting the suites and updating the linens."

Yes! She was grateful. It was a start but so much more needed to be done.

"That's a great start…" Molly's words trailed off.

"But?"

"But we still need to get to get a lot of people here, fast. Our bookings are down for the summer and we won't cover costs if we don't do something."

"Yeah, I realized that." Mack rubbed his jaw. "My brothers and I could give the resort a cash injection if it needed it."

So he'd considered that option, too. Molly was pleased to know he was prepared to part with his cash, that he would do anything to keep Moonlight Ridge going. But as nice as that would be, it wasn't a long-term solution, as she told him. "We need guests, Mack. That's what must change. We need feet through the door."

"Let me look at the finances and see how much more money we can release to throw at a marketing campaign. Hopefully, I'll be able to make sense of the bookkeeping system. It's a goddamn mess."

Molly sympathized. "I know. Do you want some help?"

Mack nodded. "I'd like that. Do you want some help finessing your marketing ideas?"

There was so much history between them, so much pain,

but she had to put that away and concentrate on what was important and that was saving Moonlight Ridge. "Yeah, we can do that."

Mack stared at her for a minute, maybe two, before standing up and placing one hand on the arm of her couch and looming over her. His penetrating eyes searched her face and, lifting his other hand, he swiped his thumb across her bottom lip. "I want my friend back, Molly. The friend I lost because I was young, dumb and an ass. And that means facing what I did and how I did it. And then I look at you and all I want is to kiss you senseless and strip you naked."

They were words she'd long thought she needed to hear; words she'd dreamed of. But they also scared her because Molly knew that it wouldn't take much for her to fall under his spell again. And she refused to do that; she didn't think she could handle Mack loving and leaving her again.

Molly resisted the urge to touch his thumb with the tip of her tongue. "Let's leave the past where it belongs, Mack."

Mack's smile was gentle and a little sad.

"Normally, I'd be the first to agree with you but with you, I can't do that."

"Mack…"

She needed to tell him, to explain that nothing was going to happen between them, that they could be colleagues who worked together and that was all. But when Mack looked at her like he was doing now, cataloging her features, soaking her in, her words stuck on her tongue.

Mack dropped a light kiss on the corner of her mouth before pulling back to look at her. "Get some sleep, Curls. And, yes, that's a damn order."

Mack kissed her again, his mouth hard and direct, before walking away from her and out the room.

Well, okay, then.

* * *

Jameson, sitting in a comfortable chair on his expansive deck, watched Molly and Mack crossing his bright green lawn to join him, each trying so damn hard to play it cool.

Morons, he thought, chuckling. Since they first met, they'd never been able to ignore each other.

Mack was looking more relaxed, thank God. His oldest, Jameson admitted, worried him. Mack played his cards so close to his chest, and his defensive walls were sky-high. Molly had been the only person, besides him, to slip under, over or through those barriers—Travis and Grey had only gotten so far—to see that, at his heart, Mack was a man who needed to be loved, who needed love. Despite his me-against-the-world stance, more than most, Mack needed a family, a wife, a place to belong. Jameson had given him that for ten or so years but Mack had been on his own for far too long.

And Molly, God, she was the daughter of his heart. Over the years there had been so many times when he wanted to stand between her and her family, to meet with them privately and tell them to leave her the hell alone. He wasn't a fool; he knew that Molly still supplemented their income. There was no way they could enjoy the lifestyle they did without a discernible source of income. He'd hired Beth in hopes the family would leave Molly alone, but Beth was too selfish and too smart to hand over her money to her boyfriend's family. The Haskells always had money and Jameson had no doubt it was from Molly.

She was their bank manager, their personal ATM, their get-out-of-jail card.

He wouldn't have a problem with her handing over her money—it was hers after all, and she was an adult—if they treated her with an ounce of respect. But they didn't. They didn't even seem to like her much because she reminded them of what they could be, could do, if they put a little effort in, made better choices.

The tall trees, Jameson thought, always caught the wind.

Jameson felt his newspaper being plucked from his fingers and turned to see Giada standing in front of him, the now-folded paper pressed against her fantastic breasts. Jameson sighed. The last thing he should be thinking about was Giada's rack.

Then again, thinking was all he could do right now. Sex, like work, was off the table for a few more months.

Giada frowned. Her dark eyebrows pulled together and Jameson knew that she was about to deliver another lecture in her slightly accented voice, her fabulous eyes flashing with impatience. God, the woman was bossy. He rather liked it.

He'd always, terribly inconveniently, liked her. And lusted after her.

"You're reading the news," Giada complained.

Something he'd done since he was a kid. "It's called staying informed."

"It's stressful," Giada shot back. "Politics, corruption, more politics, a gruesome murder."

Jameson tipped his head back and closed his eyes. "I do not need to be wrapped in cotton wool, woman. And give me back my cigars," he grumbled. Giada thought she was so clever in confiscating his cigars but she didn't know that he had secret stashes all over the house.

The fact that he had to resort to sneaking around to take a puff pissed him off.

Giada placed the newspaper on the side table next to him and slapped her hands on her hips. Round hips, sturdy hips… hips that could handle his broad hands on them, a body that could handle his bulk and strength, as he pushed into her.

Jameson wiped his hands over his face at the image of

a naked Giada under him. There was only one thing worse than fantasizing about a woman he couldn't have and that was knowing it would be months before he could even try.

God, he was done with feeling like crap.

"What are you thinking about?" Giada demanded, her eyes drilling into him.

He'd never admit the truth so he gestured to M&M. He lowered his voice to make sure that they didn't hear him; if they did, being stubborn fools, they'd do everything in their power to prove him wrong.

"They are perfect for each other. I am so glad he's home. She needs him and he desperately needs her."

Giada put herself between Jameson and his children. Because Molly was, in every way that counted, his. She lifted a finger and poked him in the chest, sending ribbons of electricity skating over his skin. "Do not interfere. They are adults and are perfectly capable of making their own choices and decisions."

Sure, but where was the fun in that? "I have no problem nudging them," Jameson replied.

"No nudging," Giada warned as Molly and Mack called out their greetings. As they approached, Giada sent him a victorious smile and turned to face his visitors.

Before he could greet his son and the woman he hoped would one day be his daughter-in-law, Giada spoke again. "I'm so glad you are here. I need help."

Molly bent down to kiss his cheek and when she stood up, she kept a hand on his shoulder. She looked at Giada and nodded. "What do you need? What can I do?"

Giada handed him a smile that stopped his heart. It was sexy and sneaky. And savage. "You can help me search the house for Jameson's contraband cigars."

Shee-it. Busted.

Six

Molly juggled the heavy files in her arms as they walked away from Jameson's house and back toward Moonlight Ridge, Mack carrying a heavy box of ledgers and files like it was a box of light-as-air biscuits. When Giada offered to accompany Jameson on a slow, short walk through the wild garden and back, they'd raided his study for any paperwork relating to Moonlight Ridge. There had been more than they expected.

The man, Molly decided, was strong. Like pick-me-up-and-haul-me-away strong. And yep, she was having a few fantasies of him doing exactly that. Preferably when they were both naked.

Molly dropped back a step to eye his exceedingly nice ass. Unlike so many men's butts, his wasn't flat; nor was it too round. It was just, well, *perfect*. His broad shoulders and muscular back told her that he wasn't a stranger to working out and his long, muscular thighs reminded her that he'd been, back in the day, an excellent swimmer.

Her teenage boyfriend was now a hot, sexy, powerful man. And he still managed to set her panties on fire.

Shouldn't that ship have sailed, had a mutiny, burned out and been scuttled? But no, it seemed not.

Because his butt, his entire body, just did it for her.

Mack stopped abruptly and spun around to look at her. "Are you checking out my ass?" he demanded.

Oops, busted.

Molly made a show of juggling the files in her arms. "Just trying to get a better grip on these."

Mack's eyes danced with amusement and she caught a brief flash of bright white teeth behind his blinding smile. "Liar, you were *so* checking me out."

"So checking me out..." Molly mimicked him. "You sound like a teenage girl."

"Maybe, but I'm still waiting for you to disagree."

Molly scowled at him. "Okay, princess, your ego obviously needs a bit of stroking." Her next words gushed out as she tried to imitate an over-the-top teenager. "O! M! G! You are so hot! Do you work out? Can I get your autograph? You are sooooo cute. Can I try and bounce a coin off your butt?"

Mack laughed at her, amusement making him look ten years younger. Molly stared at him, her heart thumping, as she saw, for the first time, the laughing boy she remembered. Yeah, there he was... Mack. Her friend. The boy who'd introduced her to love.

Hello...

Mack's smile faded as he tipped his head to the side. "Why are you looking at me like that?"

"Like how?"

"Like you are seeing me for the first time."

Ah, because maybe she was? Molly ignored his question and resumed walking, her arms burning. "So how do you keep that fabulous bod in great shape?" she asked, still curious. "Do you still swim?"

"No." Molly saw a flash of embarrassment hit his features and wondered what he was hiding.

"Running? Gym? Weights?"

Mack jerked his head to where a large tree stump sat in the middle of the lawn, decorated with a weathered copper birdbath. "What happened to the oak tree?"

"Big storm six months ago. The trunk cracked and it was deemed to be a safety hazard so we had to cut it down. And stop changing the subject...what do you do for exercise?"

"Yoga."

Molly wasn't sure she'd heard him right. Mack and his brothers were men's men, guys who relished close-contact sports. The nittier, grittier and dirtier, the better.

She could not imagine Mack Holloway twisting himself into a human pretzel.

"Yoga? Gentle stretching resulted in those muscles? No way!"

"I do advanced Bikram Yoga. It's intense and we practice in a hot room. It's physically demanding. Bikram Yoga is what I do religiously."

"And what do you do nonreligiously?" Molly asked as they approached the back door to Moonlight Ridge.

Molly wasn't looking forward to trudging up all those narrow steps with her arms full of heavy ledgers.

"I also practice Krav Maga," Mack admitted.

Now that made sense. And typical Mack, he wasn't one to settle for a judo or karate class; he had to attempt to master the hardest self-defense discipline in the world.

"You're nuts."

"It's been said before," Mack said, resting his box on his knee to push open the door to let her enter the inn. "You're still in pretty good shape yourself...how do you stay so slim?" She was happy he'd noticed. But only because she wanted him to appreciate what he'd never lay hands on again.

Well, that was the plan but her body, and libido, had different ideas. It had been a long time since she'd had a man's hands on her, an awfully long time since Mack had seen her naked.

He'd been good at sex back then; she had no doubt that he'd be brilliant at it now.

Molly cursed herself as she stepped into the inn and immediately turned right to hit the stairs. She was not going to sleep with Mack...

Absolutely, categorically, definitely...

Maybe.

Arrgh!

"You didn't answer my question, Mol," Mack said from behind her.

Ah, what had he asked? Oh, what she did to keep in shape. She looked around and shrugged. "I run up and down these steps a hundred times a day."

She resumed her climb up the familiar staircase, each crack and knot a familiar friend.

"You don't dance anymore?"

Molly immediately stiffened. She'd been waiting for him to broach the subject of her dancing, the other great passion of her teenage life.

God, everything changed after that hot, sexy summer.

"I left ballet behind a long time ago," Molly stated, her voice barely above a whisper. And God, how she missed it. She'd been, over the years, so tempted to pull on her tights and ballet pointes, wanting to do grand jetés or to pirouette across a studio.

But she'd been warned that her knee was too weak for her to return to classical ballet so she assuaged her need for dance by joining modern dance, tap and hip-hop dance classes.

For someone who could once make her body fly, not being able to do grand jetés and grand adages was torture.

"Why?"

Molly stopped her climb and leaned her back against the cool white wall behind her. "I tore the anterior cruciate ligament in my knee. And when I say tore, I mean I ripped it to shreds."

Mack grimaced. "Nasty. What happened?"

Molly wanted to push her hair off her face but her hands were full so she resorted to trying to blow the annoying curl out of her eyes. Mack placed his box on the next stair, removed the books and files from her hands and placed them on top of his box. "Why didn't we get a porter to do the heavy lifting?" he ruefully asked.

"Because we thought Jameson would have a file, maybe two, not a truckload of paperwork."

Mack lifted his hand and with his finger, pushed her curl off her cheek and tucked it behind her ear. He looked down at her and, once again, wished she could tell what he was thinking. She didn't like being shut out, not by Mack, not by the man whom she once knew inside out. "You were telling me about your dance injury."

Molly rubbed her left wrist with the curled fingers of her right hand. When she saw Mack looking at the action, she immediately stopped. He knew it was something she did when she was feeling anxious or out of her depth.

"It was dress rehearsal and I caught my foot in my dress and I went down. I heard the pop and I knew it wasn't good. I was helped off stage and then they started phoning around for someone to pick me up and take me to the hospital."

She wouldn't tell him that, delirious with pain, she'd

told them to call him, insisting that he'd come and get her. The EMS techs tried him but he hadn't answered. Then they tried her mother and her brothers, none of whom they could reach.

Eventually, it was Jameson who met her at the same hospital Travis had recently left. And he'd held her hand when they told her that dance, like Mack, would never be part of her future again.

She felt its loss like a body blow.

Molly shrugged off those bitter memories. "They did reconstructive surgery but it will never be as strong as it was so pirouettes and arabesques are solidly off-limits." She gestured to the narrow stairs above them. "So I now mostly climb stairs."

"I'm so sorry, Mol," Mack told her and her eyes burned at the emotion she heard in his voice. He'd loved to watch her practice, had encouraged her to pursue her passion when her mother and brothers dismissed her talent. He'd understood, on a fundamental level, how important it was to her...

"I do still dance, modern and hip-hop mostly, but it's not the same. I loved ballet."

"I know," Mack said, looking and sounding serious.

"Yeah, well, hell happens," Molly said, ducking behind flippancy.

"Yeah, it really does," Mack said, his hand cupping her cheek, his thumb sliding over her cheekbone. His eyes drifted over her face, his stern mouth relaxed. "At seventeen I thought you the most beautiful creature I'd ever set eyes on. But you are lovelier today than you were back then. It's blowing my mind."

Molly rested her palms flat against the wall behind her, watching as his mouth descended toward hers. He smelled different, Molly thought, his scent more subtle but powerful, a dizzying combination of citrus and spice. His beard was stronger, his cheekbones more defined, those eyes shuttered, but God, his lips, when they touched hers, were still the same. A little sweet, a little soft, devastating and demanding at the same time. Mack placed his thumb on her chin, an unmistakable command for her to open up so she did, letting him slide inside.

Unable to stop herself, Molly placed her hands on the balls of his shoulders, feeling his heat beneath the material of his casual, expensive shirt. As he took a long, languid discovery of her mouth, she ran her hands down his arms, feeling the bumps of those impressive muscles, the raised veins in his forearms. Needing to explore herself, she slid her hands across his wide, hard chest and danced her fingers over his ladderlike stomach, until she hit the button of his jeans. Later, she wouldn't be able to decide whether she touched accidentally or on purpose, but when the side of her hand brushed his erection, she heard his swift intake of breath.

Mack whipped his head up, stared at her, his eyes wild and wicked and then his mouth, hot, sensual and rather wonderful, covered hers again. This time he used his big body to gently press her against the wall, and while his tongue was dancing with hers, she released a breathy moan. His scent rolled over her, earthy and primal and hot as fire. Molly gripped his shirt, twisting the material as he dragged his stubble across her jawline, stopping to pull her earlobe into his mouth. A little tease and a little taste and he was off exploring again, his mouth trailing down her neck, nudging aside the material of her loose silk T-shirt to expose the skin of her shoulder.

They shouldn't be doing this; it was a lethal game. They were tempting a tornado, flirting with a firestorm. Too much had happened between them—hurt, anger and disappointment—but Molly couldn't force herself to verbalize the words that would make her drop out of the game.

Desire shimmered between them, hot and feral and uncontrollable. If she made the slightest move, if she gave in to temptation and allowed her hands to roam, her mouth to feast, she'd tumble into a situation that would spin, rapidly she was sure, out of her control.

It took everything she had to stand still, to harness herself...

"Come on, Curls, give me something. Anything," Mack muttered against her lips, his teeth gently nipping her bottom lip.

It was that small bite, that sexy nip, that shattered her control. Swamped and slapped by passion, she gripped his shirt, twisted it and pulled her to him, feeling his hard body pushing her to the wall again. Her tongue slipped into his mouth, and he moaned when she feasted on him, needing more, needing everything.

She'd missed this; she'd missed him. He knew how to touch her—his hand on her breast, capturing her nipple between his thumb and finger proved that—knew when to advance, how to retreat. Molly sighed when his hard shaft pressed against the juncture of her thighs and, oblivious to where they were, she opened her legs to give him better access. Frustrated, she lifted her knee to curl her leg behind his thigh, thanking God she was still ballet flexible. Mack's hand ran up and down the back of her thigh, his fingers curling inward, coming dangerously close to her happy spot. Mack bent and held the backs of her thighs, easily lifting her, and it was the most natural thing in the world to wind her legs around his trim waist, to hook her ankles in the small of his back.

They were groping on the back stairway of Moonlight Ridge and she didn't care. At all.

They shared another hot, hard and wild kiss and Molly lifted her hips to scrape her core against his erection. Man, he felt so good. Nothing made sense but for them to get naked, immediately.

The slam of a door below them made them flinch, and the sound of heavy footsteps on the stairs below them, a floor down, had Molly dropping her legs and Mack bending to pick up the heavy box to hide his erection.

As the footsteps reached them, they continued their slow walk up the stairs, standing to the side to allow the fit, and young, porter to pass them.

Neither of them looked at each other; they didn't speak.

And when they hit their floor, Mack pealed left to go to his office and she went right to hers.

But really, the only place she wanted to be was in his bed.

Molly left her apartment around nine and walked through the soft, fragrant night, navigating her way to the guesthouse by the light of the moon. Since their hot kiss on the stairs, Molly felt hot and horny, and she was sick of waiting for him to come to her so she'd decided to take the initiative.

But what if he'd changed his mind? Molly winced. She was ninety percent sure he wouldn't; his kiss had been demanding and ferocious.

You're overthinking this, Haskell. Just tell him you want a one-night stand and see what he says.

Molly looked over her shoulder and considered retracing her steps back to her place. Good girls didn't ask for sex; men should make the first move…

Molly released a silent curse, annoyed that she was listening to the old-fashioned voice in her head. She was a woman in her early thirties. She was allowed to want sex.

It was a natural, biological urge and she was single. Mack wasn't married, engaged or in, as far as she knew, a relationship. If they ended up in bed, and there were no guarantees that would happen, she wouldn't be doing anything wrong.

They were both adults…

She could have sex with him without needing a commitment, without expectations. That was what modern, emancipated women did these days and, as far as she knew, she was one of the tribe.

So then why did she feel nervous, like her heart was about to bounce out of her chest and roll around on the floor?

Molly halted at the bottom of the short steps that led up to the porch on the guesthouse of what used to be her old home.

Would this be a one-night stand? Or would they keep sleeping together until he left? What if he didn't want her…?

For God's sake, Haskell, stop! She'd seen the attraction and desire in Mack's eyes; there was no doubt that he'd be fully on board with her idea. They'd sleep together, have a fun time and they either would, or wouldn't, have sex again. Either way, she'd be fine.

She could do this.

She *would* do this. *So move your feet, Molly.*

"What are you doing, Curls?"

Mack's voice, drifting over in the darkness, wrapped around her like a warm, sensual piece of silk. Molly squinted through the darkness. His vague outline told her that he was sitting in one of the big, comfy chairs in the corner of the veranda.

"I'm not actually sure," Molly said, annoyed to hear the tremble in her voice.

"Then why don't you come up here and we can figure it out together?" Mack suggested in that low, sexy voice.

Molly walked up the steps and crossed the veranda to where he was sitting. When she reached him, his hand wrapped around her wrist and he tugged her to stand between his thighs.

Molly looked down at his masculine face, wreathed in shadows, and shuddered when his hands moved to her hips and he rested his forehead on her stomach. "I want to take you to bed, Molly."

So direct, so…adult. But could she do this…could she sleep with him and keep it simple? She was desperate to believe that she could keep all the messy emotions out of it. But this wasn't any man; this was Mack and he was, always had been, hard to resist. As kids, they'd shared a powerful connection, and she'd loved him with an intensity that still, even in hindsight, scared her. When he moved on, her heart died.

Her body was demanding sex but her mind kept insisting that getting naked with him was dangerous. He called to her; he always had. And not only because he had the face and body that could stop traffic at a hundred yards. No, she liked his scalpel-sharp mind, the way his feelings ran deep, his loyalty to Jameson. She liked the way his focus sharpened when something caught his interest, his offbeat and dry sense of humor and his calm confidence.

Mack tugged her down so that she sat astride his thighs. His mouth touched hers and something fierce, primal and deeper than attraction flared between them as Molly fell into his kiss. One arm tightened around her waist and his hand held the back of her head as if she might—crazy thought—consider removing herself from his embrace.

Mack's hand drifted over her hips, down her thighs, slid

under the soft cotton of her dress and curled around the back of her knee. "What do you say, sweetheart?"

She made herself say the words, to remind herself that this could never be more than some bed-based fun. "A few hours, no expectations and no drama?"

"Works for me," Mack said, his skilled hands running up the backs of her bare thighs and flirting with the curve of her butt cheek. Mack's fingers slid under the band of her bikini panties, a small promise of what was to come.

Molly expected him to stand up, to lead her through the house to the main bedroom, to the room her parents used—thankfully redecorated—but Mack surprised her by keeping her on his lap, her knees on either side of his strong thighs. He reached up to hold her nape, gently pulling her down so that their lips could meet, and his kiss was tender, sweeter than she expected.

She expected…she didn't know what she expected, Molly thought as his skilled tongue played with hers. She'd expected assertive and confident, a little crazy, but his kiss was an exploration, a rediscovery. Sexy, hot, a little sweet.

Molly needed to touch him so she placed her hands on his chest, feeling hard muscle under her hands and she sighed, her lips opening to allow that puff of air to escape. Mack used the opportunity to slide his tongue between her lips. A flame immediately rushed along the detonator cord and ignited a fireball of crazy want and need. Molly slid down his thighs, pressed her breasts into his chest and her hips met his, her core coming to rest against his steel-hard erection.

Perfect.

As their kiss deepened, became wilder and wetter, their hands skated from body part to body part, searching for skin. Mack shifted forward in the chair, perched on the end and dragged her dress up her butt, and Molly felt the warm night air on her lower back. His hand slid down the back of her panties to cup her bare ass. Needing to touch him, she pulled Mack's shirt out of his pants to run her hands up the dip of his spine, over his muscled back, slowly making her away around to his ladderlike stomach. She could feel her heart thumping erratically, or was that Mack's?

She didn't know and it didn't matter; all that was of importance was that he was as out of control as she was. Molly ground herself against his shaft, desperate to be rid of the barriers between him.

Mack's hand covered her breast and soon his mouth was there, too, sucking her through her dress and bra. Frustrated, he pulled her dress down and then the bra cup, and dragged his hot tongue across her nipple.

Moisture flooded her panties and Molly knew that, just by riding his shaft and having him tongue her breasts, she could come.

"You are so damn sexy, Curls," Mack muttered against her skin.

And in his arms she felt sexy, a little wild, a pagan goddess intent on pleasure. Molly whimpered when Mack's hand dived between her thighs to pull the seam of her panties to one side so that he could stroke her bare, throbbing flesh. He rubbed his thumb across her bundle of nerves and she tipped her head back. The world narrowed to his touch and he slid one finger inside her, then another.

Molly, insensible to the fact that she was half-dressed, that her breasts were bare to the night air, closed her eyes, swept away on a rising tide of passion. Mack knew exactly how to touch her; she was so close to gushing all over his fingers, to spinning away on a whirlwind of sensation.

And he was still fully dressed…

She needed more so she forced herself to slide back, her hands going to the button on his shorts, flipping it open.

With hands that were very out of practice, she slid down his zipper, needing to feel his silky shaft in her hands. For him to be inside her...

Molly freed him from his underwear and shifted so that her core was riding his shaft. She groaned, tilted her hips and released a small scream when pleasure ricocheted through her.

"Want you, want you, want you," Molly chanted, feeling fireworks building behind her eyes as she rubbed his shaft. "Mack, I'm so damn close."

"I know, Mol. Use me, any way you want to." She wanted him inside her but she didn't want to stop doing this, either. She was one move, maybe two, from the most delicious orgasm and, because it had been so long, she couldn't stop. Didn't want to...

"Use me, sweetheart."

She'd be happy to. Molly ground down on him, pushing herself down, wishing she could fall into him. Working her hand between them, she palmed him, amazed at the warmth they generated. Another slide, another kick of pleasure, and Molly groaned when Mack lifted his hips to increase the pressure. She looked down into his eyes, saw the pain and pleasure on his face, and dipped her head so that her mouth could meet his. Mack stabbed her mouth with his tongue, echoing the rhythm down below, and Molly knew that she was nanoseconds from coming.

"Harder, baby, yeah, that's it."

Molly rocked herself against his shaft and everything coalesced into a thin, pulsing band of pleasure. She felt her womb contract, the gush of heat and she spun away, lying as pleasure overtook her. She felt Mack surge against her, felt his body tense and his masculine and hot release.

Molly slumped against him, his arms tightened around her, and she buried her face in his neck as her nerve endings buzzed. As the roaring in her ears subsided, she heard Mack's erratic breathing and his superfast heartbeat.

Feeling like she was losing the feeling in her trapped hand, she pulled it out from between them and scooted off his lap, turning away to rearrange her clothing and underwear.

When she turned back, Mack was dressed and his expression had returned to impassivity.

He probably had encounters like this all the time. Unlike her, he wasn't an inexperienced, churning, electrified mess of need and want and hormones.

Molly shoved her hands into her hair, wishing she knew what to say, how to act. They hadn't made love, in the traditional sense, but she did feel like Mack had taken her apart and slapped her back together again. She wasn't who she was before. She was a little off balance, felt different.

If she felt like this now, how would she feel after they made love?

Mack stood up, held out his hand to her and sent her a smile. "Come to bed with me, Mol. Since we've both taken the edge off, I want to take my time rediscovering every inch of you."

Saying no wasn't an option; she needed to be with him, in every way, so Molly put her hand in his and followed him inside the house.

Seven

Mack heard the beat-up truck long before it arrived. Standing on the driveway at the bottom of the steps leading up to the portico, he—and two guests who'd just arrived in the latest Mercedes AMG—turned to watch the truck emerge from the tree-lined driveway.

Mack stiffened as he recognized Grant and Vincent Haskell, Molly's brothers, and his least favorite people. Jerking the truck to a stop a few inches behind the Mercedes, giving the couple near heart failure, the two brothers looked at Mack through the cracked windscreen, sizing him up.

Oh, crap. Trouble had arrived.

Mack turned to look at the couple who was eyeing Molly's brothers with obvious distaste. He gestured for the porter to lead them inside. Despite not having had any contact with Molly's siblings for fifteen years, he knew, thanks to their belligerent expressions and annoyed eyes, they were happy to cause a scene.

Mack knew, via Jameson, since Molly refused to discuss her family, that they'd been banned from the property years ago and had been told if they returned, they'd be charged with trespassing. Something must've happened for them to take that risk…

Mack hoped Molly's mom was okay. Vivi wasn't a great mom but she was the only one Molly had.

Mack spread his feet apart, kept his arms loose and ready—the Haskell brothers were volatile, threw punches without thinking and the blood between them had always been bad—and watched as the two men left their vehicle.

"Holloway," Vince said, folding beefy arms over his chest. "I'm looking for my sister."

Mack kept his expression bland. "You're trespassing," he stated. "Leave now and I won't press charges."

Grant's chin jutted out, his blue eyes cold as ice. Mack could cope with Vinny, he had an impetuous temper, but Grant worried him. Even as a kid, he showed no remorse and worse, no empathy. Grant's favorite hobby was tormenting Molly. He loved, and lived for, seeing her cry.

Mack was quite sure nothing had changed.

"Molly isn't taking our calls and we need to talk to her." Grant looked at him, smiled and shrugged. "Our mom's sick and Molly needs to know."

Bullshit. In triplicate. He wasn't buying that, not for a minute, but before he could give them another chance to leave, he heard the front door open behind him. Turning, he watched Molly fly down the steps, her eyes full of fear.

Still.

The Haskell boys had gone back to hassling Molly after he'd left town; that much was obvious. In his quest to put distance between him and the accident, he'd left her to fend for herself. Mack tasted remorse at the back of his throat and glared at the two men. Brothers were supposed to protect their sisters, not tease or torment them. A part of Mack wanted to taunt them, to force them into throwing a punch, purely so that he could beat the snot out of them. With his Krav Maga training, he no longer needed his brothers for backup and could take them with one hand tied behind his back.

For every insult they tossed at her face, every demand they made on Molly, he'd make them pay.

Molly skidded to a stop beside him and slapped her hands on her hips, undiluted fury replacing fear. "Why are you here and why did you park here? We have guests arriving, you idiots!"

Grant shrugged. "Saw Holloway, wanted to say hello."

Mack called BS. Again.

"You are not allowed here, you know that! You've been banned from the property!" Molly reminded them. "Get in your truck and go before someone calls the cops."

"I'd be happy to do that," Mack growled.

"Not helping, Holloway," Molly snapped. She pointed to the truck. "Go! Now!"

"Need to talk to you," Grant said, hooking his thumbs into the pockets of his grimy jeans. "You're not answering our calls so we came out here."

"I'm busy, dammit!" Molly snapped.

"Still need to talk," Grant stated, his eyes growing colder. Mack felt the hair on the back of his neck rising and searched for some sort of emotion in his eyes and found nothing. He knew that Grant wouldn't move until he was damn well ready to.

Molly, obviulsy coming to the same conclusion, hauled in a deep breath. "Okay, I'll hear what you have to say but not here." She gnawed at her bottom lip. "I'll meet you at the old barn near the entrance in ten minutes and we can talk."

Grant stared at her before nodding. A smile, if one could call it that, lifted the edges of his lips up. "Fine. But if you don't arrive, you know what's going to happen, right?"

Mack didn't need to see the color draining from her face to know Grant had just threatened her. He stepped forward, his hands bunched. Before he could speak, Molly lifted her arm to slap her hand against his chest, halting his progress. "I've got this, Mack. Please don't make it worse." Molly looked at her brother. "Ten minutes. I'll see you there."

Grant sneered. "Make it five. And you know what we need so bring that, too," Grant said before catching Vinny's eye. "Let's go, dude."

Mack watched them until the rust bucket disappeared from view. When he thought his temper was vaguely under control, he turned to talk to Molly, wanting to know why she was still interacting with her waste-of-oxygen brothers.

But Molly was gone.

Damn, the girl could move fast.

Molly, standing next to Vincent's truck, darted a look toward Mack, who watched from his seat on a dirt bike he'd commandeered from Moonlight Ridge.

He'd pulled up behind her golf cart a few minutes after she approached her brothers, who were still sitting in their vehicle, and she was glad that she had some sort of backup. Her brothers had never physically hurt her, but from a young age, she knew that Grant wanted to. He'd bullied her mercilessly as a kid, but he'd never quite crossed the line into violence.

But the urge was there.

"This is all the money I have," Molly warned them, nodding at the envelope of cash. "And you should know that the next time you put a foot on this property, I will have you arrested."

Grant laughed at her. "You can do that but if you do, we won't have any reason to keep your secret, will we?"

This. Always this. She was the girl who'd called wolf once, or a few times, too often. They didn't believe that she'd cut ties with them because she hadn't followed through. And that was on her...

God, she couldn't keep living this way, feeling like the sky was about to fall on her head. She needed to confess, but Jameson couldn't take any stress so she couldn't, not yet. Not until he was a lot better.

Not only would her news upset him but she'd probably lose her job. And that would mean he'd stress about having a new manager running his beloved resort when he should be relaxing.

No, there were reasons to keep the truth from him for a little longer...

Molly scowled. "And, God, stop talking about me to your girlfriend, Grant! What the hell were you thinking, telling Beth about what happened back then? Life is tough enough without you making it a lot more difficult!"

Grant rested his arm along the back of the bench seat. "But I like making your life miserable, Molly. You should know that by now. Thanks for the cash but we need more. We'll see you soon."

Molly watched their truck roll away and resisted the urge to rub her eye sockets with the balls of her hands. She wanted to cry, to howl, to stamp her feet and beat her fists on the ground, but Mack was watching so she couldn't indulge in an old-fashioned hissy fit.

Damn him. What did he think he was doing following her down here? She was an adult and fully able to deal with her brothers on her own.

Molly stomped over to him, feeling her temper bubble.

Before she could speak, Mack did. "Please tell me that there wasn't money in that envelope, Mol."

He was really going to lecture her on what she did with her money, how she dealt with her brothers? The sheer nerve of the man. "Why are you here, Mack? This was my private business."

Mack didn't look remotely embarrassed about sticking his nose in where it didn't belong. "If you think I was going to let you confront those two on your own, then you are nuts."

Really? Now he was getting protective? "I've been dealing with them on my own for a long time, Holloway."

She'd been spoiled in those years before Mack left. She'd not only had Mack as a backup, but Travis and Grey, too. They'd been her own little protection crew and her brothers, mostly, left her alone. They'd hassled her for a year and a bit, until she left for college. On returning to Asheville, she'd thought it was all behind her, that she and her family could find a better way forward, that they had to change the dynamic between them. She'd invited them out for a meal and told them, as kindly as she could, that she was done supporting them and they had to do without her financial contribution.

Her mom's response was to tell her, blatantly and without remorse, that she had a choice: she could either keep feeding them money or she'd go to Jameson and tell him about the money Molly stole from him. Vivi insisted Jameson wouldn't care that she had a valid reason for doing what she did. And, because her father stole from Jameson, he'd never trust her again. He might even press charges against her...

That day Molly learned from whom Grant inherited his ruthlessness. And her last ounce of respect for her mother evaporated. But a small part of her, tiny but loud, still wanted to be part of a family, to not be on the outside looking in.

Molly drilled her finger into Mack's big biceps. "Stay out of my personal business, Holloway."

Mack's eyes flashed with anger. "They were on my property, Molly."

"Your property?" Molly released a high laugh. "Your property? Are you kidding me? You haven't spent more than a night here for years, Mack!"

Mack ran a hand through his hair. "Okay, if you want to be pedantic, then it's my father's property. My dad's land, his business, his hotel. I'm just here to look after it while he's sick."

Molly watched as Mack climbed off the dirt bike. God, she was so tired. She was done with fighting, with the stress, with waiting for the shoe to drop, the sky to fall in. She was done. She just wanted it over.

Mack's hands settled on her arms and Molly forced herself to look up into his face, trying to work out what he was thinking. She hated that he managed to keep his thoughts from her, and that she'd lost the ability to read him.

But his touch was gentle, his anger gone. Mack rubbed his hands up and down her arms to comfort her, before pulling her close and embracing her, holding her tight. She tried to pull away but Mack held her tighter, dropping his head to place his mouth by her ear. "Let me hold you, Mol, because, God, you need someone to."

Molly stopped resisting, his words touching her deep in her soul. Needing to lean on him, just for a minute, she rested her cheek against his chest and hung on, desperately trying to suck in his strength.

She was so tired of being alone.

Molly felt the burn of tears in her eyes, the tightness in

her throat. She couldn't cry now; if she started she doubted she'd stop. But despite her best efforts, her tears started to fall...

And then she started to sob...

Mack came from a family of men who seldom cried. Emotions were expressed by yelling, by slamming doors and, with his brothers, an occasional clout around the head or a fight outside. Sarcasm and shouting, punches and pranks, yes...tears?

Hell, no!

He didn't know how to deal with this outpouring of... whatever was causing Molly to fall apart in his arms. Oh, her brothers were pricks, but Molly had never reacted like this, not even when her brothers decapitated her Barbie dolls or tore pages out of her beloved books. Molly was a fighter, strong as hell, and to hear her sobs coming from a place deeper than pain, scared the crap out of him.

What was going on with her?

Oh, he knew she was a workaholic and a perfectionist and that she had an overdeveloped sense of responsibility. Had her long work hours caught up with her? Were her brothers the final straw of what had been a long few weeks and months? Was she worried about Jameson? Had his return stressed her out?

What was going on behind her pretty eyes and underneath her gorgeous hair? He needed to know. Because, God, he needed to fix this. As quick as he could. Because he'd still do pretty much anything for Molly.

She was still, despite years and time and distance, his best friend.

And the woman he very badly wanted to see naked again. And as soon as possible.

However, this wasn't the time to think about the way

she smelled—delicious—the way she tasted—fantastic—and the low, breathy, soft moans she made when she came.

Wrong time, wrong place, Holloway. Get your act together.

They weren't far from the steel bridge and if they crossed it, it was a short walk to the pond. The pond was their special place, where Mack taught her how to skip stones and to swim. On the banks of that pretty pond, sitting on the branches of the cypress tree hanging over the edge of the pond and later in the treehouse he'd built with his brothers, they'd shared their fears, their deepest desires, their dreams and their hopes.

It was where they'd lost their virginity that summer night… He'd been so damn nervous, in awe of her and the passion between them.

If there was one place on the property he could get Molly to talk, the pond was it.

Ten long minutes later Mack sat on a cushion on the smooth deck of the fantastic treehouse that had replaced the one he and his brothers built as teenagers. Following Molly up the spiral staircase, he took in the cheerful interior complete with a comfortable couch, easy chairs and a galley kitchen. Beyond the lounge was a bedroom and a bathroom, and a wraparound deck gave them three-sixty views of the pond and the mountains. Where they sat was directly over the pond, and a misstep could result in a dip right into it.

It was fabulous.

Mack looked at Molly, who'd stopped crying but her face was still pale, her eyes fixed on the clear water of the pond below. "When was this built?"

"Five years ago. We thought it would be a fun place for teenagers to camp out on summer nights," she said with a shrug.

Mack nodded to the open deck and the lack of a safety railing. "Isn't that a safety violation?"

"The contractor fell ill before he could finish the job and since there has not been a single booking for the tree-house in all that time, we haven't bothered to get it fixed. I think I'm the only one who ever spends any time here."

"I should get back to work," she added, a few minutes later.

She'd said variations of the same sentence five times since she stopped crying and, just like before, Mack ignored this version, too. She'd bitched about taking the time, about coming to the pond, but Mack ignored all her protestations. He was going to discover what was going on with Molly Haskell and if that meant keeping her in this treehouse for the foreseeable future, that was what he'd do.

Mack stared at her lovely profile, her skin still a little blotchy from her earlier bout of tears.

"Spill, Haskell," he told her.

Molly turned her face to him and lifted her eyebrows, trying to hit arrogance and missing by a country mile. "Excuse me?"

Mack ignored her frigid voice. "What's going on with you?" Her mouth opened and he carried on speaking before she could. "And don't you dare tell me *nothing*!"

"I'm not sure what you are talking about, Mack. I apologize for crying earlier."

Okay, they'd start there. "So why were you crying?"

Molly turned her attention back to the water. "I'm a little tense."

Pfft. "Nice try, Curls. You're not a little tense. You are massively *stressed*. You work insane hours. You don't stop. You have no social life and rarely leave the premises. I thought I was committed to my job but you're twice the workaholic I am."

"Jameson is sick. I've been trying to do his work as well as mine," Molly said, defensively.

"But I'm here now and one of the reasons for me being here is to take the pressure off you. That hasn't happened and I'm wondering why not. Have you always been like this?"

"I work hard. It's what I do."

Mack recalled the occasional comment Jameson had made about Molly over the years; how he worried about her, that she pushed herself too hard, that she thought she owed him the world. She was overqualified and could be climbing the corporate ladder at another company. Jameson was convinced the resort was too laid-back for her.

Jameson, he suddenly realized, had been worried about Molly for a long, long time.

Seeing the stubborn look on Molly's face, he knew that he was venturing down a closed-off path. Hoping to catch her off guard, Mack changed tack.

"Why the hell are you still giving your brothers money, Mol?"

Molly's head snapped up, her delicious curls bouncing with the sharp movement. Molly sent him a cold look. "Mind your own business, Holloway."

Not a chance. Because her business was starting to become his. Whatever made Molly sad, mad or crazy was his problem to solve. Not because she couldn't—Molly was one of the most capable, independent people he knew—but because he cared for her. She'd been a part of his childhood, had been and was still, his best friend, the person who knew him best. He was also her lover and was, and always would be, protective of her.

Nobody messed with Molly.

"They are adults, Mol, and shouldn't be asking their baby sister to bail them out."

Mack, watching her body language, saw the tension seep back into her body. It was in the way her hands tightened, in her suddenly clenched toes, the way her back hunched over.

Oh, yeah, her family was a major cause of stress. They always had been but this was harder and deeper than before.

"God, Molly, talk to me. You know you can!"

"I don't know that, Mack!" Molly responded, her tone sharp. "How can I trust anything you say? You said you'd love me forever but you left me, without a word. Without a goodbye or an explanation. *You. Left. Me.*"

Mack sighed. He'd been thinking about this lately; being back in Asheville had forced him to dig a little deeper into the past and his actions. He was big on control; there was no getting around that, but his need to protect was almost as strong.

And Molly had always been under his protection.

Mack leaned forward, captured her chin in his hand and gently pulled her on it, forcing her to meet his eyes. "I left you without a word because I knew that if you asked me to stay, if you asked if you could come with me, I would've said yes, either way. And neither of those options was best for you, Molly. You needed to stay. You needed to be in school. You needed to dance, if you'd left with me you would've given up all of that!"

"I—"

"I couldn't stay. I was, in a clumsy, crazy way, trying to protect you because I could never say no to you, Mol."

And he probably still couldn't. Mack knew that no matter what Molly asked him now, there was a good chance he'd move heaven and earth to give it to her.

She was that important to him.

Mack allowed his thumb the pleasure of drifting over her full bottom lip. "I would've given you anything you wanted, Mol. But right now I want something from you."

Molly's green eyes turned wary. "What?"

Mack kept his fingers on her face so that she kept looking at him. "I want you to trust me, Molly. I want to know what's driving you, what's hurting you, what's making you crazy. And, God, if you tell me *nothing*, I swear I'll boot you off this deck."

It was an idle threat but Molly seemed to take it seriously, possibly because he'd tossed her into this pond a hundred times when they were kids. Molly brushed an irritating curl out of her eyes before scowling at him. "You play dirty, Holloway."

Ah, but he wasn't playing at all. Not this time.

Could she trust him? Could she share her deepest secret with him? She was so damn tired, a battery whose energy was slowly being drained, with no hope of been recharged. She felt lonely and sad, and hostile, angry and guilty.

Yet, a part of her, *most* of her, would prefer to live like that to avoid seeing the same expression she remembered seeing on Jameson's face when she was six and dealing with her dad's betrayal: confusion, pain, disappointment and anguish jumping in and out of his eyes.

She'd been so young yet she understood, at a fundamental level, that her father's actions had eviscerated Jameson.

And when he'd hear about her theft, she'd be reopening, deepening and expanding that wound.

If she didn't tell him, she'd slowly fade away. If she did, she'd lose everything she loved. It was a hell of a choice…

Molly tipped her head to the side, considering the idea of telling Mack, thinking he could be her trial run for telling Jameson. Mack would be horrified and wouldn't want anything to do with her; he'd immediately hit the brakes on their relationship—if that was what it was—and start backing away. And yeah, that would suit her because a) she didn't have the strength to walk away from Mack on her own and b) at least she'd see this split coming and could be, somewhat, prepared for it.

After calling her a thief and a dozen other names—all of which she'd called herself over the years—Mack would reject her and walk out of her life. His dislike and disgust would prepare her for losing Jameson's love and support.

She hoped.

Should she do it? Could she do it? Molly didn't know.

After a few minutes more of silence, she looked at Mack, knowing her expression was granite-hard. "If I tell you something, do you promise not to tell Jameson?"

Mack's eyes darted across her face as if he was trying to judge how serious she was being. "What could be so bad that you can't tell my dad? He adores you."

Right now he did. When her secret came out, Jameson would look at her the same way he looked at her father, with confused disgust.

"Jameson can't handle stress right now so I need you to promise not to tell him." Once Mack gave his word, he never reneged on it.

"Are you, or is he, in danger or in legal jeopardy?" Mack demanded.

"No."

Mack nodded. "Then I promise."

She couldn't believe that she was finally going to allow her secret to see the light of day. Molly sucked in a deep breath, knowing that her life, from this point on, would change again, that she was all but pushing Mack through the door, ending whatever it was they'd managed to find again.

And that was okay; it was going to happen at some point so it might as well be now, when the pain was anticipated and manageable.

"A few weeks after you left, my mother was out of money and we were about to be evicted. She kept asking me to get the money from Jameson. I was desperate. They were pressurizing me and I didn't want to have to move again so I stole two thousand dollars from Jameson. It was the end of my shift, he'd gone to visit Travis and I went into his office and took it from the Chinese tea caddy on the windowsill behind his desk."

Mack's expression didn't change. He just looked at her, his face inscrutable. In searching his eyes, she didn't see disgust or anger, just curiosity.

"That's my big secret." Molly shrugged. "My family knows I took the money and whenever I don't do what they want, that is, when I balk at giving them money, they threaten to tell Jameson."

"Nice," was Mack's only response.

Molly frowned, confused. "Okay, you can start yelling now."

"Why would I yell at you, Molly?"

Was he messing with her? "I *stole* money from *your* dad, just like my dad stole money from him. I've never come clean, never told him, never confessed."

Mack nodded, obviously agreeing with her. "No, you didn't do any of those things. But from what Jameson told me, you did refuse to let him pay for college for you, choosing instead to work your butt off to get a scholarship and working as a bartender to put yourself through school. And then, instead of joining a corporate company, you came back to Moonlight Ridge to work for Jameson, to work your *ass* off for Jameson."

His next words nearly knocked her off the deck. "Your actions speak far louder than words, Mol, and they reflect your remorse."

Molly just stared at him, still waiting for him to casti-
gate her, to yell and scream at her.

"Why didn't you hunt Jameson down and ask him for
the cash? He would've given it to you, no questions asked."
Mack bent his knee, placing his forearm on it.

Good question. "He was so stressed, Mack. You'd left
and he was so worried about you. Grey was spending more
and more time with friends, and Travis was angry and
dispirited. And still in the hospital." She bit her lip. "He
looked gray and tired, as if another crisis would drop him
to his knees. I tried, for a couple of days, to ask him but he
was snappy and brusque and then we were told we were
getting kicked out…"

"So you just took it."

She didn't want to put lipstick on a pig. "I didn't take it,
Mack, I *stole* it."

Mack acknowledged her words with a slight dip to his
head. "Why didn't you tell Jameson at some point? I mean,
with a decent conversation, you could've averted a lot of
stress and anxiety. And told your brothers to go to hell,
which had to be a great incentive."

Ah, another great question. And one that would be so
much more difficult to answer. Molly rested her chin on
her bent knee. "I came back to the resort as a penance, I
suppose. I wanted Jameson to see how hard I worked, that
I could do a good job so that when I told him, because I've
always planned to, he'd take that into consideration when
he was debating whether to fire me or not. But I love it here,
Mack. I love working here."

She really did. Moonlight Ridge was her place, where
she belonged.

"I don't think he would've fired you, Mol."

"I'm my father's daughter, Mack. He was a thief and now
I am one, too. My mother is a perpetual victim and I've just

given my brothers money, not knowing what they are going to do with it. Buy drugs or guns, play blackjack, who the hell knows? I don't ask and they don't tell me. That's the family I come from."

"But it's not who *you* are."

"It's not who you want me to be but yes, it is who I am," Molly stated.

"I was supposed to have a meeting with Jameson, the day he had his brain episode," Molly continued her explanation. "We were going to discuss the resort and I was going to tell him everything, come clean. I knew he would fire me. Stealing is the line you can't cross with Jameson. I'd saved enough to rent an apartment, to pay for movers, to reestablish myself. I was going to break ties with my family, to start again…"

"But then he ended up in the hospital."

"Yeah, and I'm back to where I was. I can't tell him. I can't afford to stress him out. But I will tell Jameson at some point, I have to." Molly looked him in the eye, straightened her shoulders and lifted her chin. "You have Jameson's full authority to act on his behalf, so what are you going to do?"

Mack lifted his hands, looking confused. "About what?"

"About me, you idiot! Are you going to fire me?"

"I am not firing you because you did something stupid when you were under pressure and were a kid! That's between Jameson and you, Molly."

Molly's shoulders dropped and a little tension slid away. "Will you tell Grey and Travis?" she asked in a small voice.

Mack shook his head. "What part of *that's between you and Jameson* did you not understand, Mol?"

A curious combination of hope, relief and astonishment flowed through her. "I didn't expect you to react like this, Mack. I expected—"

Mack waited for her to finish her sentence but when she just shook her head, he filled the silence. "You forget that I know you, Mol. I know who you are beneath your spreadsheets and your lists, your constant push for perfection—"

"The accounting system is far from perfect."

"The accounting system is a freakin' mess but that's not on you. That was Jameson's responsibility and Beth's." Mack stared at her before shaking his head. "She's not only shitty at her job but she has questionable taste in men, too, if she's dating your brother."

Molly handed him a small smile. "You're not wrong."

Mack stood up and offered Molly a hand to pull her up. "I seldom am."

Mack turned to walk off the deck but Molly's hand on his elbow stopped his progress. He looked over his shoulder at her and raised his eyebrows.

She swallowed and rapidly blinked, trying to disperse the sheen of tears in her eyes. "Thank you. For believing in me."

Mack touched her cheek with gentle fingers. "Oh, Mol. You are so damn tough on yourself."

Molly's eyes connected with his. "And you aren't?"

"Touché. We are, in so many ways, our own worst enemies." Mack held out his hand and Molly slid her fingers between his, feeling for the first time in forever, a little hopeful, optimistic.

Maybe, just maybe, there was a tiny chance the sky wouldn't fall on her head.

Because Jameson's office was next to hers and only thin drywall separated the two, Mack could hear everything that went on in Molly's office. Well, not conversations but voice tones and types, and his door creaked every time the door to Molly's office opened.

And that was all the damn time.

Nobody gave her much of a break. Every half hour someone was knocking on her door, asking her a question, demanding something from her.

How did she get any work done?

Hell, he was next door and the constant traffic in and out of her room disturbed his work and broke his concentration...

Mack leaned back in his chair and eyed the many piles of paper on his desk, floor and on the small conference table in the corner. He could not believe that Jameson had let the paperwork run away with him. How did Jameson pay accurate sales and use tax, income tax? How did he know whether he was paying creditors accurately, whether his invoices matched the deliveries?

He now realized why Molly had been so reluctant to allow him to look at the paperwork; she knew it would deeply offend his anally retentive, need-control-at-all-costs soul. And he also knew she felt embarrassed, felt that it was her fault that the accounting system was in such a mess. Molly had an overdeveloped sense of responsibility; if any blame was to be laid, he'd drop it at Jameson's, and their useless bookkeeper's, door. From his observations, it seemed Beth liked to do as little work as possible, but still collect her large paycheck.

Jameson, bless him, was a brilliant host and exceptional at PR, but book work bored him. All his personal expenses were paid for by the business, and as long as there was a little money left in the bank account for some monogrammed shirts and fancy shoes, for him to buy an occasional antique or painting, and his damn Cuban cigars, he was happy.

Mack glared at the spreadsheet on his computer, conscious of the headache pounding behind his eyes, wishing he was looking at the color-coded, immaculate spreadsheets of his own business, able to pick up any information at a moment's notice.

He liked neat, he liked tidy and he liked control.

None of which he'd found here at Moonlight Ridge.

The books were a mess, and so was his head. He was crazy in lust with his ex-girlfriend, his one-time best friend, but she started work at seven and finished after six, sometimes seven at night. He suspected that if he wasn't in the picture, her working hours would be longer.

And that had to stop. Sure, he worked hard, but he made time for yoga, for exercise, for sex. His life, a long way from perfect, was a little more balanced than hers was.

Mack heard her door opening again, heard footsteps crossing the floor to her desk and heard low, rumbling masculine tones. It was the fourth time she'd been disturbed in twenty minutes and it was enough.

Mack understood that Molly adored Jameson, she felt guilty for stealing from him and was trying to redeem herself, but she was slowly, by degrees, killing herself.

That stopped. Right now.

Mack pushed back the leather chair, stood up and walked around his desk to the door connecting their offices. Not bothering to knock, he opened the door and two heads shot up to look at him. Molly frowned at him but Ross Barnes managed to flash him a smile. Mack replied to his greeting and walked to stand behind Molly, resting his shoulder against the wall.

He didn't speak but kept his eyes on Barnes, knowing that silence was an excellent way to demand an explanation. And while he waited, he reviewed what he knew about Ross. In his midthirties, he was Moonlight Ridge's catering and events manager and had years of experience in the field.

Since he'd heard his voice at least three times on separate occasions this morning, Mack had to wonder why, after years in the same position, he needed to speak to Molly so often.

He had many, many managers and he left them to get with their jobs and only interacted with them on a need-to-know basis.

"I was running some ideas by Molly for a fiftieth wedding anniversary party we are hosting in two weeks," Ross explained.

Mack's frown deepened. He'd seen the booking; it was a simple brunch for twenty people. Surely, someone with Ross's experience could handle that without Molly's input?

"You found it necessary to disturb Molly three times to discuss a minor event?" Mack asked, sounding skeptical.

"Uh—"

Molly turned around and nailed him with a hard look. "The mayor of Asheville will be attending. It might be a small brunch to you but it could lead to bigger functions."

No, the more likely explanation was that Moonlight Ridge's managers were, subtly and sneakily, delegating their work to Molly, using her loyalty and love of Jameson and the hotel to lighten their own loads.

Well, screw that. That stopped right now.

"I've been working next door and, by my account, Molly has had ten visitors in the last hour. She has her own work to do and every interruption adds ten or fifteen minutes to the end of her day. You all work seven-to eight-hour days. Molly works a lot longer than that. It stops right now."

"Mack!"

Mack ignored Molly's furious expression.

"I want a meeting with all the heads of departments this afternoon at three. I will tell them the same thing. I think it's high time we instituted different protocols around here."

Barnes's mottled face reflected his anger and embarrassment. Mack didn't give a rat's ass; nobody was going to take advantage of Molly while he was around. And if he could reduce her stress and reduce her working hours, all the better.

"Jameson—"

Mack deepened his scowl and the rest of Barnes's sentence died on his lips. Good to know he wasn't losing his touch. He jerked his head toward the door and Barnes stood, rose and with a sour look at him, left Molly's office.

Molly spun around in her seat and looked up at him with her beautiful, intense, amazing eyes. In those clear depths he saw frustration, anger, and, was he imagining this, a little relief? Because there was no way Molly would take his high-handedness lying down.

Mack folded his arms, feeling defensive. "Before you cut me off at the knees, nobody gets to take advantage of you, Mol. Not Jameson, not your family and definitely not the staff. They are paid good salaries, have the experience and should be working independently of you."

Instead of lambasting him, as he expected, Molly just rested the back of her head on her leather chair and nodded. "I know. I should be tougher but I like being involved, I like knowing what's going on, feeling useful and being Jameson's eyes and ears."

Mack knew that for Molly, the hotel and Jameson represented stability and solidity, the one place and the one person that didn't change.

His father, for most of her life, had been her rock—and she felt she owed him—but that didn't mean she had to sacrifice her mental and physical health for him. And it was obvious that she was doing both.

What she needed was a break, some sun, to breathe fresh air. Grateful they weren't arguing, he pulled himself off the wall and held out his hands. "Let's go."

"Go where?" Molly asked, putting her hands in his and allowing him to pull her to her feet. Man, the woman was a feather. Along with working less, she needed to eat more.

He noticed the three dirty coffee mugs and shook his head. Too much work and way too much caffeine.

That, he decided, was going to change.

"Let's take a walk."

Molly nodded, reached for her cell and radio but Mack snatched them away before she could pick them up. Removing his phone from his pocket, he dumped all three devices in the top drawer of her desk and slammed it closed.

"I have to be available." Molly looked panicked, her corkscrew curls shaking.

"The world won't stop spinning if we take an hour off. Giada is with Jameson and everyone else can either find their own solution or wait until you return." Still holding her hands, Mack rested his forehead against hers. "Come walk with me, Mol, and let's check out for a little bit."

He saw the acquiescence in her eyes before he heard her small yes, saw her nod. Feeling like he'd both dodged a bullet and won the battle, Mack led her from her office, her hand warm and soft in his.

Eight

Her hand in his, Molly and Mack didn't speak as they walked down the long driveway toward the main road leading into Asheville. It felt strange not to have her phone in her pocket, her radio in her hand.

Strange but good.

The old cypress trees that lined either side of the driveway were showing off their bright new leaves and she could hear the brook chortling on its way to the lake. In the distance she could see two guests hiking up the steep hill to Tip's Point, a favorite walk of hers. From the lookout a few miles up the hill, they'd have an awesome view of the Blue Ridge Mountains.

She hadn't done that walk for ages, maybe a year. Two? Three? God, could it possibly be that long?

"You're frowning," Mack said, squeezing her hand. "You're supposed to be relaxing, not thinking."

Right. Molly tucked her free hand into the front pocket of her pants, conscious that her shoulders were up around her ears. She rolled them back, straightened her spine and made a mental note to find time for a deep massage.

But she knew she wouldn't; she hadn't visited the spa for an indulging treatment—waxing didn't count!—for many months. Possibly even a year or more.

Despite his high-handed manner on this subject, Mack did have a point. She allowed the staff to take advantage of her and she worked too hard.

But it was hard to change the habits of a lifetime. And she owed Jameson her loyalty and her effort—to work for her redemption. Without him, God knew where she'd be.

Mack nudged her shoulder, bringing her back to the present. "Just breathe and, for God's sake, stop thinking."

Molly sent him a wry look. That was easier said than done.

"Yeah, I know that's like asking for the moon but can you at least try?"

Stopping, Molly faced him. "Why are you doing this? Why do you care how stressed I am? Why are you trying to get me to relax?"

"Because you are wound tighter than a spinning top and you have no balance in your life."

"But why do you care?" Molly demanded. They'd had no contact for so long and it didn't make sense for him to slide back into his role as protective-in-chief. "I've been on my own for a long, long time, Mack, and I can take care of myself."

Mack lifted his hand to squeeze her left trapezius muscle. His fingers encountered a rock-solid wall and she pulled away from the pain. "You're stressed to the max, Molly, and, while I'm here and have some sort of power, I *will* make life easier for you. It's BS that you work such long hours and that you juggle a hundred balls, ninety of which don't even belong to you."

Underneath his designer clothing, expensive cologne and the urbane mask was still the boy who would move heaven and earth for her. It was both wonderful and terrifying.

Mack, she had to remember, had left her, breaking her heart and her spirit. She would not allow that to happen again.

They were temporary colleagues, temporary friends having a temporary fling. End of story.

Mack placed his hand on her back, steering her down the road toward a rambling stone structure. The barn, standing to the side of the road, was empty, its roof still intact. It was part of the history of the farm and an interesting feature and while it was pretty, it wasn't useful.

"I've tried to talk to Jameson about knocking it down but he won't hear of it," Molly told Mack.

Mack walked down the overgrown driveway and stepped up to the front door, warped by the weather. "He promised Tip he'd never pull it down because it was built before the main house."

Tip O'Sullivan's parents, professional socialites, built the house a century ago. They added one wing to accommodate their incessant stream of guests and within a few years converted the estate into a hotel and resort. Tip added on another wing and Jameson built the pretty lakeside cottages to accommodate more guests.

Yet, in all that time, this stone barn stood untouched on a rise overlooking the lake.

Molly watched as Mack put his shoulder to the door and pushed. The door opened with a loud complaint and Mack stood back and gestured her to precede him.

"After you," Mack said.

Molly heard the tremble in his voice and swallowed her huge grin. "No, please, after you," she insisted.

Mack glared at her. "Hah, funny. Get in there and do your thing."

It was a long-held agreement between them that Mack would deal with all critters they found on their adventures—from frogs to snakes to bugs—but she was the person in charge of exterminating spiders.

Mack loathed spiders and it seemed nothing had changed. Before he would step into the barn, she'd have to do a recce and tell him, exactly, how many spiders she could see and where they were. Mack, tall and broad and tough as hell, was deathly scared of arachnids.

"Wuss," Molly said, brushing past him. Stepping into the empty structure, she placed her hands on her hips, looking at the stone walls, the exposed timbers of the roof and the way the sunlight streamed through the windows on the side of the building looking out to the lake. It was a stunning spot and Molly thought it would be lovely if it was converted into a private, self-catering villa.

But the conversion would cost a bomb, or two, and the business didn't have the credit or cash flow to support that sort of expansion. And, since they had too many rooms open too often, she couldn't justify any expensive renovations.

"Spiders, Mol," Mack reminded her, still standing just outside the door.

Molly did a cursory look around, didn't see any spiders and gestured for him to come in. Mack did his own quick sweep and he gradually relaxed.

Coming to stand next to her, he whistled as he took in the huge space and the lovely light. "Wow, it's amazing."

Molly trailed her hand down a stone wall, wondering who built this place so long ago. "Isn't it? I was just thinking that it would be awesome as a private villa. With clever renovations it could sleep six or eight." She gestured through the broken windowpane to the clear lake. Two guests were idly rowing across the lake, their faces tipped to the sun.

Molly caught the quick shake of his head and sighed. "I know. Until we fill up every room every night, I can't think about converting anything."

"It would be a really good idea…if we had the guests," Mack replied.

Molly darted a look at him. "Can I run something by you?"

"You know you can."

"I'm standing by all the ideas in my proposal because they are necessary."

Mack gestured for her to carry on talking.

"But I'm thinking that we should make Moonlight Ridge even more exclusive, more difficult to get into. I think we should hike the prices, reduce the numbers and turn it into a boutique hotel, a place people should be fighting, and definitely waiting, to get into."

Her desire to run an exquisite, exclusive place, providing her guests with the best of the best, burned in her soul. This was the way to go, she was certain of it. But would Mack agree?

Mack thought for a moment. "I think it's a great idea, I do. But we still need to get people here, a reason why they'd choose Moonlight Ridge over a hundred others," Mack pointed out.

"If only Travis would come back and open a world-class restaurant here. That would bring the guests in. I've heard that his Traverser restaurants are booked up for months and months in advance," Molly said.

"Yep, they are. Travis is a fabulous chef and he's making a name for himself in the haute cuisine world."

Molly heard the pride in his voice and hid her smile.

The brothers' relationship might be strained but it wasn't completely broken. She was glad for Mack; family was important and she hoped that Mack, Grey and Travis found their way back to one another. Back in the day, they'd been a tight-as-hell team.

"All of his restaurants are in great cities—Atlanta, LA, London. Asheville is hip and trendy but I don't know if it's sophisticated enough for a Traverser," Mack stated, his brow furrowed.

Damn.

"But you're right. An excellent restaurant could bring guests to Moonlight Ridge."

Molly watched as Mack paced the room and saw the intense look of speculation on his face. His face held the same expression it did when he was ten and contemplating building a ramp for his BMX bike, plans for the treehouse, how to raise enough money to buy the F-150 truck he'd been eyeing since he was twelve.

Mack had hit on a plan; of that Molly was certain.

Mack paced out the width of the barn, then the length, coming back to stand in the middle of the room, his expression thoughtful.

"Are you going to share what's going on in that big brain of yours?" Molly asked, leaning her back against the stone wall and lifting her booted foot to rest its sole on the wall.

Mack turned around to face her. "Actually, I was thinking this would be a perfect spot for a Corkscrew Craft Beer brewery."

"I never understood why you chose that name." Molly wrinkled her nose. "I mean, a person associates corkscrews with wine bottles, not craft beer."

When he looked at her, his face was inscrutable. "It has nothing to do with wine or corkscrews."

"Then I really don't understand."

Mack took two steps, lifted a strand of her hair and wound it around his index finger, watching as the curl hugged his finger. "Corkscrew curls, Mol. I've always loved your hair."

Molly sucked in her breath, completely blindsided by his admission. He'd named his company after her? What the hell? Why? "I don't understand why you would do that."

Mack dropped his hand and turned away. Ignoring her silent plea for an explanation, he pointed to the back wall, where there were no windows. "I'd add on space at the back, for the processing and distribution of the beer, but I'd put the tanks there where the diners could see them. In front of them, a really long statement bar. A small, open kitchen in the corner, and we'd have a small, beer-inspired menu. I'd go for an industrial look inside, to contrast with the wooden beams and the stone walls. Heavy tables, a concrete floor. I'd leave the stonework exposed. Maybe we could open up that far wall, make a deck and put tables out there, too. The customers would enjoy the view."

Forcing herself not to grab his shirt and demand why he felt the need to name his company after her hair—her hair, for goodness' sake!—Molly struggled to think. It wasn't easy when she wanted to beat an answer out of him.

Pulling up her business brain took far more effort than she expected.

"And how, exactly, would your brewery benefit the resort?"

Mack took a moment to digest her question, his thoughts obviously a million miles away. "Well, I'd have to buy the building, giving Jameson an immediate and rather substantial cash injection."

Which would be lovely but she needed more than cash; she needed guests, as she'd told him.

"I don't own and run Traverser-like restaurants but actually, people do travel to visit my breweries. I have no doubt that some people would choose to stay at Moonlight Ridge. Some would stay over, visit the spa, want to take a hike…maybe we could do joint promotions between Moonlight Ridge and the brewery. The point is, we want to up the visibility of the resort, and the brewery would be a good way to do it."

Molly wrinkled her nose. "Aren't we looking at two different segments of the market? The resort caters to the very rich while the brewery is more middle-of-the-road, isn't it?"

Amusement flashed across Mack's face. "Actually, you would be surprised at the demographics of who visits my breweries. According to the expensive company I recently hired to do consumer research, the young and wealthy account for at least half of my customer base. And isn't that the segment of the market you are looking at attracting?"

He had her there. "Fair point."

Mack looked around the space again and Molly could see his mind working at warp speed. "I'd need an architect to help me plan the space."

Molly had spent too much time taking virtual tours of his many breweries on the Corkscrew Breweries website—and really, every time she remembered that he'd named his business after her hair, her heart did a strange triple thump—and all his places carried the same subtle branding and design elements.

He'd call in his usual design team and within months the brewery would be up and running. When Mack wanted something, he didn't let anything get in his way.

"I need to talk to Jameson and if he agrees, I'll get my senior management team out here to do some market research and viability studies. Asheville has many craft breweries but my gut says mine will be a welcome addition. But I'd like the research to confirm my hunch. Once we make the final decision, I'll get Vanna out here to inspect the building, to start working on some design plans."

"Is she an architect?"

"Yeah, she's worked on most of my breweries," Mack responded, his thoughts miles away.

Molly knew that she was wandering into a minefield but they couldn't keep avoiding the subject forever. "Why did you never ask Grey to do any work for you? I mean, he is one of the most in-demand, award-winning architects around."

Guilt and annoyance replaced excitement. "I try to keep family and work separate."

Molly rolled her eyes and made sure he saw her dramatic gesture. "Thousands might believe you. I don't."

"Drop it, Mol," Mack growled.

That wasn't going to happen. "Why are you three still not talking? It's ridiculous, Mack!"

Mack made a show of looking around the empty, decrepit building. "How did we go from talking about this barn to my family?" he asked, his tone suggesting that she back down.

She never had and never would.

"Why aren't you and your brothers talking, Mack?" Molly persisted.

Mack started to walk away but Molly placed her hand on his roped-with-muscle forearm. She ignored the flash of heat and the corresponding lust. This was more important than the still-bubbling desire.

"I confided in you, Mack."

She had him there and he knew it.

"We do talk."

That was such a lie. "I'm not talking about quick conversations about Jameson and you know it. You guys were tight, best friends as well as brothers, but now you are little more than strangers."

"Yeah, well, nearly killing them in a car crash tends to change the dynamic," Mack muttered, grief and regret coating the bitter words.

Had he spent the past fifteen years blaming himself? Surely not? Molly chose her next words carefully. "Mack, it was an accident. Everyone knows that."

When his eyes met hers Molly saw, for the first time, the guilt lodged deep in his soul.

"I lost control, Molly, and the blame is mine to shoulder. I was behind the wheel. I put that truck into the ditch."

"I was told you were all arguing, that you were distracted," Molly protested.

Mack's expression turned hard and she could feel him pulling back, creating distance between them. "I am the oldest—"

"By months, for God's sake!"

Mack ignored her interruption. "—and I was responsible for looking after them, for their safety. I failed and Travis nearly died. I lost my right to a family because I failed to look after them. I allowed myself to be distracted, to lose control and *it will never happen again.*"

Wow. Mack had always been hard on himself but this was ridiculous. "You are being insanely tough on yourself."

"No, I'm really not."

Molly frowned, hearing the subtext beneath that hard statement. "What aren't you telling me?"

"Leave it alone, Molly." Mack turned to walk toward the door but Molly ran to stand between him and the door, stretching her arms out wide to create a barrier between him and the exit.

Mack sent her a "get real" look. "Molly, I'm bigger and

stronger than you and could just lift you up and out of my way."

Molly dropped her arms. "Yeah, of course you could." Her eyes clashed with his and she sighed at all the pain in those deep, dark depths. "Tell me, Mack."

She wanted to know; the curiosity was killing her. But more important, she sensed that, like her theft, this was a piece of the past that needed to see the light.

"My mom died at childbirth."

She knew that. He'd been raised by his dad until he was seven. One day, his father dropped him off at school and never bothered to collect him. Mack never heard from him again.

"I know, Mack," Molly replied, keeping her tone gentle and nonconfrontational.

"But I never told you it was my fault she died."

He didn't have to; it was never the baby's fault when a mother died. But instead of telling him that, she just tipped her head to the side and waited for more.

"I was a big baby, and she was tiny. I was two or three weeks late and they induced her. Officially, the cause of death was post-partum bleeding from an obstructed labor."

"That sounds reasonable and none of it your fault," Molly said.

"That's not what my father told me every single day of my life," Mack whispered, his hands clenched at his sides.

Oh, God. Molly muttered a silent string of curse words before stepping forward to place her hand on his chest, directly above his heart, needing the connection. "You know that's rubbish, Mack."

Mack raised his shoulders halfway to his ears before allowing them to drop. "Intellectually, I do. Emotionally, not so much. And the things you are told as a young kid tend to stick with you."

Mack raked his hand through his dark hair and Molly noticed the slight tremble in his fingers. "He told me that I should've died, not her."

And she didn't need to be a rocket scientist to know that he thought that he should've been injured, not Travis. "Oh, Mack, you know it doesn't work like that. It wasn't your fault."

Mack stared at a point past her shoulder, his body tight with tension. "After I came to live with Jameson, I was terrified of messing up, of doing anything wrong. I was the model kid. Jameson said jump and I leaped. I didn't want to give him an excuse to give me back."

She didn't know any of this; maybe they hadn't been as close as they thought they were. Then again, they'd been kids and Mack had never been one to wear his heart on his sleeve.

"When Grey and Travis arrived, I started to relax a little because they were far worse behaved than I was and Jameson never sent them away, or even threatened to."

Man, what had it felt like to live with so much insecurity? Molly knew how much she worried about Jameson ever finding out about the money she stole, how it would change their relationship, and it kept her awake at night. She'd been a young adult but Mack had lived with his guilt a lot longer than she had. And it wasn't his fault!

God, if she could she'd hunt down his father and slap him stupid. What a bastard!

"The accident just reminded me that it's better for people if I keep my distance, if I stay away."

Molly stared at him and shook her head. Then she lifted her hand and smacked it back down on his chest, the sound jerking his eyes back to her face. Gripping his shirt, she looked up into his anguished eyes and tried to shake him.

Because he was so much bigger than she was, she didn't move him an inch.

"All right, *enough*. Seriously, Mack, you're done with thinking like that. It was not your fault your mother died and your father had no right to blame you! Her death was horrible, but it was not your fault!"

She caught a flicker of hope in his eyes that was quickly extinguished. She tapped his chest again, trying to make her point. "*It. Was. Not. Your. Fault.* Are we clear on that?"

Mack kept his eyes on hers, his hands coming up to rest on her waist. Well, at least he was listening to her, and was she imagining the fact that some of the tension in his body had dissipated?

"As for the car accident, I know that you were all arguing and, hell, Mack, you know how heated your arguments could be. I was witness to so many of your fights back then. Testosterone was raging, you all wanted to be right and God, you were all as stubborn as each other. I can easily imagine the argument in the truck and I'm not surprised you got distracted. It's a horrible curve, it was dark and raining and you were all yelling at each other. You were *all* stupid, *all* irresponsible and if there is blame to be assigned, it should be shared. But you were kids and it was an accident, for God's sake."

Mack shook his head. "I was driving—"

Molly stepped back and folded her arms across her chest. "I can't change your mind about how you feel about the past, Mack. Only you can. All I can tell you is that your father's stupid words and an accident a long time ago shouldn't still have so much power."

"But it does," Mack told her, his words coated with sorrow and grief.

Molly rested her hand on his cheek, feeling the stubble under her hand, the hard line of his jaw. "Only you can change that, Mack. Not me, not Jameson, not your brothers. Only you."

It would be easy to change the subject, to brush aside the emotion and flit onto another subject, but Molly liked Mack too much—more than she should—to allow that to happen. She stepped closer to him and wrapped her arms around his trim waist, hoping to hug away the desolate look on his face.

Unlike her, Mack had nothing to be ashamed of.

Mack didn't say much on their walk back to Moonlight Ridge and when they reached the third floor, he disappeared into his office without a word. Knowing that she needed to give him space, Molly immersed herself in her own work. When she finally stopped, somewhere around seven, she noticed that the light was off in his office.

She returned back to her apartment, saw that the guesthouse was in darkness and assumed Mack was with Jameson. She cooked, ate, drank a glass of wine and wondered whether Mack would come to her tonight.

And she kept wondering for another hour, then two. At half past ten, minutes before she was about to give up on him and go to bed, she saw the lights come on in the guesthouse and she debated whether to go to him or to give him space.

But like her, Mack tended to spend too much time in his head, and she knew of a truly excellent way of getting him to step outside his big brain. It involved getting naked and Molly knew Mack had no problem with that...

Minutes later Molly found herself standing at his closed door and lifted her hand to knock. But before her hand could make contact with the wood, the door opened and Mack stood there, looking at her like she was wholly unexpected.

"Ah, you're here."

"I am."

Mack rubbed his jaw, then pushed his hand through his hair. "I was just coming to you," he said, not sounding very enthusiastic. "Just so you know, I'm not in the mood to talk."

Ah. He assumed she'd come over here to revive their earlier conversation.

"Well, if you don't want to talk, what would you prefer to do? Play Monopoly? Drink wine? Cheat at poker?" she teased him.

"Strip poker, maybe," Mack growled, tugging her into the hallway. Placing his hot mouth on her bare neck, he shuddered. He lifted his head to speak again. "I just need to lose myself in you, Curls."

"I think I can make that happen," Molly told him, her lips curving.

Mack, not wasting any time, immediately pulled her dress up the back of her thighs and palmed her butt with his broad hand. He pushed his other hand into her hair, gripping her head and angling her face to receive his demanding, possessive kiss. Tongues dueled as he explored her mouth, rediscovering her, learning about the woman she was today.

It was enthralling to be the object of so much focused passion and the reason for his brief, husky statements of appreciation. Needing to feel him, Molly pulled his shirt up so that she could touch his hot body. Her fingers traced the rows of his six-pack and the long muscles that covered his hips, before drifting over the hard erection that tented his jeans.

Ooh, very nice. She traced his long length with the tip of her finger. And, because she could, did it again.

"Love that, baby," Mack muttered, bunching her dress up to her hips, revealing her white bikini panties. Annoyed

with the barrier, he pulled the dress up and over her head
and dropped it to the floor. Resting his forehead against
hers, he looked down her body, past her flat stomach to her
long legs. She was still in her heels.

"Ah, Mol. You...this..." He shuddered. "You in my arms
is everything, and more, than I imagined."

"Is that a good or a bad thing?" Molly asked as her bra
fell to the floor.

"It's a very excellent thing, Curls."

Mack slid his hand between her legs and cupped her,
his thumb immediately finding and brushing her sensitive
bundle of nerves. She released a soft yelp and immediately
wanted more.

"Mack, I need you," Molly moaned against his lips, lifting her hips to push herself against his shaft.

Mack's hand stilled and his breath against her nipple
was fire hot. "If we don't slow down, I'm going to take you
right here, right now."

"So do it," Molly challenged him, tipping her head back
to connect with his deeply dark and passion-soaked eyes.

"Good thing I came prepared." Mack smiled and pulled
a strip of condoms from the back pocket of his jeans. He
ripped a packet off with his teeth and allowed the rest to
drop to the floor. He pressed the condom into her hand.

As Mack pulled off his shirt, Molly opened the first
button of his jeans, then the second, and when they were
loose around his hips she shoved her hands inside his briefs
and pushed both underwear and jeans down his hips. His
erection stood tall and proud, and Molly sighed at how big
he was...

She couldn't wait for him to be inside her. She wanted to
be filled, stretched, taken to the limit. She wanted him...

Molly pulled out the condom and swiftly rolled it over
his erection, sucking in her breath as he hardened even fur-

ther. Mack released a soft curse before hooking his hands under her thighs and lifting her, spreading her legs to either side of his waist. The head of his penis pushed against her wet, warm core.

Mack pressed her against the front door and pinned her there with his body, sliding into her with one long, confident, sexy stroke. Her world narrowed, everything faded away and there were only Mack's hands on her thighs, his tongue in her mouth mimicking the thrust of his hips, the hot strokes inside her as he pushed her higher and higher.

She whimpered, stretching for that ultimate release, wanting to step inside pleasure, to become pleasure.

Mack dropped his head to murmur encouragement in her ear. "You are so damn sexy, baby. I can't wait to feel you come on me, around me."

"Mack!" Molly yelled, reaching for her release.

Molly shouted as stars exploded behind her eyeballs and her body splintered into a million pieces. She vaguely heard Mack's yell in her ear, felt him shudder as he fell apart, his fingers digging into her hips.

Mack pushed into her and connected with something deep inside. She flew again, pleasure fueling her flight. She screamed his name again before fracturing once more.

Molly had no idea how much time passed when she returned to earth, her face in his neck, still pinned to the door by his hard body.

"I don't think we did that properly, Mol. I think we might have to do that again." She heard Mack's laughter in his words, felt the curve of his lips against her temple. "And again, until we get it right."

The problem was that she thought it might take the rest of their lives to get it *exactly* right. And, even more scary, she was game to try.

Nine

Mack stared at the spreadsheet he'd spent the past few weeks working on, the numbers dancing in front of his eyes. He pushed his thumb and index finger into his eyeballs, hoping to ease the burn.

Dropping his hands, he stared at the total at the bottom on his column and cursed violently, the words bouncing off the walls of the office. The total was still the same and he knew it would never change.

Before he could second-guess himself, he opened his browser and did a large file transfer, sending a copious amount of scanned documents and spreadsheets to Grey's email address, hoping his brother would find a reasonable explanation for what he'd discovered.

Mack spun around in his chair and stared out the window behind his desk, into the dark shadows of Moonlight Ridge's extensive gardens below. In the distance he could see the yellow lights of one occupied cottage on the edge of the lake but otherwise, the grounds were in darkness.

Mack looked at his watch, saw that it was nearly eleven and thought of Molly, curled up in his bed in the guesthouse, hopefully fast asleep. They'd been sleeping together for the past six weeks and, strangely, he still hadn't tired of her. Usually, by this point in a relationship he'd be looking for an easy exit, concocting a strategy to slide out of his lover's life.

Truthfully, he couldn't remember when, if ever, he had a fling that lasted this long. Ironic that his two longest relationships were with the same woman.

Mack turned back to his screen and frowned, wishing he could avoid having to tell her what had taken him weeks to discover. With her history, Molly would take it personally, would blame herself for what had happened.

She needed to know as quickly as possible, but before he told her, he needed to tell his brothers so Mack picked up his phone and shot off a text to them, asking if they were able to talk.

Grey replied immediately, saying he was free but Travis's message went unanswered for a couple of minutes. When he did reply, he said that he was in the middle of service and couldn't talk right now.

After telling Travis to call him when he was free, Mack started a video call to Grey and within a minute his brother's face appeared on his monitor, blue eyes wary. God, he was so sick of seeing the distance, the cool composure on his siblings' faces.

He wanted his brothers back. They needed to talk, to discuss that night so long ago, to, if they could, put it behind them. He missed them, intensely. Horribly. Being back in Asheville, living and breathing the air and atmosphere of Moonlight Ridge, made him realize that they'd wasted so much damn time.

He wanted his family back...

Grey's question broke into his thoughts. "Mack, what's up?"

It wasn't the time or the place for a heal-the-past type of conversation; he'd prefer to speak to his brothers in person, to apologize to their faces and not to a screen. And he would apologize and ask for their forgiveness. He hoped, prayed, he got it.

"Mack?"

Mack met his brother's eyes. "Hey, thanks for taking my call." So formal, so stiff. That had to change. And soon, dammit. "I hope I'm not interrupting anything important."

The corners of Grey's mouth lifted, somehow knowing that Mack was referring to a date or sex. "I'm in my office, at my desk, working."

"Busy?" Mack asked, hoping Grey wouldn't shut him down.

"Yeah, always," Grey replied, looking a little surprised at his question. He didn't blame him since they only ever discussed Moonlight Ridge or Jameson.

Mack rubbed the back of his neck, wanting to delay telling Grey the bad news. Instead, he decided to broach an idea he'd been considering. "Do you remember the old barn at the bottom of the property?" It was a stupid question; of course Grey would remember the barn. It had only stood there all their lives.

"Sure," Grey replied.

"I spoke to Jameson and I'm thinking about repurposing it, establishing one of my breweries there. What do you think?"

Grey thought for a minute before smiling. "I think it's a great idea. It needs to be used, to be lived in again."

"It's a great space but it needs to be reworked." Mack

sucked in a deep breath, annoyed to realize that he was nervous. "I need an architect. You interested?"

Grey's eyes widened, and astonishment jumped into them and fluttered across his face. "You want me to bid for the job?"

"No, I want *you* to design my new brewery. I don't care what you charge. I just want my brother to work on this project with me."

Grey's astonishment didn't fade. "It's been a while since you've called me your brother, Mack," he quietly stated, sounding bemused.

Mack rubbed the back of his neck again, feeling his skin prickling. "Yeah, I know. Look, we need to talk but I'm done with this cold war. Can we talk sometime, about you working with me on the brewery?" He hesitated before deciding to dive in. "I also want to talk about the accident, to find a way to move forward?"

Was that relief he saw in Grey's eyes or was he imagining it? Grey nodded. "Yeah, I think that's a good idea. Let's talk, Mack."

"I'd like to get the renovations to the barn done as soon as possible but I will wait for a gap in your schedule," Mack told him, feeling a warm wave of relief sliding through him.

"I could work on the design when I take over from you at the end of the month," Grey told him. "It's going to be a real pain moving back to Moonlight Ridge but I promised to do it."

"When you get here, listen to Molly. I mean, *really* listen to her and support her ideas. No one knows the resort better than she does, and her ideas will put Moonlight Ridge back on the map."

Grey looked amused at his words and Mack saw the he's-getting-lucky thought cross his mind.

Mack ignored Grey's curious expression and thought

about going back to Nashville, resuming his normal routine, and his stomach clenched. The life he knew two months ago no longer seemed normal; waking up with Molly seemed right; sharing a carafe of coffee on the porch seemed normal; chatting with her throughout the day was what he wanted to do. But he did need to check on his brewery in Austin and to investigate why his Santa Fe operation was experiencing a huge dip in turnover. He had to go back to work. But he didn't, necessarily, want to return to Nashville.

Asheville, dammit, was starting to feel like home again. That wasn't what he expected when he made the long drive from Nashville weeks ago.

Grey asked Mack how Jameson was and they passed a couple of minutes discussing Jameson's health. Mack told him that Jameson fired Giada every other day but his nurse simply ignored their father's fiery declarations. Giada was also refusing access to his cigars, another battle in an ongoing war.

They both agreed that Giada was tougher than she looked and could handle their grumpy, stubborn father.

"Dad wants us home for a Sunday lunch like we used to have," Grey told him.

"I heard," Mack replied. "I'd like that, actually."

"I would, too. But is there any chance his cooking has improved?"

Mack smiled at Grey's grimace. Jameson loved Sunday lunches and insisted on cooking for his family. Unfortunately, they were always a disaster with burnt duck, undercooked potatoes and overcooked vegetables. Sunday lunches, and Henri, the resort's previous chef, were the reason Travis started cooking and launched his love affair with food.

"Maybe we can persuade Travis to cook," Grey mused, "if we can get him home."

"We both know Trav will find a way to get out of it," Mack quietly stated.

Grey nodded. "Admittedly, with his insane work schedule, we were damn lucky to get his commitment to do a look-after-Moonlight Ridge shift after me. He won't come back before he has to."

Of the three of them, Travis was, by a hair's breadth, the most stubborn. If, and when, the three of them got together next, he'd find a way to get through to his stubborn-ass baby brother. He was tired of living his life without them in it.

Grey gestured to his desk. "I've still got a few hours' work ahead of me, M. Send me the dimensions and any ideas you have on the barn and I'll mull over some ideas of my own."

"Sounds good," Mack said before grimacing. "But actually, that wasn't why I called you, Grey."

Grey's eyes sharpened. "Then why did you call me?"

"I've just emailed you a lot of paperwork, including accounts, payments and reports. You've always been great at numbers and I need a second opinion. I hope I'm wrong, but I think someone is stealing from Moonlight Ridge."

Grey returned his call an hour later and this time Travis was able to join their three-way video call.

"So I hate to confirm your suspicions, Mack, but yeah, from what I can see, money has been taken from Moonlight Ridge."

Mack winced, wishing that he'd been wrong. This was going to kill Molly.

Mack gripped the bridge of his nose with his finger and thumb. "Are you sure?"

Grey nodded. "Yeah. Look, I did a cursory look at the material you sent through but I picked up quite a few instances of double dipping—"

"What the hell is double dipping?" Travis asked.

"Basically, the thief submits a claim for an expense on a credit card and gets reimbursed. Later, she—he—submits a cash reimbursement request for the same expense. Double dipping," Grey explained.

"Okay." Travis rubbed the back of his neck. "And how long has this been happening?"

Grey shrugged. "At a guess? Years and years. Jameson also made it easy for the thief to operate because, by God, I have never seen such a crazy accounting system in my life."

Neither had Mack.

"Talking about our father, are we going to tell him about this?" Grey asked.

"Hell, no. He's not supposed to be stressed, remember?" Mack snapped. Hearing that there was another thief at Moonlight Ridge would cause Jameson to stop convalescing and start bashing heads together.

Mack looked at his computer monitor. On the left side was Grey's face, on the right Travis's.

"I agree," Travis said, his deep baritone a lot like Jameson's. Despite them not sharing any DNA, Travis and Jameson had the same deep voice and the same build, and Travis learned how to be tenacious and stubborn from watching their father.

They all had.

He was so sick at being at odds with his brothers, Mack thought. Tired of wasting time, seeing another week, another month, go past without them connecting.

He'd reconnected with Molly and he now knew how great that felt. He wanted more of it, wanted his family whole and happy again.

Even if it meant eating Jameson's terrible food, he wanted those Sunday family lunches, Molly at his side, his hand on her thigh under the table.

He could see it, almost taste it. Jameson sitting at the head of the table, refusing to allow anyone else to carve the duck. The table would be piled high with dishes; Grey and Travis would be arguing about something because, hell, that was what they did. But it would be a friendly argument, a lot of teasing and trash-talking. He didn't know whom his brothers would end up with, not yet, but he could sense their women at the table, laughing and drinking wine together, discussing clothes and babies and art and politics.

Smart women, fun women.

And his hand would be on the thigh of the smartest, loveliest woman he'd ever met. The only female who'd ever touched his soul.

His first love and his last love.

The feeling that he only ever wanted to be where Molly was had been steadily enveloping him the past few weeks. And if Molly wanted to be here, then he had to consider making some changes including moving his company headquarters to Asheville. If he wanted to be with Molly, and God, he did, then that was the only course of action that made sense. He'd still travel but maybe he could buy a small piece of land behind the pond, build a house for him and Molly, and their kids, to share. He'd travel for work but he'd always come home to Moonlight Ridge, to Molly.

If she'd have him…

"We need a forensic accountant to dig deeper, to do proper accounting," Grey suggested.

Mack pulled his attention back to the problem at hand. "I presume it will take some time to get a forensic accountant in place. So what can Molly and I do to try and find out who is the embezzler in the meantime?" Mack asked.

The look on Grey's face had his heart plummeting to his toes. "That's not a good idea, Mack."

"Why not?" Mack asked, though a part of him knew what was coming.

"Molly is in charge of the company credit cards and it's her signature on some of the claim requests."

Ah, hell, no.

"I'm grateful that I'm on the other side of the screen and you can't hit me as I ask this..." Grey grimaced, hesitating. "But are you sure it isn't Molly who is the embezzler, Mack? From the reports you sent me, she looks like the most likely person to have done this."

Mack swallowed down his instinctive response, which was to rip Grey's head off for the suggestion. Mack ground his back teeth together and forced the words out. "Of course it's not Molly, Grey. Despite what it looks like."

A cold fist slammed into his sternum, expelling his warm and fuzzy feelings. Was he wrong to instinctively defend her? Was he blinded by lust, by memories, by their shared history? Was he looking for a reason to absolve her because he didn't *want* her to be guilty?

But dammit, because of her confession, there was a tiny flicker of doubt.

Mack forced himself to think, to be the coolheaded, rational, thinking person he normally was. If this was anyone else but Molly, how would he respond to Grey's statement?

With skepticism and doubt and with a burning desire to know, one way or the other. Guilt rolled over him, hot and sour. Mack felt the pull between blind faith and loyalty and his own innate suspicion and cynicism. After all, she had stolen from Jameson before...

Guilt crashed over him and he was glad he was sitting down.

"It's not Molly," he stated, wondering if he was trying to convince himself or his brothers.

"How do you know that, Mack?" Travis asked. "It's been

a long time since she was part of your life and you don't know her anymore."

Oh, yes, he did. But doubt, insidious and relentless, mocked his loyalty. "It's *not* Molly."

Did his brothers hear the note of hesitation in his voice? Because he sure as hell did.

"I'd like to believe that," Grey replied, his voice steady. "I've always liked Molly but it would be nice to have some proof."

"What happened to innocent until proven guilty?" Mack demanded. His hesitancy about her integrity would be something he kept to himself. *Always.*

"It's a nice concept but this is real life, Mack. If this gets out, and it will, it will become news. Jameson is hugely popular in Asheville and the press loves him. They will go nuts when they discover that there's another thief at Moonlight Ridge and that the chief suspect is his protégé and the daughter of the man who embezzled from him before. And we all know that bad publicity is the last thing Moonlight Ridge needs."

Mack looked at Travis. "What do you think, Travis?"

Travis nodded. "I agree with Grey. It's been a long time and the Molly we knew could be long gone."

Mack ran a hand over his face, feeling sick to his stomach. They had, dammit to hell and back, a point. If Molly were any other employee at Moonlight Ridge, they'd put that person on a leave of absence until they could get to the bottom of the mess.

It would take a lot of time, effort and knowledge, forensic accounting knowledge, to find some solid proof, and that leave of absence could be weeks or months. If he did that to her, Molly's reputation would take a hell of a hit. If she was innocent, she'd feel betrayed and mentally eviscerated. And she'd never forgive him…

His rational, business brain—the part of him that looked at the world without emotion—accepted that his brothers had a point. His intuition, his soul, dammit, was screaming at him to trust Molly, to remember what she told him about why she stole from Jameson before, reminding him how gutted and guilty she felt for her actions as a young adult.

Beth could be the thief; after all, it wasn't a big jump from blackmail to theft. She was bright enough to make it look like Molly was the thief...but then Mack remembered that Beth hadn't been at Moonlight Ridge that long and the pilfering had been going on for years. Not Beth then. Damn.

Could it be Molly? Was she playing him? She'd taken money before; she could do it again, if the stakes were high enough. Her reasons would be good; it wouldn't be for her personal gain. Had her brothers got into some sort of debt they couldn't repay? Was her mom sick? Was she still paying off her student loans...?

No, none of that felt right. Or was he just wanting her to be innocent? Molly was trustworthy, he was sure of it. But what if he was wrong and she wasn't?

What then?

Molly ran up the back stairs to her office, feeling light and a little lovely on this bright, early-summer morning. She'd heard Mack rolling out of bed, felt his kiss on her cheek, his murmured instruction for her to sleep in. Happy to listen, she'd rolled over and slid into a deep sleep, the best she'd had for months, maybe years.

Mack returned home extremely late last night and she'd woken to his mouth on the ball of her shoulder, his hand between her legs. She'd tried to talk to him but he'd told her to hush and slowly, thoroughly made love to her. Time and time again she fell apart in his arms. No wonder she'd slept like the dead.

There was magic between them and being together made sense.

It always had.

Molly stopped on the landing, placed her hand against the wall, remembering the first time she felt this sense of "rightness." She'd been eight and Mack reattached the head of her favorite Barbie Grant decapitated in a fit of rage. There were a thousand little moments from then on—him helping her with math, looking down into the front row from the stage to see his eyes on her, the first time they made love—and, hopefully, there would be tens of thousands of those moments in their future.

She was his and he was hers; they'd always each been one half of a whole.

Maybe it was time to stop fighting that…

Mack loved her, of that she was certain. He knew her and, when she confessed her sins, he'd chosen to believe the best of her, not the worst. It would've been so easy for him to judge her actions and paint her with the same brush as her dad, but he'd dug deeper, peeling back the surface to discover her motivations.

And maybe, with his understanding and forgiveness, she could, sometime soon, forgive herself and accept that she'd been pushed into a horrible position; a child who'd felt alone and abandoned.

In showing her compassion, Mack taught her to be compassionate to herself.

As soon as Jameson was stronger, she'd have a chat with him, confess her sins and let go of the guilt. She'd hand him a check, plus interest, and he'd, hopefully, be as understanding as Mack. Jameson, burly, big and gruff, had taught his sons tolerance so Molly was hopeful that everything would be okay.

Oh, she had no idea what the future held, how she and

Mack would make this work going forward. Or even if they could. In a few short weeks, he'd be back in Nashville, and then he'd be back on the road, whipping around the country to check on his businesses. Molly was under no illusions that they'd have a traditional relationship, or that a white wedding or 2.4 kids were in her future.

She could drive herself crazy trying to figure out the future. The past was behind her, the future was unknown so all she could do was to give this moment, today, her entire attention.

And yes, let's be honest here, after being thoroughly loved last night, today she was feeling pretty damn fine.

Molly walked into her office, dumped her laptop bag on her desk, grimaced at the folders she saw there and resisted the urge to walk into Mack's office and try and talk him into playing hooky with her today. They could hike up to Tip's Point, make love in the back meadow nobody knew about. Or they could try out the new east-meets-west fusion restaurant in downtown Asheville.

They could drink wine, take some time…

But hell, it was the end of the month and they'd taken most of yesterday off. Mack not only needed time to do whatever month's-end duties he had for his own company, but he had payroll checks to sign for Moonlight Ridge, supplier payments to authorize and, as he'd mentioned, a series of online meetings scheduled.

And she had her own work to do…lots of it.

Being responsible was such a pain in the ass.

Molly stood in the doorway of the door that connected their offices and took a moment to study Mack, whose attention was on his monitor, fingers flying across his keyboard. A pair of black-rimmed reading glasses sat on his nose and he looked like a sexy scientist or a hot accountant.

And Molly fell in love, once again. At the rate she was

going, by the time Mack left—and he would leave—he was going to, yet again, own all her heart. If he didn't already…

Molly walked over to his desk, surprised that he'd yet to hear or sense her. He was in the zone, she realized, concentrating so deeply that he'd shut out the world.

Amused, Molly tiptoed into the space next to his chair, bent down and ran her hand down his chest.

Mack's head jerked back, missed her nose and caught her cheek in a glancing blow. Molly released a quick hiss of pain, more surprised than hurt.

Molly held her cheek, breathing deeply. Mack stood up and gently peeled her fingers away from her face. "Mol, are you okay? Jesus, I didn't know you were there. What the hell were you thinking sneaking up on me?"

Molly winced as his fingers prodded the area on her cheekbone his hard head connected with. "Ow, dammit."

"I don't think it will bruise but maybe we should get you some ice," Mack said, his expression grim.

The pain was already fading and Molly waved his suggestion away. "I'm fine. It's not that bad."

Mack raised one eyebrow. "Are you sure?" he asked, his lips gently touching her cheek as if to kiss it better.

"Very." Molly turned her head to drag her lips against his. "Let's try this again… Morning, Mack."

Mack smiled, his dark eyes tender. "Morning, Curls. Did you enjoy your late start?"

"So much. Thanks for letting me sleep," Molly replied. She lifted her hand to touch his jaw, saw his concern and smiled. "I'm fine, Mack, really. And you're right. I shouldn't have snuck up on you."

Mack placed his hands on either side of the desk and kissed the side of her mouth, gently moving his lips across hers in a kiss that was sexy as it was sweet. It was an "I missed you" kiss, a "hi, there" smooch.

Completely perfect.

When Mack pulled back, Molly remembered his earlier jumpiness. "What on earth are you working on that held your complete attention? I could've set off a bomb in here and you wouldn't have heard a damn thing."

Mack took a step back, then another and, before her eyes, he morphed back into being the supersuccessful business-man, the tough-as-nails negotiator. As his eyes darkened, her heart sank.

"There's a problem, Molly." He nodded to one of the visitors' chairs. "Take a seat."

Molly stiffened at his suddenly cold tone, his bleak eyes. Her cheek forgotten, she walked around the desk and perched on the edge of the seat, pressing her knees together. She knew, from a place deep inside her, that what-ever came out of Mack's mouth next would crack their shaky foundation.

"You're starting to scare me, Mack," Molly said when he didn't speak. "Is it Jameson? Has he taken a turn for the worse?"

"No." Mack turned his computer and tapped his key-board before placing his hands flat on the desk, his expression intense. "As you know, I've been trying to make sense of Moonlight Ridge's accounting system—"

Molly grimaced. "The books are in such a mess, I know. I've been pushing Jameson to hire an outside accounting firm but I haven't gotten anywhere. Maybe you can talk him into doing that or, since you have power of attorney, you could just get it done."

Mack stood up and folded his arms across his chest. "Grey has been tasked with hiring an accountant."

"That's a great idea," Molly replied. When Mack's hard expression didn't change, she frowned. "Why do I think there's still something you aren't telling me?"

Mack hauled in a deep breath. "Grey is hiring a forensic accountant, Molly, because a considerable amount of money has been siphoned from the company."

Molly felt the room spin and Mack's tall figure faded in and out. This could not be happening to her, not now. Any minute now Mack would tell her he was joking and, after he did, she would, without a doubt, punch him.

She knew he liked to tease but this was, well, hurtful and…cruel.

Mack was impatient and a hard ass, sometimes ruthless; she'd never thought him to be cruel.

"Mack, that's not funny!" Molly stated, her voice trembling with rage.

"I. Am. Not. Joking." Mack elucidated every word, his voice deep and hard and so very intimidating.

Molly closed her eyes, hoping that when she opened them this would be a bad dream. Forcing herself to look at him, she wrapped her arms around herself, hoping to melt the icy core that was growing inside her. "God, you really aren't. How much?"

"I'm not sure yet. We need a forensic accountant to get an accurate figure. But at least tens of thousands of dollars."

"God." Molly lifted her hands to her lips as if she was praying. "But how?"

Mack stared at her, his expression resolute. "Shouldn't you be asking who, Molly?"

Of course, but she didn't want to go there. The people who were in the position to steal money were her friends, people she'd worked with for years and years.

"Look, Beth has horrible taste in men but she pushes paper, she doesn't sign any checks or anything. Fern, our exec chef has worked here for more than two decades. Harry has been here forever. Ross doesn't have a long history with us but Jameson and I both trust him. Our staff is loyal, Mack. They wouldn't have done this."

"You left someone out, Molly."

"Who?" Molly demanded, running over her list. No, she hadn't; not really. Those were the only people who dealt with paperwork, who could pull off some illicit scheme.

"You, Molly."

At his two-word sentence, her world as she knew, cracked and crumbled.

"You, Molly."

Mack kept his eyes on hers, watched as shock consumed her features and her knees wobbled. Her irises dilated and he could hear the harsh sounds of her irregular breathing. He knew that if he put his hands on her skin, she would be clammy and cold and her hand pressing into her stomach suggested that she was feeling nauseated.

As if she'd heard his silent thought, Molly's eyes darted around the room. "I think I'm going to be sick."

Mack bent down to pick up the trash basket and thrust it under her nose. Molly bent over the basket, heaved and he winced when she expelled her coffee into the trash receptacle.

It wasn't pretty, it wasn't nice—some would even call him cruel—but yeah, he needed to get her immediate response...

Mack glanced at the small camera within his state-of-the-art laptop, which he'd angled to point in her direction. Its flashing light told him it was still recording.

He'd spent another few hours in this office last night, running through what he did and didn't know, what he suspected and what he could prove. Despite his earlier, and brief doubts, he absolutely knew Molly wasn't the thief but what he knew and could prove were very different.

And the real thief had done, on the surface at least, a damn fine job at pointing the finger at her...

He needed to control the situation but more than that, he needed to protect her. It was, after all, what he did.

Moonlight Ridge was an Asheville institution and Jameson was one of the city's favorite citizens. He'd also been a source of good copy—starting with inheriting the place from the billionaire Tip O'Sullivan when he was in his early thirties. He'd been regarded as an extremely eligible bachelor and speculation was rife as to who would wear his ring. Instead of producing a wife, he fostered, then adopted, three boys, raising eyebrows. Molly's father's embezzlement caused an uproar, and Jameson's recent ill health made headlines again.

Jameson was interesting and the reporters would be all over this new drama. When news of the theft became common knowledge, and he had no doubt it would, fingers would be pointed in Molly's direction. She had access to the inn's bank account; she was in the position to steal from him; she was her father's daughter.

And, because the Haskell family couldn't keep their damn mouths shut—Grant's pillow talk with Beth was a great example—the world would soon know Molly stole money from his dad when she was a scared teen.

The press would eviscerate her unless he protected her. He could shout it from the rooftops that Molly was innocent but everyone at Moonlight Ridge knew they were sleeping together and his defense of her would mean nothing. No, Molly was her own best defense.

If it became necessary—when the reporters started circling, or the police came calling—he could show them a video of her unfiltered, instinctive response.

No one who saw her reaction, her shock and physical reaction to being accused, would doubt her innocence. Protecting and loving Molly was what he was put on this earth to do and this, unfortunately, was the best way he could.

It was a temporary pain for a long-term solution. This way he'd be in control of the narrative…

Molly finally dropped the basket, her face white. Mack quickly walked across the room to the bar fridge in the corner and pulled out a bottle of water, cracking the top and holding the bottle for her to take.

He expected her to take it, to drink some water to remove the foul taste in her mouth, and to sink to the chair.

Instead of doing that, any of it, Molly slapped the open water bottle from his hand. When her eyes connected with his, he realized that her blistering anger coated soul-deep hurt. "You son of a bitch! How dare you accuse me of stealing from Jameson? Especially after what I told you about what I did and how guilty I feel."

Mack winced. Yeah, explaining his actions wasn't going to be easy. Or any fun at all.

Mack picked up a small remote off his desk, the one that controlled the camera, his finger on the pause button. But he needed one more reaction from her; one sentence that was a decent denial, hopefully bellowed at the top of her voice. "How much did you steal from Jameson, Molly?"

Molly, her temper erupting, picked up a stapler from his desk and hurled it at his head. "I didn't steal a damn thing, you prick! I don't know what you are talking about and I'm gutted that you think that I had. How dare you think I would do that?"

Good enough, Mack thought, cutting the recording. Now it was time to do some damage control, to make Molly understand that he'd led her down this rocky and thorny path to help, not hurt her.

But judging by her heaving chest and flamethrower eyes, that was going to be harder than he anticipated.

"Sit down, sweetheart."

This time an empty coffee cup flew past his head, narrowly missing his ear. Her aim, dammit, was getting better.

"Don't you dare call me sweetheart, you two-faced pile of cockroach vomit!"

Mack winced.

"I know that you didn't steal the money, Molly!" Mack bellowed. She stared at him, her mouth falling open.

"What?"

He held up the remote in his hand, quickly explaining that he'd recorded her reaction, that he'd defy anyone to think she was guilty after seeing the footage.

"This is so bad. I cannot believe this is happening," Molly whispered, her voice breaking.

"It'll be okay, Molly. I believe in you. We'll fight this, together."

"The hell we will."

Mack frowned at her response, thinking that he was missing something here. She wasn't reacting anything like he'd expected her to.

Molly gripped the back of the chair with white fingers, staring down at the floor. When she finally lifted her face, Molly's eyes were dry and, at that moment Mack realized her pain was too deep for tears. She lifted her index finger, cocking her head to the side.

"Question…instead of this crazy scheme, why didn't you sit me down, tell me what was happening and let us come up with a plan to prove my innocence together?"

Uh…good question.

"Fifteen years ago you left my life because *you* decided, without consulting me, that was the best for me. You've just done that, *again*. Who gave you the right to take control, to find a solution and to make decisions without me?"

Molly's intense eyes stood out in her still-white face. "How dare you!"

Whoa, wait, hold on...

But before he could respond, words started flying out of Molly's mouth. "I am not a child. Nor am I a ditsy girl who needs you to make decisions for me. You arrogant bastard! This is *my* life, *my* reputation and *my* career. If I am being accused of theft then I will fight it. I will react and respond the way *I* feel is right!"

"I was trying to help you," Mack protested.

"No, you were trying to control the situation and control *me*," Molly replied, her tone bitter. "I've come to terms with you leaving me then. I can forgive that young and stupid boy, but you treating me like this, it's unacceptable, Holloway. It's hurtful and disrespectful, controlling—I said that already—and incredibly patronizing. I thought that maybe there was something building between us again, something wonderful and worthwhile. But you don't love *me*, you love the girl you used to know, the one you used to protect. You don't see the woman I am today, the one who is capable and smart and determined and independent."

"I—"

"Don't you dare say a word." Molly whipped out the words, cutting him off. "You've lost the right to take part in this conversation! I have lived my life without your help and guidance for fifteen years and I think I've done okay. So, screw you and screw your need to control everybody and everything."

"I'm better off on my own, I always have been. Thanks for the reminder." Molly turned to walk toward the door, her back stiff and straight.

"Jesus, Molly, will you listen to me?" Mack bellowed, not knowing what he would say if she gave him even half a chance.

Molly just shook her head and walked away from him. And Mack knew that, in his cockiness, in his hastily concocted need-to-control-everything plan, he'd gone too far. He'd hurt her, badly.

And while Molly had an enormous heart, she wasn't stupid and she tended not to repeat past mistakes so she'd never love him now and she'd never trust him again.

He was—what was the word he was looking for?—screwed.

Ten

Later that afternoon Mack left yet another message on Molly's voice mail system. "Dammit, Molly, call me! It's about Jameson. He's back in the hospital."

Giada placed a hand in the center of his back and Mack looked down at the tiny woman standing next to him. He could see his fear reflected in her eyes, and Mack pushed a fist into his sternum as he dropped into one of the plastic seats in the hospital waiting room.

"I can't get a hold of her." Mack dropped his head, his forearms on his thighs. "She needs to be here."

With him. Because that was where she belonged. He needed her, craved her, loved her and he wanted her by his side riding every wave life sent their way. The small ripples, breakers that could be easily surfed, the storm-whipped monster waves.

He could live his life on his own, taking his chances, but he didn't want to. He wanted to share his journey with Molly. As a team, a partnership, equal in every way.

And he wanted everything with the woman who was not currently speaking to him. And might never again.

In the hours between Molly's storming out of his office and Giada's frantic call, he'd examined his actions and had a couple of come-to-Jesus moments. As hard as it was to admit, Molly had been entitled to rip six layers of skin off him. She wasn't a child; his actions had been high-handed and the I'll-protect-you dynamic that characterized their childhood didn't apply anymore.

Molly wanted, and deserved, someone who respected and valued her input. If she ever forgave him, he'd never forget the lessons he learned today.

The phone in his hand buzzed and Mack hit the green button without looking to see who was calling. "Mol?"

"No, it's me... Grey."

Mack rubbed his fingers across his forehead. He'd left messages for his brothers, telling them Giada found Jameson on the floor of his bedroom, conscious but mentally confused.

"How is Pops, Mack?" Grey demanded.

"They think it might be a stroke but the tests will confirm that. If it is, then they can treat him immediately and he'll have a great chance of recovery," Mack told his brother.

"And if it's another bleed?"

That was a question Mack didn't want to answer. "Let's just wait and see, bro. Are you on your way?"

Grey told him that he was boarding his flight and would be with him in a few hours. Mack disconnected the call and his phone rang again. He felt the same flare of hope that it was Molly but it was Travis. After a brief conversation with him and confirming that he was also en route to Asheville, Mack tried Molly again, to no avail.

"I can't get a hold of her," he told Giada again.

"You will." Giada patted his hand. Her eyes went to the door, willing a doctor to walk into the room to give them some news.

As if she manifested him, a small woman walked into the room, a satisfied smile on her face. Both Mack and Giada sprang to their feet, anxious for news.

"Mr. Holloway is fine," she told him.

"He didn't have a stroke or a brain bleed?" Giada demanded, her voice shrill with anxiety.

"Nope. We ran the tests, did an MRI and we can't see anything that indicates a serious neurological event."

Mack's heart rate dropped to a more regular rhythm and he took his first full breath in what felt like years.

"Come with me." Dr. Bell gestured them to follow her, which they did, Mack following a step behind the two small women.

Dr. Bell led them into a private room and Mack looked over to the bed, where his father sat, resting on a mound of pillows. He glared at Giada and then at Mack. "Get me the hell out of here," he growled.

Mack smiled. If Jameson was feeling uncooperative, then he would be fine.

"We want you to stay overnight for observation. I'm sure you will be able to go home tomorrow," Dr. Bell told him, not at all intimidated by his gruff father.

Mack walked up to Jameson and dropped a kiss on his bald head, smiling when Jameson told him to stop being sloppy. But he saw the tiny smile on Jameson's face, the hint of pleasure. Yeah, his dad was still a sucker for affection.

Mack folded his arms and looked at the doctor. He was about to ask what caused his setback when Molly ran into the room, her face blotchy and red, her eyes frantic.

She immediately rushed over to Jameson and threw herself onto his chest, burying her face in his neck. "You can't die, dammit! I won't let you! I need you, Jameson."

Jameson's big hand curled around the back of Molly's head and his eyes cut to Mack's face, his expression as black as thunder. He could easily read the silent demand in his eyes. *What the hell did you do to her?*

Yep, Molly was definitely his favorite child, the one who could do no wrong. And really, since she was his favorite person in the whole world, he had no problem with that.

Giada, calm and practical, rubbed her hand over Molly's back, just like she'd done to him earlier. "Jameson is fine, darling. Dr. Bell wants to tell us what she discovered."

Molly stood up slowly, wiped the tears from her eyes with a tissue Giada handed her and slid her hand into Jameson's.

She hadn't once looked at him since she'd run into the room. He was all but invisible. It was clear that Molly had cut him out of her life. And, really, he couldn't blame her.

He'd been given a second chance with her and he'd blown it. Badly. Because he was a control freak moron.

Molly looked at Dr. Bell. "So what put him in the hospital?"

Dr. Bell jammed her hands into the pockets of her white coat. "As I said, the MRI scan and the tests we did showed no neurological issues. I think Mr. Holloway is looking good, brain-wise."

"That's up for debate," Giada quipped. Mack frowned, wondering if he was imagining the flirtatious smile she sent Jameson. But maybe, because he had love on his mind, he was imagining something that wasn't there. And, let's be honest, he didn't think he could cope with Jameson and Giada acting like besotted teenagers.

Though, given their combative personalities, any romance between them would be full of sarcasm and snark.

Anyway, that wasn't important. Not right now.

"Mr. Holloway, I consulted with my colleagues and we all agree you had a reaction to the new drug we prescribed for you. One of its side effects is confusion and instability."

"Then why did you prescribe it?" Molly demanded, her voice irate. Yeah, she'd go to war for Jameson.

When Molly loved, she loved hard and fiercely and with everything she had. He needed that, for himself, and for the family he wanted to create with her. Because there had only ever been Molly, would only be her.

Dr. Bell shrugged. "It's effective for managing seizures and that's what we are trying to prevent. But there are other drugs as effective and I'll prescribe those instead. They have fewer side effects."

"Maybe that's what you should've given him in the first place," Molly told her, chin up and green fire blazing from her red-rimmed eyes.

Giada rubbed her arm. "Everyone's body chemistry is different and reactions to medicine can differ from patient to patient. Dr. Bell is doing the best she can, Molly dear."

Molly's expression clearly stated her disagreement with Giada's statement.

"I know that you would like to be at home, Mr. Holloway, but as I said, I'd prefer it if you stayed the night," Dr. Bell said, ignoring Molly.

"He'll stay," Molly and Giada chimed at the same time.

Jameson rolled his eyes at Mack, who just lifted a shoulder in a "what can you do?" shrug. He wasn't brave enough to take on Molly and Giada at the same time and, when Jameson's shoulders slumped, realized his father wasn't up to the task, either.

As Dr Bell left the room, Jameson turned his attention to Molly. "You've been crying," he accused.

Molly swatted a curl away. "That's what happens when I get a million calls telling me you are back in the hospital."

Jameson narrowed his eyes at her. "That's not why you were crying."

Molly mustered up a smile. "I'm fine, Jameson. I promise."

Jameson's frown deepened as he looked from Molly to Mack and back again. "Look, I know you are all trying to keep me wrapped up in cotton wool but I won't have it! What is going on?"

They'd been told to keep his anxiety levels down and that was what they'd do. Judging by Molly's attempt to smile, she agreed. They both loved Jameson and would do anything in their power to shield him from stress.

Jameson slapped his hands on his thighs. "I demand to know what made you cry."

Molly's frantic eyes met his and he caught the small shake of her head. They were on the same page; she wanted to keep the embezzlement at Moonlight Ridge quiet.

"If one of you doesn't start talking, I'm going to get out of bed and beat it out of you," Jameson told them. Mack recognized it for the idle threat it was since Jameson never once raised a hand to any of them.

"Pops, just relax. We're handling everything," Mack said, trying to soothe him.

"I don't want you to handle it. I want to be involved. I want to know what's going on!" Jameson shouted, gripping the bed covers with a tight hold.

Mack winced. Jameson, whenever he got the bit between his teeth, refused to let go. He'd yell and shout until he got an answer. And if they tried to leave, he was stubborn enough to follow them out the door.

They had to tell him something…something he'd believe. But Mack didn't know what.

Molly took the decision out of his hands by sitting on the bed facing Jameson, her thigh next to his hip. Mack knew she was going to confess and he wished she wouldn't; not because Jameson couldn't take it but because he didn't want to alter the relationship between Jameson and Molly.

"Mol, *don't*."

Molly didn't drop her eyes from Jameson's face. "I have to, Mack. I can't live with it anymore and he deserves to know."

Jameson's huge hand covered Molly's, making hers disappear from view. "Is this about the two grand you stole when you were a kid?" he asked.

Molly's mouth dropped open, the shock causing her features to slacken. Mack was better at masking his emotions but he felt his eyes widen. So the old man knew all along? What the hell? Mack looked at Giada, who didn't look too surprised, either. She hadn't been around at the time so that meant Jameson told her.

How close were these two anyway?

"You know?" Molly whispered.

"I've known since the day you took it."

"But…how?"

Jameson shrugged. "It wasn't hard to figure out. You were the only person besides the boys who knew I stashed money in that Chinese tea caddy."

"Everyone knew you did that, Jay," Giada told him.

Jameson rolled his eyes at her. "Okay then, smarty-pants, Molly was the only person who knew, had access to my office and who was in a jam."

Mack leaned his shoulder into the wall and dropped his head to hide his smile. Damn, the old man was sharp. And how stupid were they to think that they'd pulled one over on him? He always knew everything…

A tear ran down Molly's cheek. "I'm so, so sorry. I know it was wrong but—"

"But you were being evicted and your family made it your problem to find the money," Jameson said, sounding disgusted. "You were a kid, Molly. They had no right to put pressure on you to find a solution."

"Still, I stole from you," Molly said, her voice breaking. "I have the money. I put it into a savings account and its earned interest. I'll write you a check." Molly pulled her hand from Jameson's and stood up, her body shaking with tension. "Why didn't you say something?"

Jameson pulled a face. "I kept expecting you to admit it. You never could keep a secret. I nearly told you when you refused my offer to pay for your college expenses— you are stupidly stubborn by the way—"

"I learned it from you," Molly shot back.

"I expected you to tell me when you first started working for me but you didn't. So I respected your privacy and decided that you would tell me when you were ready. Or you might not. Either way, it didn't change how much I loved you, how proud I was of you."

Molly dropped her head and stared at the floor. "How can you say that? I did what my father did. I stole from you."

For the first time Mack saw the anger in Jameson's eyes, but quickly realized it wasn't directed at Molly but at her father. "Your father was an adult, who chose to steal to fund his gambling habit. I offered him help. He chose to steal from me instead. The only person in your family who understood the gravity of his crimes was you, Molly. You were so young but you instinctively knew the difference between right and wrong. Your family, not so much."

Jameson patted the space next to him and when Molly sat down, he cupped her cheek with his broad, gentle hand.

Mack swallowed, touched by the tenderness in his father's eyes. "It was such a bad time, Mol, and I was off my game. I focused all my attention on Travis and I neglected my other boys."

Jameson's eyes connected with Mack's and he saw the deep and intense apology within those dark depths. Mack acknowledged his apology with a nod and a small smile.

And in one look, Mack released that his past was over and it was time to create a better, brighter future.

Jameson looked at Molly. "I neglected you, too, Molly darling. I know that you felt lost and alone. I'd heard your family was in financial trouble again and I paid the rent for six months a week or two before you took the money. Because I was juggling so many balls in the air, I forgot to tell you.

"But you should've come to me, Molly," he added, his voice a little stern.

"I know. But you had your own family stuff going on—"

Jameson released an irritated growl. "You are a part of my family, Molly. You always have been. From the moment your father died, you became mine. Not in a legal sense, but here." Jameson thumped his chest, his eyes bright with unshed tears. "And you should've confessed a long time ago."

Molly sucked her bottom lip between her pretty teeth. "I know. I'm so sorry."

"So you should be," Jameson grumbled. He crooked his finger at her. "Come here, baby girl."

Molly dropped back down to the bed and rested her head on his chest, her closed eyes leaking tears. Mack looked at Giada, who was dabbing at her own eyes with a tissue. His eyes were also, annoyingly, damp.

Mack walked over to the window and stared down into

the parking lot below, his thoughts whirling. Jameson and Molly would be fine but he wasn't fool enough to believe she'd forgive him that easily. But now that they knew his dad would be fine, his only goal was to win Molly back.

He wanted, needed, her in his life, in his bed, as the mother of his children. Because frankly, he couldn't conceive of a life without her in it. He'd only existed the past fifteen years, but over the past two months, he'd lived and laughed and loved.

This was going to be the fight of his life and winning her back was all that mattered.

Molly left the hospital feeling mentally exhausted and physically drained. But knowing this dreadful day couldn't get much worse, she decided to head across town to confront her family, to end her relationship with them...

Permanently.

From her seat behind the wheel of her car, Molly stared at the small house she'd purchased for her mom, noticing the grass lawn hadn't been cut for a while or the shutters repainted. Vincent's truck sat in the driveway, a trickle of fresh oil running down the pavement. A rusted bicycle still sat under the tree, as it had for the past ten years, maybe more.

She didn't belong here. These weren't her people. Oh, not because they were poor but because they refused to *try*. Because they'd always take the easy way out, they couldn't stop playing the victim and because they made such damn awful decisions.

And because they routinely lied to her. And used her.

Molly left her car and walked up the cracked path to the door. On hearing an expensive engine, she turned and sighed when she saw Mack's Mercedes pull up behind her car.

She couldn't deal with him now. Or, possibly, ever.

Molly glared at him as he approached her. "What are you doing here?" she demanded. Then she waved her question away. "I don't actually care. Just go away, Mack."

"There is no way I'm going to let you confront your family alone. I told you that before and it still holds."

"How did you know I was going to be here?"

"I know you, Molly. I knew that when you left the hospital, this would be your first stop."

He knew her? Really? What rubbish! "Yet, you don't know me well enough to talk to me when a problem arises, to work with me to find a solution. No, you thought you could just charge in and make decisions for me like I'm an incompetent idiot!"

Before Mack could respond, the front door opened. "Will you two please stop yelling? Vince is asleep."

Molly stepped onto the porch and addressed her mom. "Then I suggest you wake him up, Mom. We're going to have a talk and I'm not leaving until I've said what I need to."

"You can't just come over here and make demands," Grant told her, his face contorted into an ugly sneer. He pushed past Vivi to step onto the small porch.

Mack stepped forward, putting himself between Molly and her brother. "She can do whatever the hell she wants to since she's the one funding this suckfest. Go get your brother because, by God, if I have to haul him out of bed, he'll regret it. So will you."

Molly had never seen such a cold, hard expression on Mack's face and when Grant disappeared back into the house, she knew her brother felt it was prudent not to argue.

A few minutes later Vincent, half-asleep, joined them on the porch. Her mom, looking anxious, gestured for them to go inside. Molly shook her head. This last conversation could take place on the porch.

"So I found out something quite interesting today," she said when she had their attention. And, as annoying as he was, she was glad to have Mack standing next to her.

The next few minutes wouldn't be pleasant.

"What would that be?" Grant snidely asked.

"I found that you never needed the money I stole from Jameson. He'd already paid the rent." Her eyes darted from her mom's face to Vincent's, to Grant's and then back to her mom's. Nobody rushed to deny her words; nor were they shocked by her statement. Molly felt fury bubble up her throat. "I was seventeen and I didn't want to take the money. You all told me that if I didn't, we'd be evicted. Yet the rent had been paid, for several months."

Molly felt Mack's hand on her back and immediately felt steadier, more in control. She slapped her hands on her hips, keeping her attention on her mother. "You've blackmailed me for years! Why would you do that to me?"

Vivi shrugged. "Jameson had money. We didn't. And he caused your father's death and took away our only source of income."

"Dad stole from him, Mom!" Molly yelled. "Do you not get that?"

Another shrug. "Jameson was adamant that he wouldn't drop the charges. If he'd just let your father resign, he could've landed a job and we wouldn't be here, living in this crappy house."

"A house you didn't pay for! A house I bought, with the money I worked my ass off to make. What have any of you done?" Molly shouted.

"Sponged off you," Mack said, his tone withering.

"You manipulated me, played me, let me believe something that wasn't true for all these years and I will never,

ever forgive you for doing that," Molly said, her voice cracking. "Why would you do that? I'm your daughter, your sister."

Vivi snorted. "You were your daddy's girl and then when he died, you attached yourself to Jameson."

"Because he, at least, seemed to love me," Molly shouted.

Mack placed his hand on her shoulder and gently squeezed. Molly leaned into him, just for a minute. It felt so damn good to lean, to soak in his support. But then she remembered what he'd done and reminded herself that she didn't need him, just like she didn't need her family.

She was better off alone.

Molly lifted her hands, palms out, in a just-stop gesture. "I'm done. Don't ever contact me again."

"But—"

Molly forced herself to look at her mother. "But what?"

Vivi gestured to the house. "What are you going to do about this house? It's in your name but you gave it to me."

Why was she surprised at the lack of reaction, of feeling? Why was she shocked by her mom putting herself first?

"I'll sign it over to you," Molly said, feeling completely wiped out. "Do what you want with it. Just don't ever call me again."

Vincent and Grant exchanged a long look and Molly knew that they weren't done with her yet.

"Then what about a goodbye present, sis? Something to wish us well as you leave our lives?" Grant asked, his eyes dancing with maliciousness. "We still need that ten grand for my new business."

God, you couldn't make up crap like this. Shaking her head, she turned to walk down the steps, trembling with rage. But not with surprise. Her brothers were the ultimate scavengers, after all.

Molly heard a hard smack and whirled around, just in

time to see Grant sliding down the wall next to the front door, blood flowing from his obviously broken nose. Vincent, ever loyal, jumped on Mack's back but was easily dislodged with a jab of Mack's elbow to his gut, quickly followed by a punch to his kidneys. Vincent followed Grant to the floor.

It was all over in ten seconds.

Vivi released a harsh cry as she took in her white-faced sons. "I'll press charges," she told Mack. "I'll have you arrested for assault."

Mack just handed her a cold, hard-as-steel smile. "Your threats don't scare me, Vivi. They never have. Do not contact Molly. Do not let your sons contact her. No text messages, no emails, no visits. If any of you come within a mile of her, I will destroy you." He smiled again and Molly shivered. "Are we clear?"

Vivi, her hand to her throat, nodded.

Mack joined Molly on the path and placed a hand on her lower back and urged her forward. As they walked to their cars, Beth stepped onto the path, looking vaguely amused.

"Ooh, drama. And damn, it looks like I missed it," she said. Then she caught sight of Vincent and Grant on the floor of the small porch, Grant's shirt splattered with blood.

"What the hell happened?" she demanded.

Mack kept moving Molly forward. "You can get the story from them. Oh, and, Beth?"

"What?" Beth asked, glaring at him.

"You're fired."

Despite being furious with Mack and feeling sick and sad from her encounter with her family, Molly silently cheered his blunt declaration.

Beth sneered at him. "You can't fire me because I am sleeping with your girlfriend's brother."

"I'm not. I'm firing you because you are a piss-poor

bookkeeper. Don't bother to collect your final check. I'll have it delivered."

"But…but…you can't!" Beth wailed.

"I just did." Mack's mouth lifted at the edges in the tiniest of smiles. "Jameson always used to tell us that if you lie down with dogs, you get up with fleas. My advice to you? Disinfect."

Mack didn't bother to follow Molly home. He knew exactly where she was going and when he saw her car parked in the space next to the road leading to the steel bridge, he drove his car to the villa and parked it in the garage.

He slowly made his way down the road toward the steel bridge and, ultimately, to the pond and the treehouse where he knew Molly would be.

It was her thinking place, their special place. But as much as he wanted to be with her, he also knew she needed a little time to calm down, to pull herself together.

He'd give her some time but before the sun set, they'd have an understanding between them.

He wasn't leaving her life again; he'd never underestimate her or try to control her again. And he was prepared to spend the rest of his life proving that to her.

Mack heard his ringing phone and pulled the device out of the back pocket of his khakis, knowing he couldn't ignore his father's call. He swiped the green button and his father's face filled his screen.

"How did it go? Have you two kissed and made up yet?" Jameson demanded.

"Stop bugging me or I'll tell Giada that you keep a secret stash of cigars in the inside pocket of your winter coat," Mack retorted.

Mack heard Giada's triumphant shout and Jameson scowled. "Dammit, Mack! You have a very big mouth."

Jameson turned the phone and Mack saw that his dad wasn't alone in his hospital room. Travis and Grey, trying hard to ignore each other, stood on either side of Jameson, while Giada sat in the visitor's chair, glee on her face.

"You shouldn't be smoking anyway," Mack told Jameson.

"Yada yada," Jameson said. "Did she confront her family?"

Mack nodded. "Yeah, she did. It was pretty ugly."

"They are ugly people," Jameson agreed.

"How many Haskell brothers did you deck, Mack?" Grey asked.

"Both of them." Mack looked down at his swollen knuckles, suddenly conscious of the insistent throbbing in his hand. Worth it, he decided.

Silence fell between them and Mack sighed, over it. This couldn't go on. Molly, obviously, was his top priority, but getting his family back ran a close second.

Stopping, he stared down at the screen, noticing that Travis had turned away to look out the window and that Grey was staring at his own phone. Nobody was talking to each other and he was over it.

He was so done with this cold war.

"I have a few things to say," Mack stated, determined. When Travis didn't turn around, Mack sighed. "Travis, look at me, dammit."

His brother resumed his place behind Jameson's shoulder, his scowl telling him he didn't appreciate his barked order. Mack didn't much care. "About our conversation last night, we were wrong to even consider that possibility."

"What are you talking about?" Jameson demanded.

He wouldn't explain but Grey and Travis knew that he was referring to Molly's innocence. "Are you sure?" Grey asked.

"Very," Mack emphatically stated. Grey nodded, accepting his word, but on seeing Travis's hesitance, Mack spoke again. "I need you to trust me on this, Trav. Please."

Travis nodded and Mack released a sigh of relief. On his word, his brothers accepted Molly's innocence. The realization both humbled and touched him.

But there was more to say and Mack spoke before Jameson could demand another explanation for their obscure conversation.

"I'm done with this cold war between us. I miss my family," Mack told his siblings. "I'm so sorry I lost control of the vehicle. I'm still gutted that you were injured, Trav. I'm also gutted that you lost your football scholarship and that you never got to play pro ball. I fully accept all responsibility for the accident."

Grey looked like he was about to speak but Mack's hard look stopped whatever he'd been planning to say. "I'm also sorry for running instead of sticking and staying. But it's been fifteen years, dammit."

Mack rubbed the back of his neck, tasting tears in the back of his throat. "Fifteen years of not being able to grab a beer, a late-night chat, of not being able to tease you, talk you down or talk you up. Fifteen years of not talking and I'm goddamn sick of it!" Mack shouted, the dam bursting on his carefully held back emotions. "You're my brothers and I don't care what I have to do but we *will* be a family again."

Travis shook his head. "We can't just go back, Mack. It doesn't work like that."

"I don't want to go back, Travis. I want to go forward," Mack told him. "Give me a chance. Give us a chance."

Travis lifted and dropped his massive shoulders. "I don't know. Maybe."

From his stubborn-ass brother, a *maybe* was a very good

place to start and more than he expected. Mack smiled at him. "I'm gonna wear you down."

A smile touched his eyes. "You can try."

Mack, feeling lighter, just managed to stop himself from doing an air punch.

"So does this mean I can host a Sunday lunch this weekend?" Jameson demanded.

On cue, Mack and his brothers shuddered and groaned. Jameson wasn't a great cook and his roast duck was always burned on the outside and raw on the inside.

They exchanged anxious looks and Mack finally nodded. "I'll be around."

"I can fly back on Saturday, stay over and fly back on Sunday evening," Grey said.

Travis rubbed the back of his neck. "I'm not sure I can make it. I have a lot on my plate. I can try."

Mack knew that there was little chance of Travis breaking bread with them on Sunday. He wasn't, he knew, ready to bury the past or to revive family traditions.

"I'll make my famous roast duck." Jameson looked excited. Oh, God. It sounded really awful but he'd eat a hundred awful ducks if it meant having his family back together again.

"You are not nearly well enough to cook," Giada told Jameson, her tone suggesting he not argue. "I will cook. Lunch will be served at one. If you are going to join us, do not be late. Asparagus salad with parmigiana, seafood pasta, tiramisu. Yes?"

"Yes!" Mack and Grey chimed in unison while Travis remained silent.

It would be wonderful, Mack admitted, to spend some time with Grey, but let's be honest here. Sunday lunches wouldn't be the same until all three of them were back in their chairs, eating at their father's table.

* * *

Molly knew that Mack would join her at the treehouse, so his sinking into one of the huge cushions on the deck wasn't a surprise.

The fact that he just sat quietly, waiting for her to speak, was. Mack didn't usually hold back; he was in-your-face assertive. But she refused to look at him, refused to try and work out what he was thinking. Along with her family, she was done with him.

Or, more honestly, she *wanted* to be done with him.

Molly rested her chin on her bent knee and stared at the calm waters of the pond, wondering whether she should stay at Moonlight Ridge or try and forge a path somewhere else. Jameson would understand if she left. He had, after all, encouraged his sons' efforts to fly harder, farther and higher and he'd afford her the same respect and consideration.

A part of her wondered if she could cut it in a competitive environment; wondered if she could hack a corporate culture. Then she remembered that she'd survived thirty-plus years of her family's backbiting and manipulation. She'd be fine.

She was a hard worker, was smart and canny and her BS meter was well tuned. She'd make it anywhere.

But did she want to go? When Mack left—and Molly prayed that would be soon—did she want to stay at Moonlight Ridge, help Grey and then Travis, discover who the real thief was? She rather thought that she did. She was, after all, being set up to take the fall. She wanted to help nail the perp's hide to the wall. And, she adored Moonlight Ridge. It was her place and she was the best person to manage it.

But that meant working and dealing with the oldest Holloway brother, for a few more weeks at least. "When are you going back to Nashville?"

Mack considered her harsh question before answering her. "Grey is taking over from me soon, I do need to get back on the road so that'll suit me."

Mid-June was just ten days away; she could tolerate him for that long, surely? She'd have to...

"But I'm seriously thinking of relocating my Nashville headquarters to Asheville," Mack added.

Molly banged her forehead on her knee. Why was life punishing her like this? "Why?"

"I want to be around more, hang out with Jameson, bug Grey. And, when it's Travis's turn to look after the resort, I want to spend some time with him, too," Mack said, his voice even.

"Making amends, Holloway?" Molly demanded.

"Yeah. But that's not the biggest bridge I need to re-build."

Molly didn't pretend to misunderstand him. "Good luck with that."

She could see the remorse in his eyes, his expression frustrated. "I messed up, Molly, I know that. I absolutely should've brought my concerns to you before going off half-cocked."

"Did you suspect me of taking the money?" Molly demanded. "Even once?"

"Yes," Mack replied, his expression grave.

She thought she'd be angrier but she respected his blunt admission of the truth.

"And no..."

Well, that was a confusing answer. Molly raised her eyebrows in a silent command to explain.

"Maybe a part of me wanted you to be guilty because then I could go back to my boring, staid and uneventful life. Maybe I was looking for a way to put distance between us. There's a chance that I chose to act like I did because I knew it would infuriate you and you'd call it."

"Congratulations. You succeeded in getting me to do what you wanted," Molly stated, her tone flat.

"But that's not what I want, Mol." Mack stretched his legs out, crossing his feet at the ankles and resting his weight on his arms. "The real reason I didn't want to come back to Asheville was because I knew I wouldn't be able to resist you, Curls."

Molly scoffed at that statement but Mack ignored her. "Over the years I didn't engage with you, couldn't spend any time with you because I, subconsciously, maybe even consciously, knew I would fall for you again. And that's exactly what happened."

Mack turned to face her and rested his forearms on his knees. "I'm so in love with you, Molly. And loving you so much scares me. It scares me enough to run because if I run, if you're not around, I can't lose you."

Molly's heart bounced off her chest. "You lost me once through your own choice and you lost me again because you acted like a controlling ass."

"Noted. Accepted." Mack picked up a twig from the deck and pulled it through his fingers. "Congratulations on confronting your family, Mol, and on confessing to Jameson."

"Thanks," Molly replied, caught off guard by his change of subject.

"You are so much braver than I, sweetheart," Mack stated. "You stand and fight. I—like my sperm donor—tend to run when life gets tough or inconvenient or too real. I did that years ago as a kid, and I'm ashamed to say I was going to do it again."

"You don't need an excuse, Mack. Just leave. I'm giving you permission to go. Trust me, I'll be fine."

"Except that I would rather chew my wrists off than leave you again," Mack softly said. "I want to stay. I want to fight for you, for our happiness, for our future. I want to be brave like you, Mol. I want to dig my heels in and get stubborn. I want to plant roots and a garden, build a relationship and a house with you. I want to earn your forgiveness, wake up with you in my arms, put a ring on your finger, catch our babies as you give birth to them."

"I'm sticking, Mol. And staying," he added.

Molly fought again the rising tide of joy and tried to push down her happiness. "And what if I tell you that you hurt me too badly, *again*, that I'm not interested in anything you want to do, the life you are offering?"

Dismay and fear flashed in his eyes and, for the first time, she saw his vulnerability. He was scared, too, Molly realized. "Until some other guy makes you deliriously happy, slips into your bed and puts a ring on your finger, I'll fight for us, Molly. I'll do anything and everything to win you back, to get you to trust me again."

Molly heard the determination in his voice, awed by the intensity in his gaze. And suddenly, she knew he was speaking the truth, that she was the reason the sun rose and set for him every day.

Could she trust him, one last time? Could she risk her heart again?

Mack kept his eyes on hers, his focused gaze not wavering. "I'll be rock steady, Molly. I'll be there for you, every step of the way. I'll never disappoint you again." He grimaced. "Oh, I'm not saying I'll never mess up, but when it comes to what's important, I won't let you down, Mol. I won't cheat on you, I promise to always listen to you and take your feelings and opinions into consideration. I promise to trust you. I just need you to give me one more chance."

She felt his assurances deep in her soul and believed

every one of them. If she wanted him, Mack was prepared to dive all the way in.

And she couldn't resist him.

She shook her head. "No."

Mack's face fell and he turned away but not before she saw the gleam of tears in his fabulous, black-as-the-night eyes. His bottom lip wobbled, just for a second, and his torso slumped.

"You don't need to try and win me back, Holloway. I have been, always will be, yours."

Mack whipped his head up, his mouth falling open in complete shock. "What?"

"Do try and keep up, Holloway," Molly teased. When he just kept staring at her, Molly touched the tips of her fingers to his jaw. "I'm so in love with you, Mack. I've always loved you, all my life, but this is different. Newer, deeper, scarier."

Mack held her fingers against his face. "I know, darling. I am scared, too. Let's be scared together."

"How scared?" Molly asked.

"Rings-on-our-fingers scared, building-a-house-over-looking-this-pond scared, trying-to-have-a-kid scared."

Molly smiled at him, not feeling the slightest hint of fear. "That's a lot of fear, Holloway."

Mack nodded. "Yeah, but you make me brave, sweetheart. You make me think I can do anything." He touched his lips, gently, reverently, against hers, pulling back to whisper the words she most wanted to hear against her lips. "I love you so damn much. Be mine, Molly."

"I always have been, Mack. Then, now, forever."

* * * * *

WHO'S THE BOSS NOW?

SUSANNAH ERWIN

For Nia, Isabel and Marie—the best critique group
(and group of friends) a writer can have!

One

Breaking into the owner's private wine cellar at St. Isadore Winery was easy. The side door at the rear of the house stuck a little from disuse, but it led directly to the service stairs and Marguerite Delacroix's destination several flights below. Getting out, on the other hand…

Marguerite tried to lift the two full cases of wine at her feet and gave up, rubbing her aching arms as she considered the best way to make a quick exit. What had seemed like an excellent plan at 11:00 p.m. over a bottle—or two—of Carménère shared with her best friend, Aracely Contreras, turned out to have several flaws in its execution at one in the morning. To start, the bottles were heavy. Too heavy to carry up the stairs except a few at a time, which would take the rest of the night.

She held up her phone, with the flashlight app on, and did a slow, albeit unsteady, 360-degree pirouette, shining the light around the dark, chilly cellar with its dozens of wine racks lining the walls. But this just confirmed what she already knew. Her only other option was the elevator, but it was riskier.

She sighed. Of course, this wasn't going to be simple. Things never were at St. Isadore.

Marguerite grew up on stories about the fabled exploits of her Delacroix ancestors, legendary for their winemaking prowess. She was descended from the branch of the family that immigrated to California during the gold rush, producing wine for the state's fast-growing population. One vineyard turned into five and St. Isadore was established shortly after, built to resemble a Loire Valley castle. Now it was one of the few remaining original wineries in Napa.

The winery had survived the phylloxera virus, which had destroyed most of Napa's grapevines by the turn of the last century, and sailed through Prohibition thanks to savvy packaging and not a little smuggling. However, St. Isadore had almost gone under when two brothers inherited the estate after World War II and fought bitterly over how to run the business. Eventually, one brother had kept control of the winery while the other took the vineyards to manage for himself.

The two branches of the family had remained at odds until Marguerite's father, who had inherited the vineyards and then sold them ten years ago to the late Linus Chappell, who owned the winery. Marguerite had begged her parents to keep the land until she could take over its management, but neither of her parents had much interest in viticulture, and early retirement in Arizona had beckoned. She'd returned home after her junior year at UC Davis to find that the vineyards, for the first time in their history, no longer had an owner named Delacroix.

But even a reunited estate hadn't restored St. Isadore to its former glory. The more Northern California's wine country thrived off increased tourism and demand for its wines, the further St. Isadore seemed to fall behind.

New equipment did on occasion make its way into the winery, but the elevator in the cellar dated to the mid-1930s. It was as beautiful in its art deco detail as it was rickety and noisy. The engine room was underneath the owner's living quarters and could be heard—and felt—through several floors and walls. The family liked it that way. It served as another control on who accessed their private stash of rare and experimental wines and when.

At least the elevator was reliable; Marguerite knew from long experience. Besides, who was around to hear her use it? Linus had died six months ago without a will, and his entire estate had gone to his closest relatives, two great-nephews who'd immediately put the winery and its vineyards on the market. The sale of St. Isadore to a Silicon Valley tech CEO had been completed last week, and according to local gossip, he hadn't taken possession yet. And the local gossips would know. He was an object of intense interest, not the least because he was reputed to be ridiculously good-looking and single.

But the detail most important to Marguerite was when escrow closed, the security guards the great-nephews had installed disappeared. Which left her this one small window of opportunity.

She propped open the elevator's wooden outer door with a nearby wedge, then pulled back the ornate steel security gate and began loading wine bottles into the small cab. This was probably the last time she would set foot in the cellar. St. Isadore was targeted to be torn down and turned into a luxury housing development, if the rumors were correct.

Her breath caught in renewed pain at the thought.

But she could save the wine. *Her* wine. Wine that she hoped would be the first step to restoring the Delacroix name to winemaking prominence. Most of it was locked up in the winery and inaccessible, but Linus had asked for a sample bottle from each batch to store in the owner's cellar. Now these bottles were all she had left after eight years. Eight years of putting her whole heart into working for Linus because they had a handshake deal: he would pay her fifteen percent of her negotiated salary. The other eighty-five percent went toward buying back the original vineyard that started it all, with its grapes to be made into wine by her and sold by St. Isadore. She would not let the Delacroix name down.

And she had come so close! She'd finished paying off the vineyard on her last birthday, of all dates, and Linus had promised to transfer the deed. But then a stroke had suddenly taken his life. After his funeral the leather-bound ledger he'd used to record her steady progression toward ownership was nowhere to be found. When she'd tried to negotiate for the vineyard with Linus's great-nephews, they'd laughed in her face before calling the sheriff to remove her from the property.

The wine she'd made was all she had left and she'd be damned if she let it rot in the owner's cellar or worse, be destroyed. She gathered up the last bottle. Beads of sweat formed on her brow despite the cold of the cellar, and she brushed them away with a swipe of her arm, the scent of old, spilled wine and damp stone cling-ing to the sleeve of her loose T-shirt. Dust covered her hands, and she wiped them on her jeans before pushing the button for the ground floor. From there, it would be a short walk to the main entrance. Aracely was some-where nearby, waiting for Marguerite's call. Together they would load the wine into Aracely's SUV and then make their getaway.

But to what? The only life Marguerite knew was here, at St. Isadore. All she'd ever wanted was to re-main here. And she'd thought her agreement with Linus meant she would be able to stay forever.

Marguerite blinked back tears. No matter how much pain St. Isadore had caused her, it was home. And now the new tech-CEO owner would destroy it.

Evan Fletcher rubbed his closed eyes. It didn't help. When he opened them again, the numbers on his lap-top screen remained the same: dismal.

When he first authorized his business manager to buy St. Isadore lock, stock and multiple barrels of wine, he had been pleased to learn not only was the win-ery fully equipped but the owner's residence came fur-nished. Then he arrived a few hours ago, finally able to inspect his purchase for himself, and learned that the photos so beautifully shot in the golden sunlight hid a myriad of imperfections and outright damage. But St. Isadore was still a working business and thus perfect for his needs. The rest was cosmetic.

"I'd love to say I told you so, but not only is it late, I want to keep you as a client," said his business man-ager from the speaker on Evan's phone, followed by an audible yawn.

"It's okay, Pia. Rub it in all you want. It's the least I

deserve after calling at this hour. I thought I'd be leaving a voice mail."

"I've learned if I don't pick up the phone when I see your number, by the time I call back you've dug an even bigger hole—like making an offer on a winery sight unseen."

"Next time I'll call during business hours. This was the first quiet moment I had today, between getting things settled here and a new crisis erupting at work."

"I thought things were calming down on that front."

"Define calm." Evan was the CEO and founder of Medevco, a fast-growing tech start-up in artificial intelligence-based medical devices that had hit a billion-dollar valuation a year ago, making it what Silicon Valley insiders liked to a call a "unicorn" because such companies were rare and exciting. But with growth came growing pains. Expensive ones. And lots of them.

He shook his head to clear it. One potential disaster at a time. Right now, the winery took precedence. "Thanks for going through the St. Isadore numbers with me. And tell me how to best apologize to Luisa for keeping you so late."

Pia laughed. "Like time has any meaning since the baby arrived. And no need to apologize. She'll thank you because I'll be up for the two a.m. feeding and she can sleep. But if you truly feel bad, send us a case of Chardonnay...but maybe from another winery."

"Ha ha," Evan deadpanned. "You'll see. By this time next year, you'll be begging me for a case of St. Isadore's finest."

"This isn't a tech company. It's a completely different industry, and you purchased a small winery that didn't produce up to its capacity even before the senior staff left. You can't expect your usual Midas touch to kick in."

"That sounds like a challenge."

"Depends on how high your expectations are. And knowing you, they're stratospheric."

Evan scratched the back of his head but stayed silent. New mothers didn't need additional stress.

"I heard that," Pia said.

"Heard what?"

"The sound of you keeping something from me."

"The Global Leader Summit is being held in Napa this summer."

Pia's exhale was audible through the speaker. "Please don't tell me what you're about to tell me."

"The organizers heard I was purchasing a winery and asked if I would be interested in hosting the kick-off social event. Of course, I said yes."

Pia groaned. "Evan, those are some of the world's most important business leaders—"

"It'll be fine."

"This has nothing to do with Angus Horne blowing off your phone calls, does it? He always attends the summit. And he's quite the wine connoisseur."

Evan laughed. "Would I buy an entire winery and the corresponding estate simply to corner an investor for Medevco?"

Pia scoffed, "You'd buy the moon if you thought it would give you quality face time with Horne to work your magic. You forget, I watch over your accounts when you refuse to. Bottom line is this, Evan. With so much of your capital tied up in Medevco, the winery purchase put a strain on your liquid assets."

"The winery is revenue producing."

He heard her fingers tapping on her keyboard. "Revenue but not necessarily profit. And you'll need to make several capital investments in the property. You can run it at a loss for a year without giving me gray hairs."

"I'll do my best." He'd hired Pia as his business manager for her cautious approach. But he hadn't sold three companies before the age of thirty, then founded and become CEO of Medevco, without having the utmost confidence in his judgment and skills. Pia might call it his Midas touch, but he preferred to think of it as creative risk-taking combined with a ruthless ability to cut his losses. "Thanks again. And hey, try to get a nap in before the kid wakes up."

He disconnected the call and leaned back in his chair. At least the place was clean, the shower had plenty of hot water—his hair was still slightly damp from the one he'd taken before calling Pia back—and the new beds had been delivered that evening and made up with fresh linens.

He rose and stretched, intending to discover if the mattress was as comfortable as it looked, and a low rumbling shook the scuffed parquet floor under his feet. "What the—?"

His gaze whipped around the room. Years of living in California with the ever-present possibility of earthquakes had taught him how to seek the safest spot to wait out the tremors. But the rumbling didn't get worse, nor did it stop. It stayed a steady hum. A machine-generated hum.

Of course. The elevator. The one that led to the private cellars built deep underground. His pulse rate fell.

Then it sped up again. He was the only person awake in the house. The other occupant had gone to bed several hours ago.

He didn't believe in ghosts, despite the furniture

in the residence resembling rejects from Disneyland's Haunted Mansion. But the elevator dated well into the last century. It was probably malfunctioning.

He sighed. Better check it out. The last thing he needed was a fire caused by faulty wiring.

He passed by the arched entrance to the kitchen on his way to investigate. Through the doorway, he spotted a heavy cast-iron frying pan sitting on top of the ancient stove. He grabbed it.

Just in case he was wrong about ghosts. And they came armed.

The elevator ground to a halt. Marguerite hit the stop button and pulled back the steel gate. Bending down, she picked up and cradled three bottles in her arms, then used her back to push open the wooden door. Mission accomplished. And no one would ever know she'd been there. She straightened up and turned around—

—and came face-to-face with a half-dressed man, his chest as bare as his feet, the cast-iron skillet in his hands aimed squarely at her head.

She screamed. Two of the bottles slid out of her arms. They landed with a thud on the elevator cab's worn linoleum floor. Pure instinct took over, her mind swallowed by a cloud of fear and panic. She grasped the third bottle by the neck, then pulled it back over her right shoulder like an extremely short baseball bat.

And swung.

The man brought the pan up to cover his face. The bottle met the heavy cast iron. The air rang with the cracking of glass.

The cool liquid cascading over Marguerite's hands caused her brain to come back online. She blinked in rapid succession, her adrenaline still surging. "Oh, no. Oh, no no *no*."

What was she doing? All her hard work, her last connection to St. Isadore, was now a spreading stain on the floor. She immediately brought the bottle to a vertical position, the cork end pointed at the floor. It was hard to tell in the darkened foyer, but it looked like she had lost a third of the wine.

She could save the rest. Maybe. Her mind raced, seeking options.

The man lowered the cast-iron skillet, letting it fall to his side. She had been so focused on the bottle, she'd almost forgotten she wasn't alone.

They stared at each other for a heartbeat, their chests rising and falling almost in unison. So this was the ridiculously handsome new owner. She recognized the square jaw with the perpetual five-o'clock shadow, the thick dark brows set atop a piercing gaze from news stories on the internet. But neither the photos nor the gossip had conveyed the breadth of his shoulders, the way he exuded power and strength, despite being clad in only low-slung sweatpants that draped off narrow hips.

And she was the interloper here, not him. "Are you going to use that thing?" she croaked, pointing at the pan.

He shook his head, his mouth working for a few beats. "What the *hell*?" exploded from his lips. "Who the—?"

"I can explain." He was furious. Deservedly so. But she had a bigger concern at the moment. "Right now, I need a new bottle. A container. Something." She started to push past him, the bottle cradled against her.

He caught her arm with his left hand. His grip was solid and warm after the chill of the cellar. Wine splashed on her shirt, and her breath caught. She wouldn't be able to break free. Not without losing what wine remained—and leaving behind all her other bottles.

"No, you don't," he growled. "Explain now."

"Let me go and I will."

His eyebrows shot toward his hairline. "Let you— Lady, you tried to clobber me!"

"You threatened me first!" With her chin, she indicated the frying pan in his right hand. "And you're right. I'm sorry. But you scared me."

"You're breaking into my house!"

"Technically, I'm about to leave your house. Which I'm still happy to do. But please. I need something to hold the wine." She met his gaze for the first time. His eyes glittered in the dim light. She took in a gulp of air. "Please."

His frown deepened, but his hold on her sleeve loosened enough for her to twist and feint right before dodging around him to the left, to find the door—wallpapered to blend in with the rest of the wall—that led to the service corridor, and beyond it, the kitchen. There had to be something she could use in there.

The heat of his fingers continued to linger on her skin.

Evan blinked. Did the thief...disappear into the wall? What the *hell*?

He glanced at the bottles still in the elevator. They didn't have labels. Instead, it looked like someone had scrawled notes on the glass with a paint pen.

That made no sense at all. The owner's cellar contained rare and very valuable wine. A thief out to make a profit would have gone for the bottles most likely to fetch a high price on the market. What was his intruder up to?

He explored the area of the wall where she had disappeared and discovered the door, left slightly ajar. A vague memory surfaced of the agent who had represented the estate talking enthusiastically about secret passageways. Evan thought it had been real estate hype, an attempt to upsell a back stairway or an attic crawl space. But no. The house did indeed come with hidden entrances and hallways. And his late-night guest knew about them.

He paused to listen, then followed the faint sound of rustling to another door. Pushing it open, he discovered he was back in the kitchen, a cavernous space with appliances that would be right at home in a 1950s sitcom. Two cabinets had their doors flung open, while a wine bottle sat propped upside down in the dish rack next to the stainless steel sink.

The thief was rummaging through a third cabinet. She threw him a glance over her shoulder. "Where are the carafes?" she asked. "Linus kept them here. Did you move them?"

Evan patted the pockets of his sweatpants for his phone, intending to call the authorities and hold her there until they arrived. However, his pockets were empty. He must have left his phone in the other room. "Talk. Who are you? What are you doing here?"

She turned to face him. He had his first good look at her in the bright glare of the overhead lights. Dark hair, more raven than chestnut, had been twisted into a bun at the top of her head, but several locks had escaped, the wavy tendrils sticking out every which way. Her skin was pale, almost translucent in contrast to the black T-shirt and dark skinny jeans she wore. Those jeans outlined long, slender legs that led to gently curved hips, but her loose-fitting top concealed the rest of her curves. He dragged his gaze back up to her face. The freezing glare he received informed him he had been caught looking. "Carafes?" she repeated.

"You don't seem to understand who I am or how much trouble you're in. I ask the questions."

Her mouth twisted. "Oh, I understand. You're St. Isadore's new owner. The tech guy. The entire valley has been wondering when you would arrive, although obviously, I didn't think you'd moved in yet. In fact, I would've put money down that you wouldn't move in at all. So, carafes. Are they in the butler's pantry?"

He shook his head, confused, but he'd puzzle her words out later. "I didn't put anything anywhere. I've barely set foot in this room." She glanced at the iron skillet still loosely held in his right hand and raised an eyebrow. He put the pan back on the blackened burner on top of the antique stove. He didn't get the feeling from her he would require it. "Except to get this. You, however, seem to know the place well. Who are you?"

"Maybe if you examined the kitchen as thoroughly as you check out women's bodies, you'd know where things are." Her tone was light as she continued searching the cabinet, but she held her head as if she were a monarch giving the annual address to the kingdom's subjects.

"Just ensuring I can give the authorities an accurate description of who broke into my home."

"I didn't break in. I have a key." She opened another door. "Most people change the locks when they move into a new place, you know."

She had a key? He added that piece of information to his mental catalog of surprising things he'd learned about his thief. "You don't have an invitation. That makes it a break-in."

"In California, I believe that makes it trespassing." She took out a small plastic water pitcher, scratched and discolored from years of use. "May I borrow this, please?"

He narrowed his gaze. "I'm not a lawyer, but if *Law and Order* reruns have taught me anything, it's only trespassing—which is still a misdemeanor—if you don't intend to commit a crime. The wine stacked in my elevator says otherwise."

She crossed the kitchen and started to pull out cabinet drawers, one after the other. Have you seen—aha!" She pulled out a corkscrew. "I'm not committing a crime. Well, okay, I'll agree I am trespassing. But not stealing." Her voice trailed off as she lifted the upside-down wine bottle from where it rested in the dish rack to inspect it. "At least it was a clean crack, which is weird because I doubt I hit the pan hard enough to cause one." She poured the contents into the pitcher and then sighed, her shoulders falling. "There. I wish the wine could age more, but at least I can taste it."

Then she turned to face him. "Thank you for not calling the sheriff. And for your patience. I owe you an explanation—"

Blue-and-red revolving lights appeared, shining through the kitchen window to cast multicolored shadows. The sound of slamming car doors accompanied them. She raised her eyebrows. "I guess you did call them."

Evan shook his head. What the hell? "I don't have my phone on me." He pointed at her. "Stay here. I want your story."

He made his way to the front entrance, flicked on

the lights and opened one of the heavy wooden doors. The chilled January night air rushed in, but his focus was on the sheriff's car parked in the circular gravel driveway with its lights still flashing. Two men stood by the car, speaking to each other. "Evening," Evan called out, although it was more like early morning. "What's the trouble, deputies?"

The taller and stockier of the two men straightened up. "No trouble. Sorry to disturb you."

The shorter, leaner man strode toward the door. As he came closer, Evan could make out his face. His heart sank past his stomach.

"Nico."

His younger brother pushed past him without a word. Evan turned to the sheriff. "What did he do?"

"Who, Nico? Oh, he's not in trouble. But he was a passenger in a car pulled over because the driver was under the influence. Now, your brother is sober, but he doesn't have a valid driver's license and therefore couldn't take over the operation of the vehicle. I was finished with my shift, so I offered to give him a ride here."

"With flashing lights?" Adrenaline still thumped in Evan's veins. The night just kept getting more surreal.

The sheriff ignored his question and waved instead. "Hey, Marguerite."

"Hello, Deputy Franks."

Evan turned to see the thief standing behind him, lit by the ornate wrought iron chandelier hanging in the foyer.

"Didn't think you still lived here," the sheriff said.

The thief—Marguerite, Evan mentally corrected himself—shot Evan a glance. When he didn't speak, she took a deep breath. "I don't."

The sheriff's gaze ping-ponged between Evan and

Marguerite, and Evan remembered for the first time since finding his thief that he was wearing only a pair of sweatpants. Then the sheriff nodded. "All right. Well. I should get going."

"Thanks for bringing Nico home." Evan shut the front door and turned to Marguerite. "I still want your story. First I have to find my brother."

"He's in the kitchen," she said. "He seems angry. That's why I came to find you."

"Nico is always angry," Evan muttered.

"Why didn't you tell the sheriff you caught me trespassing?" She cocked her head. More dark locks fell from her messy bun to frame her high cheekbones.

Evan didn't answer. He wasn't sure if he had an answer. "My brother, then you," he repeated and motioned for her to lead the way.

Nico sat at the wide oak table that occupied one end of the kitchen. He had a loaf of bread and a mammoth jar of peanut butter by one elbow, and he was chugging from—

"Oh, no," Marguerite exclaimed. She extricated the pitcher from Nico's grasp. Only a few drops remained. If Nico wasn't drunk when he got here, he was now doing his best to remedy that.

That was the last straw for a night that contained more straw than a haystack. Evan slammed his palms down on the table. Nico and Marguerite both raised startled gazes to meet his. "Start talking." He pointed at Nico. "You first. You went to bed hours ago."

"I changed my mind," Nico said, his tone as flat as the piece of bread he was spreading with peanut butter. A shock of light brown hair fell across his forehead and hid his eyes, but Evan knew Nico's gaze would be just as expressionless. "A girl I met earlier called and said she and her friends were going out and she'd come get me. You were in the shower."

"You need to tell me."

"I know you forget, but I'm twenty-one years old. So, no, I don't." Nico bit into his sandwich. "But I texted you when the sheriff pulled us over. Thanks for picking me up, by the way. Having the sheriff drive me back here wasn't at all humiliating."

"I—" Damn it. His phone was in the living room. And he hadn't looked at his messages since he first sat down to go through paperwork four hours ago. It felt like a century had passed. "We're not talking about me," he finally said. "We're talking about you."

Nico's response was to take another bite out of his sandwich. "Who's she?" he asked, jerking a thumb at Marguerite.

"Oh, no," Marguerite said again, with an entirely different intonation. She clutched the water pitcher to her chest. "I'm not a part of this. I'll grab my things and go."

"Do 'your things' include the multiple bottles of wine you're stealing?" Evan asked.

"More wine?" Nico perked up. "If it's what I was drinking, it's excellent."

"Really?" Marguerite smiled, the first real smile Evan had seen from her. And it was…amazing. He'd noted she had expressive eyes, the dark blue of an evening sky. But when she smiled, they glowed, making her appear lit from within. "That bottle was pretty young."

"Tasted great to me." Nico carried his plate to the sink.

"Thanks." Marguerite sniffed what remained in the water pitcher. "But a wine expert would say—"

"Too much tannin, so yeah, it would benefit from

more aging. But the flavors were nicely balanced. Anyway, good night." Nico left the kitchen without a backward glance.

"Hey, we're not done—" Evan called after him, but Marguerite's hand on his arm caused the rest of his words to die in his throat. He glanced down at where her slender fingers rested on his bare bicep.

Pink colored her cheeks. She took her hand away and stepped to the sink where she washed out the water pitcher. "Let him go. He was spoiling for a fight, but now he's thrilled he scored a point off me. Allow him his victory."

Evan still felt the pressure of her touch. "You're not only a thief, you're a psychologist? Multitalented."

Her color deepened and she held her chin up. "I'm neither. I'm a winemaker. And I was once his age." Her tone implied that Evan must not remember what it was like to be a young adult.

She was right. He didn't. Because when he was Nico's age, he was running his first company. Nor did he need to be reminded by a thief of the chasm between Nico and him, no matter how intriguing he found her. "My brother isn't your concern."

She raised her eyebrows. "Okay. So, like I said, let me get my things—"

"You still owe me your story. Let me guess—you say you're a winemaker, so you made the wine you're steal—"

"*Not* stealing."

"Liberating, then." He made air quotes with his fingers. "But I don't remember a Marguerite listed among St. Isadore's key staff. I thought the head winemaker was a Calvin or a Cassian or a—"

"Casper. Casper Vos. He's at Dellavina Cellars now."

Steel shutters slammed down behind her eyes, turning her gaze opaque.

Evan regarded her. "You don't seem to like him."

"Most of St. Isadore's staff is now gone," she said, ignoring his comment.

"I see that for myself."

"They started to leave even before Linus had his stroke. Might not be a bad thing to have to start over. Loyalty wasn't their strong suit." A bitter breeze danced through her words.

He leaned against the table. "Except for you, I take it. What was your role at St. Isadore?"

She sighed. "That's a complicated question."

He waved his hand at the dark windows. "There are a few hours left before sunrise."

She opened her mouth—

The lights overhead winked and went out. The room plunged into darkness.

TWO

Marguerite stood still, allowing her eyes to adjust to the sudden change. But apparently her companion had other ideas. She heard a thump and a crash, followed by several muttered words she couldn't quite make out, but she was sure most of them had four letters. "You okay?" she said.

"This damn night" was the response. "What the hell is happening now?"

Marguerite chuckled. She couldn't help it, even though her heart still pounded painfully from being caught trying to sneak away with her wine. Her pulse had started racing from the moment the bottom of the bottle had hit the frying pan and now continued to act as if she were competing in the last leg of a triathlon.

Or at least that's why she told herself her heart was pumping overtime. It had nothing to do with the fact Evan Fletcher wore nothing but sweatpants, which constantly threatened to fall off his narrow hips. She was almost glad the lights were off so she wouldn't have to work so hard to keep her eyes from lingering on his impressive pecs and the wall of abdominal muscles below.

"The previous owner's memory started to slip toward the end. He was afraid he'd forget to turn off lights and run up the electricity bill, so every room is on a timer."

"At two a.m.?" He sounded both put out and disbelieving.

"He was a night owl. I'll get them back on."

"I can turn on my own lights," he muttered, followed by the scrape of furniture against the floor and another thud. A loud thud.

Marguerite gasped. It was bad enough the sheriff had seen her at St. Isadore late at night. If he had to come back because the new owner was hurt while she was on the premises...it would not do her reputation, already tattered after her confrontation with Linus's nephews, any favors. As it was, she could already hear tomorrow's gossip leapfrogging from breakfast table to luncheon counter thanks to Deputy Franks spotting her with a half-dressed Evan tonight.

She struggled to distinguish shape from shadow in the dark, but Evan had to be near the kitchen table. She moved quickly—only to trip over what in hindsight she realized were his bare feet. She stumbled and went down, her hands stopping her fall. "Ow!"

"That hurt, damn it," came the grumpy voice from her left.

"Are you okay? What happened?"

"Chair. Nico didn't push it in."

He sounded so disgruntled, she had to laugh. "No broken bones, I take it."

"Just my broken dignity. What little remained. You okay? Sounded like you went down harder than me."

Her wrists stung from taking the brunt of her fall. She ran a quick check of the rest of her body. Feeling the firm hardness of his thigh under her left calf, she realized her legs were entwined with his. She quickly untangled herself. "Um. No. More shocked by finding myself on the floor than hurt."

He gathered himself together and stood. Now that her eyes had adjusted to the dark, she could see him extending a hand to her. "Here, let me help you."

She took it. His palm was warm, his grip tight and reassuring. She scrambled to her feet, but when she put weight on her right ankle, it was agony. "Ouch!"

He appeared at her side, encouraging her to lean on him. "Sprain or something worse?"

She shook her head. "Twisted. It will be okay." She tried to move away from his side but couldn't put weight on her foot.

"C'mon." He tugged her down to sit beside him. "My shins are going to be black-and-blue from fighting with the chair. And I hit my knee when I fell, so I'm not up to carrying you at the moment. May I offer you some floor?"

Not a bad offer; the hardwood was cool but rather comfortable. She picked a spot that kept her legs from touching his and propped her back against one of the cabinets. After withdrawing her hand from his, she instantly regretted the loss of his warmth.

The room was dark and still. Shadows pressed in, but they created a cocoon, wrapping the two of them together against the outside world. Without sight, her other senses sharpened. Her ears picked up his soft breaths. And her nose, trained to distinguish slight variations in wine aromas, inhaled lemongrass and basil and something else she could define as only warm, clean skin. Her pulse thudded in her veins.

All she had to do was move her hand slightly to the left and it would brush his, perhaps be enveloped again in his comforting strength. And maybe he would use that excuse to pull her closer and she could let her fingers trace in the dark what she had been afraid to explore with her gaze in the light: the smooth bronzed skin over defined biceps, the dark hair dusting his chest before it narrowed to a trail that disappeared below the drawstring of his sweatpants…

He cleared his throat, and her mind jumped back to reality. "That makes three surprises about this place so far," he said. "Four, if I count you. The elevator works despite looking like a museum piece, the secret hallway isn't real estate fiction, and the lights turn off on their own. And it's only my first night."

"That's St. Isadore. I learned something new every day. No matter how long I worked here."

He turned toward her, but she couldn't read his expression in the dim light. "What did you do here anyway? Especially if Custer was the winemaker."

She let out a mirthless laugh. "Casper. Like I said, it's complicated."

"Great. You owe me a story, might as well be a good one."

She huffed. "Fine." But there was no need to go into the details with him. "I was Linus's live-in personal assistant. Jill-of-all-trades, I suppose you could call me. As long as I did what he needed me to do, my time was my own, and I spent it making wine. The previous winemaker agreed to mentor me—" She was proud her voice didn't crack. Casper's abrupt departure for one of the premier wineries in the country accompanied by his curt dismissal of her talent still smarted "—and I experimented on my own with blends and methods."

"If you're a winemaker, why be a personal assistant? Find a job making wine."

She pressed her lips together. Her reasons for being at St. Isadore were personal and tangled and messy—although not as personal and tangled and messy as the gossip spread by others. Including the gossip spread by Casper, who ensured her reputation as an innovative winemaker was ruined. And from what she knew of Evan Fletcher, he would have zero idea why she cared so much.

She settled on: "The grapes aren't the same somewhere else." She heard his intake of breath as he prepared to speak, and she cut him off. "Don't ever say that a grape is just a grape. Not around here."

She didn't need light to see his eye roll. "Despite what you're thinking, I'm not some dense tech guy. I was going to ask why St. Isadore's vines are so special. I own them, after all."

They're special because they're mine. But saying that out loud would take explanations about her tangled family history she didn't want to give, along with admitting how she allowed others to take advantage of her good faith. And she doubted he would be fobbed off with a few vague sentences. The tech guy definitely wasn't dense—well, except for maybe his muscles. "What makes them special? The terroir."

"The terror?"

She laughed. "You're kidding, right? You know what terroir is."

"Yes. A little. Actually, let's say no."

"Terroir is the concept that the specific conditions

of where the grapes are grown—the soil, the wind, the sun, the elevation—affect the wine's flavor."

He nodded. "Terroir makes the vines unique."

She smiled. "Which means the wine made from them is unique. There's more to it, of course, but that's the nutshell." Then she sobered. "I guess this means the rumors are right."

"What rumors?"

"About you."

"Me? What are they saying?" Was it her imagination, or had he leaned closer to her? Then she felt his breath on her cheek and understood he was all too real. Pinpricks of awareness flared on her skin.

She swallowed. "Nothing, really. Nothing bad. They say you bought St. Isadore only to tear it down and sell it off piece by piece."

"*They*," he emphasized the word as he shifted away from her, "have no idea why I bought this place."

It was weird to miss someone's breath near your ear, right? But she did. "Why else would a superrich tech dude buy a winery that's seen better days? Unless maybe as a tax shelter. I'm not familiar with how those work. But either way, it's obvious you didn't buy St. Isadore because you have an affinity for viticulture. So why did you buy it?"

The brooding silence only increased the arctic temperature in the room. He finally spoke. "St. Isadore is a business. I buy and run businesses."

Her hands clenched and unclenched. "You plan to keep St. Isadore going as a winery? Produce wine? Distribute it? Not develop the land?"

"That's why I bought it. As a going business." He huffed. "If I can make it one."

Butterfly wings of hope fluttered in her chest. St.

Isadore wouldn't be torn down. Its vineyards wouldn't be sold and destroyed.

Maybe the dream that had sustained her since childhood wasn't gone for good. Maybe she could save her family's legacy. Oh, Evan wouldn't agree to the same arrangement she'd had with Linus, nor would she dream of proposing it. She trusted Linus—wrongly, as it turned out—because he had been like a grandfather to her, and Evan…was anything but grandfatherly. And look how that had turned out. She'd worked her butt off and received little in tangible reward except for bottles of wine she had to sneak in and liberate.

Marguerite tried to search Evan's gaze. But despite her eyes having long ago adjusted to the lack of illumination, she couldn't read him. She stood up, using the cabinet handles and countertop as leverage, and walked-hopped across the kitchen to the far wall, where she located the switch. Bright, hot light bathed the room as she turned back to him.

He was blinking rapidly. "You could have warned me before you did that."

"Sorry. I will next time."

"Next time? Are you planning on making this a regular thing?"

She nodded. "You're going to hire me."

He blinked again, but she doubted the glare was the cause this time. "Excuse me?"

"You need me."

He ran his gaze up and down her figure, and his mouth curved into a teasing grin. "We just met. A little presumptuous, don't you think?"

She balled her hands on her hips. "You need me to help you bring St. Isadore back up to speed. You said it yourself—most of the staff is gone."

He narrowed his gaze. "I already have an assistant."

She smiled, a long, slow smile. "I'm not going to be your assistant. I'm going to be your winemaker."

This was the strangest night of Evan's life so far. And that included when an ex-girlfriend had persuaded him to attend a private séance at the Winchester Mystery House. The last few hours had delivered far more surprises than that evening had.

But it had also been one of the more intriguing nights of his life. And exciting, even though he didn't want to examine the physical side of his reaction to Marguerite too closely. Yes, he had a tendency to fall hard when dark eyes that spoke more eloquently than words ever could were involved. But this night, for all its surprises, made one thing clear: Pia wasn't wrong.

He was in uncharted waters. He might have bitten off more than even his vaunted business skills and reliable intuition could handle. And if he failed, his plan to solve Nico's problems would disappear down the drain like the remnants of Marguerite's wine.

But was Marguerite the life preserver he needed?

"First, you're a thief—" He held up his hand to stop the protest forming on her lips. Her plump, lush lips. "Fine. You weren't stealing. But you agreed you were trespassing."

"Because I thought you were going to tear down St. Isadore. Look, if I'm an actual thief, would I take the bottles worth gazillions of dollars that are sitting untouched in the cellar or the 'unmarked swill,' as you put it?"

He'd made the same point to himself earlier. "Then you said you were the personal assistant to the previous owner. But the business was about to go under. Why

should I turn it over it you?" The one thing he did understand about wineries was the winemaker was a key
role in its success or failure.

"It's true St. Isadore didn't live up to its potential.
Linus didn't believe in introducing new technologies,
no matter how hard we tried to change his mind. But I
worked here for eight years. I know the winery. I know
the vines. Above all, I know what St. Isadore is capable
of becoming." She raised her eyebrows. "And in case
you haven't noticed, you don't have anyone else."

"I can hire someone."

She shrugged. "You could. But they won't have my
experience or specific knowledge of this place." She
smiled, and he could swear the light in the kitchen increased by one hundred watts. "Besides, your brother
likes my wine."

She probably meant the last as a joke, but it was a
strong argument in her favor. Evan was still figuring
out who Nico was, but he knew one thing: his brother
was a wine savant, whether he came by it genetically
or thanks to growing up with their Italian grandparents
and their ever-present bottle of wine at the dinner table.
Nico had a palate that sommeliers at Michelin-starred
restaurants would envy.

And a chip on his shoulder big enough to be seen
from the International Space Station, but Evan would
find the key to removing it. Somehow.

His gut told him Marguerite wasn't lying. It was
evident she cared about St. Isadore. She would be as
invested in the winery's success as he was. And his instincts hadn't betrayed him yet. "As it so happens, I do
need to hire someone—"

"At the going market rate. Benefits included. And a
contract. A signed contract."

He bit back his smile. "You didn't let me finish. Yes, St. Isadore needs a winemaker. But I need someone to ensure the winery is able to hold a prestigious event in six months."

Her gaze narrowed. "Six months?"

"I'm hosting the opening kickoff for the Global Leader Summit here."

"Global Leader Summit…wait. I've heard of that. Isn't that where CEOs and world leaders get together for a week of secret meetings and when it's over, the public finds out Amazon agreed to buy Disney?"

"Amazon and Disney remain separate companies, but yes. The event will put St. Isadore on the map if it goes well."

She nodded. "And if it doesn't, you face-plant in front of some of the world's most powerful people."

Not that he would admit that. "So, if you want to stay at St. Isadore for longer than six months? Make sure the event is flawless."

Her chin jutted into the air. "Six months puts us before harvest. The winery has a bare-bones staff at the moment, so we need to hire more people immediately. At good salaries with excellent benefits. And if you want a flawless event, you need to hire a flawless event planner. Luckily, I know the best one in wine country."

"I believe in compensating my teams very well. But in return, the only acceptable outcome is success."

"*I* know what I'm doing." Besides, your event will be a good dress rehearsal for the annual harvest dinner, which will make or break St. Isadore's reputation under your ownership."

"Harvest dinner?" He searched his memory of the buyer's paperwork and came up blank.

"It's a winery tradition, has been for over a century.

Tickets go for hundreds of dollars. We debut the new wines and it's heavily covered by the industry press. You will definitely need someone who understands St. Isadore." She assessed him from under thick eyelashes and held out her right hand. "Deal?"

He closed the distance between them and shook. "Deal."

This close, he could see her eyes were several shades of blue, from almost navy on the rim to the color of afternoon sky nearer the pupil. She pushed a lock of hair off her cheek, and he caught the strawberry scent. This was either going to be one of the smartest hiring decisions he'd made or it might sink him. Personally.

"I guarantee you'll be pleased," she said. Was it his imagination or did she linger on the last word? A wicked light danced in her gaze as it met and held his. "Here's to a mutually successful outcome."

He wondered what it would be like to kiss her. To taste her mouth and see if wickedness had a flavor. Feel her open beneath him, inviting him in. See if her lips and tongue were as playful as the words they formed.

He owed a huge debt of gratitude to whoever first came up with sweatpants and made them loose enough to avoid possible embarrassment.

A cell phone rang and she jumped. He blinked, the sound dumping a bucket of cold water on his overheated imagination. "I...don't have my phone with me."

"It's mine." She pulled an older model cell from the back pocket of her jeans and glanced at the screen. "Oh, no. I can't believe I forgot." She answered the phone. "Hey, Aracely."

Whoever was on the other end was not happy. And did not let Marguerite get a word in. Evan walked to the sink, ostensibly to pour himself a glass a water.

And to let the rest of him catch up with the change in the atmosphere. Yes, his libido wanted to kiss her. But his intellect said he needed to employ her. And the two actions did not, would not mix.

Marguerite finished her conversation and hung up. "That's my ride. She'll be here in a few minutes." She put her phone away and turned to face him. "I'll see you first thing in the morning? Nine o'clock at the winery offices?"

"Make it noon. Get some sleep."

"Noon, it is." She hesitated for a second, then seemed to think better of what she was going to say. Instead, she gave him a half wave. "See you then." She ran-walked out of the kitchen, his gaze following her until she disappeared.

His instincts never failed him.

He only hoped it was his *business* instincts that had hired her, not something more primal.

Three

"If I were a ledger no one can find, where would I be?" Marguerite tapped her finger on her chin as she stood in the doorway of Linus's old office at the winery. Her gaze wandered over shelves that needing dusting and the collection of paperweights, still where Linus had left them, on top of the ornate mahogany desk. Marguerite had barely slept after she said goodbye to Evan the night before, so her vision was a bit blurry. But she didn't need it. She could describe every inch of the room in detail even if she wore a blindfold.

It was harder than she thought to cross the threshold. Not that she thought she would find the ledger in the room. The last time she'd been in the office, it was to pack all the winery's business records under the watchful eyes of Linus's grand-nephews. The ledger had been missing then, although Marguerite had been too shell-shocked by grief to give it more than a cursory thought.

Later, of course, she'd realized without it she had no proof of her deal with Linus.

Marguerite willed the moisture forming in her eyes to go away. She'd never known her grandparents, and Linus had been the closest thing to one she'd ever had. She still missed him. She probably always would. But he had also been her boss. And now his office was hers. She sat down in the immense leather chair behind the desk, ignoring the chill that climbed up her spine and settled on the back of her neck at hearing the upholstery creak, like it had all those times Linus had leaned forward to catch Marguerite's eye and solemnly impart a line of wisdom.

She shook her head. The office needed redecorating. The past would be the first thing to go.

"Good morning. The security guard said you were here."

She jumped and looked up. Evan stood in the doorway, leaning a shoulder against the jamb, his arms casually folded. She almost didn't recognize him, dressed in the Northern California business casual uniform of khakis and a button-down shirt. A part of her missed being able to feast her eyes on his rather glorious pecs and well-defined abs, but the crisp dark blue shirt provided its own visual pleasures, contrasting with his tanned skin and wavy dark hair.

Any lack of sleep from last night's encounter didn't show on his face, making Marguerite all too aware of her own tired appearance. His smile was warm, reminding her of how much she'd wanted to flirt with him the night before and how she had failed at it—luckily. Workplace romances were Not a Good Thing.

She offered a quick prayer of gratitude that she'd

remembered to put on mascara before leaving for the
winery.

"Good morning," she responded. "I know we said
noon, but I thought I'd arrive a little early."

"Now works better for me, if it's okay with you?"
At her nod, he crossed the room and placed a manila
folder on her desk. "Here's the employment contract
you asked for."

"My contract? Don't I get to negotiate my own—"
She took the document out of the folder and glanced
at the top page. A dollar sign followed by a very large
number leaped out at her. "Oh."

"We can renegotiate if you like," he said with a
straight face, but a glint in his eye betrayed his humor.

She blinked several times. No, she wasn't imagining
the number. "I'm sure you don't often hear these words,
but this is too much. I said I wanted the going market
rate. This is at least twice that."

He sat down in the guest chair opposite her desk,
his broad frame filling it completely. Evan owned his
surroundings with a breezy confidence that made him
even more attractive—and when he smiled at her, her
stomach squeezed in the most delicious way. "Are you
saying your time and effort aren't valuable?"

"No, I—" She stopped and took a deep breath, getting her unruly feelings under control. "You just met
me. I have yet to work one day for you. Why are you
paying me this much?"

He shrugged. "I asked around first thing this morning. Everyone I spoke to said you were the one who kept
St. Isadore running these past years. I'm still curious
why you were only the assistant, however."

Because that was the bargain. "Only the assistant?"
She stared over the top of the document at him. "Does

your assistant know you have so little regard for the role?"

"I promote mine," he responded. "I don't keep them in what amounts to indentured servitude. I looked up your salary, and you were badly underpaid. Think of this as the back pay you're due"

"There are other forms of compensation besides money."

He shook his head. "In my experience? Not really."

She opened her mouth to defend Linus by explaining their agreement. Then she closed her lips with a snap. She'd just met Evan, but it was clear he dealt in hard logic and cold cash. Telling him might make him doubt her business skills at best. At worst, he could have her thrown her off the premises, like Linus's grand-nephews had when she told them. And Evan had even more cause to bar her from St. Isadore, since he'd caught her red-handed breaking into the owner's residence.

She tapped the contract. "I see that. So there must be a catch somewhere…" She read on. "Ah. Found it. I see there's a performance review at six months and I can be terminated at will without cause until then."

"The Global Leader Summit event, as we discussed last night. I told you I cut losses fast and early."

She waved off his concern. "Don't worry, your rich friends will be impressed. Is that all it will take to pass the performance review? A successful event? It's a pretty simple ask."

He gave her a one-shouldered shrug. "I'm a simple man with simple wants."

"That's not what you said last night. I highly doubt there's anything simple about you. Including your—" she paused but hopefully managed to recover before he noticed "—wants."

"True," he agreed. "I do like things that are…complicated. Hard to figure out. Makes the moment when you realize how to get what you want that much more rewarding." He grinned, the smile of a big bad wolf luring girls in red cloaks off the forest path. Despite the bright sunshine and summer temperature, Marguerite's skin prickled with awareness as if they were back in the dark, cool kitchen of the night before and his muscled thigh was warm beneath her leg.

"Have you ever failed?" she asked.

He shook his head slowly.

Of course it was a rhetorical question. She placed her elbows on the desk and leaned her chin onto her interlaced fingers, the better to keep her gaze steady. There's always a first time, you know."

"There's always the first time you approach a new situation. But you experiment. You learn. Take this, for example." He picked up a rose-colored foam ball from the desktop.

"Linus used that for stress relief. Do you need instructions?"

He turned the full force of his wolfish grin on her, and the ember of excitement, burning since the night before, kindled into a deep glow. "I'm familiar with stress relief. Although this? Not my preferred method."

Her throat was dry. She swallowed, hard. "I'm sure. Please, go ahead. You were saying?"

"It's a matter of action and reaction. For example, if I press here—" and his thumb made an indentation on the ball "—then I learn how soft it is. How pliant. And if I move like so…" His thumb made small circles on the surface of the ball. She couldn't tear her gaze away if she tried. Underneath the desk she crossed and uncrossed her legs, hoping that the movement would relieve the tension beginning to pool between them. It did not. "…now I know how the ball reacts to my touch."

She leaned back in her chair, hoping to affect an attitude as cool as the rest of her was hot. She wanted this job. She needed this job.

And mixing flirtation with business—much less going beyond flirtation—was a recipe for disaster. "Seems to me that ball is just lying there. Not quite sure I'd call that a reaction. Unless that's what you're used to. If so, no wonder you think you've never failed." She smiled, saccharine sweet.

His gaze flared with surprise and he laughed, placing the ball back on the desk. "As I said, I learn from whatever situation I'm in. Like what I've learned about you."

"Me? What could you have possibly learned about me in—" she checked her watch "—less than ten hours?"

"You don't take enough credit or compensation for your work. You're patient, or you wouldn't be in an industry that requires its product to age. You're a planner and don't follow your impulses—except maybe when your wine is involved, and then you had a plan for breaking in and taking it." His grin reappeared, big and bad and full of wicked promise. "How did I do?"

Better than she'd expected. She thought tech guys cared about only code: cold, lifeless numbers that flashed by on a bright screen in a dim, lonely room. But he'd laid her bare, one personality trait at a time. "That's not learning." She pretended to yawn. "That's amateur pop psychology."

He leaned over the desk. Only a few inches separated their mouths. He fixed her with his hazel gaze, a mesmerizing tumble of jade green, amber and russet. "And you don't like it when people get too close."

"Excuse me?" He wasn't wrong, but he also wasn't

right. She did like having close relationships. The problem was when other people knew how much she cared, they used that knowledge to manipulate her. Betray her, even.

"Like now. You don't like it that I've picked up so much about you."

"Really."

He nodded. "Your lips," he rumbled, the vibrations putting the tiny hairs on her arms on alert.

"My lips?" She used her tongue to trace them.

His gaze followed the same path. "You purse your lips. When you're annoyed."

Her lips were indeed pursed. But it was also the shape of a mouth anticipating a kiss. And the light in his gaze told her he knew it, too.

She leaned back in her chair, seeking to get some distance from his delectable scent. This morning he was a cross between freshly laundered cotton, a hint of the lemongrass and basil from the night before, and a touch of black pepper and cardamom. For the first time in her life, she regretted having a finely attuned sense of smell. "That just means you can pick up on other people's tells. You must be one hell of a poker player."

He laughed. "True. My friends won't play with me."

"But I could be annoyed for a variety of reasons. For example, this is an annoying conversation."

"Annoying because I'm right." His grin was self-satisfied.

Their gazes battled. His was amused and...not unappreciative. He clearly enjoyed sparring with her. Learning how to get a reaction out of her.

She'd walked right into his trap. And unfortunately, she didn't mind at all. She could make herself very much at home, sharpening her wit to better play with him, watching the colors in his eyes shift and change as he responded.

But she also knew from experience how fast relationships could change, and one day she'd wake up and find herself shut out and left shivering, miserable and bereft. Casper had been her mentor and Linus a substitute grandfather, but while her caring for them had been platonic, when they left her, each in their own way, it had still been devastating.

Her initial reaction to Evan was anything but platonic. That spelled more potential trouble, and the situation had an even greater capacity to hurt her. The only way to deal with the heated charge hanging in the air between them was to spell out the rules of engagement from the start. She rose from her chair.

"Where are you going?"

"You don't already know? Since you know me so well." She pulled off the elastic band holding her messy bun in place, and her hair tumbled down. She then raised her arms to gather her hair back behind her neck, knowing the movement would display her chest to its best advantage. Sure enough, that caught his attention. She then walked around the desk and, facing him, hopped up on the surface, kicking off her sandals before crossing one leg over the other. The foot on top came perilously close to brushing his thighs when she swung it. "I'm being impulsive. Although—" she ran her gaze over his impressive physique, allowing it to linger on the areas that most interested her "—not as impulsive as I want to be."

"Oh?" His voice was a deep rumble. "What's stopping you?"

She shrugged. "Well, for one, it would involve the other party giving their consent."

"Let's say the other party does. Then what?"

"But it's more complicated than that, isn't it?" She tapped the manila folder containing the employment agreement. "I don't kiss coworkers. Or do anything else with coworkers, for that matter."

Recognition dawned in his expression, followed by a burst of horror. He ran a hand through his hair. "I don't, either. This is…not my usual behavior. I know better. I apologize. If you are having second thoughts about working for St. Isadore—"

"I'm working for St. Isadore." That was nonnego-tiable. "It was my idea, remember? But—" she let her foot swing even closer to the top of his thigh "—I think we're both enjoying this…would you call it a flirtation?"

He didn't say anything, but the heat in his gaze gave her his response.

"So. Once I sign this document, I'm your employee. But until then—"

"—you're not." His slow smile made the breath catch in her throat.

"I'm not." She used her foot to spin his chair, so he faced away from her.

He leaned his head back so his upturned gaze could catch hers. "That wasn't what I was expecting."

She hopped off the desk. "Told you. I'm being im-pulsive."

Then she held his head steady with her hands. And lowered her mouth to his.

Embers exploded into fire. No wonder the upside-down kiss scene in the first Spider-Man movie was iconic. It turned the known geography of mouths into virgin territory, ripe for exploring.

He made a sound, or she did, she wasn't sure. He disengaged his mouth from hers, shrugging free from her light grip. But before she could register the loss of his heat against her, he was on his feet, tugging her to him, his grasp firm as he held her hips tight against him so she felt the solid shape of his arousal. Then it was his turn for his mouth to crash down on hers, demanding, insistent.

She'd been kissed before. By expert kissers who knew what they were doing and never gave her cause to complain. But Evan... Evan was in another class altogether. If kissing were an Olympic sport, they ultimately would have to force him to retire because no one could ever be better than him. And he was right. He did learn. Fast. He read her gasps and her sighs and knew exactly how to make her nerves sing.

She pulled away before her rational mind was taken over by pure want, while she could still control her hands and stop them from unbuttoning his shirt and roaming over his wide chest to explore the muscled skin that had haunted what little sleep she'd had the night before.

"Still think I can't act on impulse?" she said, struggling to return her breathing to something resembling normal.

He broke into a breathless chuckle. "Did I prove to you how much of a quick learner I am?"

"Your point is made." Her veins would not stop fizzing.

"So, if neither of us gets involved with colleagues..."

"Right." She walked back to her chair, hoping he couldn't tell how much her legs quivered, how her knees felt as if they would give way at any moment. "That was fun. But we also agree we don't kiss—or engage in any other physical activity—with coworkers." She pulled the employment contract toward her. He watched her through hooded eyes as she flipped to the last page, took out her pen and let it hover about the line for her signature. "Once I sign this, our relationship is strictly professional. Agreed?"

A light flared in his eyes but was quickly extinguished. "Two consenting adults had a good time, but now comes the hard work. I won't lie. I do find you attractive. But I also promise you can trust me. My self-control is rock-solid."

That isn't the only thing about you that's rock-solid... She shook her head. They had a moment, they sated their curiosity, and now they could work without constant static disrupting the atmosphere. Her libido would stay locked up in solitary confinement for the duration of her employment contract. She would not be thrown off track from her goal of restoring the Delacroix name to wine-making prominence.

But she also wouldn't lie. She found Evan damn attractive.

"I look forward to a productive working relationship." She scrawled her name and dated the document before handing it to him. "Let's start."

Four

Evan leaned back in his desk chair and stared out the window of his San Francisco office, high in a tower that afforded him a prime view of the bay. It was a clear, bright summer day, absent the fog for which the city was famous. Sailboats blew this way and that over the water's surface as ferry boats took tourists to and from Alcatraz Island, but he didn't see them. Instead, his mind fixated on the distant Golden Gate Bridge and the rolling hills on the opposite side. It was Friday afternoon. If he left now and took the bridge, he would be in Napa in ninety minutes and have the whole weekend there…

"The meeting with the suppliers is Tuesday. We need to nail them down before we speak to the bank next week and—" Luke Dallas put down his electronic tablet and looked up from where he sat in the guest chair opposite Evan's desk. "Evan? You with me?"

"Huh?" Evan dragged his gaze away from the window and the route that would take him to St. Isadore. Although technically Luke was the chief operating officer and Evan was the chief executive officer of Medevco Technologies, they ran the business as a team. A smoothly operating team, so Evan didn't know why Luke sounded so testy. "Sure. I'm with you. The meeting is Thursday."

"Tuesday," Luke corrected. He leaned forward. "Anything you need to tell me?"

"No. Why? The distribution situation is finally in hand. Three weeks of round-the-clock worry I'm never going to get back, but otherwise, a return to optimal. But it underlines why we need to nail down that investment from Angus Horne." Evan glanced out the window again. A flash of sunlight off the water caught his gaze. He followed the trail of light to the bridge again. Traffic would be dense, but it would be worse if he left an hour from now. If he wrapped things up—

"So you keep saying." Luke didn't sound happy, but Luke usually sounded terse. The only times Evan heard him laugh was when Luke was with his wife, Danica.

"You don't need me for anything for the rest of the day, right? I'd like to head out to the winery." Evan began to organize his desktop, straightening papers and putting away unneeded items.

Luke's gaze narrowed. "The company needs us to figure out this supply chain problem. Or we won't have a company."

Evan closed his top drawer and locked it. "Alarming. Also, not true."

"But now I have your attention." Luke tapped on the surface of his tablet. "I sent you the information for the supplier meeting on *Tuesday*—" he stressed the last word "—so don't extend your stay in Napa past Monday. No matter how attractive she is."

"Don't worry. I'll be ready—" He froze, his laptop half in, half out of the carrying bag. "What makes you think there's a she?"

Luke never rolled his eyes. But his expression was the closest thing Evan had seen to an eye roll in their year or so of partnership. "You're moody and easily distracted. There's no other logical explanation."

"There are plenty of explanations. Nico, for example. Nico is more than enough of an explanation."

"Right. Nico. The brother I didn't know you had until you brought him to the office last month. Yes, you've always been concerned about spending as much time as you can with him."

Ouch.

Evan liked Luke. A lot. He was the best business partner Evan had ever had in two decades of creating start-ups and building them into success stories acquired by larger companies for hefty sums of money. He'd envisioned being partners with Luke for a long time. Until now. "Just because I don't turn into goop when my family is mentioned—"

"Goop? What are you—?"

"Danica," Evan shot back at him.

A warm smile replaced Luke's taciturn expression.

"See?" Evan said. "Goop. As soon as you hear her name."

"I wasn't aware *goop* was the technical term for caring about one's wife." Luke rose from his chair and crossed the room to leave. "Enjoy the weekend. But don't forget about Tuesday."

"I won't." Evan waved Luke off and went back to packing his work bag in preparation for the trip ahead.

He wasn't leaving now to see Marguerite. He did need to spend time with Nico. Nico, whose resentment of him must be ready to erupt like a geyser for dragging him to Napa and dumping him in an ancient mansion while Evan went back to San Francisco to work. Nico, who—

Images of tousled waves of dark hair piled into a messy bun crowded everything else out of his brain. Dark brown eyes, so dark he almost missed the dilation of her pupils after she kissed him. Pale skin that, no matter how nonchalant and unaffected she pretended to be, betrayed with a flush her true emotions.

He'd spoken on the phone with Marguerite every day during the last three weeks. Her conversation revealed her bright wit, delivered through dry asides and wry jokes that kept him laughing. He found her intriguing— after all, she'd broken into his house and he'd ended up hiring her—and he wouldn't be averse to kissing her again and letting things build to their inevitable conclusion, preferably in a nearby bed. But that's where any entanglement with her stopped.

There would be no goop—aka mooning after a hypothetical wife—in his future. He would not walk around the office with a goofy smile on his face like Luke did after receiving a text from Danica. Not now, and not in the future.

Relationships took time, energy and resources. He was only human and he had limited supply of each. He knew his strengths and where he could maximize his returns. If he had returned home after his parents died and taken custody of five-year-old Nico as his grandparents had suggested, he wouldn't have been able to develop his ideas, work on the code, hire additional developers, network with investors, meet with buyers. And he wouldn't possess the money now to ensure Nico didn't need to struggle the way Evan had. To set Nico up in a career he loved, to pave the way so his journey would be far smoother than Evan's.

He'd done the right thing then, and he was doing the right thing now. Nico had had a good childhood with their grandparents, and now that he was a young man, Evan would help him find his way. Therefore, he was eager to get to St. Isadore for one reason only: to ensure his investment was in good hands as long as it took for either Nico to take over or for Evan to sell it at a profit and reinvest the money in another occupation for his brother.

Besides, Marguerite was his employee. They had a contract. They'd both made it clear they did not indulge in personal relationships at work.

By the time he crossed the Golden Gate Bridge, visions of tumbled black curls and darkly slumberous eyes, dazed with passion, filled his head.

Marguerite stared at her computer screen. Her entire day had been spent answering questions. Her in-box should be nearly empty. But as she scrolled, the number of unread emails continued to climb. She picked one at random, read the first line and clicked away almost immediately, screwing her eyes shut.

With Evan called back to San Francisco for an emergency at his tech company, the responsibility for St. Isadore's day-to-day operations fell on her shoulders. Although they talked every day, what Evan knew about the industry would fit on a wine label and still leave room for the logo and the government warning about sulfites. She had assisted Linus, but she hadn't realized until now how much work Linus kept to himself. No wonder the winery had suffered as Linus's health declined.

There was so much that needed to be accomplished. Aside from ramping up the winemaking operations, the tasting room needed to be remodeled and brought into the twenty-first century. The main building required a laundry list of repairs. And their distribution network was on life support and must be rebuilt, along with their sales team.

They were close to hiring a director of operations, and she had a stack of resumes to give to Evan for the other open jobs. Once St. Isadore was fully staffed, things would run more smoothly, but what made Marguerite think she could get the business to that stage? And what had possessed her to tell Evan she could?

Her own damn pride, that's what. And loyalty. Family honor. At least as long as she was at St. Isadore, she could continue her quest to return the Delacroix name to its legendary winemaking status.

Assuming she kept her job through the next few weeks, much less the next six months.

She groaned and folded her arms on her desk, the better to pillow her forehead while she tried to decide which urgent priority to tackle next.

"I have broken down the event for the Global Leader Summit into steps." Aracely breezed into the office, looking like she was ready to take her seat in the front row at Paris Fashion Week instead of an office in Napa. Her dark olive complexion was flawlessly made up, her ebony hair piled on top of her head in a complicated twist. She stopped short and her long skirt billowed around her legs. "You haven't spent the entire day napping, I hope?"

Marguerite raised her head. "Steps? You have next steps?" Something like hope blossomed inside her.

"Of course. That is why you recommended me to be

the event planner." Aracely put a binder stuffed with pages on Marguerite's desk and took the chair opposite her. A vision of Evan in that chair flashed across Marguerite's mind. How his mouth had opened under hers, his tongue sweeping hers, his hands—

"That is also why you're paying me the big money." Aracely wagged her eyebrows, earning a laugh from Marguerite.

"Why Evan is paying you," she corrected.

"Right, Evan. I am still impressed you turned a break-in into a job offer. Not to mention a place to live."

"The carriage house was empty and could use a paying tenant." Marguerite shrugged. "I know, because I was the last person to live in it. It was a no-brainer."

Aracely smirked as she tapped the binder. "This contains sketches for the party layout, photos of possible decorations and some fabric samples for the tablecloths as well as the shirts for the serving staff. Oh, and speaking of clothes, I dropped off a few things for you at your place. Some pieces of mine you might want to borrow for the party. Or any other occasion now that you're back at St. Isadore."

"That wasn't necessary," Marguerite answered automatically, but she gave Aracely a wide smile. Aracely's wardrobe truly was a wonder to behold. Not only did she possess exquisite taste and the funds to indulge it but she'd also inherited closets of designer clothes from her mother and grandmother, both noted socialites in their youth.

"Just a few things." Aracely pushed the binder toward her. "Here. Look."

Marguerite flipped through the pages. On top were drawings of the winery's terrace with various configurations of furniture and food stations. Underneath a divider were mood boards containing color palettes, suggested lighting configurations and flower arrangements for the tables. And below another divider, she found cloth samples and examples of various embroidery styles so the servers' uniforms would proudly proclaim they worked for St. Isadore. "All I see are decisions that need to be made." She pushed the binder back at Aracely. "My head is spinning. You do it."

"*Pobrecita.*" Aracely didn't sound sympathetic. "If you want to run a winery, hosting events will be an important part of your revenue stream. Start with the first page and go one by one."

Marguerite sighed. Aracely was right. Becoming a sought-after venue for meetings and celebrations was vital to the stability of St. Isadore's financial health. "Sorry. Momentary moment of mortification. Won't happen again."

"Yes, it will. You are human." Aracely grinned. "But this is exciting! We get to spend someone else's money. My favorite form of exercise."

"You do like to give credit cards a workout." Marguerite opened the binder to the beginning section, removing the pages so she could arrange them on her desk. "Start with the layout first, then decorations?"

"Then the details." Aracely nodded. "I will be cheeky and tell you my favorites."

"In case I choose wrong."

"But of course," Aracely agreed with an angelic smile. "My reputation is riding on this as much as yours."

Marguerite looked up from the first sketch. "What are you talking about? You've only been in Napa three years, and you're one of the most sought-after event planners around. Besides, you're going back to Chile in December. Which I'm not forgiving you for, by the way. I don't care how much your parents' business needs you."

"The business does not need me." The smile stayed on Aracely's face, but it no longer reached her eyes. "My parents want me to return."

"But to take over the business, right?"

Aracely made an impatient gesture. "It does not matter why. Now, do you prefer to set up the area for dining on the north end of the terrace or the south end? Here are several different layouts."

"If you don't want to go back, you should tell them."

Aracely kept her gaze focused on the sketches. "I think the north end. It is more protected from the wind."

"You know I'm here if you need to discuss anything."

A flash lit Aracely's gaze, so quickly Marguerite didn't know if she saw it or imagined it. "I will figure it out, like I am figuring out the wine tasting without your help. Care to join in? I am assuming Evan will want to know the plans." Her familiar smirk appeared on her lips. "Or not. Perhaps this is only pretend so he can canoodle more with you."

"Canoodle? What old movie did you learn that from?"

"Aha! This suggests I used the right word as you are not disputing the meaning."

Marguerite rolled her eyes. "There's no canoodling. Not now, not in the future. Especially not with people I work with."

Aracely shook her head. "And yet you and Evan canoodled."

"Can we stop using that word? There's nothing going on. I kissed him to prove a point, nothing more. Now he's my employer, and that's the end of the relationship between us." Marguerite stabbed at the first piece of paper she saw on her desk. "Here. Let's go with this one."

Aracely picked it up. "This is a letter from the sanitation department about the proper disposal of refuse. It will be a stretch to make this work for the wine tasting, but I have an excellent imagination."

Marguerite snatched the letter back. "Set up the food tables on the north end. Because of the wind."

"Excellent choice. So, chairs. Do you want—?"

Marguerite's cell phone rang, cutting off Aracely midsentence. Marguerite looked at the caller ID. "It's Nico."

Although Nico had stayed at St. Isadore after Evan returned to San Francisco, she rarely saw him and they exchanged even fewer words. Why would he call her? Her mind raced to several conclusions, and she didn't like any of them. "Hello?"

Nico didn't bother with a greeting. "Evan's not with you, is he?"

"Um, no." Why would Nico think that? What did Evan say—?

"I was hoping he was back from San Francisco." Nico's voice was strained as if he were in pain.

"Sorry, I haven't seen him. Are you okay?"

He was silent for a few beats. "There was a…thing. I need a ride."

"Are you hurt? Do you need to go to the hospital?"

"I'm fine. My friend, too. We just need to get out of here. We tried to order a rideshare, but no cars are available."

"Are you safe?"

He huffed into the phone as if catching his breath. "Yeah. Now."

"Do you know where you are? Give me the address." She wrote it down. "I'll be right there." She got up from her desk, grabbed her purse and car keys. "If by any chance you see or hear from Evan, let him know I'm on my way to get Nico," she called to Aracely as she exited.

Nico was in a community over forty-five minutes away, which wasn't so much of a town as a collection of gas stations, food markets, and the odd restaurant and wine-tasting room. Luckily, the traffic was light on the back roads skirting the various vineyards, and she was able to get to him in record time.

He paced outside a convenience store, his hands thrust in his jeans pockets, his thin shoulders hunched around his ears. She pulled into the parking space in front of him. "I'm here," she called out the window.

Nico's shoulders fell, but he retained his air of guarded wariness. "One minute," he said, and he disappeared into the store. When he emerged, he was escorting a young woman. He didn't touch her, but it was evident from the way he bent his head to listen to her and curved his body as if to shield her that she must be the friend he'd mentioned on the phone.

Or more than a friend.

Nico opened the rear passenger door and escorted the woman inside the car and then came around to the other rear door and slid in behind the driver's seat. "Thanks for picking us up," he said. "This is Gabi. Gabi, this is Marguerite."

Gabi raised her head and caught Marguerite's gaze in the rearview mirror. "Thanks for taking time out of your day. We appreciate it. I called my friends but they're all at work and couldn't leave."

Marguerite could see why Nico liked Gabi. She was a pretty brunette with dark brown skin, a direct gaze and straightforward manner. Marguerite nodded. "No problem. So, what happened?"

Nico peered out his window. "Do you mind if we start moving first?"

"Sure." Marguerite reversed out of the parking space and put the car in Drive. When they reached the main road, she threw a glance via the mirror at the couple in the rear seat. "This is all very cloak-and-dagger-ish. Want to tell me what happened now?"

Gabi leaned forward. "I'm an intern at Dellavina Cellars. In winemaking."

Something slithery crawled in Marguerite's stomach. "You work for Casper Vos."

"Right. Anyway, we all went out for drinks the other day—all the interns, that is. And Nico was at the same place and we…"

"Started talking," Nico supplied.

"Yes. And we both had to leave, but we've stayed in touch. So when I had today off, I suggested Nico and I meet up this afternoon to go for a bike ride, explore some more of Napa." Gabi sighed.

The uneasiness in Marguerite's stomach expanded, although at least it was no longer connected to Casper. "I didn't see bikes when I picked you up."

Gabi shook her head. "No."

Marguerite glanced at the couple via the rearview mirror again. "Were they stolen?"

"I got a flat. We pulled off the road to patch the tire." Nico's voice was a good impersonation of a volcano struggling not to blow and let loose lava flows of hot anger. "Then these guys drove by, yelling trash at Gabi. We didn't think anything of it. Fifteen minutes later, they came back from the other direction."

"How awful." Marguerite kept her focus on the road, but her heart was with the couple in the back seat. "I'm so sorry."

"They probably had too much to drink. But when they drove by the third time, we decided to ditch the bikes and hike across some fields to the nearest safe place," Gabi said. "And that's when we called you."

"I'm glad I answered. Do you want me to send a truck out to collect the bikes?"

"If they're still there." In the rearview mirror, Nico's lips pressed together in a thin, hard line. "They belong to Dellavina, so we should try to return them."

Marguerite nodded. "I'm going to call the sheriff. Do you have a description of their car?" Then she realized she was almost at the turnoff for the long driveway that led to St. Isadore. "I'm so sorry, I'm driving on autopilot. Gabi, where should I take you?"

"Gabi's staying with me." Nico's tone was ironclad. "And I memorized the license plate number."

Marguerite bypassed the turnoff for the winery and kept going. "Why don't you both come to my place? It's more comfortable than the winery office, and we can call the sheriff together."

Every San Franciscan in possession of a car had decided to visit Napa for the weekend, or so it seemed to Evan after it took three hours—spent on phone calls trying to schedule a meeting with Angus Horne's people—to reach St. Isadore. He couldn't wait to get out of the car, pour himself a glass of one of Marguerite's wines and spend some time catching up on what had happened at the winery in his absence.

It was only eight o'clock. Marguerite tended to work late. Perhaps she wouldn't mind coming up to the house, with its dark corners and overstuffed furniture creating an intimate atmosphere no matter the size of the rooms. A vision of her sitting next to him, a circle of warm light encompassing both of them as they discussed her plans, danced in his head.

For once, he didn't mind the Gothic haunted house aesthetic.

But when he entered the owner's residence, there was a stillness to the rooms that indicated no one was home. And when he pulled back the curtains to check on the winery offices across the large flagstone terrace, Marguerite's window was dark. Nico, sure. He didn't expect a young adult male to hang around an empty house waiting for an older brother when there were bars and clubs and other people his age not too far away. Marguerite, on the other hand... Her absence delivered a right hook that he hadn't seen coming.

He rolled his eyes at himself. Of course she had better things to do on a Friday night than sit at her desk, waiting for her boss to arrive so she could debrief him. But he'd thought...maybe...she'd want to see him since it had been three weeks since they were last in a room together.

He looked at his phone. There were several missed calls from Nico. Well, at the least, the kid was keeping him informed of his comings and goings after that first night. Evan pressed the callback button as he searched the meager offerings in the refrigerator. Looked like Nico hadn't grocery shopped, either. Again, not that he blamed him.

"Hey," Nico answered. There was laughter and even music in the background, but it didn't sound like he was at a club. Someone's house?

"Hey," Evan replied. "I'm home. Where are you?"

"Marguerite's place." Someone said something to Nico Evan couldn't quite hear. "Got to go. See you later." He hung up.

Evan stared at the phone in his hand. Nico was at Marguerite's apartment? At eight o'clock on a Friday night?

What the hell was going on? And why was there music?

Not that he was jealous of his baby brother. But were they having a party? Without him? They both knew he was returning tonight.

This was why he'd made the right decision all those years ago. He should be spending his Friday night out with business associates, wining and dining, building his networks of contacts, working ever closer to his goal of creating a multinational empire. Medevco was the closest he had come so far to starting something that might actually still be a major corporate player in people's lives twenty years from now. And while much of its product success was due to Luke and his technical genius, Evan had brought in the investors who provided the money to keep the company growing. He'd partnered with Grayson Monk and his venture capital firm. He charmed the banks. He made the rounds of Wall Street firms. He was going to bring Angus Horne on board for their biggest round of financing yet, thus solving several of their growing pains.

That's what he was good at. That's how he provided value for the people in his life.

Evan grabbed a beer out of the refrigerator, slammed the door shut and headed for the back door and the mile walk to the carriage house. He could drive, but the thought of being behind the wheel again so soon made his spine ache. Besides, he could use the exercise. And the cool night air.

By the time his destination was in sight, he had worked up a sweat and finished the beer, which provided him with a thin layer of calm. Until he got close enough and saw a sheriff's car pull away from the converted stables that held garages for various winery vehicles, with Marguerite's apartment above.

He broke into a run, somehow not tripping on the cobblestones that made up the courtyard entrance. The ground floor front door was unlocked, and he took the stairs two at a time to the residential quarters on the second floor, bursting into Marguerite's living room and almost falling on his face at his abrupt stop. He windmilled his arms to keep his balance.

Three heads swiveled as if one to gape at him.

"Why was? The sheriff here?" he gasped between gulps of needed oxygen. "Again?" His vision recovered enough to take in the sight before him. Marguerite was standing in the middle of the room, her arms akimbo as if striking a pose. A young Black woman about Nico's age sat on the sofa. Nico lounged in an armchair opposite, while the empty chair next to him held what looked like a pile of dresses. The low coffee table held three wineglasses and a mostly empty wine bottle as well as bowls of popcorn and potato chips. Music softly played in the background.

He had interrupted some sort of gathering.

Marguerite recovered her aplomb first and lowered her arms. "Hello, Evan. Welcome to my home. As for your questions, the sheriff was in the neighborhood and stopped by to take Nico's and Gabi's statements," she said as if that explained everything. She frowned and plucked the empty beer can from his nerveless grasp, holding it up. "Seriously?"

"What? Why? Who?" His lungs still felt as though a brush fire had been kindled inside them.

"Nico and Gabi." Marguerite indicated the young

woman next to her. "Evan, this is Gabi Watkins, Nico's friend. She's a college intern at Dellavina Cellars. Gabi, this is Nico's brother, Evan. The new owner of St. Isadore." Gabi waved hello as Marguerite continued, "They were out for a bike ride this afternoon, and men in a car harassed them. The sheriff has a description and license plate number and said he would keep an eye out."

"Wait. Slow down." He got his breathing under control. "One thing at a time. Bike ride?" He turned to Nico. "You were supposed to shadow the accountants while I was in the city."

Nico's lower lip jutted out. "That's what you took away from what Marguerite said? I didn't do as you told me?"

"I said one thing at a time. That was the first thing." Evan ran a hand through his hair. Why was it so hard to hold a simple conversation with his brother? He never had this problem talking to his staff.

"Maybe 'Are you okay?' should be the first thing. Or 'Sorry that happened to you.'" The darkness clouding Nico's expression was turning into a full-blown storm. "No, the first thing should have been 'Hi, Gabi, nice to meet you.'" He got out of his chair and extended his right hand to Gabi. "Come on, let's go."

"Nico—" Evan sputtered.

"Nico." Marguerite's soft tone seemed to cause Nico to visibly relax. "Evan just got here. Give him some time to catch up. Gabi, why don't you see if a friend is available to pick you up?" She pointed at Evan. "You. Come with me, please."

"You know I'm the boss, right?" Evan grumbled, but he followed her.

Marguerite led him to a small balcony off the dining room. After sliding the glass door shut behind them, she turned to him with a magnificent scowl on her face. "Of course, I know you're the boss. Until now. I quit."

"Good. So, as the boss—" His ears caught up with her words. "Wait. You what?"

"You'll probably fire me anyway. I'm just saving you the trouble." Marguerite took a deep breath, willing her voice not to tremble. She was taking a huge risk. He might indeed demand she leave St. Isadore. But she had spent the last two hours getting to know Nico better and he deserved a champion. Which meant inserting herself into the brothers' private lives. "We agreed that after we signed the agreement our relationship would be professional only. But this is about your personal life."

He narrowed his gaze. "I doubt I'd fire you for voicing your opinion, personal or not. Go for it."

"You must stop treating Nico like a child. Or like someone you pay." She folded her arms across her chest, the better to hide her still quaking fingers, and gave him her best glare. "You're his brother, not his boss."

She expected his anger to flare or perhaps his disdain. Instead, his eyebrows rose as his gaze swept over her. "I'm familiar with casual Friday, but this is the first I've heard of formal Friday. St. Isadore tradition?"

What was he—? "If this is an attempt to deflect the conservation away from you and Nico—"

He waved a hand at her outfit. "You look great, by the way."

She glanced down and her cheeks filled with heat. "Right. Sorry. I was trying to take Nico's and Gabi's minds off what happened. Aracely dropped off some dresses for me to try on for the event, so we were playing fashion show." She smoothed her hands over the full skirt of the 1950s-era emerald green cocktail dress she wore. "You should see Gabi in this Pucci minidress that used to belong to Aracely's grandmother."

He ran his gaze over her one more time, slow and deliberate. "I like what I'm seeing now. Since we're being personal."

Her cheeks were hot enough to start a brushfire. "We're talking about you, not me."

He cleared this throat. "Go ahead. You called me out here to yell at me."

"Not yell. I just don't understand why you and Nico constantly go from zero to being at each other's throats in five-point-six seconds." She tried to search his gaze, but he evaded her attempts.

"I wasn't at his throat. I asked him a reasonable question." He leaned against the sliding glass door. The lamp glow from inside threw his muscled physique into silhouette.

"They were scared today. Badly. You didn't even ask how they were."

"You all seemed perfectly relaxed when I came in."

"After I distracted them and got their minds off what happened! You need to pay more attention to him."

He straightened up. "I do pay attention. Why do you think he's here? Why do you think I bought St. Isadore?"

"Honestly? I have no idea."

"It's for him. He flunked out of college and needs an occupation. That's why we're here. For Nico to learn a business. Get his hands dirty. You say I'm not his employer. But I am."

"Wait. You bought St. Isadore for Nico? As a…toy?" Her voice rose on the last word. All of her hard work. Her family's history. But to Evan, St. Isadore was nothing but a plaything?

"No, not as a toy—"

"You run a tech company. Why not find a job for him there? You think you can throw anyone into running St. Isadore?"

"I threw *you* into running St. Isadore."

She scoffed. "That's different."

"How?"

"Because I…" She stopped, worrying her lower lip with her teeth. Earlier, she'd wondered if she was the right person to oversee St. Isadore. But she'd raised her hand for the job. Evan barely acknowledged Nico's presence. She doubted if he had even asked Nico if this was what he wanted. She tilted her chin high and met his gaze. "Because I know what it entails. I have experience."

"Exactly. And so will Nico if he would wake up." He made a sweeping motion with his hand, indicating the bulky shadow of the winery in the near distance. "How many kids his age are given such an opportunity? He's squandering it."

"He took one afternoon off to spend time with a woman he likes."

"And then one afternoon turns into a week. Then a month. Before Nico knows it, the year will go by and he'll have nothing to show for it."

"He might have a relationship to show for it."

Evan laughed, a deep belly guffaw. "Right. That's supposed to make up for wasting the chance to learn how to run a company from the ground up. What's he going to do when she goes back to school? You said she was an intern, right?"

"Yes, but you're missing the point—"

"She'll go back to her classes and friends. Nico will be nothing but a brief memory. And he'll have no education. No school no school of hard knocks."

"You don't know that—"

"You think I need to pay attention to Nico? I am paying. Attention and money. Lots of money. This place sucks up resources like a tornado. But I'm willing to throw cash at it so Nico has a future. A future that wouldn't be his if I didn't care so much." He gave Marguerite a firm nod.

She regarded him for a beat. "Can I speak now?"

"What more needs to be said?"

"Do you genuinely think Nico should be, what was it, stuck inside all day with accountants—?"

"Shadowing accountants. So he can learn. Man, I wish I had done that when I started out. If you can't read a spreadsheet or understand a financial report, you are—"

She cleared her throat, cutting him off. "I thought there was nothing left to be said."

He held both his hands up in a gesture of apology. "Sorry. You were saying."

"Is this what you did when you were Nico's age? Spent your time indoors pouring over numbers instead of going out? Falling in love?"

He grinned. "I fell many times. Several times a night. I'm all for Nico enjoying himself as much as he wants."

Good thing she gave him her verbal notice and could consider herself officially unemployed. This was definitely not terrain she should be exploring with her boss. No matter how interested she was in his side of the conversation. "I'm not talking about sex. I'm talking about love."

"There's not a lot of difference between the two at the age of twenty-one."

"Of course there is! Nico and Gabi are exhibit A."

Evan scoffed. "This is the first I've heard Gabi's

name. Sure, Nico might be infatuated. She's very attractive. But love? They just met. He's too young to know if it's love."

Marguerite stopped herself from rolling her eyes. "And what is the age for knowing your own heart, O wise one? Twenty-five? Thirty-two? Fifty-seven?"

"You know I'm right. You don't want to admit it."

"Have you ever been in love?" This time she caught his gaze. His eyes were dark and unreadable in the dim light. The longer their gazes held, the faster her pulse sped up. He wouldn't break the connection, and she couldn't.

He looked away first, to her satisfaction. Or her disappointment. It was hard to tell with her heart threatening to jump out of her chest. "Hasn't everyone? After one breakup, I even grew a beard and bought out an entire liquor store of its whiskey."

"I'm sorry. That sounds like it was painful."

"Then I shaved and threw a party. My friends drank what was left in the liquor cabinet, and that was that." He shifted his position to lean on the railing next to her. "What about you? When were you old enough to know if you were in love or only in love with the, let's say, physical feeling?"

The night breeze carried his scent to her. Still the hint of basil and lemongrass but with a deeper, richer base note she was coming to think of as "Evan." She inhaled deeply before she knew what she was doing. "I think…you're born knowing. But it takes the right person to switch it on, no matter how old you are."

"And have you been switched on?" he rumbled.

The night breeze had subsided, leaving the world still and hushed. Stars glowed high overhead in a moonless, dark indigo sky, leaving the light spilling from the sliding glass door as the only source of illumination. She was keenly aware that Evan was less than an arm's length away, so close she could reach out and hold his hand.

Draw him to her.

She shook her head to clear it. "I'm not the subject here. Look, I don't know the history between you and Nico. And maybe it's the age difference that makes you two butt heads every time I see you together. But even as his employer, you can't stick him in an office and walk away and not expect him to be resentful. You especially can't fault him for spending time with Gabi. He has genuine feelings for her."

The moment—if there had even been one—dissipated. He leaned away from her. "I know where those feelings originate, and it's not his heart. It's another organ. That's fine, as long they both consent and take necessary health precautions. But spending time with her when he should be working isn't going to pay his bills. He needs to learn that. And he's damn lucky he has me to give him that opportunity."

The wind blew Marguerite's hair into her face, and she pushed it back with an impatient movement. "Okay. Fine. You're his brother."

"Yes, I am." He threw her a side-eyed glance. "But. You're not wrong. We do butt heads whenever we're together. Tonight is the most relaxed I've seen him since he came out to California."

"I spent the last two hours talking with him and Gabi." She reached over to touch Evan's hand but chickened out and drew back at the last second. "You should try it."

"I didn't mean to leave him here by himself for so long, but—" He shrugged. "Things at Medevco seem to be in constant crisis. We grew very fast. Now we need to secure another round of money so we can continue to expand, or we need to make cuts. And we're not making cuts." His tone was final. But she didn't miss the almost imperceptible flash of concern in his eyes. Perhaps he was capable of deeper caring, after all.

"Nico knows how important your company is to you. He does. But while he's here in Napa and you're there in San Francisco, have you thought about having him work in hospitality or retail instead of accounting? The gift shop, for example. He likes people and he's knowledgeable about wine. He'd need a refresher course on St. Isadore's offerings, but then he'd be ready to give people recommendations."

Evan shook his head. "I've got a better idea. Nico reports to you."

"Me? You forgot. I quit."

"Your contract requires a written letter of resignation with fourteen days of notice. Until I accept it, you're still employed." He smiled.

She laughed. "I guess we're back to being professional colleagues."

His little finger brushed hers. Accidentally, she was sure. Her heart skipped a beat nonetheless. "I like to think this conversation took place between friends," he said.

"Friends?" Her laughter faded. "I don't know. Work and relationships, even when it's friendship, don't mix well in my experience—"

He nodded. "Right. Our contract talk. I remember." The deep rumble of his voice, accompanied by the devilish glint in his gaze, told her exactly what he remembered. Her knees turned to water. Thankfully, her fingers were locked in a death grip on the balcony railing. "Outside work. During work, I need to pretend

I know what I'm doing when it comes to St. Isadore. For the sake of my poor, deluded ego."

She laughed to buy herself time and give her legs a chance to recover their strength. "See, this is why I would never claim to be able to read you. You say things like that out of the blue."

"So, what do you say? Friends?"

She shouldn't say yes. Being friends with Casper had led to letting her guard down, only to be sucker-punched when he took credit for her ideas and used them to secure a more prestigious position, bad-mouthing her in the process. She thought Linus had cared for her as a family member instead of just a disposable employee, and it had nearly broken her when she discovered how wrong she had been.

But being friends with Evan had its appeal. Especially if it meant she could help him with his relationship with Nico. And she had to admit she liked spending time with Evan. She wouldn't mind getting to know him better.

To make her job easier, of course. No other reason. Or so she lied to herself.

She mimed raising a glass in a toast. "To friendship. After hours."

He held up his own imaginary glass, and in the process, their hands briefly tangled. Heat flared where his skin slid against hers.

She was pretty sure friends didn't feel a friend's touch hours later.

It was a long, sleepless night.

Five

Marguerite crossed another day off the wall calendar hanging behind her desk and leaned back in her chair. Nine weeks ago, she'd broken into St. Isadore. Six weeks ago, she and Evan had decided to be friends.

That left three months to go until the Global Leader Summit event.

Would she make it?

St. Isadore wasn't the cause of her concern, for once. After reviewing the business plan she drew up, she and Evan agreed the winery needed more staff. They'd recently finished the interview process and made a series of job offers, including a director of operations who would take some of the day-to-day responsibilities off Marguerite's shoulders. The winery would soon operate at full capacity again, and the upcoming harvest crush and fermentation no longer featured prominently in her nightmares. And despite being looked after by a near-skeletal operation after Linus's death, the wine aging in barrels was promising. The Cabernet Sauvignon still needed more time, but the Chardonnay was almost ready to be bottled. They wouldn't produce nearly as many cases as they should this year, but St. Isadore was in better shape than it had been for some time.

But before she could get to harvest in late summer, she had to get through the upcoming Global Leader Summit event.

Which meant spending more time with Evan, who'd called ninety minutes ago to say he was leaving San Francisco for St. Isadore.

Gone were the often stilted conversations of her first few weeks working with him. Since that evening on the balcony, their phone discussions ebbed and flowed naturally.

But talking long-distance only went so far. Although they occasionally used video when Marguerite needed to run items past him for approval, for the most part Evan remained a disembodied presence in her ear. He usually called late at night after marathon hours at Medevco, and at first, his tone would be terse, even impatient. But after an exchange of pleasantries and comparison of their work schedules, he'd slow down, his voice deepening, his conversation turning thoughtful or roguish, with the occasional rumbling of laughter.

It was the best part of her day. Alone in her room, tucked in her bed, the lights out and only his voice tethering her to the world, it was so easy to pretend she and Evan were actual friends.

Or more.

Which was why she had yet to tell him about her agreement with Linus granting her ownership of the original Delacroix vineyard. Or even to confess that she was descended from St. Isadore's original owner. She didn't want to do or say anything that could damage the growing but fragile trust building between them. And she certainly didn't want to throw any wrenches into the relationship tentatively forming between him and Nico.

A knock sounded at her door, and as if her thoughts had summoned him, Nico appeared. He carried a large box in his hands. "Okay if I take off a little early? Gabi's parents are in town. They scored reservations at La Blanchisserie and asked me to join them."

"Wow. Those are difficult reservations to get. Parents, huh?" Marguerite couldn't help the large smile spreading across her face.

Nico ducked his head. "Not a big deal."

Marguerite rarely saw the family resemblance between Nico and his brother, but she heard it in their speech. Nico had the same don't-push-any-further warning tone in his voice as Evan whenever the subject got too close to his personal danger zone. She nodded at the box in his hands. "Is that the wine aroma kit?"

Nico put it down on her desk. "Thanks for letting me borrow it. Gabi and I have been practicing. I thought I had a decent nose, but hers? Wow."

"I bet yours is pretty good." Marguerite glanced at the clock. Evan could arrive at any minute. Or he might be stuck in traffic and not arrive for hours. She was too jumpy to sit at her desk and pretend to answer the emails that had come in while she was out in the vineyards. "Do you have time before you go to show off what you learned?"

Nico's eyes lit up. "I've got a half hour. What do you have in mind?"

"Want to help with my Chardonnay trials?"

"Sure. Are we going to the cellars?"

She shook her head. "I'll have samples brought up to us. I don't want to miss Evan." She fired off a message, catching a glimpse of her reflection in the computer monitor. She smoothed her hair, gathering up loose locks and tucking them back into her ponytail. She wouldn't be able to do anything about her wrinkled shirt. She brushed at it anyway.

Nico sat down in the guest chair. The chair she still couldn't look at without blushing. "Don't want to miss him, huh?"

She glanced around the monitor and caught his smirk. "He's my boss and he's been in San Francisco all week. I have some items to discuss with him."

"You could send him an email." Nico's grin grew, threatening to reach his ears.

Two could play that game. "So, Gabi's parents. First time meeting them?"

Nico wiped his expression clear, and he scratched the back of his neck. "I was thinking, if it's okay with you, my next rotation could be in the tasting room."

She hid her own smile. "Tired of winemaking already?"

He gave her a one-shouldered shrug. "There's a lot of chemistry involved. And math."

She nodded her head. "Indeed."

"I like talking about wine. And drinking it, of course. But maybe not making it. Not the way you and Gabi like making it. It's like a calling for you two. For me it's more of a...fun hobby."

She inhaled. "You know why Evan bought this place, right?"

A knock on her door heralded the arrival of the wine samples. She thanked the messenger and took the eight small, labeled glasses, placing them on her desk. Four for her, four for Nico. "Saved by the bell. Or the wine, as it may be."

Nico straightened up. "What are we looking for?"

She regarded the glasses. "I started a trial to test the effects of using different barrels to age Chardonnay. St. Isadore wine is known for being buttery and oaky, but consumers are trending toward brighter, crisper flavors."

Nico nodded. "Got it. Gabi mentioned Dellavina is also evolving its flavor profile."

Marguerite suppressed her eye roll. Of course they were; Dellavina and St. Isadore had similar Chardonnay styles. But when Casper had been at St. Isadore, he'd pooh-poohed all her suggestions.

"All the wines came from the same lot," she continued. "The first sample was aged in a five-year-old French oak barrel. The second one, in a new American oak barrel. The third one, I used a hydro barrel, which means water was used to form the staves instead of fire. And the fourth is the Chardonnay we're bottling now."

Nico leaned forward. "Where do I start?"

"Start with our current wine. Then let me know which sample you think would push St. Isadore in the right direction."

They picked up the glasses and began tasting, their conversation relaxing into jokes and laughter as they compared notes. Marguerite was in the middle of telling Nico a story about one of her biggest mistakes in winemaking "—and that's why you never add a large amount of yeast too quickly to an already fermenting tank—" when she looked up and saw Evan in the door, watching them.

She wasn't sure how long he had been there. He

looked tired; even from where she sat, she could see the deep grooves worn into his cheeks and how the corners of his mouth drooped. But he was still more attractive than any human had the right to be, with his button-down shirt open at the throat to reveal a triangle of skin and his jeans seemingly tailored to show off his narrow hips and well-muscled thighs. Then their gazes caught and held, and everything else disappeared. "Hi," she said slowly.

He nodded. "Hi."

She could get lost in his eyes.

Nico stood. "I'm going to be late. Thanks, Marguerite."

She snapped out of Evan's spell. "You didn't—"

"Two is my choice," he shot back, and pushed his way past Evan.

Evan stared after him. "Good to see you, too," he called.

"He does have a date," she offered. "At La Blanchisserie."

"La Blanchisserie? Didn't know I paid him that much."

"He's been invited to dinner." She lowered her voice to a stage whisper. "By Gabi's parents."

Evan crossed the room and dropped into the chair that Marguerite would always think of as his. "Sounds like you, at least, are making headway with him. Good work."

She cocked her head and gave Evan a side-eyed look through narrowed eyes. "Pretty sure that isn't my job." She paused and added, as much for her sake as for his, "Boss."

"So, fill me in. Where are we on the Global Leader Summit event?"

They discussed the plans, locking down decisions

that required his personal approval. The party was taking shape nicely thanks to Aracely's meticulous planning, so Marguerite was startled when she glanced up and found Evan frowning. "Anything wrong?" she asked.

"How did you get Nico to laugh like that?"

She blinked. "I talked to him. I told you, you should try it."

"I've never heard him laugh like that before."

Never? She frowned. "It was a pretty normal laugh."

Evan rose from the chair and closed the door to her office, then started to pace around the room. "You may have noticed Nico and I aren't close."

"I think it's safe to say the entire winery staff has noticed. Probably most of Northern California."

"Right." He ran a hand through his hair. "This is the first time Nico and I have spent extended time under the same roof."

"The first time? What about when you were kids? Although it's obvious there's a big age gap."

"The last time we lived together, he was a baby. I started college at seventeen. I was out of the house around the time he turned two."

"But what about holidays? Summers? Surely you went home to see your parents."

He stopped circling the room and stood so still, that for a second, she was tempted to wave her hand under his nose to see whether he was breathing or had been turned to stone. "My parents died in a car accident the start of my sophomore year."

She gasped. "I'm so sorry. For you and Nico."

He suddenly looked very young, and very broken. She yearned to reach out and comfort him. But although their friendship had settled into a comfortable rhythm and they spoke every night, that was a boundary neither of them crossed. They were careful not to touch each other. "I can't imagine how hard that must have been. For both of you."

He shrugged, his expression settling back into the Evan she knew. The Evan who would rather joke or retreat into bluster than admit he was an everyday mortal with emotions. "Save the condolences for Nico. He lost his parents when he was five. I'd already started my first company out of my college apartment."

"Eighteen is still young. You must have been devastated." She would've been if she'd lost her parents at that age. She had her differences of opinion with them, and they certainly didn't understand why she felt so strongly about Napa and the family winemaking heritage, when they couldn't wait to get out and move to Arizona, but she loved them deeply.

"I was running a business." His tone kept any emotion trapped under its surface. "A business I later sold for nine hundred thousand dollars. Pretty good money for someone in college."

She resisted pointing out even successful student entrepreneurs were allowed to mourn. "And Nico? What happened to him after you lost your parents?"

Evan resumed pacing. "My maternal grandparents raised him." He turned his flat gaze on her. "He had a good life."

She wasn't sure if he was trying to convince her, or himself. "I don't doubt it. But why did you say this is the first time you've lived under the same roof? Didn't you visit?"

He kept his head turned from her as he continued to treat her office like an oval track. "Sure." Another turn around the room. "I went to his high school graduation."

She didn't say anything, just watched him.

"I couldn't take time off," he said after three more revolutions around the room. "I sold that company and moved to California and then began and sold three more. Each more lucrative than the last. But each requiring hundred-hour workweeks." He turned back to her, his gaze holding hers hostage. "I sent my profits to my grandparents. Nico wanted for nothing."

She nodded, her throat too tight to speak.

"He had a good life," he repeated. "But then last year—" he balled his fists at his sides "—he flunked out of college. Stopped going to classes. My grandparents didn't know what to do. I stepped in."

"Do you know why he stopped?" she finally managed.

"It wasn't partying or drugs. He drinks but not to excess. And before you ask, he didn't break up with anyone so it's not 'heartache.'" He made air quotes around the last word.

She ignored his derisive snort at the thought of suffering from a broken heart. "Many find college isn't the right fit. You dropped out, too, right?"

Evan laughed, a bark devoid of mirth. "I dropped out to run a company. He flunked out without a plan. When I asked what he wanted to do, he said he wanted to be paid to drink wine. So here we are." He finally stopped wearing a path in her faded rug and pulled out her guest chair, settling his muscled bulk in it. "Tell me how you got him to laugh."

"Evan, I…" She didn't know what to say. Didn't know what the current state of her relationship with him allowed her to say. Her heart squeezed as his hazel gaze lasered in on her, as if she were a glass of water and he was stranded in the middle of the desert. "How

I got Nico to laugh isn't the issue. You need to learn how you can make him laugh."

"I've tried. He rolls his eyes at my jokes."

"Because your jokes make dad jokes seem edgy."

He scowled at her, but she was glad to see a glint of humor return to his expression. And something else. A light of appreciation she both wanted to bask in and was afraid of exploring too much. She dropped her gaze and it landed on the wine aroma kit. "One of the reasons why I love working in wine is because of my family. We've been winemakers for generations. What about your family?"

Evan shrugged. "My mom was a teacher. My dad owned an auto shop. We don't have a family trade."

"What about hobbies? Do you and Nico share any?"

Evan's blank stare returned. "I don't have hobbies. I work."

"You…" She let it pass. "What about taking up Nico's interests? Nico and I get along because we share an appreciation of wine. I could teach you about it."

He smirked. "I prefer beer."

She gave him a mock frown. "I've noticed." She indicated the box. "Nico just returned this aroma kit. It's a tool used for training people's noses to identify different scents found in wine. Want to try? At least you'd have something to talk to Nico about."

His gaze sparked to life. "How does it work?"

She opened the box and chose six small vials, uncapping one before passing it across the desk to him. "Take a sniff. What do you think it is?"

He inhaled deeply, then coughed.

"A sniff," she said.

"Right." He tried again. "Um…strawberries."

She smiled. "Correct." She took it back from him and handed him another. "Now this one."

He waved it under his nose. "It's the same one. Strawberries."

"No. Although it's also a fruit."

He put his nose closer to the vial and then shook his head. "This is a trick, right?"

"The differences can be subtle. I promise, not a trick."

He leaned back in his chair, his gaze catching hers. The dark gold flecks in his eyes glowed in the late afternoon sunshine streaming through the windows. "Maybe it's because when I'm with you, all I recall is how your hair smells of strawberries."

She struggled to find her best schoolteacher voice. "You're supposed to be concentrating on the scent I gave you."

"Sorry." He lifted the vial to his nose again, then put it down and gave her a slow, crooked smile. "Still strawberries. My favorite."

Only Evan Fletcher could make a simple summer fruit sound oh-so-tantalizingly dirty. "Perhaps your sense of sight is overwhelming your sense of smell."

"Are you suggesting I close my eyes?"

"Would you keep them shut?"

He thought for a second, then his smile widened as his gaze traced the contours of her face, causing heat to rise in her cheeks. "No."

She stood up, thankful her knees still possessed enough structural integrity to hold her weight. "I might have a better idea. It's after five o'clock, right?"

Evan frowned. "It's almost six. Why?"

She opened a cabinet. If she wasn't mistaken, Linus had stored fabric wine bags for use when giving impromptu gifts…yes. She pulled out a black velvet bag and a length of satin ribbon, then held them up for Evan to see. That means it's after work hours. Or maybe I should give you a letter of resignation first?"

He watched her through hooded eyes. "You're fired until tomorrow morning."

She laughed. "Good. Because blindfolding the boss definitely violates the employment contract." She stepped to his side and placed the velvet against his eyes, tying the ribbon to keep it loosely in place. Her fingers brushed the rough stubble of his cheeks, the silky softness of his hair. She held her breath so he wouldn't hear it shudder and then stepped back. "Can you see?"

The makeshift blindfold only enhanced the curves of his well-shaped mouth, threw into relief his chiseled jaw and sharp planes of his face. "No. Let me have the scent again."

"I'll hold it for you." She placed the vial under his nose. His right hand came up to hold hers steady, his touch warm and firm. She swallowed. "Anything?"

He inhaled, then exhaled. His breath wafted over her skin, causing a shiver. "Still strawberries. And maybe sugar cookies?"

He was describing her. Her shampoo. Her body lotion. "You're peeking," she accused.

"No," he rumbled. "But your skin smells of cookies. I like it."

His voiced caused tremblors deep in her belly. "It's vanilla. But if you're not taking this seriously…"

"I am. I'd like to see you tell the difference between the scents." His hand was still cupped around hers. His grip changed, his thumb rubbing ever so slightly against the sensitive skin on the back of her hand.

She got her breathing under control. "Please. Part of my job is identifying aromas. I could identify all the scents in a kit like this in elementary school."

His beautiful mouth quirked into a half smile. "Show me."

In response, she untied the ribbon and pulled the velvet bag away from his eyes. The kaleidoscopic mix of green, amber and russet was even more mesmerizing than earlier. It took her a second before she remembered to straighten up.

"Turn around." Evan stood, took the bag and ribbon, and re-created the makeshift blindfold on her.

The velvet was soft against her skin, the nap of the fabric tickling her eyelids where the ribbon held the bag in place. Evan guided her to the guest chair, the heat of his hand on her arm burning through the thin fabric of her blouse.

"I'm ready," she said. For what, she didn't know and couldn't name. She leaned forward, only to realize she was straining against a restraint that didn't exist. The blindfold really did transform how she processed the world around her. Without sight, her ears filled in the details of the scene: the clack of glass as Evan picked up various vials and placed them on the desk, the soothing, regular sound of his breathing. Then he was next to her, the air thick with his presence even though he had yet to touch her.

"Here."

Anticipation caused her stomach to squeeze. He picked up her hand, and the brush of his skin against hers made her nipples pebble even though all he did was place a cold glass vial in her fingers.

He guided her hand with vial up to her nose—

She sputtered and frowned in his general direction. "Horse sweat? Really?"

He took the vial from her. "I'm sorry. That was for me. I'm fascinated to know what horse sweat smells like. I'm even more fascinated why wine smells of horse sweat."

She laughed, unsure whether to be disappointed or relieved that the spell was broken. "The scent is caused by a type of wild yeast called Brettanomyces or Brett for short. It's found in red Côtes du Rhône, or it could be a sign something is off in other varietals—" She stopped. The atmosphere in the room had changed. "You're silently laughing at me, aren't you?"

"Believe me, laughing is the last thing I'm doing."

His rough whisper sent a rush of slick heat between her legs. "You glow when you talk about wine, did you know that?"

He reached for her hand, his warm fingers curling around her, guiding her to hold another cold glass bottle. "What about this one?"

She sniffed. "Bay leaf."

His chuckle was more vibration than sound. "Now who's using their memory instead of their sense of smell?"

"It's bay leaf, Evan."

He leaned closer to her, the molecules in the air charged with his presence. "Are you so sure? My aftershave is bay leaf."

She laughed. "No, you smell of basil. And lemongrass." Not needing to see Evan to know where he was, she reached out, picked up his wrist and brought it to her nose. She closed her eyes, the better to learn him, grateful he couldn't see the pleasure on her face. "And here—" she traced his skin, identifying the ridges and valleys marking veins and tendons "—cinnamon and cloves, with a touch of orange. You used the soap sold in the winery gift shop."

Evan was still, only the pulse in his wrist beating against her fingers. She dropped his hand, panic starting to rise. She'd given herself away. Now he knew she was as keenly aware of him as he appeared to be of her. Only he was flirting for flirting's sake and she was… not flirting. She was a terrible flirt, in fact. She was incapable of keeping her emotions separate from her words and actions. Look what had happened when she tried to dissipate the tension between them by kissing him before signing her contract. The awareness only continued to build…at least on her side.

She was attracted to Evan. It wouldn't take much to fall for him, head over heels. But experience had taught her when she let others into her heart, she ended up shut out in the cold. She would not make the same mistake again. Especially not with her future at St. Isadore on the line.

Reaching up, she yanked off the blindfold and blinked as her eyes adjusted to the light.

"So," she said brightly, rising from the chair, "do you want to take the kit home? Practice on your own?"

He shook his head, his gaze unfocused. "Thank you, though. You definitely made me appreciate my sense of smell."

"Anytime. That's part of my job, after all. Teaching others about wine, that is. A good winemaker should always be able to explain their process and describe what others are drinking." She was babbling. Anything to pretend the scent of his skin didn't cause a rush of warmth deep in her belly. Anything to get back to a state of normalcy between them. "Do you think this will help you with Nico?"

He shook his head slowly. "No. Definitely not."

"Oh." She felt deflated. "It was worth a try—"

"I don't think Nico would appreciate it if I rhapsodized about how his skin smells." Evan grinned, his gaze devilishly appreciative. "But I enjoyed it. Very much."

The heat between her legs blossomed. She leaned on her desk for support. "Glad you didn't think it was a waste of time."

"Except I still don't know what horse sweat smells like."

She indicated the kit. "You can learn."

"Next time." His expression sobered. "Thank you, by the way. For being concerned about Nico. For wanting to help."

She smiled at him. "Of course. It's easy to care about him." Acting on impulse—acting as she would for any friend—she leaned up to kiss Evan on the cheek.

He turned his head at the last second. Their mouths met. His lips were firm, hard, and then he opened his mouth under hers, and all was warmth and wetness. The impact rocked her, sending her several steps back.

Too late, she realized what she'd done. She'd crossed the line. She'd touched him.

She'd kissed him.

Her hand flew to her mouth in shock. "I'm so sorry—"

He shook his head once, twice, in brisk, precise movements. Then he reached out and drew her close, his hands closing on her waist. "Strawberries and vanilla," he ground out. "You taste like you smell."

She got her breathing under control. "You don't taste of cinnamon and basil. Thankfully."

"Huh. Maybe you should try again. Make sure you're getting the right notes. That's the correct term, isn't it? Notes?"

He wanted to kiss her again? Every nerve ending screamed "yes!"

"Notes are very important. You're right, it would be a shame to miss them."

He didn't require another invitation. His hands tightened on her waist, drawing her against him. She wound her arms around his neck, daring to press even closer. Then she raised her head to his, eyes closed, lips parted, anxious for the urgency of his kiss.

But he took his time. His mouth landed everywhere but on hers: on her cheekbones, along her jawline, gentle as goose down on her eyelids. He lingered on the stretch of her neck, on the sensitive area behind her ear. He used his lips and his tongue and the scrape of his beard, lighting fires wherever he roamed, building a conflagration deep inside her that demanded more, now, here—

Something buzzed. Something had been buzzing, she slowly realized. Evan must have heard it, too. He lifted his head, his gaze black and unfocused. "Phone."

Her heart raced as if she'd just finished a triathlon. She found enough air to gasp, "Not mine."

"Mine." Keeping one hand on her waist to hold her to him, Evan reached into his jeans pocket and pulled out a sleek smartphone. He answered with a curt, "Yes?"

Marguerite couldn't hear the other end of the call, but whoever it was didn't seem to be bearing good news. Evan let go of her and stepped away to the farthest corner of the room to finish the conversation.

She turned away, both to give him some privacy and to try to return some semblance of order to her hair and clothes. Her shirt was untucked, her hair mostly down instead of up, and she was missing a shoe although she couldn't remember how it had come off her foot. She'd probably kicked it off when she wound her leg around him...

Evan cleared his throat and she glanced up from her search for her shoe. He, too, had tidied up his appearance, although his dark curls looked far more windswept than when he'd first showed up in her office. But his shoulders were rigid and his jaw set, while apology was evident in his gaze.

"We need to talk about what just happened but—"

She knew the look on his face. "You need to go back to the city even though you just got here."

"We're having ongoing issues with one of our suppliers and the CEO is unexpectedly flying in. If I leave now, I'll be there in time to have a nightcap with him, and then Luke arranged a last-minute weekend of golf at Pebble Beach. I'm sorry. Can I call you later?"

She nodded. "What about Nico?"

"I'll talk to him."

She threw him a look from under her eyelashes.

"I will," he insisted. "Wild horses can't stop me."

"Since untamed equines are in short supply in Northern California, that's a pretty safe promise. Medevco, on the other hand..." She smiled, to take any sting out of her words.

He rolled his shoulders a few times. "I know. If we can straighten out this issue, then—"

"You'll need to make Nico a priority at some point." She touched his right hand with hers, and he stilled under the contact. "If you want to get to know him, that is," she finished.

He nodded, but she wasn't sure if her words had

reached their target. "Can you continue to look out for him?" he asked.

"Of course! Besides, Nico reports—oh." She smiled up at Evan, her expression steady even as his fingers caressed her knuckles, her insides melting anew. "I guess he doesn't report to me."

"Right. You're re-hired as of this moment." Evan squeezed her hand one more time, then he let go.

"I have to run. But you and I—"

"No buts. And, honestly, you don't have to gird your loins for a big conversation. You and I are good." She paused. "Boss," she emphasized.

"Boss." He considered for a minute. "I guess that means no goodbye kiss?"

She burst out laughing. "Go. Drive safely. I have my own work to finish."

But after he left she sat motionless at her desk, her thoughts tumbling after each other, like kittens playing in a box, until the sun had long vanished and darkness covered every inch of the room.

Her mind could lie to itself. Outside of work, she and Evan were friends. Friends who found each other attractive and occasionally kissed, but it didn't mean anything.

Her heart knew better.

Six

Marguerite closed her eyes and leaned under the shower's spray, enjoying the leisurely start to her Saturday. Then her eyes flew open, and she turned off the water and stuck her head outside the curtain. Was that…the sound of her front door opening and someone coming up the stairs? She was sure she'd locked it. What the—?

"Hello?" Aracely called. "You here?"

Marguerite exhaled, the adrenaline surge receding, though part of her wished she'd heard a certain male voice instead of her best friend's. "You scared me! I almost regret giving you a key," she called back, and then quickly dried off before slipping into a robe to greet her guest. "You better have brought coffee after nearly giving me a heart attack."

When Marguerite got to the kitchen, she saw Aracely standing by the kitchen table, holding a carrier tray with two cups of coffee in one hand and a white paper bag in the other. "And freshly baked doughnuts."

"I take it back. You can keep the key as long as you want." Then Marguerite frowned. "But why are you here? I thought you had an early morning meeting with a client." She took the bag from Aracely and sat down.

Aracely took the chair on the opposite side of the table. "I do. But I want to make sure I heard you correctly on the phone. You kissed Evan last night, and then he ran out the door? Do I have that right?"

Marguerite paused, a chocolate cruller halfway to her mouth. "And good morning to you, too."

"This is not normal boss-and-employee behavior."

Marguerite put the pastry down. "Did I miss a holiday? Is today Obvious Day?"

"No, it is I-care-about-my-friend-and-want-to-make-sure-she-is-okay day." Aracely's dark brown gaze met hers. "Are you okay?"

"Of course. Why wouldn't I be?"

Aracely crossed her arms over her chest, her expression the definition of skepticism.

"It's all good. In fact, yesterday I received this month's wine quality analysis from the lab, and everything looks great. It's such a relief since I wasn't sure—"

"And what did the analysis of the kiss with your boss say? Panties melted or merely socks knocked off?"

Marguerite choked on her coffee. "I told you, he fired me before we kissed. Technically, he wasn't my boss."

"Right. The game you two play. Technically, the game does not change reality. You know this, yes?"

"And we're back to Obvious Day." Marguerite bit an end off the cruller. "I know that. It just…"

"Makes it easier to not have a conversation."

"I told him we didn't need one. And we don't. Yes, he signs my paycheck and I like him—"

"Enough to kiss him several times—"

"Twice. But we both know it's not going to go any further." Marguerite put down the rest of the doughnut. She couldn't really taste it anyway. "He's still figuring out his relationship with Nico, and he thinks parking Nico here at St. Isadore is the solution. It's not, but he has to learn that for himself. But it's obvious his first priority is his company and the Silicon Valley business scene. And I'm not leaving St. Isadore."

"What if he sells it?"

Marguerite stared at Aracely. "What do you mean?"

Aracely shrugged. "You said it yourself. He bought St. Isadore as a place to put Nico while he is busy elsewhere. What if circumstances change and Nico does not stay here? Evan would sell it, no?"

"He bought St. Isadore to be a going business. Plus, there's the event. You know, the one you've been hired to plan."

"But is that not what you said he does? Sells his companies?" Aracely put her doughnut down. "Have you made any progress in finding the ledger?"

"No. I've searched the winery from top to bottom several times now. And I doubt it's in the owner's residence. I looked there after Linus died and besides, he never took business documents out of the office." Marguerite shivered despite the apartment's warmth. Evan wouldn't divest St. Isadore. Would he?

If only she had found the ledger. She knew she should have demanded a signed agreement from the beginning, but Linus prided himself on his old-fashioned values. He insisted his word was his bond and she'd had no reason to doubt him until...well, until she did. It hurt to believe

he took advantage of her good faith, even going so far
as to create a record, but with no intention of following
through and turning the vineyard over to her.

She could still hear the jeers of Linus's great-nephews. Why would he agree to give his young female assistant ownership of the winery's premier vineyard?
If Marguerite wasn't paid a fair wage for her services
while Linus was alive, that was her problem, not theirs.

If the ledger hadn't shown up by now, it probably
never would. Which meant Linus threw it away or otherwise destroyed it. Tears pricked her eyes.

She took a sip of coffee and decided to change tack
before her memories led her deep down a disquieting
rabbit hole. "Have you spoken to your family about
staying in California instead of returning to Santiago?"

Aracely laughed. "Perhaps the reason I know you
need to have a talk with Evan is because I am avoiding
my own with my parents."

She rose from her chair. "I have to run. Talk later?"

"Of course. And thanks. For everything."

"*Claro, po*. Always." She waved and left the apartment.

The room was still after Aracely left. Too still. And
Marguerite's thoughts about Evan came roaring back.

It was clear their current status was unworkable. For
her peace of mind, if not her peace of libido. As she saw
it, there were three choices moving forward. One, she
quit working at St. Isadore, for real. Two, Evan stopped
coming to St. Isadore. Three…they had that conversation after all and established new ground rules, as it was
obvious the original rules would continue to be broken
every time they were alone together.

The first option was out. She loved working at St.
Isadore. And now she had far more responsibility than

she'd had as Linus's assistant. She called the shots when it came to winemaking, now that Casper was gone. Evan gave her free reign to be as creative as she wanted to be. He may hold the purse strings, but when it came to the winery, she called the shots.

She doubted Evan would agree to the second option. Nor did she want him to.

That left the third. But while she was excited— well, excited and scared—to explore more fully the chemistry that exploded every time Evan was near, she was petrified to tell him her entire history with St. Isadore. Would he suspect her interest in him was driven solely by the prospect of material gain?

She'd like to think not. But then, once upon a time she believed Casper was a trusted mentor and Linus supported her aspirations. She was wrong on both accounts. Did she dare trust Evan? Not only with her future and her family's legacy, but with all of her?

Maybe she didn't need to own the vineyard to fulfill her ambition. Maybe what she had right now was enough. Enough that she could still achieve her long-cherished goal of restoring the Delacroix name in winemaking and, perhaps, create a new dream. One that involved Evan Fletcher, his dark curly hair and broad shoulders and firm lips she wanted to kiss for hours on end and...

She stood up. She should get dressed and start her day. She didn't need to puzzle everything out right away. Evan was in San Francisco and would probably stay there until the following weekend. She had plenty of time to—

A rap at her front door interrupted her thoughts. "Now you knock?" she called, crossing to open the door. "Why not use your key—oh."

Evan stood on the front step. She drank in his appearance. He wore khaki trousers and a hunter green button-down shirt that turned his hazel pupils to deep jade. But lines of exhaustion furrowed his forehead.

"I thought a knock was more polite." He glanced at her, then quickly looked away toward the colorful potted plants that lined the courtyard. "Sorry. I should have called first."

"I thought you were Aracely. She was just here." She clutched her robe closed at the throat. Why was he at her apartment? On a Saturday morning?

He nodded, scratching the back of his neck, his eyes still averted. "This was probably a bad idea. I'll go, give you your privacy."

"Wait—I thought you were playing golf this weekend. With the supplier. Is something wrong?"

"No. Yes. I mean, I was supposed to play, but…" He took in her bare legs, his gaze lingering on the sash loosely tied at her waist. "After yesterday and we… You know what? Let's discuss it later."

They could. They could talk in her office on Monday. She could offer to quit or he could fire her temporarily, although Aracely was right. The game didn't change reality.

Or she could put the third option she had just been mulling into motion. Now.

She let go of her robe and opened the door wider. "Come in. There are still a few doughnuts left, and I can make fresh coffee."

"I don't think that's a good idea. Maybe when you're dressed."

"Please. You're right. We should talk. We need to set some new rules."

"Right now, with you looking that way, there won't

be much talking. The only rules I want to discuss is how to break them. For good."

His words were all it took. She let go of the door, winding her arms around his neck to bring his head to hers. Then she kissed him, hard, and let go. "Great. I feel the same way. Now, will you please come inside before we scandalize the neighbors?"

He smiled for the first time since he'd arrived as he pulled her tight against him. "Nico spent the night at Gabi's, so I'm the only neighbor. Scandalize me as much as you want."

"That's the plan," she whispered against his lips. And she kissed him again. Softly this time. Taking her time. Inviting him to stay and explore, much like he had the night before. Only this time...

His lips were still, just for a second. Then he opened to her and she wasn't sure who was kissing who, who was taking the lead and who was eagerly following. Tension pooled in her center, melting her limbs, and she locked her arms around his neck so she wouldn't be prone on the courtyard flagstones.

His mouth was hot, insistent. One of his hands traveled from her waist to wrap around the back of her head. She relaxed into his hold, intent on making him relinquish the rigid control she could sense was keeping him from fully letting go. Unlike their earlier kisses, there was no reason to hold back. No need to pretend.

She rose up on her bare toes, her robe falling open, her breasts and stomach pressing against him. She wriggled, seeking out the hard ridge in his trousers. "This is what I wanted to happen the first time I kissed you."

"This is what I wanted when you fell on top of me in the kitchen," he growled, and she laughed as he nuzzled her ear, her throat. Then his hand slipped inside her robe to find her right breast, his thumb weaving worshipful circles around it, and laughter was forgotten.

"If we don't go to my bedroom right now—" She gasped as his hand moved lower, brushing over her abdomen, trailing lightning storms in its wake—"I'm going to scream and scare anyone out in the vineyards."

He laughed against the side of her neck. "A bed might be nice." He reached around her for the doorknob. Then he frowned.

"What's wrong?" She turned in his arms and tried the door herself. "What the—? How is this possible?" But even as she asked the question, she knew how. She hadn't unlocked the door from the inside. They were locked out.

"I don't suppose you have a hidden key out here?" he asked. "An open window?"

She shook her head. "I don't suppose you have your set of keys?"

"I've dreamed of being in your bed, but only if invited. So no, don't have them on me."

"Argh." She rattled the door again.

"It's okay. This is probably for the best, all things considered. I'll go to the main residence and get the key ring. Then you can get dressed, we can go out for breakfast and talk." He lifted her right hand to his mouth and pressed a kiss into her palm.

But she'd be damned if she let this encounter be swept under the rug. Let it be chalked up to "we're just friendly work colleagues who sometimes get carried away but then remember who we are."

"I've already had breakfast." She caught his gaze, insisting that he really see her. "I want you."

Still keeping her gaze locked on his, she undid the

belt of her robe, letting it fall open. Then she shrugged it off her shoulders. It pooled at her feet, leaving her bare.

His gaze darkened despite the bright morning sun. In his throat, his Adam's apple bobbed.

"Did you know I'm the happiest when I'm outdoors? It's my favorite place to be." She stretched, her arms reaching to the blue sky above.

The air shifted. She could smell the change. "It's beginning to be my favorite, too," he said, his gaze drinking her in, lingering on her breasts, the curve of her stomach, the nest of curls at the juncture of her thighs.

She smiled, enjoying his reaction, and leaned up to kiss him anew. Then she pulled back slightly.

He quirked an eyebrow. "Second thoughts after all?"

"No. But before we go further, maybe we should discuss past partners? Healthwise?"

He shook his head. "Last real date I had was before I bought St. Isadore. Clean bill since."

"I haven't been on date in over a year. All good at my last exam." She kissed Evan, and he groaned into her mouth, their tongues exploring and tangling as she unbuttoned his shirt and tugged it free of his trousers. Her hands traveled across his lightly furred chest, her fingers rubbing across his flat nipples before finding the trail that led down his six-pack abs to the waistband of his khakis. Then they traveled lower and she gasped, gulping in air as she learned the size and the heat and the steely hardness contained within.

Soon his hands were helping hers and before she knew it, he had divested himself of his clothes. She stepped back, for only a second, so her eyes could enjoy what her touch already told her: it was the most magnificent erection she'd ever witnessed. Then she fell to her knees, her robe acting as a cushion, and took him into her mouth.

Intimacy came in many forms. But of all the acts possible between partners, she enjoyed this one especially. Not just because she controlled Evan's pleasure, using her mouth's heat and wetness and pressure to discover what made him gasp, what made him groan, what made him dig his nails into his palms and strain not to lose all control. Not because she could also use her hands to caress and stroke, pinch and pull, learning what combination made him moan her name as a profane prayer.

But because it was the most personal and private place to learn his scent.

Evan overran her senses, bringing them achingly alive. She ran her tongue along his length then suckled on the satiny head, marveling as he swelled even more, his harsh breaths music to her ears. His hand fisted in her loose hair, and he gently urged her up.

"My turn," he said simply, kissing her deeply while guiding her to the courtyard bench.

She'd always loved the bench. It was one of the things she'd missed most after Linus's nephews threw her out of the carriage house. Trellises of grapevines surrounded it on three sides, meeting high overhead to make an arch. It was a favorite place to read or daydream or even take a nap.

But when Evan tugged her down to sit on the bench, then knelt before her, using his mouth…

Dear heavens, his mouth. His talented, wicked, relentless mouth. He lapped and encircled and sucked, following her gasped directions, learning her cues, varying the rhythm and intensity, demanding she soar higher, faster. She tried to hold back, to savor the unreality of the moment—this was Evan between her legs, Evan worshipping her with his tongue, his fingers—but the pressure kept building and building until she had no choice but to come apart, every molecule fizzing and sparking.

Evan guided her through the waves, gentle now, slower, and when she could finally open her eyes, he was there, holding her, gathering her into his lap as he sat on the bench, his shirt as his cushion. He had the most enormous, self-satisfied grin on his face.

"Proud of yourself, aren't you," she muttered, but she was aware she probably wore the same expression.

"You have no idea," he breathed in her ear.

"I hope you have a condom in your wallet." She snuggled against his chest, the sunshine warm on her bare back.

"As a matter of fact—"

The sound of a car's tires on the gravel drive leading to the carriage house penetrated the fog of pleasure blanketing Marguerite's senses. She hopped off Evan's lap. "Car. Someone is here."

He immediately understood. Bending down, he handed Marguerite her robe and then pulled on his trousers. He had one shoe on and was searching for the other when they heard the gate to the courtyard opening. Marguerite sprang in front of him to intercept their guest.

Aracely came around the corner, her gaze locked on her phone. When she looked up, she froze in place for a minute, then gave a tiny smirk that gradually grew to encompass her entire expression.

"Hi," Marguerite said, begging Aracely with her gaze not to mention the obvious. "Meeting over so soon?"

Aracely cleared her throat. "Did I leave my portfolio here this morning? I seem to have misplaced it. Hello, Evan."

"Hi," he returned, putting his second shoe on.

"I don't think you left anything. Or at least I didn't notice," Marguerite said.

"You do seem rather…preoccupied." She glanced at the door and raised her eyebrows in a question.

Marguerite continued to stare her down.

"May I look for it?" Aracely said. "Inside?"

"Oh, sure." Marguerite exhaled. The key. Aracely had a key. "Be my guest."

Aracely's narrowed gaze ping-ponged between Marguerite and Evan. "I will," she said slowly. "I will be inside for fifteen minutes."

"Okay," Marguerite agreed. "Take your time."

"The time is not for me. It is for you, so you know how long you have to make yourselves more presentable." Aracely swept past them and unlocked the door. She turned around before entering. "There are socks underneath the bench and what appears to be boxer shorts in the trellis."

Aracely shut the door behind her with a decided slam. At the sound, the nervous giggles Marguerite had been struggling to contain broke free, and she collapsed with laughter. Evan joined in, his strong arms holding her up when she would have melted to the ground, and the courtyard rang with mirth.

"This was not how I anticipated my morning to go," Marguerite finally said, wiping tears from her eyes.

"I didn't anticipate it. Fantasized about it, maybe. But the reality was better."

Marguerite swallowed the last of her laughs and straightened up. "So. Um. Door is open," she finished.

"I see that."

She pulled her robe tight around her and tied the belt with a double knot. A ridiculous move, considering what they had just been up to. But she appreciated the armor, flimsy though it may be. "I can make the coffee I offered earlier."

"Marguerite." Her name was both a caress and a warning.

She glanced up from the contemplation of her bare feet to catch his gaze. She read—oh, she read so many things in his eyes. Desire and hope and happiness, but also not a little trepidation. It matched the apprehension threatening to swamp her stomach. "Yes?"

"About that conversation." He retrieved the missing articles of clothing and stuffed them in his pocket. "I've been thinking about next steps."

Her heart began to race again, but this time not only due to his physical proximity. *Right. The conversation.* "You mean other than the one we just took?"

"Including the one we just took. You were pretty clear about not engaging in personal relationships at work. Are you okay with this?"

"Pretty sure you could tell how okay I was."

He smiled. "I mean about continuing to work together. I don't want people to get the wrong idea about us. That I coerced you into this."

She loved that he cared about her reputation. She loved him—no. She couldn't fall in love with him. Or at least, she could never let him know it. She was aware of the power differential in their relationship. Until she could prove her claim on the Delacroix vineyard, Evan was the ultimate arbiter of St. Isadore's future—although when it came to making day-to-day decisions about the winery, he ceded control to her. But if he knew how much she was starting to care about him, she would be utterly vulnerable.

"Or maybe people will say you're the victim, that I'm

chasing you for your money," she said lightly. "We can't control what others think. But we're also not wrong to worry."

"Which means…?"

"Wine is big business but a small industry. We should continue to keep our distance at work and especially when we're around other people. But that's not too hard…" She reached up and kissed him, because she truly meant no sting in her next words, but he finished them for her.

"That's not too hard because I'm rarely here." His mouth twisted. "Speaking of—" He stopped when Aracely appeared in the doorway, a leather portfolio case held high in one hand while the other covered her eyes.

"I found it," Aracely said. "May I safely exit now?"

Marguerite laughed. "We're decent. It's safe to go into the courtyard again."

"Well…define *decent*," Evan said, a devilish light in his gaze. Marguerite elbowed him in the side.

"I do not want to know." Aracely let the hand covering her eyes drop. "But Evan, if you are sticking around, at some point the three of us should sit down and go over the latest plans for the Global Leader Summit event."

"How about Monday afternoon?" he suggested.

"Monday?" Marguerite turned to him. "You're not heading back to the city?"

He caressed her cheek with the back of his right hand. "The deal we're pursuing is currently on hold. The investor I told you about, Angus Horne? He had a family emergency. I told Luke I was going to work from here until we can get back to the negotiating table."

You're going to work remotely from here? Where is Evan Fletcher and what did you do to him?"

He shrugged; his body language was the perfect picture of casual indifference, while his gaze was anything but that. She shivered. "I want to learn more about St. Isadore and wine. Someone suggested that might even help me get to know my brother."

"I can't think of anything that would be better for St. Isadore."

"Just St. Isadore?"

She shook her head, not trusting herself to speak.

She wound her arms around his neck and kissed him in reply. As the kiss deepened and his grip tightened on her robe, she heard Aracely's departing laughter ring through the courtyard. Then Evan commanded her full attention, and her senses could discern only him.

Seven

Marguerite reclined on the new leather sectional sofa, sinking into the overstuffed cushions as she watched Evan and Nico argue over who deserved the last piece of the meat lover's pizza, ending with Nico offering to arm wrestle Evan for the spoils. Gabi caught her gaze and they shared an eye roll and head shake of commiseration over the men's antics as the match began. But Marguerite also couldn't help grinning. Evan and Nico competing to see who could cheat the most at arm wrestling was not something she'd ever expected to witness.

It was Friday pizza night at the owner's residence, a tradition that had sprung up shortly after Evan started working from St. Isadore. Nico had taken advantage of Evan's increased presence by asking for weekly meetings with Evan and Marguerite to discuss his work at the winery. They'd quickly determined the meeting required refreshments, which then morphed into ordering take-out pizza. At the first meal, Evan had brought out beer and Marguerite had recoiled in horror. But then she'd decided to use the occasions to teach Evan more about wine. He might still prefer beer, but at least now he could hold a conversation whenever he ran into another winery owner.

She still couldn't fully believe Evan had made good on his stated intent to work from St. Isadore. He spent his days holed up in his home office, emerging only to sign off on requests from Marguerite or the director of operations. But the nights...the nights, he definitely made his presence known. To her. At her apartment. On more than one occasion, taking advantage of the guest chair in her office. Even in the pickup truck Marguerite drove to meet with vineyard managers and walk the grapevines.

The memory of what his mouth and fingers had done to her under the open sky, with nothing but green leaves and budding fruit all around them, caused her to shift on the cushions. Evan glanced up from his match with Nico. When their gazes met he smiled, the devilish quirk of his lips telling her he knew what she was thinking. He always knew, but then Marguerite's thoughts were rather predictable ever since the morning in the courtyard.

"I win!" Nico shouted. Evan's arm was pinned to the coffee table.

Evan kept his gaze on Marguerite. "I had my eyes on a greater prize." He passed the paper plate to Nico then took a slice of margherita pizza for himself. "Enjoy."

His elbow came perilously close to the open wine bottle on the coffee table as he levered himself from his seated position on the rug. "Careful!" Marguerite reached down and moved the bottle. "This is good stuff."

He joined her on the sofa. "Then, we should finish drinking it."

"First, pop quiz. Why did we have the Cabernet Sauvignon with the meat lover's pizza?"

Evan thought for a minute. "Tannins," he replied. "The tannins offset the fat in the meat."

"And a fruit-forward wine like this particular Cab Sav pairs well with the flavor."

"I'm good at pairings," he whispered in her ear when the younger couple wasn't looking. "Quiz me more when we're alone."

Gabi finished consolidating the remaining pizza into one box and closed the lid. "We're meeting friends from my internship program." She patted the lid and grinned. "They thank you for the sustenance."

"Speaking of interns…" Nico drawled. He and Gabi exchanged a glance heavy with meaning.

Marguerite sat straight up. Evan's body language also shifted, from relaxed to attentive. "Something you two have to tell us?" he asked.

"Well…" Nico kept his gaze on the wine bottle on the coffee table. "I've been thinking. I like working here. With you," he said to Marguerite. "I'm really enjoying my rotation in the wine tasting room."

"I hear a but," Evan said.

"But." He took a deep breath. "Gabi is returning to Cornell in August. And the more I've gotten to know the other interns, the more I think… I need to go back to college." He grinned, if a bit sheepishly. "I really want to go back, despite not giving it my all before. I've decided I want to work in hospitality. For a big luxury chain. So I need those business classes after all."

Evan answered his brother with a grin of his own. "That's terrific."

"I'll still be at St, Isadore for the rest of the summer. And there are a lot of details to work out. I'm not sure Boston University will take me back, but I'm going to try."

"Nico can finish his general education courses at a junior college and then transfer to another four-year school, too," Gabi interjected.

"And that junior college wouldn't happen to be near Cornell, would it?" Evan teased.

Gabi and Nico exchanged another look. "A lot of things to work out," Nico repeated. "But maybe."

Gabi looked at her phone. "We better run if we want to catch up with the others. See you both later."

Marguerite managed to wave goodbye, still struggling to process Nico's words. Evan poured what was left of the wine into their nearly empty glasses. "Cheers," he said, holding his up. "Here's to having the place to ourselves for the next several hours."

She could only blink at him in response.

He lowered his arm. "Something wrong?"

"No. I mean, what could be wrong?"

He searched her expression. "You don't think Nico should return to college?"

She shook her head. "It's a great idea. He's doing a spectacular job in the wine tasting room. Guests love him. He'd be a great restaurant or hotel manager, if that's what he wants."

"Then what is it? You're biting your lower lip."

Dammit, he always could read her tells. "It's just…" She hesitated, unsure how to put her initial burst of panic into words. "Well, if Nico isn't here to learn the winery business…would you still need to own a winery? We're a few years away from turning a sizable profit, and you've been spending a lot of money on something that isn't your passion."

Now it was Evan's turn to blink at her. "That's a new thought to me," he finally said. "On several fronts."

"Oh? Which ones?"

"To be honest, I never dreamed Nico would want to finish his degree. So, I haven't considered St. Isadore without him. And the second..." He shrugged. "I spend money on businesses to make money. Passion doesn't enter into the equation."

"What about Medevco?"

"I want Medevco to succeed, and right now that means a lot of long hours to put out hot fires. But am I passionate? Not the same way you are about wine."

"When I was eight, I announced to my parents I was going to be a winemaker." And she would one day restore their family name to preeminence in the field. "Of course, I had never tasted it. But I knew. What did you want to do as a child?"

"Make lots of money. My parents fought over bills at the end of the month. Then Nico came along and the fights got worse. Don't get me wrong, they didn't fight all the time. But the end of the month was rough, especially if my dad's customers didn't pay on time." He was silent for a moment, his gaze falling on his wine glass. "Anyway." He put it down and turned to face her. "Speaking of Medevco, Luke called just before Nico and Gabi showed up with the pizza."

Her stomach, which had started flopping about the time Nico made her announcement, now plummeted to the ground. "Angus Horne is back from his emergency?"

"Not yet, but he will be soon. We need to be ready. And Luke and I aren't agreeing on what ready means.

Some discussions need to be held face-to-face." He pulled her into his arms and nuzzled her neck, his five-o'clock shadow pleasantly scraping her skin.

She laughed despite the trepidation starting to crawl down her back. "I hope you're not using the same approach on Luke that you use on me."

You're the only one I want to have full body conversations with." He leaned back, his gaze searching hers. "I'm leaving for the city on Monday, and probably won't be back until the summit."

His pronouncement hit her harder than it should. Of course he would return to San Francisco. Medevco was his true priority.

It hadn't escaped her notice that he didn't really answer her question about St. Isadore's future after Nico left. Nor that his story about his parents placed a premium on making money from his businesses. She didn't have nearly enough money saved to buy the vineyard she was owed outright. Asking him to sell it to her for a below market price—much less give it to her a gift—seemed...crass.

"I'll miss you," she said, the words escaping her lips before she could stop them from forming.

His gaze traced the contours of her face. "Then come with me."

"To San Francisco? So close to the event?"

"You and Aracely have the party nailed down. I'm not worried. Besides—" and he grinned, that roguish expression that always made her heart beat far faster than it should "—there are no prying eyes and ears in the city."

She grabbed her glass off the table and took a large sip, for once not tasting the spice and ripe berry note in her wine. "To be clear, Nico spends so much time at Gabi's, that's not necessarily an issue here."

He made an impatient movement. "But wouldn't it be nice not to worry? Plus, next Friday there's a charity gala I need to attend. And I don't have a date yet."

He leaned over and whispered in her ear, the low timbre of his voice causing her to shiver. "I'll leave on Monday, get as much work done as possible. You drive down on Thursday and become intimately acquainted with every room in my house. When we're tired of my place, we'll explore the city and then go to the gala on Friday night."

He did make it sound enticing. "Tell me more about the gala. Who will be there?"

"Silicon Valley types. Bay Area society types. The types that like to dress up and go to parties." He shrugged. "It's to raise money for local nonprofits, so it attracts a broad range of people."

"Wine industry types?" She kept her tone light.

"Ah." He nodded. "We'll say you're representing St. Isadore, to check out what's being served at the gala and keep tabs on the competition."

At St. Isadore, they could pretend the outside world didn't exist. Pretend they followed the new rules they established: they were strictly work colleagues from nine to five, while after hours they were friends with very specific and pleasurable benefits.

Pretend she wasn't falling in love with him.

Pretend she wasn't petrified he would decide he didn't want St. Isadore after Nico went back to college and dump it and her, leaving her back to square one yet again.

"Come to the city," he said against her lips. "I don't want to go two weeks without seeing you. You can take

the time off from work. I'll arrange it with the boss."
He wagged his eyebrows.

She laughed, helpless to resist. And maybe it wasn't
a bad idea to visit San Francisco. To be part of his life
in the city, if only for a few days. And perhaps to use
the time to persuade him that St. Isadore was worth
keeping, was worth his investment. "I'll have to drive
back Saturday morning. Aracely and I have some last-
minute meetings with vendors."

He picked up his glass and drained it before turning
so he faced her on the sectional. She shifted to match his
position, her light cotton skirt riding up and revealing a
portion of her upper thigh as she moved. With his right
hand, he began to trace abstract designs on her newly
bared skin. "You'll have fun beyond your expectations."

His fingers brushed higher and she closed her eyes,
the better to experience the swirling fire his touch so
expertly kindled. "I can't imagine how you can exceed
them when you've already set them very high."

"Let's see how high they can go." Then he kissed
her, his firm mouth closing over hers and demanding
she concentrate on only the pleasure he made her feel.

She gave in to his kiss, and the panic rattling her
nerves was overtaken by the rising tide of arousal. Evan
wasn't Casper and he wasn't Linus. She didn't need
to fear having the rug pulled out from underneath her
hard-fought goals again. Borrowing trouble only caused
stress for the borrower.

But a tendril of trepidation curled up at the base of
her spine and refused to go away.

The drive to San Francisco was both interminable
and over far too soon for Marguerite's nerves. On the
one hand, she would get her first glimpse of Evan's

life outside St. Isadore, meet his friends, gain a deeper insight into what made him, well, Evan. On the other hand, they would be together for the first time without being wrapped in their St. Isadore cocoon.

Evan lived in Cole Valley, at the top of the hill, adjacent to Golden Gate Park. The neighborhood was a mixture of Victorian, midcentury and contemporary styles, with his house definitely falling into the last category. The sleek glass, metal and cement four-story structure stood out for its elegant if severe facade, all squared angles and hard surfaces. She marveled at it through her windshield as she pulled her car, dusty from the road, into the pristine driveway.

Using the app Evan had installed on her phone, she unlocked the towering frosted-glass front door. Inside, the house was even more modern. And more impressive, with understated but obviously expensive furnishings that reminded her of TV remodeling shows featuring celebrity residences. No wonder he was less than complimentary about the dated—if still grand—decor of St. Isadore.

She put down her bag in the expansive main living quarters, which stretched the entire length of the second level, the floor-to-ceiling windows offering views of the city with the Golden Gate Bridge in the distance. The kitchen, with its sleek European appliances, flowed into the dining area, which was separated from the main room only by a fireplace that appeared to almost float in the middle of the room. The entire space was big enough to fit her apartment with room left over.

The sound of the front door opening made her jump. She whirled around from taking in the view, expecting to see Evan. Instead, it was woman, around Evan's age, with precision-cut hair framing her high cheekbones and piercing dark eyes. Her sharply tailored suit probably cost more than the entire contents of Marguerite's closet. "Oh, you're here already," the newcomer said. "Good."

Marguerite's heart thumped hard against her ribcage. Who was she? Where was Evan? "And you are...?"

"Didn't Evan tell you? No, of course not. Men." The woman rolled her eyes. "On the other hand, he and Luke have been busy, so perhaps it's forgivable. I'm Finley Smythe. A friend of Evan's—well, my brother Grayson is his friend, but Evan knew I was in town, and he asked me to look after you." She held out her right hand to shake.

Marguerite looked at Finley's hand but didn't offer her own. "Marguerite Delacroix. I wasn't aware I needed a nanny."

Finley smiled, displaying even, white teeth, and dropped her hand. "We're going to get along fine. And of course you don't need a babysitter. But Evan thought you might want a shopping companion for something to wear to the gala tomorrow."

"I don't understand." She'd borrowed an evening gown from Aracely. "I should be set. Evan knows that." She took out her phone to call him.

Finley shook her head. "He's in a closed-door meeting, will be until this evening. I know, it's annoying. My brother is in the same meeting, even though it's vital I talk to him about upcoming events. So, since I can't move forward until Grayson is liberated and you don't need to go shopping, want to show me your masquerade costume?"

"Masquerade? What masquerade?" Marguerite's head swam. It had been a long drive, and she was hungry, thirsty and overtired. Maybe she'd misheard the other woman.

Finley's gaze narrowed. "The gala. It's a masked ball."

Marguerite continued to stare at her.

Finley reached out and patted her shoulder in commiseration.

"Men." Several hours later, Marguerite had a masquerade costume assembled thanks to her companion's strategic knowledge of where to shop for supplies. The gown she'd borrowed from Aracely was a simple long slip of pale gold silk when on the hanger, but on Marguerite, it became a marvel of draping, emphasizing her curves. Taking her cue from the color of the dress—and her work—she decided the theme of her costume would be champagne. Finley found a stole of pale cream chiffon in a local boutique, and a helpful assistant at a craft store attached oversized pearls and translucent baubles to its surface. When wound around Marguerite's shoulders and trailing down her arms, the decorations resembled bubbles rising to the top of a champagne flute. Smaller pearls and clear beads decorated the simple mask, and for her hair, they rummaged through the marked-down items at a party store and found a headband with a large paper champagne cork on top, left over from New Year's Eve.

Finley also persuaded Marguerite to buy cosmetics in various shades of gold, including glitter for her face and body. When they arrived back at Evan's house, Marguerite took her newly purchased bounty into the powder room off the living space to experiment with different looks. She then slipped on the dress to get Finley's opinion, which she had come to value during their marathon shopping expedition. "Ready?" she called through the closed door.

"Ready," replied Finley.

Marguerite stepped out. Finley clapped her hands. "Perfect," she pronounced.

But Marguerite didn't hear her. Her focus flew past Finley to alight on the person coming through the front door.

Evan stood in his foyer, his gaze locked on the vision that was Marguerite. He thought her beautiful at any time of day or night, seated behind her desk in her customary trousers and blouse or sporting jeans and a T-shirt covered in dirt from inspecting the vineyards. And of course, Marguerite in his bed, wearing nothing but her wicked grin and the light of passion in her eyes, was his favorite sight in the world.

But now she glowed, as the setting sun poured its amber rays through the windows, lighting her from behind. Her gown outlined her curves, the fabric almost appearing molten as it skimmed and dipped over her skin. Just fifteen minutes ago, he had been irritable and tired, thanks to a long day spent in a windowless conference room not making any progress on the negotiations. Now—now Marguerite would be lucky if that dress stayed on her for more than five minutes.

And from the way her mouth hung slightly open, her gaze warm and welcoming, she knew it, too.

"This is my cue to go," he heard Finley say. At least he assumed it was Finley. He hadn't taken his eyes off Marguerite to confirm the other woman's presence. "I'm not going to the gala, so this is farewell. Nice meeting you, Marguerite. I had fun playing fairy godmother. I'll have to find a way to do it again." Finley patted him on the arm as she passed by. "Don't bother seeing me out."

"Bye, Finley," Marguerite said. "Thank you for everything."

"Don't let him rip the dress after all my hard work," Finley called, and he heard the front door open and close.

He closed the distance between him and Marguerite in seconds flat. But when he would have taken her in his arms, she held up a hand and stopped him. "The gala is a masquerade," she said. "Were you going to tell me before we arrived?"

"It's a masquerade? Huh." He assumed it was black tie, like all the other galas he had to attend for business. Then he squinted at the silly party hat in her dark hair. "Is that a cork?"

"I'm champagne." She did a slow twirl, the silk of her dress lifting to show off her toned calves.

"You're intoxicating, all right." He made another attempt to draw her close, but she evaded his grasp.

"Finley will kill me if I let you destroy my outfit." She removed the headband and took off the filmy piece of fabric she wore draped around her shoulders. "Okay...now. But mind the dress. It's Aracely's."

He didn't need another invitation. He had dreamed of her mouth all day, to the point that Luke had made him the presenter so he would be forced to pay attention at the meeting. The heat and the wetness, the thrust of her tongue as she played with his, the way she bit gently, then suckled on his lower lip. He made his dreams a reality as his hands, jealous of the silk caressing the curves beneath, traced paths across her back, held her waist, cupped her rear and brought her tight against his increasingly impatient erection.

She pulled back slightly to grin at him, her lips red and swollen, her gaze hot and bright. "Hello. I take it you're glad to see me." She wriggled against him, and he had to count to ten backward before he could respond.

"Happy to continue to show you how much," he growled, but when he would have captured her mouth with his anew, she started to laugh. "What is it?" he asked.

"You have glitter all over your face," she snort-giggled. "In your hair, too. And on your shirt. I think it was on my hands."

No wonder she glowed. This close, he could see tiny metallic sparkles shining all over her, from her dark tresses to the shadowy valley revealed by the deep V neckline of her dress.

"Sorry, it's a pain to get rid of." She brushed at his shirt, leaving more glitter behind than she removed.

He caught her hands in his. "I have a plan."

He led her to the staircase that connected the main living floor with the bedrooms above and urged her to go first, admiring how her dress clung to her rear. Now he was going off script for the evening. He had a carefully orchestrated itinerary, everything planned and ordered to dazzle Marguerite. Drinks at a speakeasy bar, tiny and dark and private. Dinner at a Michelin-starred restaurant where he had arranged for the sommelier to bring out a bottle of Cabernet Sauvignon from St. Isadore as a surprise. Wandering the city after dinner while exchanging bites of handcrafted ice cream from one of the city's premier small-batch creameries. Then home, to—

Home. He'd never thought of the word as it applied to him. Sure, he owned residences. Two at the moment. But they were places to store his clothes and grab a few hours of sleep between work and meetings. He'd bought this place for its investment value, and the clean, modern aesthetic appealed to him. But it had come fully furnished and he never thought twice about changing the decor.

What would it be like to have a home, not just a house?

Especially if Marguerite were by his side as he turned off the lights each night. Across from him at the dining room table. Bustling in comfortable silence while they made meals together. Holding the hand of a little girl with dark curls who clung to his fingers with her other hand.

It was a nice vision. A good one. But homes were not for the likes of him. He needed to be able to pivot quickly, take advantage of opportunities, build his companies. He would never be a mow-the-lawn-on-Saturday kind of guy. He couldn't be and still be able to provide for Nico and his grandparents the way he wanted. The way he had to.

Then Marguerite reached the top of stairs and turned back to catch his gaze, her eyes glinting with mischief and passion. She slowly raised her hands to her shoulders and, her fingers lingering on her skin, pushed the thin dress straps down her arms. The silk slipped and fell away, revealing the perfect globes of her breasts, tipped with rosy pebbled peaks. "Which way to your bedroom?" she asked.

All thought fled. "First things first," he growled and took her hand, leading her to his bedroom suite and its immense bathroom.

She gasped. "This is bigger than my bedroom and living room put together."

He took out his phone, grimacing because his jeans were far too tight, and pushed a few buttons on his home app. The lights dimmed as the shades rolled up, revealing a wall of continuous glass and the city lights twinkling in the valley below.

Marguerite held her dress up to her chest. "Wow. But holy exhibitionist, Batman."

He crossed to stand behind her, his hands coming up to cover hers and gently urge her to let the dress fall, down to her waist, and then farther, to the heated tiled floor. "The glass is treated," he murmured in her ear, taking a second to bite, ever so gently, her earlobe. She shivered and pressed her back against him. "We can look out. No one can look in."

"Then, you're overdressed." She turned around in his arms, stepping out of the pooled dress and her panties. He helped her make equally quick work of his clothes. But when she took his erection in her hands, he gathered up his self-control and moved out of her grasp.

"Glitter," he said, and drew her to the shower that occupied the far end of the room.

Evan never had any particular fantasies about showers. They were utilitarian, meant for removing the day's grime. As long as there was enough water, showers didn't occupy his thoughts.

That was all changing.

He turned the shower on, the recirculation system ensuring immediate hot water. "Right temperature?" he asked Marguerite.

She responded by moving past him to stand under the rain-forest spray, her head back and her eyes closed as the water ran over her hair, over the tips of her breasts, rivulets dancing down the curves of her belly, hips, thighs.

He'd never seen anything so achingly beautiful.

Marguerite opened one eye. "You're wearing glitter, too," she said with a slow smile. "You should wash. All over."

He didn't need additional encouragement. He joined her, pulling a washcloth from a basket of fresh ones on the nearby counter. Then he squeezed a good amount of body wash onto the cloth from a decanter mounted on the shower's one tiled wall. "Turn around."

He gently ran the cloth over her back, soaping her skin and then rinsing the suds away. She shivered as he found ticklish spots. Then he filled his hands with shampoo and began to wash her hair, drawing circles on her scalp and letting the wet strands spill through his fingers.

Her breathing became rasps. Her hands flew out to brace herself against the glass wall, her body silhouetted by the city lights.

And she was his. Right now. He almost fell to his knees.

"You've ruined me," she said. "I am never letting anyone else wash my hair." She turned, the hard pebbles of her breasts rising and falling against him. "Let's see if I can ruin you."

She found his erection with her hands, which were slick and slippery with soap. She knew him by now, and he welcomed her knowledge, the steam and the spray and the wet heat surrounding them adding an extra dimension that caused his eyes to roll back in his head far too quickly. He wanted this to last, damn it, but it was hard to think with her clever fingers knowing just where to rub, to pull, to linger. His erection swelled to almost painful dimensions, the pressure becoming unbearable. She was going to ruin him far faster than anticipated—

He blindly reached out, found the valve controls and turned the water off. Marguerite stopped her ministrations, just in time. "What happened?"

"I want to make it to the bed," he ground out. "But first, I have an idea." He tugged her toward the shower bench and had her sit down. Then he unhooked the handheld sprayer from its holder next to the bench and turned a different switch.

The pressure was light, the temperature warm but not too hot. He sat down beside her and pulled her onto his lap, her legs straddling his. Then he pointed the stream of water at them.

At her, specifically. At the beautiful triangle of tangled dark curls between her legs and the delicate exposed flesh underneath. He held her open, finding the spot where the water pressure would be the most appreciated.

He would never tire of hearing her scream his name.

Later that night, after Evan called the restaurant and had his planned menu delivered to his door, after another courier brought some of San Francisco's best hand-crafted ice cream, after they turned Evan's bed into a demolition site of blankets and pillows, Marguerite collapsed against him. He stroked her back, luxuriating in the weight of her, the warmth, the tiny tremors that still shook her. She eventually calmed, her breathing slowing, and when he was pretty sure she was on the threshold of sleep, he settled her gently next to him, finding the covers and pulling them over both of them. She curled into his side with a sigh, her left hand resting on his chest.

Right over his heart.

He kissed the tip of her ear, intending to follow her into slumber. And that's when she spoke. Quietly, so quietly he could tell himself he didn't hear her correctly, that she was sleep-talking, that she didn't mean it. "I love you."

He stilled. "Marguerite?" he whispered, once he had worked up enough moisture into his mouth. "Did you say something?"

"Wha…?" She blinked sleep-filled eyes at him. "I love your bed. Your sheets must have a gazillion thread count." Then her breaths turned into tiny snores. He'd always found her snores—snuffles, really—adorable, but they barely registered.

She'd said she loved him.

So maybe she didn't say what he thought he had heard. But now that the thought was in his head…it would not leave. What if she had said it? What would it mean?

After all, people said they loved all sorts of things, all the time. Baseball, for example. Kittens. His sheets. It was a strongly worded phrase of appreciation, nothing more. There was absolutely no reason why they couldn't continue as they had been, conducting business during the day and having fun after hours.

Then Marguerite shifted, her left leg tangling with his, her tousled hair tickling his skin, and his heart twinged in pleasure-pain at her expression, open and vulnerable in sleep.

He could no longer deny it. She might love his bedding, but he was falling in love with her.

This was a disaster.

When the screen on his phone told him it was 5:00 a.m., he carefully untangled himself from Marguerite and left the bed.

Eight

Marguerite awoke with a start. For a second she didn't know where she was, then she relaxed and sank back into the down-stuffed pillows. San Francisco. Evan's house. And it must still be the middle of the night since the room was so dark. She closed her eyes and prepared to drift back to sleep, her hand reaching out for Evan's comforting bulk—

No Evan.

Now she was fully awake. She turned over and looked at the clock on the bedside table. Eight o'clock? She blinked. That was well past the time she usually woke up. The last thing she remembered was closing her eyes after falling apart in Evan's arms. Well, he'd promised to blow her mind—and he had, wiping it so clean she'd forgotten where she was. The blackout shades covering the floor-to-ceiling windows helped add to the confusion.

There was a note on Evan's pillow that read simply,

"Didn't want to wake you. Come downstairs when you're ready." So she showered and put on the casual sundress she'd packed, and eventually made her way to living area.

Evan sat at the kitchen table, intently focused on the open laptop in front of him. Shaved, showered and dressed in his usual work uniform of button-down shirt and dark jeans, he appeared as if he had been up for hours already. She hesitated on the threshold, not wanting to interrupt him, aware she had just literally tumbled out of bed. It was an odd feeling, as in Napa, she had no trouble making her presence known at any hour of the day.

He looked up and caught her gaze. His intense expression transformed into a grin, although it didn't reach his eyes. "Morning, Sleeping Beauty," he said. "There's fresh coffee in the kitchen. And my housekeeper stocked the pantry with the best pastries in the city. Help yourself."

She nodded, her bright mood upon awaking starting to dim. Sex with Evan was always amazing, and last night hadn't been an exception. In fact, last night their connection seemed to be…one of souls, as well as their physical bodies. She wasn't sure what she expected from him this morning, but it certainly wasn't an Evan who looked like he barely remembered that he'd left her slumbering in his bed

But he was deep in a work crisis, so perhaps he had no choice. She walked farther into the kitchen but wasn't sure where the coffee maker was, much less the pantry. The counters were bare expanses of gray-veined, white marble, the floor-to-ceiling cabinetry finished in dark gray with no visible handles. "Um, Evan? Where is the coffee?"

"Allow me." Evan got up and reached behind her to touch what looked to Marguerite like part of the kitchen's backsplash then returned to the table and his laptop. A door, seamlessly concealed, rolled up to reveal a chrome-and-brushed-metal coffee maker, as sleek as everything else in the room. She would never have found it.

After filling a heavy stoneware mug she found on a rack next to the coffee maker, she clung to its handle. It felt good to hold onto something solid. Evan's house was gorgeous, but it felt like a stage set. Just this side of too perfect to be real.

St. Isadore's cozy if worn decor said, *People live and love and lead full lives here.* Evan's house said, *The photographer from* Architectural Digest *will be here any minute.*

The tendril of trepidation present ever since Nico had announced he was returning to school blossomed anew. She loved St. Isadore despite—or rather because of—its flaws. Could Evan?

Or would he sell it, disposing of a flawed and no longer necessary business asset?

"Hey," she said into the silence. "You're staring at your computer screen as if it's the only thing standing between you and disaster. Work causing a headache?"

She didn't mean it literally. But the more she took in the set position of his jaw, the slightly ashy undertone to his complexion, she wondered if she had discovered the cause of his earlier distance.

"Definitely a pain, but lower. Like, in the ass."

"Sorry. Anything I can do to help?"

"Want to build a valuation model?"

"Does it involve LEGOs?"

A bark of laughter escaped him. "I'd love to see

Luke's face if I walked in with a LEGO kit for our meeting."

"Then, no, I'm afraid that's the only model building I do." Her phone buzzed and she pulled it out of the pocket of her dress. "It's one of the vineyard managers." She answered, "Hi! What's going on?"

Evan watched Marguerite as she spoke into her phone, her dark blue eyes sparkling in the morning sun that streamed in from the floor-to-ceiling windows. But it was her bright smile that lit her face. Lit the room, for that matter, the sunshine a pale source of illumination by contrast. For the first time that he could remember in a long time, he enjoyed being present in the moment, not concentrating on what he had to accomplish and where he needed to be next.

Now that he had a few hours to become accustomed to last night's revelation, Evan could finally stop the thoughts in his head from crashing into each other without a trace of coherency. So, he didn't plan on falling in love with her. He didn't plan on falling in love with anyone at any time. His life was purposefully built to exclude any entanglements that might pull him off track from his goals. He resolutely stayed clear of the door in his mind marked Do Not Enter and surrounded by neon-red flares and bright orange caution cones. The same flares and cones that had blocked off what remained of his parents' car—

No. Not opening that door.

"Talk to you soon. Bye." Marguerite put her phone away and turned to him. Excitement danced in her gaze. "Veraison is starting."

"Very what?"

"Veraison." She pronounced the word with a Parisian

flair. "It's when the grapes start to ripen." She opened up a note-taking app on her phone. "Let me jot down some thoughts while the conversation is still fresh in my head."

"Cool. But...isn't that what grapes are supposed to do? You look like you spotted Santa on your rooftop."

A full smirk twisted her lips. "Yes, wise guy, grapes ripen, and that's exactly why veraison is thrilling. This is our first indication of what kind of harvest we'll have this year, which will determine how much we bottle and when."

He nodded. "Got it. Your French accent is excellent, by the way. But then, it should be, considering your name."

She stopped typing on her phone and looked up. "Oh. About my name..."

He frowned. "What about it?"

She half smiled, half grimaced. "Marguerite is my middle name. My first name is Daisy."

"Your name is Daisy Delacroix?"

"I know, it sounds like a cartoon character."

"I think that's Daisy Duck."

"Same difference. Anyway, when I was a child my parents told me stories about my family's French wine-making history, and I was so enthralled I insisted on being called Marguerite. And Marguerite means *daisy*, so I am using my first name, just in a different form."

"Your parents named you Daisy Daisy?"

"Or Marguerite Marguerite," she pointed out. "But that's my parents for you. They're wonderful, and I love them, but they don't think things through all the way." There was a slightly bitter note to her last words but before he could puzzle it out, she continued, "They moved to Arizona when I was in college, where the only

things they grow are tumbleweeds and rock gardens."
She threw him a look from under her eyelashes. "You
might like them."

He knew the expected response. The proper response. *Sure, I'd love to meet them.* Or even, *Let me
know the next time they are in town.* She would probably be happy with a smile or a wink from him. Something. Anything.

But the alarms next to the sealed door in his mind
started to clang, loudly. It was all he could do to nod
his head. "If you think so."

A faint crease settled between her eyebrows and her
gaze searched his. "Sorry. Parents might not be the
best subject."

He scratched the back of his head. He was usually
the one who read other people. But Marguerite was almost too perceptive when it came to him. It was part
of the reason why he fell for her, despite every intention to fight against it.

He knew his strengths and his weaknesses. He ex-
celled at building successful companies, selling them,
and investing most of the proceeds in his next start-up.
Now Medevco was poised to move to the next level. To
go global in a way his previous enterprises hadn't. And
to do more good. To provide new advances in medical
technology. Better and more cost-efficient equipment.
Expand their gift-giving program and ensure hospitals
and medical centers in underserved communities were
brought up to the same standards as their wealthier
counterparts. But if he took his eyes off the prize, his
goals may never come to fruition.

And buying and selling companies was how he provided for the people in his life, like Nico and his grandparents. He ensured the people he cared about wanted

for nothing. That's how he kept them safe. If he took his focus off—

The alarms in his head sounded again. Louder. He hit a few keys on his laptop, not caring which letters he pressed.

"Parents. Sure. I'd like to meet yours. Someday."

"Someday." She nodded, her smile as bright as ever, but some of the light winked out of her eyes. A sharp arrow of regret hit him square in the chest.

Medevco's crisis wasn't solved, but the company would continue to be his. Marguerite was here, now, and he should spend every minute he could with her, to store up memories for when she would inevitably be gone. He closed his laptop and put it in the bag at his feet. "I'm sorry. I should never have left the bed. Not with you in it."

She lit up, a glorious glow suffusing her from within. "Bed's still there."

He fake-pondered for a minute. "True. But if I remember correctly, I promised to acquaint you with every room in my house." He stood up and crossed to where she stood, cupping her gorgeous face, reveling in the satin smoothness of her skin beneath his touch. "Let's start…" He bent and picked her up, her gasp of surprise joyful in his ear, and placed her so she sat on the table, her legs dangling off the edge. Then he knelt, pushing the skirt of her dress higher, revealing her rounded thighs, the scrap of lace covering her mound. He moved the lace aside and grinned up at her. "Here."

In the end, it was Marguerite who was delayed by work and arrived at the gala long after it started. The world-renowned chef hired to cater the Global Leader Summit wine tasting had a conflict come up with his television filming schedule and was forced to cancel. Marguerite and Aracely worked the phones from their respective places to find a replacement and negotiate the fees. Evan didn't want to leave the house without her, but Marguerite knew it was important to him to be present for the speech by his friend Grayson Monk, who was being honored by the philanthropy hosting the gala. So she sent him off, unbearably handsome in his tuxedo and plain black half-mask, and continued to nail down the details. Thank goodness for Aracely, who was a model of organizational efficiency. She smoothly swapped in the new chef's proposed menu and kitchen requirements without increasing the budget. They finished in time for Marguerite to throw on her champagne costume—foregoing the glitter—and make her way across the city to the Ferry Building to enjoy the last hour of the event.

The party was in full swing by the time she arrived, the riotous cacophony of music and laughter and conversation swirling around her as she searched for Evan among the dazzling lights, colorful decorations and glittering costumes. Finally, she spotted him at a table off to the corner, away from the dancers gyrating on the dance floor and the crowds lining up at the bar. He was deep in conversation with another man.

Her knees literally went weak at the sight of him. She'd thought the phrase was an overblown cliché but it was reality. Evan turned her legs to water. A nearby chair provided some momentary support.

"Marguerite. This is a surprise." The male voice came from behind her.

She schooled her expression to be still, to not reveal the immediate blooming of hurt and shock. And then she turned, knowing whom she would find. After all, she'd hung on his every word for nearly seven years. Until she learned he was stealing her ideas and passing them off as his own.

Casper Vos was an imposing man. Well over six feet tall with a helmet of bright platinum hair, he was easy to pick out in a crowd, which made avoiding him at wine industry gatherings easy to accomplish. She wondered that she had missed recognizing him tonight, especially since Casper was one of the few people not wearing a mask. But then, she'd only had eyes for Evan. "Casper. How are things at Dellavina Cellars?"

"Dellavina is the wine sponsor for tonight. Quite the coup for us. What are you doing here? This is an exclusive event." Being direct to the point of rude was another Casper trademark.

"I'm attending a party," she said, proud that her voice remained cool and steady. "And I see my date, so if you'll excuse me—" Casper followed her gaze and too late, she realized her mistake. Of course, Casper would recognize the current owner of St. Isadore.

"Your date?" He smiled. It was a rather unpleasant smile. "I see."

"It's not what you…we're here to make connections for St. Isadore." She raised her chin. "The winery is well on its way to surpassing its output of the last ten years. Both in quantity and quality."

"Quantity, perhaps." Casper shrugged one shoulder, a smirk on his lips. "Quality, impossible." He gestured at himself. "St. Isadore lacks…proficiency."

She knew he would eventually attack her talents and skills. Say what you would about Casper, at least he attacked her to her face as well as behind her back.

Anger joined the hurt, always a bad combination when it came to holding her tongue. "Therefore we

aren't set in old, tired ways and St. Isadore has nowhere to go but up. But congratulations on your success at Dellavina. Tell me, which young winemaker are
you stealing from now?"

The smirk disappeared, but only for a moment. Then
it reappeared, deeper and more twisted than before.
"You've grown claws. Brava. But you are still the same
Marguerite. Still attaching yourself to St. Isadore's owners, still hoping they will throw crumbs your way, but
always doomed to disappointment." He plucked a glass
of red wine off a passing waiter's tray and handed it to
her. "Enjoy some award-winning wine while you can.
Until next time. I'm sure I'll see your resume floating
around town again sooner rather than later."

He walked off and Marguerite immediately put the
glass down. Her hands were shaking and the last thing
she wanted to do was stain her borrowed dress.

To think she and Evan had been so careful not to reveal their personal relationship to anyone in Napa outside Aracely, only for to tip her hand to Casper Vos. Of
all the unforeseen disasters. She needed to tell Evan.
And then she should return to St. Isadore as soon as
possible, do as much damage control as she could.

She made a beeline toward Evan's table, but as she
came closer she realized Evan was not deep in discussion, he was deep in an argument.

"If we want to jump on this deal to maneuver Angus
Horne into an investment, we have to move fast," he
insisted.

"I've run my own analyses," his companion said. He
was a dark-haired man, who, even wearing a half-mask,
still managed to look ruggedly handsome. Luke Dallas,
Evan's business partner, Marguerite guessed. "I'm not
so sure we need Horne in the first place."

"We need him." Evan stared Luke down. "Horne is our best opportunity to grow and achieve maximum returns now."

Luke shook his head. "Only if we decide that's the right direction for the long-term health of the company. My numbers say we're better off concentrating on the markets we're in. We won't see the same immediate revenue jump, but it's more sustainable."

"I'm the CEO. We're entering the international market. It's not negotiable."

"Uh oh." A pretty blonde woman in a black and silver flapper dress appeared at Marguerite's side. "Now Evan has done it." She turned to Marguerite and held out her right hand for a shake. "Hi. I'm Danica. I'm married to the one doing an impersonation of a volcano struggling not to blow its top."

Marguerite shook the woman's proffered hand. "Marguerite. You're Luke's wife. I'm so happy to meet you."

"Likewise." Danica turned her gaze back to the table and Marguerite followed suit. The men seemed oblivious to their presence, intent on their argument. "Do we go in and try to diffuse the situation, or let them hash it out?"

"Do they often argue like this?"

Danica frowned. "No. Never. They usually see eye to eye. But since Evan bought the winery—" She stopped. "Not that the winery is the issue per se. I know you work there. But the purchase coincided with Evan pushing the idea that Medevco needs to grow bigger, faster. I wonder if he overextended himself." Her mouth twisted. "Or maybe the idea came first and the winery was the result. Evan is keen on bringing Angus Horne on board and Angus does like his wine. Maybe Evan bought it to impress him."

Marguerite shook her head. "He bought St. Isadore to give his brother a business to learn."

Danica laughed. "Please don't tell Nico that and give him false expectations."

"Don't worry. Nico decided he wants to pursue something else, anyway." And Evan had yet to discuss with her his plans for St. Isadore once Nico left. Casper's words rattled in her head. *Still attaching yourself to St. Isadore's owners, still hoping they will throw crumbs your way, but always doomed to disappointment.*

A slam on the table brought both women's attention back to the men. Evan and Luke were on their feet, their hands on the tabletop, their heads held low and down like bulls about to charge. "I don't like this," Danica said, and started to move toward Luke.

But then the tension broke, and the men's stances relaxed, although Marguerite got the distinct impression they were calling a time out, not a truce. Danica reached Luke's side and he drew her close, kissing her cheek. Evan looked around and, for the first time since she arrived at the party, caught Marguerite's gaze. A wide grin broke across his face. "You're here."

"I am." Her arms hung awkwardly at her side. Should she kiss him hello? Or go for a hug? Or—

"I'm glad," Evan said simply. "I missed you." And he took her hand in his and twined their fingers as if they were always meant to fit together. Her ribcage was suddenly too small to contain her heart.

Denial was no longer an option. She was head over heels in love with her boss. The man who also held the future of her family's legacy in his hands. And who gave her no indication this was anything but a pleasurable fling between two consenting adults.

Tonight, wrapped in a new cocoon of music and colored lights and fantastical costumes, she would allow herself to indulge in pretense one last time. Pretend that Casper's taunts hadn't found their target. That she and Evan had a future. That they could build a life together that included St. Isadore.

One last time, and then she would accept prosaic reality.

Nine

A week later, the wine tasting for the Global Leader Summit was shaping up to be the social event of the summer. Marguerite smoothed her hands over her dress, a simple sheath of dark crimson with long sleeves that clung to her arms until they reached the elbows, then belled into loose, flowing ruffles that covered her wrists, and made one last inspection of the scene.

Strings of crisscrossing globe lights had been installed on St. Isadore's large flagstone terrace. They would illuminate the various areas arranged for conversation and eating. Cocktail tables in two heights, chairs to match, and sleek, comfortable sofas would invite maximum mingling and conversation. At one end of the terrace, a deluxe Santa Maria–style grill had been installed, providing the guests with tri-tip barbeque and other delectable California-inspired dishes. And all of this would take place against a stunning backdrop of rolling hills lined with verdant grapevines.

The additional staff hired for the party gathered around Nico as he walked them through the order of events for the night, with Gabi by his side as his volunteer second-in-command.

Ted Sato, the director of operations, was setting up the wines for the formal tasting to be held later. Aracely, dressed in a flowing pink-and-purple-paisley caftan that had once belonged to her grandmother, seemed to float above the smooth stone floor as she ensured every detail, no matter how minor, was perfect: the flower arrangements, the position of the wineglasses on the catering staff's trays, the order in which the appetizers were to come out of the kitchen and be passed to the guests.

And the wine. St. Isadore may have fallen on hard times during Linus's last years, when he'd refused to make changes or cede control, but the wine had always been consistently good. Not world-class, at least not in Marguerite's estimation, but pleasing to drink and accessible to a wide variety of aficionados. Most of the guests should enjoy the bottles she chose to serve. And for those who required a more challenging tasting experience, she'd brought out some of her newer wines that were ready to drink now, like the Sauvignon Blanc, and added some of her red-blend experiments that had aged enough to be opened by Evan to share as he thought necessary.

Nothing had been overlooked. Every contingency had a plan. There was no reason why her heart should be pounding in her ears one minute, her stomach aching dully the next.

Well, there was one reason. Tonight marked the end of her employment contract with Evan. And she didn't intend to enter into another one.

She'd spent her long drive from the city back to St. Isadore contemplating what to do next. She loved Evan. But she could no longer pretend. It was tearing her soul apart, to be with him, to touch him, to shudder in his arms but know she didn't have his heart.

She couldn't make him love her. But once she stopped pretending, other things became clearer, too. She would rather die than admit Casper Vos was right about her, but one of his barbs hit true. She had to stop hoping for a future at St. Isadore and to go after what she wanted.

Last week, between last-minute preparations for the party and the usual winery business, she drew up a business proposal and payment plan for the original Delacroix vineyard. She intended to present it to Evan tomorrow morning. Along with confessing how much she loved him.

Evan might laugh at her. Or be mad, or dismissive. Or he might immediately reciprocate her feelings and make her kick herself for being so scared. Whatever happened, at least she would have taken her future, and that of her family's legacy, into her own hands.

Her gaze found Evan almost immediately, his unruly hair under a touch more control than normal. He'd arrived that morning, having stayed in San Francisco the past week to, as he put it, "knock sense into Luke," who was also due at the party. She drank in his appearance. He wore a variation of his usual tech industry work uniform, but the khaki trousers were well tailored to skim just so over his powerful thighs, the fine cotton shirt was equally fitted, and the addition of a sports jacket only emphasized his broad shoulders. He raised a hand and then pointed at her, signaling for her to stay put as he walked toward her. As he drew closer, he smiled. "There you are. I've been looking for you."

Her pulse fluttered, as it always did when he was near enough to touch. She kept her hands clasped together behind her back. "What do you think of your event?"

"Stunning."

"It is, isn't it? Aracely and her team did an amazing job." The sun moved lower in the sky, its bright, golden light throwing a burnished glow over the winery's stonework and the vineyards beyond. A gentle breeze played with her hair, lifting the strands that refused to stay put in a bun. The smooth stone floor, which had seemed so cold and empty before the guests arrived, now appeared warm and intimate as people broke into small conversational groups and took advantage of the chairs and tables dotted around the perimeter. She turned back and caught Evan's gaze.

He wasn't looking at the Napa scenery. His attention was fixed on her. "Beautiful. Absolutely."

Normally, she loved it when Evan flirted with her. But acknowledging that his flirtations would never lead to anything more than the friends with benefits arrangement they currently enjoyed sucked some of the joy out of it. "Glad you approve. Of the party." She nodded at Aracely, somehow simultaneously greeting guests, whisking away empty glasses and handing out new ones. "Speaking of, I should go help her."

He grabbed her hand. She steeled her heart against the fit of their fingers. "Come join my table for the wine tasting later. Luke will be there. And you never did meet Grayson."

"Evan." She hesitated, digging deep for the resolve she'd found on her drive back from San Francisco. "I work for St. Isadore. You're the owner. This is a work event." She glanced at the terrace, now packed with faces she recognized from news articles she'd read on her phone. "Tonight, I'm your winery employee."

A shadow passed over his expression, but it disappeared so fast she wasn't sure if she actually saw it. "Sorry. I forgot. Professional. In fact, until the party is over, I'll act like I barely know you."

She laughed. "Good luck acting like you don't know your own winemaker."

"But tomorrow," he said, his voice dropping to the bass rumble that made thrills run up and down her spine, "tomorrow we need to discuss your new contract. I look forward to the part before we sign it."

"Speaking of," she started, only to be interrupted from a shout coming from behind Evan.

"Hey, Fletcher! I like your wine. So let's talk."

She peered over Evan's shoulder and saw a man, about Evan's age, grab a glass of wine off a passing tray and then veer toward them. Even without the shouting, he would still draw a second glance from her, thanks to his shock of bright red hair. He was popular, too. He barely took two steps before one guest after another came up to engage him in conversation.

Evan turned around and waved to acknowledge the shout. "Angus."

"That's Angus Horne?" she stage-whispered. "I was expecting someone…older. More established-looking."

"The older, more established people all said no to the amount of investment I'm looking for. But Angus likes risk and Medevco fits into his international strategy." Evan glanced down at her, calculations already forming behind his eyes. "I need to meet with him and Luke."

He let her hand go, but not without one final squeeze,

and began to make his way toward the clump of people surrounding Angus Horne. "Until later."

"You have no idea," she muttered to herself. But until then, she had to get through the party. She turned to find Aracely, only to hear her name called. "Marguerite! So good to see you're still here."

She smiled as Orson Whitaker approached her, his wheelchair lightly humming. Owner of the Adrasteia Group, one of the largest beverage alcohol companies in the world—which included Dellavina Cellars among its brands—he and Linus were of the same generation and had run in the same social groups.

She smiled. "Mr. Whitaker. A pleasure." She grabbed a nearby unused chair and sat down next to him.

He shook her proffered hand, holding it with both of his. "Call me Orson. The old place looks amazing. I'm so sorry I missed Linus's memorial, but work took me to Europe and I only now returned for the summit. My condolences, again."

"Thank you. He would've been happy to hear your compliments, although he would have thought them naturally his due."

"Now, we both know Linus would've never approved of the barbeque. Even the strings of lights, pretty as they are."

"True. He would have said they were below the dignity of St. Isadore."

"I also hear you're doing interesting things with wine. Dellavina Cellars hired the wrong person." Orson chuckled. "Don't look so surprised. My granddaughter Gabrielle is impressed with you. And not impressed with Vos."

Marguerite raised her eyebrows. "Gabrielle... Gabi is your granddaughter? She hasn't said anything."

"Gabrielle earned her internship. She's a natural winemaking talent."

"I agree."

"Yes, it takes one to know one. But you also understand why Gabrielle doesn't volunteer the information."

"I do know something about keeping relationships quiet out of fear of people getting the wrong idea." Marguerite said, her gaze searching out Evan.

Orson nodded and turned to look over the terrace and the vineyards beyond. "Pity I didn't pursue this place when it was up for sale. I assure you Adrasteia Group would have been a better fit for St. Isadore instead of selling to Evan Fletcher. I would have given you a fair price."

"Given *me* a fair price? You mean Linus's great-nephews."

Orson swiveled his head to look at her, his eyebrows raised. "No, my dear, I mean you. Linus was clear you should receive what you deserve."

Despite the warm temperature, Marguerite's teeth chattered as if she were in the Artic. "You must be mistaken."

"Young lady, I am rarely mistaken. Which is why I am a charter member of the group gathering here today." He looked at her closely. "I see this is news to you. Ah. Well, perhaps he thought better of it. Forgive me if I spoke out of turn." He turned his chair to leave.

"Wait—when did he say that?"

He thought for a moment. "It was the last time I saw him. Shortly before his stroke, I believe. But people do change their plans, you know." He reached out and patted her hand where it lay on her chair's armrest. "However, do not doubt he knew the value of your contributions. I may have hired Vos, but Linus was adamant you were the true talent. Not that he was about to let you go, of course. A good man, Linus was, but he had his selfish streak. Now, if you will excuse me, I should say hello to others." He wheeled away. Rather jauntily, Marguerite thought, for someone who'd just thrown a grenade into her life and shredded it.

She rose from the chair and put it back where she'd found it, leaning on its back when tears sprang into her eyes. Linus had appreciated her. He meant to upheld their bargain and turn the Delacroix vineyard over to her after all. A piece of her soul she hadn't been aware was missing clicked back into place.

He should have told her to her face, and she should have insisted on a formal agreement from the start. She'd allowed sentiment to lead instead of logic. And while it was good—oh, so good!—to learn from a third party he'd meant to keep his word, he hadn't followed through.

Still, the angry hurt that punched holes in her heart whenever she thought of Linus folded up its daggers and faded away.

"All is well?" Aracely materialized next to her.

"Huh?" Marguerite shook her head to clear it. "Yes. Of course. Why?"

"You have impersonated a statue for ten minutes."

Marguerite relaxed her shoulders, but they almost immediately sprang back to their previous position around her ears. "I'm fine. Just…thinking."

Her gaze found Evan again, standing in a tight knot consisting of Angus Horne and Luke. They were deep in intense discussion, the crowd ebbing and flowing around them like a river around a rock.

This was going to be the longest party she'd ever attended, and it had just started.

* * *

Evan sat down in the creaky leather chair and dropped his head into his hands. How had he not foreseen this? He was dealing with Angus Horne. It was a given the negotiations would not be straightforward.

He had to hand it to Angus, however. Horne loved creating chaos, but even he couldn't have known how much mental turmoil he was causing Evan.

The hour was late. The wine tasting was long over, and the cleanup crew was gone. Only the barbecue pit on the terrace, waiting to be removed in the morning, provided physical evidence the party had occurred. The guests had dispersed to the nearby summit host hotel, most of them probably asleep in order to get an early start to a weekend full of keynote speeches, exclusive roundtable discussions and chance encounters that would shape the direction of global business for the year to come. Those that weren't asleep—well, they were no doubt engaged in far more pleasurable activities than sitting in the dark in a faux Gothic library, contemplating the best choice between a rock and a hard place.

Evan had picked the library in the owner's residence for soul-searching in the wee hours of the night because it was the one room at St. Isadore that he had yet to touch, in part because the furnishings were massive and would require teams of workmen to remove—and perhaps necessitate rebuilding the entire room. The heavy oak bookcases stretched from the floor to the ceiling high overhead. The reading nooks—there were three—featured armchairs that could accommodate two people plus a good-sized dog. The desk he sat behind was solid wood on three sides, with sizable drawer pedestals. If he put it in his San Francisco office, he'd barely have room left over for a potted plant.

And grapevines were everywhere. Carved into the crown molding. Painted on the sides of the bookcases. Woven into the rugs.

The room had nothing to do with Silicon Valley, not even a computer to remind him of tech-world wheeling and dealing. But it had everything to do with St. Isadore.

And Marguerite. Whom he'd managed to avoid ever since he, Luke and Angus had shaken hands on the outline of the deal to put Medevco on the international map.

In the past week, he couldn't shake himself of certain visions. Marguerite falling asleep on his shoulder after a long day, laughter around a fully occupied dinner table, a small child with dark curls tugging on his hand. He even began to wonder if he could make those visions a reality.

But he should have known. His life was not meant to have such things.

He should have known. His life wasn't meant for such things.

His hands would not stay still. He picked up the paperweight sitting on the desk, looking for something to occupy his fingers while his mind built and discarded one decision tree after another. But the paperweight, a crystal globe encasing a miniature version of the winery, was lighter than he'd anticipated, the smooth surface more slippery. It rolled out of his grasp and under the desk.

"Damn it." He had no idea if the object had any monetary or sentimental value. He turned on the lamps and to get a better look but the paperweight had rolled to the far corner. Nothing to do but crawl under the desk.

The desk was tall enough for him to be on his hands and knees with headroom to spare. Using the flashlight app on his cell, he reached for the paperweight with his other hand but his fingertips put enough spin on the globe to shoot it out of his grasp. He sighed and rolled his eyes, waving the phone around for illumination Then he stared.

Something white was sticking out from behind the drawer pedestal on the left side. Several somethings. The desk had been emptied before he moved in, but some items must have fallen behind the drawers and been overlooked. He reached out and pulled.

The flashlight app revealed a motley collection of flotsam and jetsam that had been shoved in drawers, fallen behind them and then forgotten over the years. An invoice addressed to the Kennedy-era White House for several cases of Chardonnay. Bills of sale for new oak casks. Faded drugstore receipts, mostly illegible. A small leatherbound ledger with "M. Delacroix" inscribed on the front. A ticket stub from opening night of the San Francisco Opera, dated 1987. More receipts—

Wait. Evan found the ledger again, using the flashlight on his phone to look at it more carefully.

M. Delacroix? As in Marguerite?

He opened the ledger and a handwritten note on a piece of lined legal-size notepaper, folded into threes, fell out.

He unfolded the paper and started to read.

Marguerite couldn't sleep. Not only was she still keyed up from the party—St. Isadore had worked its usual magic on the guests, who'd raved about her wine and Hunter Chase's food and the overall ambiance—she was acutely aware Evan was in the owner's residence, only a brisk fifteen minutes' walk away.

She hadn't had a chance to speak to him after their

brief conversation on the terrace. Despite receiving two bottles to take home as party favors, many guests had asked to purchase additional wine as well as St. Isadore souvenirs. She had been pressed into service at the second cash register in the gift shop when she wasn't busy giving impromptu tours to people who requested them. Evan had seemed equally preoccupied even after his conversation with Angus Horne had concluded, dashing about the party, flashing his grin as he mingled with guests, but his gaze never finding hers. By the time she'd finished helping with cleanup, he was nowhere to be found, and she'd assumed he was having a nightcap with his fellow titans of industry or perhaps turning in early to attend the summit meetings the next day.

But the thing about revelations—like the one she'd been sitting on all week—was that they had to be shared. Casper's taunts and Orson's kind words and her own heart, demanding to be heard, were not going to let her sleep.

So when she looked out her window and saw light coming from what had to be the library, she didn't hesitate. Nico had pretty much moved into Gabi's apartment, so the lit lamp had to signify Evan's presence. She threw on sneakers and a long cardigan over her knit pajama pants and camisole and, after grabbing a flashlight on her way out of the apartment, ran down the stairs and into the main garage on the other side of the courtyard.

The quickest way to the library, she knew from her previous role as Linus's assistant, was through the secret passageway that connected the former stables to the main building. The winery maintenance staff continued to keep the tunnels in decent shape, so she arrived on the other side of the secret door without any mishap or unwanted encounters with four-, six-or eight-legged creatures. She paused, twisting her hair into a semblance of a bun on top of her head and using the time to bring her breathing under control. Although, if things went as she hoped, she would be plenty breathless soon.

Then she knocked. "Evan? It's me."

She heard a loud thump, followed by a groan. She wrenched the door open, revealing the life-size portrait of Linus on the other side. "Evan? Are you okay?"

She blinked several times as her eyes got accustomed to the light, dim as it was. Where was he—*oh*. She blinked again, this time at the sight of Evan crawling out from under the desk commissioned by the original founder of St. Isadore. He held one hand to the back of his head.

She crossed the room, leaving the secret door open. "What happened? Are you hurt? Let me see."

But when she reached for him, he evaded her touch, retreating into the shadows as she advanced. His eyes were dark and unreadable. "I'm not imagining this. You really are here."

It was a flat statement. No, more than flat. His voice was controlled. And that scared her. Evan didn't do controlled. He bantered and, on occasion, blustered. The lack of emotion stopped her cold. "I am."

His gaze flicked away from her and he laughed, but there was no mirth in it. "Should have known. Another late-night break-in. How many times didn't I catch you?"

"I… I haven't… I saw the light on and the secret passageway was the fastest way to reach the library—"

"Of course. Secret passageway. Another of St. Isadore's secrets."

"Evan, you're scaring me. What's wrong? Did Angus

say no to the investment?" It was a possible explanation for Evan's behavior. Although she doubted a business deal, even a deal that turned sour, would cause this reaction.

Ha! If only." The derision in his tone turned her from scared to petrified. "That's good, right?" She wrapped her arms around her, both to stay warm and because the atmosphere required armor of some sort. "Congratulations. I know how hard you've worked."

"You might want to hold your congrats."

"He would only invest in Medevco if I included St. Isadore in the pot." Evan fell into the chair, pressing his fingers hard into his temple. He wants me to sell the entire estate to him."

Sell St. Isadore? Was she too late? Marguerite took the guest chair from its place, pulled it around to the other side and sat next to him. Her hands were numb. She didn't know if they would ever warm up. "Have you given him a response?"

"My first thought was to counteroffer." He continued as if she hadn't spoken. "Maybe give him a partial interest. Or the wine-distribution rights. Or sell him the private residence, since he kept talking about the winery's 'chill vibes' and 'potential for social,' but I'd keep the rest." He shook his head. "Something. Anything to satisfy Horne's deal requirements but maintain control of St. Isadore."

The pressure on her chest making it difficult to breath lessened. Evan didn't jump at chance to sell. Maybe St. Isadore meant something to him more than dollars and cents. She tried to smile. "It's disappointing you didn't get what you wanted from Horne right away, but this is just the opening salvo in the negotiations."

"There won't be another round of negotiations." His

tone was final. And that was the scariest thing she had heard all night thus far.

She rose from her chair and started to pace along the rug. "So, what happens next? You'll sell St. Isadore to him?"

Her voice cracked on the word *sell*, but she recovered by the time she finished speaking. The thought of losing St. Isadore anew caused her skin to prickle as though punctured by thousands of straight pins. It hurt, damn it.

But it was nothing compared to the pain caused by the ice in Evan's gaze. He'd never looked at her that way—not even when he first caught her taking her wine from the owner's cellar.

"Why are you here, Marguerite?"

She blinked at the non sequitur. "I'm here because I wanted to talk to you, and I didn't want to wait until morning."

"No. Why are you here, at St. Isadore? Why did you break in that night?"

She frowned. What did he mean by his question? "I told you." She rubbed her hands together, trying to restore feeling to her fingers. "I thought the new owner would tear down the buildings, and I wanted to save the wine I made."

He scoffed and stood up. "At least your story is consistent."

"What the hell does that mean?" The anger was quick to spark, and she welcomed its warmth. Anything to counteract the wall of frost Evan had built around him. "You've known me for six months. Of course I'm consistent. I've been consistent from the moment I met you. You know that. We talk every day."

"But not about everything. Not about the things you leave out."

A hot flush settled in her cheeks. "What things do I leave out?"

He shook his head, closing his eyes as if he couldn't bear to look at her. And it was the disappointment written deep in his expression that hurt the most in a night of very sharp and deep hurts.

She swallowed. What had changed? What brought this on? Maybe…maybe he had his own revelation during the past week. Maybe he decided he, too, was tired of the pretending. True, he didn't seem upset when she saw him earlier, but that was hours ago when they were surrounded by the world's VIPs. Maybe, with the stress and anticipation of the party now over, he'd had time to think. Reconsider.

And she was disappointed in herself, too. She'd chosen to hide instead of stepping into the light, afraid to tell him how she felt because he might reject her. Afraid to trust him, allowing the way other people treated her to color her perception of him.

She took a deep breath. It was now or never. "You asked me why I'm here tonight. I came to tell you I can't keep pretending there's nothing between us but sexual attraction, and someday it will go away and we'll be fine with that. I want a real relationship. One we don't have to hide."

She stepped closer to him, so close she could lift her hand and caress his cheek. "I love you, Evan Fletcher." She smiled. "I literally fell for you from the moment I tripped over your legs in the kitchen."

They stood in the circle of the lamplight, its glow surrounding them. His gaze, which had traveled over every inch of the library except the spot where she stood, now flew to meet hers. In it she read all she could have ever hoped for, and more.

He loved her, too. His caring was as deep as the ocean and as expansive as the sky. The emotion was real and rich and rooted in his soul.

She reached for him, her hands yearning to caress, her mouth eager for his.

He stepped out of her grasp. The icy shell that had cracked open enough for her to glimpse the truth of his heart re-formed, thicker and more opaque than before.

Her hands fell away. Somehow, she kept breathing despite the hurt slamming down on her hopes and severing them like a guillotine blade.

"I want to believe you." His words barely penetrated past the metallic ringing in her ears. "Because I fell for you. Hard. I even had these dreams—" He stopped. "It doesn't matter." He turned back to the desk and stooped to pick up a crumbled letter and a small book from underneath the desk, handing them to her. "I'm guessing this is what you are truly after."

Somehow, she made herself take the things from him. Somehow, her eyes managed to focus on the top item. The missing ledger, with her name embossed in gold on the cover.

"Where did you find this? I've looked all over." Her voice was raspy from holding back tears. "But what's this letter?" Linus's signature, bold and black, was unmistakable. The date was just before he died. She unfolded the papers and started to read as he spoke.

"I asked you to hold the congratulations earlier because, as you see for yourself, they properly belong to you." He mimed raising a glass in celebration, his gaze flat. "Cheers. You're the proud owner of St. Isadore."

Ten

Once, when he was a small child and still believed in things like the Tooth Fairy and families that stayed together forever, Evan had walked in on his parents arguing in the kitchen. He was too young to understand the topic, but the memory was seared into his brain. Years later, he understood they'd been discussing money. Or rather, their lack of it. But at the time, all he knew was that his father—his tall, strong, superhero father—was crying.

The sight had shaken the bedrock foundations of Evan's young world. He cried, but his father? Adults didn't shed tears. And when his mother caught sight of him, standing shell-shocked on the threshold, she'd been so flustered she shut the door in his face. She opened it again almost immediately, but Evan had gotten the message.

Never let others see your emotions. Remain cool.

When feelings take control, calamity follows.

He'd clung to that lesson when he viewed the wreckage of his parents' car. He'd remained stoic at their funeral. His control had remained solid, even when Nico was hospitalized during high school with a fever of unknown origin, even when girlfriends left him.

Tonight threatened to destroy his perfect record.

He wasn't upset the ownership of St. Isadore might be in question. The physical discovery of the will was upsetting only because it meant Marguerite had been cheated out of Linus's bequest. A large bequest, one that would have made her life financially secure.

But he was furious—the rage lighting up his insides like an out-of-control forest fire—she'd never told him about her arrangement with Linus. Never mentioned to him she was related to the winery's founding family. He would have ensured she received her fair share. He would have made it right.

Finding the handwritten will as he was contemplating not only the future of St. Isadore but his own possible future with Marguerite was a coincidence, nothing more. But if he did give credence to the idea the universe was sentient and could speak to him, tonight would be a sign—and the sign would say he was right.

Relationships, family: they were not meant for him. His feelings drew him off course, distracted him from his goals. If he hadn't been concerned about Marguerite and her future should he sell St. Isadore, he wouldn't have been up late in the library. The paperweight would still be on the desk, not under it. He wouldn't have made his discovery. The deal with Angus Horne would be underway. Nico, his grandparents, Marguerite—he would finally have enough resources to assure everyone's financial future.

He wouldn't have this burning hole in the middle

of his chest, a sucking wound that made it difficult to breathe.

Why hadn't she told him? What else was she keeping from him?

Marguerite looked up, her eyes wide and wild. The paper shook in her hands. "I... I don't...what is this?"

"You tell me." His voice was steady, thanks to long practice controlling his emotions. "If I had to guess, it's a holographic will written by the prior owner of St. Isadore. Leaving the entire estate to you."

"I have no idea what *holographic* means."

"Handwritten will. Valid in California, if that's his signature."

"Um..." She stared at the paper. "It looks like Linus's handwriting. But... I don't...where did this come from?"

"Does it matter? The real question is if you knew it existed." He was surprised at how calm he sounded.

"No! I had no—" She stopped. Swallowed. Put the will down on the desk and smoothed it with her hands. Turned to face him. "You know I worked for Linus."

"Linus *Delacroix* Chappell," he supplied, emphasizing the second name.

Her gaze flashed. "Yes, we were distantly related. We're both descended from the original founder of St. Isadore."

"You didn't tell me."

"Why did I need to tell you?" Her hands balled on her hips. Gentle curves he loved to hold—

No. No emotions.

"It wasn't a secret." She marched over to the life-size portrait that had concealed the secret door and pointed to a nameplate integrated into the ornate, gilded frame. "Linus's full name is right here. Has been since before you moved in."

So, he'd missed it. Apparently he missed a lot of things. So much for his vaunted powers of perception. "Fine. Go on. You worked for Linus."

"We had a deal. I would be his assistant and in my off time, learn as much as I could about winemaking and the wine business. But instead of earning a full salary, I took fifteen percent, with the rest going toward purchasing the original Delacroix vineyard." She nodded at the ledger. "That's Linus's record. You'll see I paid off the vineyard shortly before his death. You said yourself I was underpaid and that's the reason why."

He narrowed his gaze. "I bought St. Isadore from two brothers. Your name wasn't on the deed."

She sighed, her shoulders slumping. "I know. Linus was going to have the paperwork drawn up but then he died without a will, which meant everything went to his closest living relatives after probate finished. And without the ledger, his great-nephews weren't about to listen to me. They told me to leave and locked me out of the carriage house apartment. When I tried to get their attention so I could plead my case, they had me arrested for disturbing the peace." Her lips formed a trembling smile. "At least they later dropped the charges."

"The night we met. Why were you here?"

"We've been over this! I only wanted what was mine."

Right. What was rightfully hers. Which meant she would do what she needed to obtain it. Like breaking in. Or...

Or telling him she loved him.

His heart squeezed, a hard pressure that took his breath away.

He picked up the will. "Including this."

Her eyes went wide. "I didn't know."

He stared her down.

"I didn't!" she protested. "I mean, yes, I knew the ledger existed." She ran her right hand over the paper. "I had no idea he left me St. Isadore."

The last words were whispered, nearly inaudible. Her wistful expression caused something deep inside Evan's chest to twinge. He ignored it.

He'd give her one last chance to come clean. "So you didn't ask for a job at St. Isadore so you could search for this will."

"Of course not—" Her mouth closed. "Yes. I did search for the ledger. And yes, being able to search for the ledger did enter my mind when I asked for the job. But I didn't know about the will."

Her words were a meteor, creating a crater on impact. He couldn't hold her gaze.

"I wanted the ledger because damn it, I worked for the vineyard. I earned it. And it hurt to think that Linus had no intention of upholding his end of the bargain. But after—after the morning in the carriage house courtyard…" Her voice cracked, just a little. "After that, I thought I could, perhaps, build something new. We could build something together."

She huffed and picked up the will. "We're going to keep going in circles. You think this is what I want? The estate has been probated and sold. Legally, I bet this is meaningless. It doesn't matter. Not to us."

And that was where she was wrong. Because he knew his value, and it was ensuring the people in his life were well provided for. She didn't love him. Because she didn't tell him she had been cheated out of the vineyard. "No. It matters to me. You didn't trust me to make this right."

She took a step back. Her chest rose and fell several

times. Then she reached around the desk, opened the drawer nearest to her, and took out a black permanent marker. She scribbled on the will, folded it up, and held it in her right hand before turning to face him.

Her gaze burned bright. "Yes. I didn't tell you. But not because I didn't trust you. Instead, I didn't trust myself. Linus and Casper made me doubt my abilities, and I was afraid if I told you Linus reneged on his promise, you would doubt if I was capable, too."

Something inside him started to unbend. "I would never—"

"I know. But tonight? This discussion isn't about me." She shook her head, sending black tendrils falling down her cheeks. "It isn't even about who owns St. Isadore. This is about you. And your fear."

"My *what*?" Now he was back to fury. It did taste better than bitterness. Barely.

She defiantly lifted her chin and stared him down. "You're afraid to let people get close to you. You push away Nico. Now you're making up a reason to push me away. For heaven's sake, Evan, you don't have a single family memento on display in your home in San Francisco."

"My house? What does that—?" The loud pounding of his pulse in his ears made it difficult to think.

"You don't want people to see you. The real you. And you think Nico and I don't need you because you gave us buildings and businesses to run, perhaps because buildings and businesses are the only things you will allow yourself." She held out the will. He automatically reached out to take it, but she didn't relinquish her grip. "If I didn't trust you, I wouldn't have worked for you. I definitely would not be here telling you I love you. Because when you tell people you love them, you're en-

trusting them with your heart. And hearts are fragile."
She caught her lower lip with her teeth. "Maybe that's
why you refuse to trust yours."

Her hand dropped, and the will was in his sole possession. She continued to hold his gaze. "If you ever
decide you deserve to be loved, for you and not for your
possessions, come find me. If it's not too late."

Her words landed with the precision of a heat-seek-
ing missile, fragmenting his worldview into thousands
of sharp pieces. The shards pinned him into place, so
he was unable to think or react or respond. He merely
clutched the piece of paper, a reminder that the will was
tangible. The will, he could deal with. He unfolded it
and began to read.

In big black letters printed over Linus's handwriting, she'd scrawled, "I, Marguerite Delacroix, renounce
any claim to St. Isadore and declare Evan Fletcher to be
the sole owner. P.S. If you sell, please protect the staff.
P.P.S. This is my resignation letter. I quit. For good."

No. This wasn't what he wanted. The winery was
hers. "Marguerite, this isn't—"

But when he looked up, the library was empty. The
portrait was back in its place, the secret passage hidden
as if she had never been there.

Whoever was knocking on Marguerite's door
wouldn't quit. Marguerite moaned and put her pillow
over her ears, but it didn't stop the noise. Not that it
mattered. She hadn't gotten any sleep after arriving
back at her apartment following her confrontation with
Evan. She wasn't going to get sleep now that the sun
was well into the sky. A glance at her text messages—
Evan's name wholly absent from the notifications—
told her who was on her doorstep. She threw on the

first clothes she found and made her way downstairs to the front entrance.

"I have caffeine. And cupcakes. I have decided doughnuts do not have enough frosting." Aracely held up a large container stamped with the logo of a local coffee shop in one, a pink bakery box in the other. "May I come in?"

Marguerite motioned for her friend to enter and then to follow her up to the kitchen. "Are you sure you brought enough?"

Aracely checked the container. "It says this contains twelve cups of coffee, so I will run out to get more in an hour or so."

Marguerite chuckled, then instantly wished she hadn't. "Ow."

"Hungover?"

"Only from lack of sleep." And crying until her tear ducts were empty. "But that's enough to cause a headache." She opened a cabinet and selected two of the largest mugs she owned. "Fill them up. Then you can help me pack."

Aracely poured the coffee and handed Marguerite a full mug. "Pack? What are you talking about? I am here to celebrate last night. The party was perfect, if I do say so myself."

"It was." Marguerite took a much-needed sip. "Ah. This is spectacular. Thank you."

Aracely took the mug away from her. "No more until you tell me what is going on."

"I… I realized I've made a muddle of my entire life. Hey, do you need a traveling partner when you return to Chile? I've always wanted to learn how to make *pisco*. What better place to do so?"

Aracely handed her back her coffee and joined her

to sit at the kitchen table. "Here. I was wrong to take this away. You are not yet coherent."

Marguerite sighed. "After the party, I told Evan I loved him."

Aracely put down her mug. "Oh."

There was a wealth of understanding in Aracely's breathed syllable. "The outcome was even worse than you're imagining," Marguerite admitted.

"Are you okay?"

"I will be. Eventually."

"But why pack? He did not fire you. That would be appalling, even for—"

"I quit. Forever. I can't stay at St. Isadore." Marguerite looked around her apartment. The last time she moved out, she'd been given less than twelve hours to take away her possessions. Evan wouldn't call the sheriff on her like Linus's great-nephews had, but she also didn't want to stay any longer than necessary. One more crack would shatter her heart into so many pieces, she doubted if she could ever make it whole.

Aracely regarded her. "What about the Delacroix vineyard? Your goals?"

Marguerite pressed her eyes shut. "When you don't sleep, you have a lot of time for thinking." Yes, terroir mattered, as she'd told Evan the first night they met. But the true alchemy of wine came in the blending and in the fermentation, in combining disparate elements such as yeast and juice and adding the passage of time. "In the end, St. Isadore is just a place. I can take my skills with me anywhere." She opened her eyes and peered at Aracely. "Like, say, go to Chile with you?"

"You can travel wherever you want, whenever you want. Whether I'm going to Chile is up for discussion."

Aracely waved her hand. "But today we are packing. Where shall we start?"

"First, I'm starting with this red velvet cupcake. And then after..." Marguerite sighed again. "I guess the bedroom—"

A knock at the door downstairs caused Marguerite's and Aracely's heads to swivel as one in the direction of the sound.

"You're already here." Marguerite pointed out the obvious to Aracely. "Which means it must be..."

"Do you want me to answer the door?" Aracely asked.

Marguerite thought for a moment. The knocking came again, louder this time. She shook her head. "No. I may be leaving St. Isadore for good, but Napa will always be my home. And if Evan continues to own the winery, I'm bound to run into him either in town or at industry events. Might as well get it over with sooner rather than later."

And maybe, she thought to herself, maybe Evan had come to his senses faster than she'd thought possible. Maybe Evan was here to tell her she was right, and he was ready to let her in...

But it wasn't Evan on her doorstep. "Nico. Hi."

"Hey," Nico responded, tugging at the strap of the backpack he wore over one shoulder. "Do you have a few minutes?"

"Sure. And Aracely brought enough coffee and cupcakes to fuel an army, so you're in luck. Come in."

He closed the door behind him and trailed after her up the stairs. "First, I want you to remember that I'm just the messenger."

Marguerite waited until he was seated at the table with a chocolate-and-peanut-butter cupcake in front of him before she asked. "What message did Evan ask you to deliver? If it's about moving out of the carriage house, I'm way ahead of him."

"What? No," Nico exclaimed. "Unless you're moving out to live in the owner's residence."

Marguerite's gaze narrowed. "Evan sent you to ask me to move in with him? I doubt that."

"Sorry. No. Evan called me shortly after sunrise, woke me up. Said he was leaving this morning for Asia. Something about saving a deal? Finding a new one? I wasn't very awake. But then he said he left some papers for you and asked me to deliver them." He opened up the backpack at his feet and took out a folder, then placed it on the table in front of Marguerite. "And I, um…" He shrugged.

Marguerite stared at the closed folder. "You read them."

"I peeked." Nico took a quick bite of his cupcake.

Marguerite pulled the folder toward her. And let it sit there.

"Well?" asked Aracely. "Are you going to open it or let me perish of suspense?"

Marguerite took a deep breath. She pulled back the cover of the file.

On top was a legal document. She picked it up and discovered it was a quitclaim deed, transferring ownership of St. Isadore to her. Evan's signature was bold in black, and he'd even found someone to notarize the document in what had to have been the middle of the night.

"And?" Aracely demanded.

Marguerite handed the deed to her, not sure she'd read it correctly. "I think… I think Evan gave St. Isadore to me."

Underneath the deed was Linus's will with her

scrawled message on it. And below that was a copy of her employment contract, with a note attached in Evan's strong, confident script.

> *Marguerite,*
> *Six months ago, we agreed we would revisit your contract after the Global Leader Summit. Congratulations, you've been promoted to owner of St. Isadore. You deserve it for your hard work, and it should have been yours all along. Never doubt how talented and capable you are.*
> *Evan*

She turned the pages of the contract. Evan had written "null and void" across each one. There were more papers in the folder, but they were a blur. She thought she had no more tears left after the night before. She was wrong.

Aracely gently removed the contract from her hands and read through it. "There is also a financial overview and a phone number to call for access to St. Isadore's bank accounts and records. He left you enough cash to cover three years of operations."

Marguerite shook her head, slowly at first but then gathering momentum. "I can't accept this. Especially not—" she picked up the sheet Aracely referenced and blinked at the amount Evan had deposited into St. Isadore's coffers "—the money. Where did he say he was going?"

"He's on his way to Tokyo. Or maybe Shanghai?" Nico pondered. "He said something about Sydney, too, I think."

"Never mind. His office will know how to reach him." Marguerite gathered the papers together. "Neither of you say anything to anyone. I'll get this straightened out. Even if I have to climb Mt. Everest to find him."

"Good luck." Nico polished off the last of his cupcake. "Evan makes it extremely difficult to return his gifts. Ask me how I know."

"And what happens to St. Isadore in the meantime? Harvest is fast approaching. You, of all people, know what a critical time period this is," Aracely pointed out.

"But Evan—" Marguerite squeezed her eyes shut. "Evan needs St. Isadore or Angus Horne won't invest."

"What?" Aracely sounded truly befuddled.

Nico paused in the midst of peeling the wrapper off a second cupcake. "You don't get it, do you, Marguerite? This is how Evan shows you he cares. He gifts people things. He's not going to take it back."

"I don't want 'things.' Even when the thing is St. Isadore. I made that clear last night."

"I'm sure you did. But things are all Evan gives. My grandparents used to say he took the wrong lesson from our parents' death. When he quit MIT to work full-time on his first company, they wanted him to come home and live with us in Boston. Be a family. Instead, he moved to Silicon Valley because, and I quote, 'Nico's not going to grow up like I did.' He sent lots of money, but he was too busy to visit."

Marguerite stared at Nico, her already-tattered heart falling to pieces. "That's…awful. Poor Evan."

"I thought maybe with you, he'd… Never mind." Nico took a bite and swallowed. "Meanwhile, Aracely is right about St. Isadore. Boss," he concluded with a smile.

"Regardless of who owns the winery, it is clear you are now in charge," Aracely added.

Marguerite regarded the papers, then shut the folder

closed and shoved it away from her. "I'll talk to a lawyer on Monday. And if Evan changes his mind, he knows where I am. So for now, pass me a salted caramel cupcake."

She put a bright smile on her face and even managed to crack a few jokes as the three of them polished off the contents of the bakery box. But while she did her best to maintain a calm and even carefree facade, inside she began to shrivel, one molecule at a time.

For a very long while, owning even a part of St. Isadore had been her deepest desire. Now her lifelong dream had been handed to her on a diamond-encrusted, platinum platter. She should be ecstatic.

She would give it all up for one "I love you" from Evan's lips.

Maybe Nico was right. Maybe the deed was the closest thing to a declaration of affection she would get from Evan. Maybe it would be enough, ensuring her family's legacy would continue and under her direction.

Who knew attaining the goal she'd worked toward since childhood would be so devastating?

Eleven

Whoever said April was the cruelest month never met October. Or so it seemed to Evan, lugging his suitcase into an empty, cold house that smelled vaguely of cleaning products and little else. Of course, every month since last July had seemed cruel.

He'd mostly been away the last few months, chasing opportunities for Medevco in Asia or Europe, ever since he left St. Isadore for the last time. Nan kept his place in spotless order during his absences, but she could do nothing about the lack of warmth—and he didn't mean the heat from the furnace, which was doing its best to combat San Francisco's foggy, chilled night air. Once Marguerite had opened his eyes to his surroundings, he couldn't help but look at the rooms through her perspective. He'd made fun of St. Isadore's faux Victorian vibe, but he had to admit the overstuffed furniture and dozens of knickknacks scattered around gave it a lived-in, cared-for feeling that he only now realized was missing from this house.

House, not home.

By the time he unpacked and put his things back in their appropriate places, it was time for dinner. Or rather lunch, since he was still on Tokyo time. His housekeeper had left some casseroles in the refrigerator, but they required heating up, and besides, they were large enough to feed a family.

He didn't have a family.

He had his phone out and was about to order from his favorite takeout restaurant when his doorbell chimed. The security app showed a woman at his front door, her hair covered by a knit cap. His heart jumped while his stomach performed a somersault. Could it be…? Then, with a smile and a wave, the woman looked into the camera stationed over the door, and he could breathe easily again. "Hi, Danica," he said into the phone, knowing she would be able to hear him via the camera's speakers. "I'll buzz you in."

Evan had always liked Luke's wife. Blond and petite, she had a bubbly optimism that was the perfect complement to Luke's reserved practicality. Evan wasn't sure what she was doing at his place on a weeknight, however, especially since she and Luke lived forty-five minutes south in a tony enclave near Palo Alto. But he could guess. "I don't suppose you were just in the neighborhood and decided to stop by," he greeted her when she came in.

"No," Danica said, removing her hat and unbuttoning her coat, revealing a slightly rounded belly. "Although I am fond of the sushi restaurant at the bottom of your hill. Alas, no raw fish for me for the next several months."

"I see that. Congratulations. I had no idea you were…"

"Pregnant?" Danica raised her eyebrows. "Yes. I know you didn't know. Because Luke wanted to be the one to tell you, but you and Luke aren't talking except through memos."

Bingo. Evan's guess was correct. "I appreciate you coming all the way into the city. But this is a work matter. It'll be resolved eventually. Want something to drink before you return home? I have water—" he checked the refrigerator "—and water."

Danica followed him into the kitchen. "I'm not here because of Medevco. The company's future is between you and Luke—"

"And the board of directors," Evan muttered. In fact, he'd cut his latest business trip short after three weeks because of the emergency board meeting scheduled for tomorrow morning. And he still didn't have a replacement deal for the one he'd lost by turning down Angus Horne.

"Fine. And the board." Danica placed her hand on his arm. "I'm here as your friend who is concerned about you."

He choked on his sip of water. "Me? Why?"

"I get Luke can be bullheaded. I once didn't talk to him for about a month myself. But this current impasse between you is—" She huffed and threw up her hands. "Luke showed me the numbers. Medevco will survive with or without the investment. It's in good health. But you're driving yourself into the ground chasing these deals. I'm afraid for *your* health."

"I'm fine." He picked up the basket of mail his housekeeper had left for him on the counter and started looking through it. Bills, appeals for donations, something from Pia he put aside to read later, renewal notices—

A dark purple envelope, embossed with the St. Isadore logo, with his name and address written in metallic-gold ink.

Danica must have heard his sharp intake of breath. "What's that?"

He shrugged, trying to appear nonchalant. But his pulse knocked against his eardrums. He hadn't spoken to Marguerite since their encounter in the library, although she appeared in his dreams both sleeping and waking. He did speak several times to his lawyers, ensuring his transfer of St. Isadore and its assets was as airtight as possible. Through them, he'd learned Marguerite had tried several times to have it invalidated and returned to him, but he'd held firm.

It was the least he could do.

Danica plucked the envelope from his fingers. "Oh! I know what this is. It's an invitation to the harvest dinner at St. Isadore. Luke and I received one."

He took the envelope back from her and shuffled it into the pile of mail discards. "Thanks. Now I don't need to open it."

"Evan." Danica's brows drew together.

"You're going to be a great mother. You have the I'm-so-disappointed-in-you tone down pat."

"I'm not disappointed. I'm concerned. Luke heard you gave the winery away, yet you're single-mindedly pursuing deals to grow Medevco beyond what is, frankly, reasonable." Her green gaze met his, soft with worry. "What's going on? This isn't like you."

Danica's concern was heartwarming, and that was the problem. He didn't want his heart warmed. He wanted it to remain neutrally cool, uninvolved. "I'm ensuring Medevco is a global success. Maybe becoming a father is making Luke too risk-averse."

Her gaze narrowed. "Okay. Pretend there's nothing driving your irrational behavior."

"Success isn't irrational."

"It is when you're destroying every relationship you have."

"Not if my actions keep the people in those relationships clothed and fed. Including you and Luke, in the case of Medevco."

She inhaled, then slowly let out her breath. "Do you think you're doing this for us? For the other people in your life? Evan, that's sweet. It's also condescending as hell."

"What?" Damn it, he didn't want to lose someone else from his life. But…

"You're treating us like inanimate figurines on a shelf, incapable of speaking on our own behalf, while you appoint yourself the sole arbiter of our welfare."

"No, I'm not. I'm—"

"Doing exactly that." She unfolded her arms and moved away from the counter, buttoning her coat as she went. "Y'know, Luke and I had high hopes that Marguerite—whom I like a lot, by the way—would open your eyes to the world beyond Medevco. But you gave away the winery, and in doing so, cut Marguerite out of your life, and now you're cutting Luke out by not speaking to him."

"That's not why I gave—" he sputtered.

She shook her head. "If you keep this up, Silicon Valley machinations are all you're going to have left. By yourself."

That had to be an empty threat. "Luke's not leaving Medevco."

She turned to face him. "Tomorrow? Of course not. And Luke makes his own decisions when it comes to business. I don't speak for him. But he won't put up forever with a partner who refuses to communicate." She yanked her knit cap over her blond curls. "Life is short, Evan. It's fine to spend it alone if that's what you truly want—but is it?"

She left without waiting for his answer, the front door closing behind her with a final-sounding click. Evan put down his nearly full glass of water to search for something stronger to drink.

Danica was wrong. He appreciated her loyalty to her husband, but she was wrong. Luke would come around once Evan secured the right deal. He just hadn't managed to find the best investor yet. And the only reason he gave away St. Isadore was because it wasn't his to keep.

The liquor cabinet was nearly empty. Maybe there was a forgotten beer in the refrigerator? But when he opened the door, a bottle of St. Isadore Chardonnay, chilling in the specialized beverage drawer, stared back at him. He started to close the door, only for his gaze to fall once more on the casseroles.

Casseroles, big enough to feed a family.

A vision of eating pizza at St. Isadore flashed through his head. Gabi laughing, Nico grinning as he snuck pieces of pepperoni off Evan's slices when he thought Evan wasn't looking, and Marguerite—

Marguerite smiling at him, her gaze filled with…

Love. Pure, sincere, true love.

Love for him.

Family had been there, all along, right under his nose. Love, his for the asking.

He shut his eyes. Screwed them tight. Tensed his muscles and steeled himself as the wave of regret, anguish and not a little anger at his willful blindness rolled over him.

Picking up his phone, he punched the button to call Danica's cell and then opened the invitation from St. Isadore. The harvest dinner was in a week. That might be enough time.

Danica answered over her car's sound system, street noise in the background. "I guess you're still speaking to me."

"I know you're driving, so I'll make this quick. I'm about to hop in my car and head down your way. Can you and Luke meet me in the bar at the Rosewood in an hour? I have a proposition for him, but you should weigh in."

There was a pause before Danica spoke. "Sure, as long as you buy me as many Shirley Temples as I want. See you then."

He hung up the phone, grabbed his coat and headed to his garage. Once again, he had a week. But this time he wasn't sure if he could pull off the miracle, or if he even deserved one. Still, he had to try.

Marguerite stood on the smooth flagstone terrace of St. Isadore, once more watching as guests began to arrive under the globe lights crisscrossing high overhead. Harvest was her favorite time of the year, and this harvest had been bountiful beyond her initial expectations. The grapes had been sorted and crushed and were fermenting in various tanks. Distributors were eager for the result, with restaurants as far away as Australia making inquiries about featuring her wines on their menus. Tonight was the culmination of dreams she'd spent a long time building. A celebration, in so many ways.

If only she felt like celebrating.

She accepted she was now the owner of St. Isadore.

She'd tried various methods and ruses to reach Evan, to get him to recognize he had to take back his gift, but the lawyers were in agreement that the deed had been transferred to her, and Evan...

Well, Evan always sent very polite emails, but short to the point of being terse. And whenever she tried his cell phone, he'd seemed to be either on a plane or in a meeting.

Message received: he was avoiding her. If only her heart would take a clue and stop wanting him. But try as hard as she might, she couldn't convince herself she was wrong, that Evan didn't love her. She knew what she'd seen in his eyes that night in the library. But he wouldn't admit it, for whatever reason.

She was on track to repairing her family's legacy, but legacies did not keep her warm at night. Or make her laugh. Or challenge her. Or push her to be her best.

She'd read and reread his note, until the paper was in danger of falling apart where it was creased. She wanted to tell him that she no longer doubted herself. She yearned to tell him that she didn't doubt him or his love, either. If he would only give her the opportunity...

But that was something he had to realize by himself, for himself. She couldn't do it for him. In the meantime, there was delicious food to eat, exclusive wines to uncork and business to conduct. Evan had taught her about that, too. She geared herself up to go into the crowd—

And frowned. Aracely was running toward her. But Aracely didn't run. She ordinarily floated. "What's wrong?"

Aracely said something into the headset she wore, then turned to Marguerite. "Ted has to leave. He thinks something he ate at home did not agree with him."

"Oh, no." As director of operations, Ted was in

charge of several key aspects of the harvest dinner. "Is he okay?"

Aracely nodded. "He will be fine. He tried to muscle through, but right now he's…" She wrinkled her nose. "Not something to discuss at a black-tie dinner people paid hundreds of dollars to attend."

"Poor Ted." Marguerite screwed her eyes shut to think. "Okay, I can take over—"

"But," Aracely interjected, "before he left, he called a friend and asked him to help out. Since we are short-staffed."

"We don't have time to train—"

"Ted gave him a quick quiz before he left, and he said his friend is well versed in St. Isadore's wines. But if you would like to talk to the friend, to make sure he is knowledgeable, Ted asked him to wait in the library."

"The library? Why not the winery office?"

"The winery is being used for VIP tours. This way, no one would see Ted…" Aracely mimed holding her stomach and groaning.

Marguerite narrowed her gaze. "I'm not going to find Nico visiting from college, am I? This isn't some surprise you and he cooked up?"

Aracely's eyes widened. "Marguerite. I am shocked you would think that. The harvest dinner is the most important event of the year for St. Isadore. Would I pull you, the owner and winemaker, away from guests if this were not an emergency?" She folded her arms across her chest, the perfect picture of injured indignation.

Marguerite ran her gaze over the terrace. It was still early. The dinner itself wouldn't be served for another two hours. And if Ted was actually sick…and this mystery person could take on his duties…it would be a big assist. "Okay. I'll be back soon, with or without this person, depending on what he says."

But when Marguerite arrived in the library, it was empty. "Great," she muttered. Now she had someone she didn't know roaming the halls of the owner's residence while she needed to be with her guests. She huffed and turned to leave the room—

And stopped. The life-size portrait of Linus was slightly askew, revealing darkness behind him. Someone had found the secret passage.

Her pulse quickened. Few people knew about the hidden hallways, and most of them weren't presently in residence at St. Isadore. Maybe someone from the cleaning staff had unlatched the door the last time they were in the library.

Then the floor rumbled below her feet. Surprised, she put out a hand to brace herself against the wall. What the—?

Of course. The elevator. The one that led to the owner's wine cellar.

She smiled. Was the room brighter, or was that only her vision, the dark filter that had hung over her since late July beginning to disappear as hope began to flood her senses? This could be a coincidence, she reminded herself, a simple malfunction of the elevator's wiring. It could be a real thief, using the cover of the party to steal the valuable rare wines. Or it could really be a friend of Ted's, doing some exploring while he waited.

There was one way to find out. She slipped into the secret passage. But instead of following it to the elevator, she found the stairs. Kicking off her stiletto heels, she gathered the full skirt of her long, cobalt blue gown and descended to the cellar.

With a slight push, the door noiselessly glided open. She peeked around the edge.

The cellar lights were on, sconces of bronze and yellowed, frosted glass in an Art Deco fan shape that cast a diffuse, golden glow over the stone walls covered with racks of wine bottles. But her attention was caught by the man at the other end of the room, his black-clad back to her as he removed—

Wait. That was where she stored her experiments. She pushed the door all the way open. "Hey. That's *my* wine."

The man jumped. He almost dropped the bottle he was holding but managed to hold on to it. Then he slowly turned around.

Her breath caught. She knew who it would be, but she didn't know how glorious it would feel to be right. Evan. In a tuxedo. His smile slightly crooked, happy to see her but also a bit unsure.

"Aracely was supposed to give me fifteen more minutes," he said. "I'm not ready."

Her vision blurred and she blinked her eyes rapidly. She advanced into the room, barely noticing the cold stone floor against her bare feet. "Ready for what?"

He put the bottle down on the long wooden table in the middle of the cellar. "For my interview, of course."

"Your interview?" She wanted to smile. She wanted to do a thousand things: hug him, shake him, yell at him for avoiding her. Kiss him, now and forever. Instead, she indicated the wine. "But you're stealing my wine because...?"

He picked the bottle up again and regarded it, running the fingers of his other hand over the handwritten labeling. "I thought perhaps you might like a demonstration. Of my wine knowledge, that is."

She could no longer keep her smile buttoned down. It burst forth, stretching the corners of her mouth, digging deep into her cheeks. It was a full exhibit of the hopeful joy she allowed to bubble up. "Of course. I can't hire someone who doesn't appreciate wine. But are you sure you want to open that one? It still has some aging to do."

"Oh, I don't have to open it." He moved closer to her. "I already know it's spectacular. Complex. Assertive. Unpredictable at times. Full of rich, vivid notes that only deepen with longer acquaintance. A presence that can't be forgotten, even if you try. A wine worth fighting for."

She started to laugh. "You know all this without even opening the bottle?"

He nodded. "I know the maker. She puts herself into everything she does."

Her laughter died in her throat, replaced by a thick ball of emotion making it hard to swallow. Her nose burned, a sure sign more tears were on their way, but she forced them back. "There's one problem. You already have a job. A big one."

He shook his head. And then he came even closer. "I no longer work for Medevco. I turned over sole control to Luke. The board approved the change a few days ago."

Was the cellar spinning around her? Or maybe it was the effect of losing herself in Evan's kaleidoscopic gaze. "I don't— What?"

He reached out, and now her hands were in his. "You're freezing," he said, rubbing her fingers, wrapping his hands around hers.

"I'm okay." She did tremble but not from the temperature in the room.

Evan frowned. "Maybe we should leave the cellar."

If they left, they would be surrounded by staff and guests. She would be swept up in the bustle of the dinner. Down here, they were alone, in their own world. "Tell me now. Why did you sell to Luke?"

His gaze was focused on her feet. She pulled her bare toes under her gown but not before he noted them. He gave her a decisive nod. Then, with one sweeping motion he picked her up, pulling her onto his lap as he sat on the table.

"Evan." She wriggled to get down, then realized that perhaps it wasn't the most prudent movement. Not right now.

"You want to hear the story, I don't want you to expire of cold before I'm done."

"Fine. Speak." Truth to tell, she didn't want to be anywhere else but nestled against his warmth, surrounded by the Evan-scent she'd doubted she would ever experience again.

"You were right." His words rumbled in her ear.

"About? Although I do love it when people admit that."

Evan's arms tightened around her. "Never doubt your talents. Or how perceptive you are."

"Have you forgiven yourself for whatever it was?" she asked quietly.

He stilled, only his chest rising and falling against her. "How did you know there was something to forgive?"

"Nico said something, the morning you gave me St. Isadore. About how angry your grandparents were with you."

He shifted, and she moved to leave his lap, thinking perhaps she was too heavy, but he kept her tight against him. "If you don't want to talk about it, that's okay," she said.

Only the sounds of their breathing interrupted the stillness. "I never wanted a family," he finally said. "I didn't want to leave anyone behind like I was left. Like Nico was left."

She squeezed her eyes shut, hurting for the young Evan. "I understand."

"My dad—my dad and mom were coming home after dropping me at MIT for my sophomore year. He'd taken a second job. I don't remember now what it was. Something that kept him up all night after a long day in the auto shop. The police thought...they thought he fell asleep. He drifted into another lane and never saw the oncoming truck."

"I'm so sorry," she whispered, her lips against his cheek.

"I kept thinking if he didn't take that second job, they'd still be here. Nico would've grown up knowing them."

"You drove yourself so no one else would have to worry about extra income," she guessed. "That's why you bought St. Isadore. That's why you wanted Medevco to grow so fast. So Nico wouldn't want for anything."

"Told you you're perceptive."

"Did you give me St. Isadore for the same reason? So I'd be taken care of?"

He didn't answer.

She slid out of his grasp, ignoring his muttered protest, and turned to face him. He remained seated on the table, which allowed their gazes to be level. "Evan. I'll ask you the same question you asked me that night we first met. Why are you here?"

He shrugged, his half grin reappearing. "I have it

on good authority my drive was hurting, not helping Medevco. So I left, which means I'm jobless. You're the boss now, so I thought I'd throw myself on your mercy."

Inside, she was smiling so hard her cheeks hurt. But she managed to keep a straight expression. "Then, this is a job interview. What skills will you bring to St. Isadore? I run a lean operation, you know."

He thought for a moment. "We discussed how I'm a hard worker. I'm punctual. And I'm a fast learner."

She nodded. "Those are all admirable qualities. But I'm afraid we have no openings right now."

"I thought you might say that, so I took the liberty of coming up with my own job description."

"Really?" It was harder and harder to control her expression, so she stopped trying. Joy began to spill from every pore. "Part-time or full time?"

"Definitely full time." He jumped off the table. Her gaze followed him as he went to the section of the cellar where sparkling wines were stored. He selected a bottle and came back.

She recognized the label. "That's definitely the good stuff."

"If I don't get the job, I promise I'll replace it." He removed the foil, exposing the cork and the wire cage keeping it in place. "Did you know," he said conversationally as he turned the key to loosen the cage, "that this always takes six twists?"

She nodded. "Of course."

"But do you know the legend why?" He removed the cage, twisting it into some shape she couldn't see. Then he dropped to one knee.

She gasped. The tears that had been threatening all night breached the defenses and flowed, unchecked, down her cheeks. Her entire being trembled, and it definitely had nothing to do with being cold.

"Six is the number of extreme happiness, or so I was assured by my local wine-store owner. And while that may only be a tall tale when it comes to champagne, I know it is the absolute truth when I'm with you. You asked me why I'm here. I'm hoping you will forgive me and allow me to serve as your husband." He held out the wire cage, twisted into the shape of a ring with the cork cap serving as the stone. "I love you, Daisy Marguerite Delacroix. You stole my heart from the moment we met."

"Evan." She clapped her hands over her mouth, unable to speak, unable to move, unsure if this moment—so often dreamed of—was truly real.

His smile faltered. "I'd settle for committed boyfriend if you require a probationary period first?"

She shook her head and tugged him up, allowing him to slip the twisted wire onto the fourth finger of her left hand, her heart still too full for her brain to form words.

"This was supposed to happen in the library," he said. "There's a real ring in the desk drawer."

Finally, she found words. Just a few. "This is perfect. Yes. A thousand times yes."

Then he was kissing her and she was kissing him and the cellar spun around them until she was dizzy with love and happiness and hope. They might have stayed down there until the cleaning crew arrived the next day if Aracely hadn't poked her head into the room.

"Why do I always find discarded articles of clothing when you two are together?" she asked, holding up Marguerite's forgotten shoes. "I am so sorry to interrupt—"

"We're sorry to interrupt," said a grinning Nico, appearing from behind Aracely.

"But there is a dinner going on—" Aracely finished.

"Which I don't want to miss since I'm only in town tonight to hang out with my brother. And you of course, Marguerite," Nico interjected.

"And the presence of the owner is requested," Aracely finished.

"That's you," Evan whispered against her lips. "I couldn't be prouder of everything you've accomplished."

"St. Isadore is a group effort." She ran her fingers over his lightly stubbled cheeks, still amazed he was here, in her arms. "You're a part of it. If you want to be."

"All I want is you," he said. "Today, tomorrow and to infinity. But I'd be thrilled to be on your team. Whatever you want. After all, you're the boss now." He grinned, that devilish, cocky grin that made her heart take flight and soar into the heavens.

"Whatever we want," she corrected, and took his hand to lead him out of the cellar, following Aracely and Nico up to the terrace to join the festivities. There was more to celebrate than she had dreamed would be possible. "Together."

* * * * *

COMING SOON!

We really hope you enjoyed reading this book.
If you're looking for more romance, be sure to
head to the shops when new books are
available on

Thursday 5th
August

LET'S TALK
Romance

For exclusive extracts, competitions
and special offers, find us online:

- **f** facebook.com/millsandboon
- 🐦 @MillsandBoon
- 📷 @MillsandBoonUK

Get in touch on 01413 063232

For all the latest titles coming soon, visit
millsandboon.co.uk/nextmonth

MILLS & BOON

HEROES

At Your Service

Experience all the excitement of a gripping thriller, with an intense romance at its heart. Resourceful, true-to-life women and strong, fearless men face danger and desire - a killer combination!

MILLS & BOON
MODERN
Power and Passion

Prepare to be swept off your feet by sophisticated, sexy and seductive heroes, in some of the world's most glamourous and romantic locations, where power and passion collide.

Julia James

Heiress's
PREGNANCY SCANDAL

MILLS & BOON
MODERN

Jennie Lucas

Chosen as the
SHEIKH'S ROYAL BRIDE

MILLS & BOON

Kim Lawrence

A WEDDING *at the*
ITALIAN'S DEMAND

MILLS & BOON

Sharon Kendrick

The
SHEIKH'S SECRET BABY

MILLS & BOON
MODERN

ght Modern stories published every month, find them all at:

millsandboon.co.uk/Modern